Books by Hank Searls

The Big X
The Crowded Sky
Overboard
Pentagon
The Pilgrim Project

Published by POCKET BOOKS

OVERBOARD

HANK SEARLS

A KANGAROO BOOK

PUBLISHED BY POCKET BOOKS NEW YORK

POCKET BOOKS, a Simon & Schuster division of
GULF & WESTERN CORPORATION
1230 Avenue of the Americas, New York, N.Y. 10020

To my first and last mate.

PART I

Day

CHAPTER

1

SHE HAD VANISHED WHILE HE SLEPT, SOMETIME BE-
fore dawn, one infinitesimal speck detaching itself
from another under unseeing stars. And now as the
sun rose astern, the southeast trades began to die so
that his speed slackened and his search slowed.

He sagged nude at the helm, shivering in panic,
alone with a cat 40 miles from the nearest island. In
early apricot light, he was still backtracking. He forced
himself to look at his watch. It was 5:15 A.M. Papeete
time.

The ketch had been pounding southeast, steered
by a wind-vane, bound from Bora Bora to Tahiti, now
seventy miles away. In darkness at 3:12 A.M., he
had discovered that she was gone. At that time he
had been, roughly, fifty miles from Moorea upwind,
with Raiatea forty miles in the other direction.

When the first instant of paralysis had passed and
he found that he could function, he had dropped the

man-overboard flag, tied to a lifebuoy and a floating strobe light. He had acted instinctively, but perhaps prematurely. There was no reason to think that she was anywhere near. The strobe had begun to wink in his wake.

He had found himself whimpering in fear but capable of elementary calculations. He had reversed course instantly and set the wind-vane to steer the new heading. He avoided chaos, by force of will, long enough to plot a position. And he searched for their logbook, hoping to find her last entry because it would help to pinpoint the time when she had gone. He could not find the book.

Uselessly, he had tried to call Papeete Radio, in halting French, and then English. There was no reply. He climbed halfway up the mast to the spreader.

First he had searched from aloft, letting the wind-vane steer. He had clung to the rigging under the yardarm for two hours, scanning by starlight the path they had sailed, straining against the dark and listening. The gibbous, lopsided moon sinking to the west was useless. It was not darkness, anyway, that would hide her when he drew near; it was the unceasing swells rolling in from the east. Even from twenty-five feet up the mast, the blinking strobe had been lost within minutes, astern among mountainous seas.

It was three days before Christmas, high summer and *le mauvais temps* in the Societies. He faced a day of simmering heat and squalls. Naked and tall in the rigging, eyeballs wind-dried and stinging, he had clung to the shrouds as the sun rose. His hands and feet were already raw from the teak rungs, for the roll continually pressed him against the rough wood and then flung him side to side. His skin smelled sourly of terror. Already he was oozing sweat.

He had hung on past sunrise as Irwin, their

stainless-steel wind-vane, steered him back over the track they had come. A few minutes after dawn the breeze fell off so sharply that the boat began to wander, groping for the wind. So he had swung down, lurched aft to the cockpit, and released the steering-vane. He took the wheel.

Now he was too low to see well. For a while, he slatted along at two knots, not covering nearly enough ocean, trapped at deck-level. He had no choice: if he lashed the helm and started the engine and climbed the shrouds again he'd drift from the path they had sailed.

To fend off despair, he considered once more a hope that had helped him through the hours aloft. If she had been wearing her jacket, there was a plastic police-whistle tied to the zipper, just for this, very loud and shrill. The jacket itself, being floatable, might keep her up all day.

He moved toward the hatch, intending finally to duck below to check the foul-weather locker for the coat. Hand on the hatch-top, he stopped. He was afraid to face her bright orange jacket hanging in the locker. It was better to assume that she was in it, floating somewhere ahead.

He glanced back at the rising sun, shafting through a squall line. She could be watching it too.

"Now look," he muttered to no one, "I haven't asked a fucking thing until now . . ."

He found his eyes filling with tears, so that he could not search. Astonished, he massaged them with his fingers until he could see. When his vision cleared, he grabbed a mizzen shroud near the wheel. To raise his eye-level, he balanced with one bare foot on the cockpit rail. He steered with the other, as he did when they entered an unknown pass and she perched in the crosstrees to help. He craned ahead, sweeping the horizon. Standing this way, until fatigue overtook him, he would be able to see almost as well as if he were on the bottom rung of the ladder.

He glanced at a squall line to windward. He saw one of her cloud-people, a perfect matador wearing a scarlet-fringed hat, taunting him with a swirling cape of rain. He almost called her topside, realized she was gone, pulled back just in time from the edge of self-pity and panic and tears that would blind him. He regarded instead the threat of a squall.

The usual morning revival of the trades, which would help him cover the ocean faster, would also bring the matador sweeping down on him. She could be hidden under the bullfighter's mantle if the rain moved across his path. And meanwhile, without the trades, the boat was simply marking time, while she struggled somewhere ahead.

He was impelled to move faster. He started the engine. He jammed it full ahead without warming it up, ignoring the clattering uproar. It settled finally into its normal rumble, but its sound frightened him. His main chance was to hear her, not to see her. When he was down in the troughs, he could see nothing but dark-blue hills heaving around him. With the engine drumming at his feet he could miss her if she were screaming and shrilling in a valley fifty yards away.

He considered the odds that they might both be borne aloft at the same instant that he was looking in her direction. Most of the time he was sinking or rising on the slope of a sapphire knoll. He couldn't attentively sweep the whole 360 degrees of the skyline at one time, so he was taking it one semicircle per wave, ducking under the main boom to see to leeward before he sank into the next trough. His chances of seeing her seemed infinitely small.

But her chance of spotting him was very much

greater. The mainmast towered above the wave peaks forty feet. It would be she who discovered him. He had better be ready to hear her when she did.

He cut the engine, conceding the race to the squall. Suddenly he heard only the sound of the sails. A steering cable squeaked behind him and slow-moving water gurgled under the stern.

Now, in the silence, the boat's crawling pace chilled him. He envisioned for the first time her body somewhere ahead, trailing strands of burnished bronze, spiraling downward into water turning midnight blue. The vision overcame his fear of the unanswered question of her jacket below. He took a final sweep of the horizon, bobbed through the hatch, and stumbled down the companionway ladder into the cabin. He grasped the latch on the foul-weather locker and swung it open.

Her jacket was gone. He sagged with relief. Only his windbreaker, the identical orange color but immensely bigger, with a wine stain down its front, rocked on its hanger. Having her jacket, she had the whistle too.

He caught her scent from a plastic bottle of Sea & Ski, teetering on the shelf. It was a good omen, all around.

Incredibly, hypocritically, he found himself on his knees, head bowed in thanks. Feeling suddenly foolish, he got up, slammed the locker door, and sprung topside.

The breeze freshened, speeding the squall. From below he heard the bulkhead clock strike three bells: 5:30. His euphoria trickled away. Now he became convinced that he had passed her soon after his panicky turn, in the black hours before dawn.

Everything suddenly pulled at him to reverse course and retrace his track. He was wrenched by a gut-feeling that she was astern. The steering cable behind him began to squeal *"behind, behind, behind";* the mainsail stuttered: *"back-back-back-back."*

He fought the impulse to play the hunch.

She could be just as easily bobbing in the next five miles as in the last ten.

CHAPTER
2

SHE WAS SWEPT TO THE CREST OF A SWELL. IT BROKE in her face. Her eyes stung with the foam. She squeezed them shut, lying back in her float-jacket, always clinging to the plastic jug she had torn from the trailing line.

The morning sun was hot on her forehead. She felt feverish and let her head sink to cool it. If he didn't find her soon, she'd boil like a lobster.

She guessed from the height of the sun that it was six or seven in the morning. Her guaranteed 300-foot waterproof watch had stopped precisely at dawn. She estimated that she had been in the water for three or four hours.

Her lips were cracked and stinging. Until daybreak she had been freezing. She still shivered momentarily, but now she could not tell if she suffered more from heat or cold. In twelve months in the tropics, she had never bothered to ask him how much the water heated up by day. Maybe by noon she would be warm. But of course he would find her before then.

The floating jacket that was saving her life was the worst of her discomforts. It kept slithering up her nude body and chafing her armpits. The coarse nylon safety belt was rubbing her belly raw too. She kept it on anyway. She had some vague idea that it might help him drag her aboard; already she was too tired to be much help herself. Besides, it was proof that she had semi-followed their rules, even if she had obviously not kept it clipped to a lifeline topside.

She rubbed cautiously under the belt. Doing that, she let the plastic container slip away. The wind caught it and scooted it up the face of a swell. She expended too much energy in a fast little sprint to catch it.

She gripped it firmly, like a baby, then shifted to carry it like a football in the crook of her arm. For hours she had shifted it back and forth. When water would trickle in through its broken hollow handle, she would hold it aloft to drain it. She would plug it for a while with her finger. Then she would forget and it would fill again and she would empty it.

She valued the jug for its buoyancy, afraid that her jacket might turn soggy and that she would have to jettison it. And the jug was a link with the boat.

The whole nightmare was past belief. Safe in her bunk at 3 A.M., she had been deep in the New York subway system, reading *The Taking of the Pelham One-Two-Three,* in paperback. Fifteen minutes later she had been thrashing idiotically in their wake.

She let her mind drift back, looking for some excuse. She had been soft and snug with the cat in the forward cabin, under the bunk light. The kitchen timer had croaked from its niche above a deck beam, telling her that it was time for her half-hour survey of the horizon. She spilled M. le Chat from her bare belly, snapped off her light to save the main battery, and groped with her feet for the varnished cabin flooring.

The cabin sole, when the boat was hard on the wind, sloped almost thirty degrees. Automatically, she swung herself aft in the dark from bulkhead to handhold to shelf, making no move without a hold on something. She was as familiar with her environment as a gibbon in the jungle, alternately light and heavy as the boat pitched wildly in its normal battle with the head-seas.

She sidled past the trunk of the mast, feeling a trickle of water down its varnished face where the mast was leaking, as usual, from the cabin top. Mitch kept forgetting to tape it down.

That was her current bitch. And the stupid chirping from the steering cable, which was making a neurotic out of the cat. Tomorrow she would get him to squirt it with WD-40.

In the main cabin, by the moonglow through the skylight, she could make out his bare form, tangled with his *pareu,* on the leeward side of his bunk. His massive shoulders and the line of his butt, after almost twenty-two years of marriage, were still sexy to her.

Maybe it would all work out once they got the hell back.

She left the lights off, not wanting to hurt her night-vision or to wake Mitch. She groped for her jacket in the foul-weather locker and put it on. She picked her safety belt from the hook under the canvas dodger and cinched it on too. She drew a flashlight from a rack by the hatch, took the logbook from its niche above the chart table, and climbed to the cockpit.

The night was warm but the wind whipped her hair to leeward. Its ends stung her cheeks. She snapped her safety belt to a fitting on the mizzenmast, with slack enough to move around the cockpit but leashing her from straying much further.

She stepped onto the cockpit edge to increase her height, clinging to a shroud for balance. A three-quarter moon sagged lugubriously to the west. Carefully, keeping her eyes just above the dark horizon as he had taught her, she scanned the whole 360 degrees, stooping to see to starboard under the drumming sail. She checked for the glow of the port and starboard running lights; both OK. The sternlight had been out since Bora Bora: another little job for him.

She shielded her flashlight and shone it on the Sumlog dial by the wheel. She logged the speed—5.1 knots—and the mileage. She switched on the binnacle compass light and checked the course. SSE, right on. She checked her watch: 0304. She logged that too, as 0300, then turned off the binnacle and shone her light on Irwin.

He was steering them tirelessly, but something in the slant of the mizzensheet behind him puzzled her. She saw that it was fouled on the useless sternlight.

She was supposed to awaken Mitch if she left the cockpit, but for so trivial a problem it seemed silly. She tried first to reach the line with her foot, straining at the length of her tether. She could not quite touch it, so she stuffed the logbook under the cockpit seat to protect it from spray and unclipped the safety belt hook from the mast. She should have snapped it to another fitting on the stern before she stretched out her leg again to kick loose the line. It seemed so close that she did not.

She was balanced on one leg, clinging to a shroud and reaching out her toes for the line, when a wave smacked the port bow, sending a sheet of spray aft to soak her and the whole stern. The boat lurched to starboard under the impact, then rolled to port. It threw her off balance.

She lost her grip on the shroud and pirouetted

wildly on the slickened hatch. For a moment she tottered. She grabbed at another shroud, only tipped the wire cable with her finger. Her flashlight dropped overboard. Her butt hit the rail and for an instant she teetered there, flailing for a handhold. She screamed his name, once.

Then she was in the warm rushing sea, fighting instantly to find the safety line they trailed, just for this impossibility. She groped and swallowed water. She felt the rope brush her leg, then her arm. It was slimy with sea-growth. She grabbed it, and lost it. At the last moment she glimpsed the crazy empty plastic jug bounding at its tail.

She caught the jug but it snapped off in her hands. The line whipped away, streaming phosphorescence. She found her breath and shrieked for Mitch while the dark hull pulled off. She remembered her whistle. She fumbled for its string tied to her jacket zipper, jammed it into her mouth and began wetly to shrill.

She continued to blow long after the boat was lost in the heaving dark swells. She saw the moon, tipping precariously. It was bolted out by a wave, no worse than the one that had spilled her overboard, but monstrous from her angle. She rode up its face like a cork, glimpsed the top of the mainsail, distant against the stars. She whistled again, and listened.

Nothing. She screamed his name once more.

Then she lay whimpering passively in the swells, while the enormity of it all soaked in. Once she thought she saw a faroff flash. She could not orient it well enough even to swim toward it. But if he had dropped the strobe, at least he had heard her go, and was looking for her.

She didn't see it again. After a while she decided that she had imagined it.

When dawn came and she saw no sail instantly, she was shaken and scared, as much for him as herself. *She* knew that she was OK; *he* knew nothing.

She did not doubt that he'd find her.

CHAPTER
3

THE SUN EDGED HIGHER. HE CLUTCHED THE WHEEL, unable to shake the compulsion to turn back and retrace his track. The urge to turn was distracting him from his search. He would find himself staring blindly at water he had not really scanned, weighing the odds on her being ahead or behind, thinking when he should be watching every swell.

His guilt was enormous, distracting him further. He had brought her here and never really even told her why.

Three weeks ago they had sailed into the pass at Bora Bora and anchored behind a sandy *motu* in the lagoon, isolating themselves from the hotels and the village. They were exhausted, licking their wounds from a hurricane which had driven them to sea, licking other wounds as well. That night, as they sat in the cockpit sipping scotch, she asked him idly when their cruise had really begun.

"When we spotted the boat," he said, too quickly.
"You're not leveling," she said. "And we promised."

He had caught a quick image of himself at fourteen,
a rawboned adolescent already almost six feet tall,
reading in his bedroom of a penthouse on a San Francisco hill. It was a year after Pearl Harbor. The U.S.
Navy had crawled back into the ring, due, from his
own point of view, to his father's suicidal participa-
tion. He was sunk in the old man's leather chair,
hauled months before from the den, where his mother
sat every night in majestic masochism, listening to
radio news Mitch refused anymore to hear. Weeks
before, a sergeant whose leg his dad had saved at
Tarawa had called from Oak Knoll Naval Hospital,
across the Bay. His old man had turned down orders
to take over a battle-wagon sickbay for another tour
with the Second Marines.

Mitch's gut still twisted at the thought. Great, just
fucking great! Russian roulette would be quicker and
a lot less painful to those who must sit and wait.
Homework had become impossible. Sucking at a for-
bidden pipe, Mitch anesthetized himself with fiction,
night after night and week after week. *Esquire, Blue-
book, Adventure Magazine* were all too full of the
war. So he turned to Melville, Sabatini, Conrad, Jack
London, and Slocum. *Typee, Wake of the Red Witch,
Lord Jim,* he sucked in with the smoke. Rationally, he
knew that the islands he was adventuring were dead,
or would be ruined by the war, but he saw himself
among them anyway, skippering a trading schooner,
with a slim Polynesian mistress, outwitting pearl-traders
and rescuing heiresses.

It had all been harmless, and comforting. No South
Sea island adventure between the covers of a book
was half as lethal as what his old man must be facing
further west. Mitch had spoken to no one of his reading

tastes, not his mother, not his friends. He was isolated enough already on the hill, when half his buddies lived in shoulder-to-shoulder flats in North Beach. Who read Melville except under duress?

That was when their cruise had really started. But he could not tell Lindy this. He had held to his South Sea fantasy through his own war in Korea and two years of college, pragmatically changing his self-image to that of a Pacific Island Schweitzer doctoring grateful natives on deck, all back-lit by the sun sinking into the golden west.

Lindy already blamed herself because twenty-two years ago he had quit premed for law. To lay the death of the adolescent dream on her too would have been cruel then, and foolish now. He wasn't going to jab at old wounds when the object was to close them. Promises or not, on that he took the Fifth.

"I *am* leveling," he said flatly. "The cruise started when we saw the boat." He reached for her glass. "Another blast?"

She shook her head. In the light from the cabin hatch he could see her eyes holding his. She was not buying it. Uncomfortably, he went below.

The South Sea might have rested forever between the covers of Melville if it had not been for an unemployed housepainter with a paralyzed wife, and the sturdy Atkins ketch, painted red.

The housepainter had shambled into his law office four years ago, and the ketch had crossed his path two years later.

For the housepainter's wife, Mitch had filed the largest medical malpractice suit in the history of California law. In the South Pacific, where he no longer got even the *California Bar Journal,* he had no way of knowing whether the ridiculous million-five judgment had been exceeded since. From his ex-partner's letters, he thought not.

Without the judgment, he could not have retired at 43. He might not, in fact, have been uncomfortable enough about his law practice to want to.

He had filed reluctantly, against a fine young surgeon and the University of California Hospital. The doctor was well trained and the hospital notoriously scrupulous in its records. The patient's tragedy was real enough: she had gone in for a hysterectomy and come out in a basket. The trouble was that no one knew for sure what had happened, or even that it had happened under the knife.

Mitch had hesitated, almost too long. He had never taken a malpractice case. The lanky ghost of his father who after all the wartime heroics had died years later of a tumor in bed, still hovered, sardonic in his views of lawyers who sued doctors.

But the patient's husband had, after all, come to Mitch: there was no taint of ambulance-chasing, and the woman's plight was awful. Even her husband was part of the problem. He was an alcoholic, unable to cope. When Mitch visited his potential client in their jumbled Mission flat, she was in a leased iron lung. She was a dumpy, cheerful schoolteacher, with a little-girl smile. She had been supporting the whole family. She would make a marvelous plaintiff.

Her eighteen-year-old son, radiating hostility, and a spaced-out daughter of sixteen, pricked his sympathy even more.

Still uncommitted, Mitch drove to the hospital. He got nothing there, of course, except a hint that his prospective client's paralysis might be psychosomatic. Psychosomatic or not, everyone conceded that it was genuine.

Puzzled by his own hang-up, he agonized for weeks.

Lindy begged him to drop the whole thing if it bothered him. His partner Bernie, smelling blood, grew
restless. One afternoon the husband called. He was
thinking of going to Melvin Belli.

The next day Mitch filed. The hospital and insurance company wanted to settle: the doctor, only half-
covered, refused. This made Mitch feel better. The
surgeon was asking for it. In two years, when he came
to trial, he would probably learn to trust his lawyer to
do lawyers' work.

In the meantime, Gordon-Bertelli continued to prosper, as they had for twenty years. Mitch won a PI suit
against United Airlines and Bernie won another against
Municipal Railway. Life stumbled along. Mitch's son
graduated from high school and oozed into Berkeley,
where he lasted one semester and flunked. Mitch sent
him to Humboldt, up the coast.

The trial date was set. Lindy grew more beautiful
and took over a class of retarded children. Mitch navi-
gated his third Honolulu Race in her father's sloop,
had to skipper it, really, because this year the old
man seemed too tired and crotchety to make decisions. They placed third on corrected time. Mitch was
bored the whole passage. He felt as if he were running
on biannual rails between San Pedro and Diamond
Head, and his whole life was grooved and pegged.
On previous years he had called a Navy nurse. This
time he forewent the nurse and the awards banquet
and went Scubadiving at Maui instead.

The trial date was postponed. Mitch fell off his
Honda, hillclimbing with his son and the local teenagers. He burned his calf and sprained a wrist, pre-
cipitating a hassle with Lindy, but refused to sell the
bike.

The trial date was reset again. Their German shepherd, the soul of patience, snapped at a newsboy and

had to be checked for rabies. Lindy's brother and his wife had a baby girl.

The trial date was firmed. His partner Bernie hired a receptionist who tried to seduce Mitch and then settled for Bernie. Her typing was terrible. Her diction was worse. They wanted to fire her and flipped to see who would do it. Bernie lost, and refused anyway. They carried her on the payroll until she got married and left.

With the trial a month off, Mitch began to awaken earlier and earlier every morning. He had never had insomnia before. He lay staring at the ceiling, attacked by nameless apprehensions that he and Lindy began to call "the wamblies." Even sex didn't help. He was suddenly crummy in bed. He couldn't understand it. Lindy remained warm and eager and never complained though she seldom had orgasms any more. He resolved after the trial, to ask her about it and maybe see an MD. If there were any doctors who would take him, once they won.

Suddenly they were into the week before the trial. The defendants, to his surprise, seemed to want to take it to the wire. The tide of Mitch's own affairs ran suddenly on a particularly tight schedule, as if the benevolent programmer who seemed at times to have written his life had grown impatient and speeded the tape.

Saturday, with the trial scheduled Monday, the red ketch had sailed into his life. He and Lindy had been crewing with her brother on her father's sloop in San Francisco Bay. Puffy clouds scampered above the Bridge, burgees and pennants snapped in a force-four wind, the racing fleet drove under full sail toward the starting line.

The red ketch was a double-ended Atkins of brutal grace and beauty. She was low-slung, compact, and curiously evocative. In case he might not notice her, the celestial programmer apparently impelled his father-in-law to very nearly ram her amidships.

The ketch had been cutting scornfully through a mob of competitors jostling for the upwind end of the line. She was no racer. She was bound on business of her own, on a starboard tack, secure in her right-of-way. Lindy's father, cutting toward the start, had muttered something and driven obstinately onward. In his pre-start fever, he would have splattered them all on the plates of the *Queen Mary* before he gave an inch.

Lindy, manning the jib, saw the threat and groaned. Her brother Bobby, crouched with his curls blowing, cringed. Mitch, holding a stopwatch, squinted over a railing to get a quick bearing. The bearing did not change.

"Collision course, Shawn," he warned. "He's got the right-of-way."

"Screw him, he's not racing," muttered Shawn. White hair whipping, face pink, he looked like a demented gnome. A drop of spittle inched toward his chin. He swung his head wildly, looking for his archrival, Commodore Russo on *Pegasus.*

Mitch toyed with the unseamanlike thought of doing nothing. A little bump might wake up Shawn's tired blood. But Lindy might get shaken, and he owed the old man more than passive advice. He didn't really give a damn about *Invincible,* but it would be criminal to let the pretty red ketch get hurt.

"Bear off," he growled. The bright-red boat was broad on their starboard bow, steady on her track. "Come *up,* Shawn, goddamn it!"

The old man ignored him. Mitch yanked the wheel away and headed the sloop into the wind. In a drumroll of fluttering dacron they slowed, clearing the ketch's stern by three feet. Shawn jerked a horn from a cockpit rack and let loose a blast at the other boat.

A tall, spare figure stood alone at the ketch's wheel. He regarded them sourly from under a knitted watch-cap. Then he gave them a languid finger and bulled on through the fleet.

"Asshole," muttered Shawn. He spotted *Pegasus* making the starting line, grabbed the watch from Mitch, and peered at it. "Son of a *bitch!* He grabbed the start."

Mitch hardly heard him. He had the binoculars on the ketch, trying to focus on the name on the sternboards. A yawl slid between them. Then he had to help Lindy trim her jibsheet and by the time he looked back, the ketch was a tiny red shape astern.

He had seen the hull-shape before. Plans for her prototype, *Gundred,* lay in an old crate in their basement, with an article he had cut from a wardroom edition of *Yachting* on a carrier twenty years ago.

The ketch was a smaller version of the formidable pilot-boats Colin Archer had built for the Norwegians in the '80s. You still saw the originals, *Oscar Tibring* and *Scandia,* eighty, ninety years old, plowing on forever. Sterling Hayden had owned one briefly. Probably no one could afford to build them any more.

Lindy was watching him from the lee of the deckhouse, where she sheltered when she was forced to race. Bundled in his ancient Navy jacket, peering from the fur-lined olive hood, she looked as young as she had at eighteen, a brown squirrel peeping from foliage. She nodded after the ketch.

"Did you know that guy?"

"No."

"You look as if you'd just seen Jesus."

He grinned. He felt suddenly lighter. A solid cruising boat could do that to him, sometimes, sparking the abandoned, secret dream. "His boat, I like his boat."

She studied his face. "You're cute," she decided. She had gold-flecked, hazel eyes. They were wide and clear and quite easy to look into. "Why that particular boat, so much?"

"I don't know." His eyes flicked to the racing fleet. Any boat there could have spotted the red ketch half the distance to the Farallons and beaten her hands-down. "Didn't *you* like her?"

"I guess," she shrugged. "She looked slow. Actually, I was too scared to watch."

He asked her father if he knew the ketch. Shawn, though he grew more forgetful every year, was still an encyclopedia of yachts on San Francisco Bay. But he was too irritated at losing the start to try to remember and only shook his head.

After the race, which they lost to *Pegasus* and to practically everyone else, Mitch stopped at the Commodore's slip. Russo, a potbellied pediatrician, had cooled since Mitch had brought the malpractice suit. Coiling sheets in his cockpit while his crew sipped beer, he did not even ask him aboard. He had seen their near collision with the red ketch. He recalled that she'd been for sale, off and on over the years, but didn't remember her name, or her owner's.

"Why?" he asked caustically. "He had the right of way."

"I wasn't going to *sue* him, Doctor," Mitch responded. "Just see if his boat was for sale."

Mitch spun on his heel and left. Russo, who had sailed with his dad, had treated Mitch thirty-five years ago for whooping-cough.

A gentle doctor and ordinarily a warm old guy. Just the same, since Mitch didn't tell him how to practice medicine, Russo had no goddamn right to tell him how to practice law.

Sunday morning he dug the plans for the Atkins ketch out of the crate in the basement. In his den overlooking Raccoon Strait, he spread them on the desk, studying the scantlings and dimensions. He should have been polishing the brief for Bernie, who would argue the case. Instead, he wasted half the morning calling yacht-brokers about the red ketch. Nobody knew her.

When he gave up on the boat and tried to concentrate on the brief, his back began to ache. He blamed it on an old football injury and jammed a pillow from the couch behind it. He was studying the long typed pages when his son tapped at the door and wandered in.

Tony was twenty—a very young twenty—almost as tall as he, with gray eyes like his own and black wavy hair as thick as his own had been. He had been catting around the neighborhood for weeks. It seemed an eternity. Now he exuded charm, alerting Mitch.

"I finished the cars, Dad," he reported. "So I'll take off, OK? Nancy—"

"Yeah," Mitch murmured, "Nancy . . ." She was the neighbors' daughter, a shy girl of impeccable manners. Tony had been laying her every hour, on the hour, for two weeks. Everyone knew it: her father, her mother, the neighborhood Filipino gardener, the postman. The two could disappear into thin air when you were talking to them. When they corporealized a half-hour later, as Lindy said: "You *know,* you just *know.*"

"She on the pill?" Mitch asked abruptly.

Tony blushed. "Come *on,* Dad." He grinned modestly. "So I'll split, OK?"

Mitch raised a hand. "Did you *wax* the cars? Or just wash them?"

"I thought I'd wax them tomorrow."

By tomorrow, thought Mitch, you may have screwed yourself to death. "Today, OK?"

"Nancy—"

"Get her to help you. Do you both a world of good. Exercise *all* your muscles." He swiveled back to his desk. Something bothered him. "Hey, wait."

Tony froze. "Yeah?"

"What did you mean, 'wax them tomorrow'? Tomorrow you're heading back for school."

"Look, you're busy. Talk to you later, OK?"

There was nothing he would rather have done than to have talked to his son later, preferably in a year or two. But Tony had already dropped prelaw to major in forestry. He couldn't let him drop forestry for fornication. To procrastinate was to risk surrender. And Lindy might waver herself if the kid stayed around the house for another week.

He arched his spine, which went quickly into some sort of spasm. Heavily, he prepared his soul for battle. The attack was lately repugnant to him. He seemed to lack *l'audace,* which was the reason that he was going to let Bernie plead their biggest case in court. But the best defense was an offense, and the way to protect his flanks now was to assume that the verdict was irrevocably in.

"You packed?"

"Not exactly." Tony looked at his watch. "Look, if you want me to wax the cars, I better—"

"*Pack.* Then wax. First things first."

His son regarded him miserably. "Nancy—"

"Screw Nancy!" growled Mitch. He was instantly sorry. He tried to soften the impact. "*After* you pack. Listen, you don't have to wax. All right?"

Still, he had made a mistake. Tony's face showed shock. Wordlessly, he started out the door. "Tony?" Mitch called.

His son paused. "Um?" he croaked.

"It came out wrong. I'm sorry."

"Forget it." Tony closed the door, gently enough, behind him. Theatrics, true love? Tony probably didn't know himself.

He half rose to follow him. Maybe if he let him take the big Honda to college . . .

He'd probably spend all his time rocketing around and flunk, if he didn't kill himself. Mitch sat down.

The kid should for Christ's sake realize that at twenty he was too old to be drifting like an empty beer can in the surf. And be grateful that his father cared.

He was damned if he was going to chase him around the house groveling and wreck his back for good.

After dinner, on their enormous bed, Mitch lay belly-down so that Lindy could straddle his legs and knead his spine. Her hands, though small, were strong, and her legs were firm and solid beside his own. She was only five years younger than he but somehow, effortlessly, kept herself looking like a daughter instead of a wife. Her hair was thick and vibrant, her skin always tanned and young, her hazel, gold-flecked eyes clear as the day they had met. He thought of her as bronze and amber, lit somehow from within. He would have to tell her this, sometime when she was moody.

Justice Holmes, their shepherd, licked his arm soothingly. Mitch toyed with his satin ear. None of it was fair. The dog stayed in shape, sleeping all day and chewing on newsboys. Tony stayed in shape, diddling broads. Lindy stayed in shape, playing tennis and vacuuming the house. While *he* got fat behind a desk, supporting the whole *ménage,* and his back grew feeble and his balls dried up.

"You know why your back hurts?" Lindy murmured.

He sensed her diagnosis and didn't care to hear. "A downfield block in the USC game," he said quickly. "It hurt twenty years ago."

"You never complained then."

"I was dulling it with booze."

"Nope," she decided. "It's the surgeon."

"I'll file another suit, for sorcery."

"You know what I mean."

She didn't realize that once he had made the decision he had quit worrying about it. He reached back and patted her tail.

"Lindy Gordon," he yawned. "Girl psychotherapist. The paper-back kid. Hey, lower?" Her stubby fingers found the knot. "Thanks."

"You're not like Bernie," she insisted. "It bothers you."

"What, for Christ's sake?"

"Knowing he saved her life."

"He paralyzed her first . . . OK, lower. Hey, you've done it!"

"We think he paralyzed her," she murmured, getting up.

He felt a flash of pain and his back clenched again.

"The case," he said softly, "is solid."

He might not be the most open of men, but he seldom lied to her. He disliked himself when he did.

His back began to throb, stolidly, in time with his pulse. By strength of will he stood up without wincing.

He was damned if he'd tell her, after all her work, that her treatment had failed.

Now that she had cured his back, perhaps, and wrecked his Sunday, she felt awful. She should not question his work, and besides, she was blaming the wrong guy. He hadn't really wanted the case: Bernie had simply conned him.

She had been annoyed because he was sending Tony back to school against his will. Her pique was silly. Mitch was right, Tony had to finish, and Tony should know it too. She found him packing in his room, miraculously without Nancy. It was the first time all month she had found him alone. He was stuffing socks, shirts, and Levi's indiscriminately into an orange backpack. He could have got twice the gear into any one of three suitcases in his closet, and he never hiked where he could take a bus or drive, but she supposed that the backpack was as important to him as Mitch's old Navy duffel bag was to Mitch.

He was red-cheeked and hot-eyed, but only shook his head when she asked what was wrong. She wandered to the window and looked across at Nancy's bedroom. No wonder the poor kid was so horny: the strip-tease acts that must have gone on here all through his puberty must have been enough to strain the soul of a saint.

"You'd think," he growled suddenly, "he went through college as a Trappist monk!"

"Mitch?" she chortled. "More like Cyrano de Bergerac."

"I've gathered. But he's forgotten all that. Didn't *he* ever flunk a course, or anything?"

"No." He looked so disappointed she handed him some ammunition. "He did quit premed for law. And I quit as a sophomore, you knew that?"

"Well, but that was *me*. Right?"

Her face flamed. "What do you mean?"

He poked a finger through a hole in a ski sock. He

tossed it into a wastebasket, with its mate. She retrieved them both, silently, and looked up at him.

He muttered: "Well, you quit because you were pregnant, OK?"

Startled, she started to protest, but changed her mind. He was twenty, it was time he knew. "Yes," she admitted. She had a happy thought. "Hey, did *Mitch* tell you?" She would have liked that.

"You're kidding! No, your wedding picture, in an old *Call Bulletin,* or *Examiner,* or whatever. In a scrapbook at Grandad's apartment, before he moved to the Club. The date was wrong."

Her father had moved to the Bohemian Club ten years ago, so for at least that long Tony had sat on this one. She wondered if there were other secrets from him that were not secrets at all. "That was pretty sharp, for a ten-year-old," she suggested.

"To know my own birthday?" he smiled. "Thanks." He wanted to know if they'd lived together before, and she told him no, hardly anybody did. "He was back from Korea, he still had this kind of drink and be merry aura, tomorrow we die, and, well, I was only eighteen." Now she was apologizing to her own son.

"So you got married to be polite," he reflected. "And lived happily ever after."

"Polite?" she cried. "No! We were in love. *You* happening didn't change a thing." Not strictly accurate, maybe, but about *that* she didn't really know, herself. "It wasn't *1890,* you know. Nobody was *that* polite."

At the door, she turned. "You know," she said, "that was a pretty crummy crack." Her throat was tight and her voice sounded squeaky. " 'Polite!' "

He studied her. His eyes were as gray and soft as his father's. And as inscrutable. "I'm sorry," he said. "OK?"

"I guess." She went down to darn his sock.

CHAPTER
4

HE WAS SUDDENLY IN THE SHADE. HE DRIFTED TEN
degrees off course, and the rising sun was flirting with
the edge of the mainsail. The tempting, elusive
shadow tensed and annoyed him but brought him
back. He spun the wheel quickly and checked the
wake to see how far he had wandered from the track.
It curved significantly before it disappeared among the
swells astern.

He was still impelled to turn and follow its path,
although he had miles to search before he logically
should. He weighed his gut-feeling against common
sense. He could simply not decide unless he knew
when she had gone. It was too soon to turn without a
reason. The only documentary evidence, the logbook,
seemed nowhere.

He had awakened her at midnight, to stand her
watch. He had finished his own stint with a last sweep
of the horizon, gone below, and shaken her shoulder.

He had not even bothered to kiss her awake, as he used to do before Jean-Paul, but he must not think of that now.

She had slithered from her bunk and stumbled to the stove for the cup of coffee he had poured her. He had told her to check topside for squalls every half hour: the boat was far enough from land and steamship lanes so that she could sleep in the intervals. She would set her kitchen timer to wake up for her sweeps, but unlike him, she would not really need it. She was too conscientious to sleep deeply on watch.

Then he had crawled into his bunk. The last heart-grabbing words to the woman he loved were par for the recent course: "Every time you go topside, log the speed."

His eyes went blind again with tears. He clenched the shroud and tried to see into the rising sun. "Christ," he mumbled, half-strangled: "Holy Jumping Jesus Christ!"

He had to quit sniveling if he was going to see at all. He tried to focus his mind on the facts that would help find her, to estimate her drift and his and the difference between them, and how to handle it, but his brain refused to compute unless it knew when it had happened.

Instead it searched for a clue in his memory, a scream or a whistle half-heard in his sleep, that might have awakened him without piercing his conscious mind. If it had been a yell that awakened him, he should be ten miles astern, not here.

He forced his mind back. He had come awake suddenly, an hour and a half before dawn, lying on his back in the starboard bunk in the salon, where he always slept at sea. He had glimpsed the Southern Cross racing across the skylight. He saw it weave amid-ships, zigzag back, and finally disappear behind the starboard edge of the frosted pane.

The bloodshot eye of the compass at the foot of his bunk stared at him. It cast a glow on varnished cabin beams and tinted the clock and barometer to a brassy rose. All very shippy, he had thought. Once, one of the delights of awakening at sea. But, like everything else, dimmed with a year aboard, and too familiar.

Groggy in his bunk, he squinted at the compass heading. Still SSE. The boat was splitting the expanse of ocean between Huahine and Moorea. They were beating heavily, on the best track they could lay into the trades toward Tahiti.

He pushed himself away from the side of his bunk, where the constant heel to starboard had jammed him. The flowered *pareu* he used for a sheet was tangled around his ankles. He kicked it loose.

He was sweating greasily. The ports were closed against spray and probable squalls. From a wind-scoop set on the cabin top, gusts played over his skin, but the puffs were too moist to cool him. He groped for the fan above his bunk and let its fierce little breath whine the length of his body. Then he shut it off to save the battery.

The ketch groaned and muttered at the seas. Her starboard steering cable chirped in the stern. The sound drove the cat crazy and bothered Lindy too. He kept promising her to oil it but at anchor, or tied to the Papeete quai, the cable was quiet and he kept forgetting it.

From forward, where he assumed Lindy lay half-asleep, came the moan of a plank strained a year ago during a haul-out on a primitive marine-railway at Moorea. From aft came a familiar knock. It was the rudder, slamming back and forth. It had hurricane damage besides. He had been going to replace the massive bronze fastenings which rode in the sockets, but there was no use doing it now, if they were selling the boat.

The other sounds required no action. The bilges sloshed as always. The baggy mizzen-sail, set taut at sunset for every foot of gain they could earn during the night, thrummed nervously. From the gargle of water he could hear through the hull he estimated their speed at four and a half knots.

He braced his buttocks against the leeward bulkhead, to go back to sleep. He could not. He had to urinate.

He could go topside and chance a dash of warm spray or he could struggle with the toilet in the head. The toilet trip meant handing his way forward through the main cabin, which was heeling twenty degrees. Squeezing into the head, he would then have to flick on the light. The toilet was below the waterline, and they kept the sea-valves closed when cruising, fearing flooding through the bowl. So he would have to kneel to twist open the seacocks. Then he would have to regain his feet, adjust his trajectory for the list, the roll, and the pitch, and let fly. The problems of train and elevation were considerable.

And if Lindy, forward, was asleep, the snuffling of the pump when he flushed the toilet would awaken her. Pumping the john sounded, up forward, like a flood in a mine tunnel.

He decided to pee topside instead. He rolled from the bunk, handed himself along grab-rails in the overhead like a commuter on a lurching subway. He slid open the main hatch and climbed the companionway ladder. Ducking from the canvas enclosure into the moist night, he ignored a tug of guilt as he brushed past his web-nylon safety belt without putting it on. The belts had snap-shackles you clipped to the rigging.

He had made her promise him, and had promised her, always to wear one topside at night, but it was a lot of trouble just to take a leak, and if you were nude, the webbing rubbed at your belly. Since Jean-Paul, such promises did not seem to matter, and he had ignored his own rule.

Unbelted, he stepped to the check. Clinging to a mizzen shroud, he voided over the rail. He watched his phosphorescent trail slide astern. He re-estimated their speed at five knots. He stepped down into the cockpit. Reluctant to return to his stuffy bunk, troubled vaguely now by something wrong, he inspected the self-steering vane hanging aft.

It stood rock-steady in the unchanging wind. Irwin, as Lindy had christened it, was steering with his customary precision. Mitch flipped on the compass light and checked the tension in Irwin's sinews, thin steel cables leading aft to the small auxiliary rudder. The cables were tight and the little rudder was swinging slavishly, hard-port to hard-starboard, obeying the tug of Irwin's arms as they followed the nudge of the wind on the vane. To watch Irwin too long always made him tired, and a little guilty, as if they should feed him or keep him in booze.

He was still uneasy. Aft of Irwin, there was a tangle of lines. Hanging tightly to a mizzen shroud, he kicked it loose. For a moment he gazed astern at the living green wake they laid.

A thick yellow polypropylene line writhed in their track. They trailed it for safety. Tonight it was strangely passive and looked white in the moonlight. It was sixty feet long, secured strongly to an after mooring-bit. You were supposed to grab it if you fell overboard and try to hang on until your mate rounded up into the wind. With the boat finally stopped, the victim might even use the hawser to haul himself back.

The line should have been dragging an empty plastic jug as a buoy astern, bobbing and dancing in his wake. But he could not see it, although the line itself was wagging from port to starboard. Its listlessness bothered him. He began to haul it in. When its end was twenty feet astern he could see in the glow of the sternlight that the plastic jug was gone.

He hauled the rest quickly aboard to check it. The eye he had spliced through the handle of the missing jug was still intact. The cap of the jug must have loosened, after five thousand miles dragging in their wake. The jug must have filled with water and become so heavy that its handle had broken off.

He tossed the hawser back into the wake to let it trail without the jug. He could attach some sort of buoy tomorrow, but since the line was surfacing all right without it, he guessed that he probably wouldn't.

He was turning away when he felt rippling fur at his ankles. It was M. le Chat. Gently, he nudged the cat away with a bare foot, afraid it would be washed overboard if a wave shot over the rail.

M. le Chat was a gift to Lindy from a waitress at the Vaima Restaurant, on the Papeete quai. He had been intended as coprarat-insurance. Sure enough, they had picked up a rat in Rarotonga after the hurricane, an unassuming recluse who liked Kellogg's Special K. Mitch had glimpsed him yesterday and chased him to the bilges, where he had disappeared between the hull and inner sheathing. He was enormous.

For this rat, the cat was as useful as a high school tackle sent in to nail O.J. Simpson. He was indifferent, or scared. The stowaway was big enough to chew him up and spit him over the side. The cat's real interest lay in the imaginary bird chirping under the aft compartment.

Mitch didn't really like M. le Chat. Now he decided

to discharge him dishonorably when they got to Tahiti. He could give him back to the waitress, perhaps, and replace him with another dozen traps.

The problem would be Lindy. He organized his brief: "He still gets seasick."

Probable rebuttal: "I still get seasick, Mitch. Are we going to get rid of me?"

"He won't hunt for the frigging *rat!*"

"You won't hunt for the leak down the mast."

"If there's any kind of sea, he misses his sandbox."

"He misses his sandbox? Monsieur le Chat, listen to *that!"*

The boat, any cruising boat, was simply too small for a pet. M. le Chat slept at the foot of Lindy's bunk and resented a rival. Whenever they wanted to make love they had to lock the damn thing in the head, or it was swarming all over them, horny and purring. Mitch was surprised that it had left her bunk now.

Hell, it was all academic. They would throw in the cat as a premium when they sold the boat. Special, Christmas season only.

He looked at it uneasily. The compass light, caught in its eyes, seemed to have set fire to its brain. Its glossy flanks began to heave with excitement. Slowly the ebony belly sank to the deck. One white forepaw rose absently. It was a sitting duck for a stray wave.

"Monsieur le Chat," Mitch murmured, "there's *no* goddamn bird! *Il n'y a pas d'oiseau! Attention aux vagues!"* Mitch was suddenly impatient to return below. He picked up the cat and spilled him roughly down the companionway steps. Turning back to douse the compass light, he noticed that Lindy's safety belt was not swinging next to his under the canvas shelter. That was strange. She was unlikely to be wearing it in her bunk, and a year at sea had taught them to keep safety gear in place. She was better at this than he.

The cat scooted back up the ladder and brushed by him. It was heading aft again. Mitch grabbed at it and missed. He saw it spring at the hatch, slide across its slick surface, and thump into the leeward rail. The next wash of water could scoop it into the sea.

"Idiot," he growled, lunging to recover it. He was apprehensive now, inexplicably nervous. He snagged the cat and this time carried it below, forgetting to turn off the light. He wanted overpoweringly to see Lindy scrunched naked on her bunk, bronze hair spilled, fine hips curving to her tanned legs and her poor, sea-scarred shins.

He tossed the cat into the head-compartment, slammed the door, and ducked forward. He brushed aside the curtain to the forward compartment. Her bunk-light was not on. The compartment was pitch-black. Shaken and frightened, he groped for the light, missed, felt in the bunk itself. He found nothing. "Lindy?" Tight with terror, he found the light at last and flicked it on.

The port bunk was empty. So was the starboard. "Lindy?" he shouted, checking the head and even the clothes-locker. *"Lindy!"*

A bolt of panic tore through him, paralyzing him. He began to tremble uncontrollably. He could not budge from the spot.

When he could move again, he moved swiftly. Sometimes when it was stuffy below, she slept topside on the dinghy's plywood sea-top, her belt clipped to a tie-down line. He slid open the forward hatch, just in time to catch a warm splash of spray. He scrambled topside, too frantic to close the hatch, and lunged for the dinghy.

He could see by moonlight that it was bare. He continued aft, slipping along the deck and skinning his knee. Astern, he worked automatically. The strobe lamp, horseshoe buoy, and the man-overboard pole were all connected by a line, ready for action on the rail. He hurled the lot into the wake. He found himself sobbing quietly but working out the drill, not sure why he was dropping it all here when she could be hours away astern, simply doing it anyway.

The floating lamp, weighted to bob erect, tumbled upright and began to flash its strobe: one lightning-blink, visible for miles, every five seconds or so, so long as its battery lived. Its first flash froze the man-over-board pole, weighted and buoyed to tilt upright, with its orange flag caught in midflutter. The yellow horse-shoe buoy sat nearby. The second flash silhouetted the flag just peeping over the crest of the next swell. By the third flash the thirteen-foot pole and buoy had dropped out of sight in a trough.

He still could not believe that she was gone. He flicked on the spreader-lights, illuminating everything on deck and halfway up the mast. She might not be overboard at all: she could have come topside, fallen, be lying unconscious on deck.

So he ranged the rail, port and starboard, handing himself from lifeline to shrouds, stooping to keep his center of gravity low against the constant roll. She was nowhere topside. OK, she might be washed over and be dragging half-drowned from her safety-line: he would pull her aboard and revive her and they would laugh about it tomorrow.

Feet on the rail, hands clinging to shrouds, ass over the water, he swung far out to port, then scrambled to starboard, peering fore and aft.

Nothing. He turned off the spreader-lights, which had already wrecked his night-vision, and spun to disen-gage Irwin. He reversed course in a slamming, flapping panic of sails and sheets, so shaken that he found difficulty in adding 180 degrees to their heading of 160 to find the reciprocal. Finally, without the answer, he

simply began to turn toward the winking light. When
it was dead ahead he tried the sum again.

He squinted at the compass. It was level as the en-
circling horizon, seemed to have gone crazy. It tossed
and twisted, blurred under the ruddy little light. He
managed to steady it at last on 340, almost NNW. In
three minutes he was close abeam the strobe. The
search was starting now.

He tightened a knob on Irwin, giving the vane control and freeing himself to act. He ducked below,
checking the time on the chronometer above his chart
table. 1720 Greenwich, 0320 local. Less than two
hours until dawn.

He leaned on the chart table, chewing a pencil. He
subtracted three minutes from the present time, call it
0317. Say he had discovered her gone at 0317. He
reached for their logbook in a line of publications above
the chart table. Strangely, it was not where they left it.
He searched the cabin wildly, throwing clothes and
books and pillows everywhere. If he found the log with
its half-hour entries, it could give him a clue as to
when she had last been aboard.

The log was nowhere, and there was no more time
to waste searching for a book when he should be
searching for his wife.

So he penciled a shaky position on the chart and
labeled it 0317. He picked off the latitude and longitude with dividers. His hands trembled so badly that
he had to do it twice, and even then he could not keep
the figures in his mind and he had to check it again.

He finished. He hurtled through the cabin and
clicked on the radio-telephone. He switched to the international emergency frequency—2182—and called
Mahina Radio in Papeete, over and over.

Papeete was only seventy miles northwest, but he
got no response. He began to broadcast blindly, any-

way: *Mayday,* followed by his latitude, longitude, and present course. When his French became confused, he shifted to English.

When he still raised no reply, he decided that his signal was being blanked by the crags of Moorea fifty miles to windward.

It was then that he had lunged back topside, swung up the mast, and begun the useless predawn vigil from the shrouds. He had stayed until the failing wind forced him to take over the helm.

Now, still not knowing when she had gone, he forced his attention back to sea and the skies. The sun had finally edged its way up behind the mushroom clouds abeam, tinting their summits pink. Steering with his foot on the wheel, eyes taut with fatigue, he tried to estimate how much time he had to take down the mainsail before the first squall hit him.

The cloud-matador had somehow changed to Marie Antoinette, hair towering. She looked frail in her bustle, but her trailing skirts of rain were just as dangerous as the matador's cape. There might be enough time to drop the mainsail before the folds of her train enveloped him, but to do so meant taking his eyes again off the sea.

The sun broke from behind the roil of her coiffure and turned the water to windward into a lane of hammered brass. It was impossible to search it with the naked eye. He dashed below for his Polaroid sunglasses. When he could not find them, he tore into his drawer and flung clothes, handkerchiefs, and socks around the cabin. He discovered them finally where he always kept them, in a net above his bunk. He barged back topside.

Now there was even less time to strike the mainsail before the blow. He was afraid even to leave the wheel. The squall hit in a blinding sheet of rain and spray. For five minutes he could not see upwind at all, and to leeward not more than a hundred feet. Somehow *Linda Lee* slogged through it. The wind shifted, and when he thought they were safe, another squall blustered through, with thirty-knot gusts.

When the wind shifted again he checked the sails. Incredibly, there were no torn seams. After the squall line passed, the trades began again, gently at first, and finally enough power for Irwin.

Quickly he placed the vane in charge. He pulled binoculars from a plastic sheath on the mizzenmast and slung their strap over his neck. He climbed the ladder to the spreader, clenching the shrouds as the roll swept him port and starboard and port again. Gauging the motion, he got a foot over the yard and pulled himself to a sitting position on its flat upper surface, clinging to the mast to maintain his seat.

He glanced down at the empty cockpit. The bronze binnacle, still sparkling with rain, stood lonely in its center. He put his binoculars on it and found that he could read the after-lubberline on the compass. Irwin, towering in the stern, was holding course precisely, as if he could see the compass too.

He brought the glasses up and tried to study the water up-sun. He was dazzled by dancing gold. He let his binoculars swing from his neck and searched with the Polaroid glasses alone.

The Polaroids helped, but the glitter tempted him to concentrate on the restful blue to the west, and he had to force himself to study the water to windward.

Two white terns were flashing off his quarter, spiraling upward together to perhaps two thousand feet, striving for a wider horizon. He put his binoculars on them for a moment. They were delicate, ethereal creatures with translucent wings, always in pairs. The Tahitians called them the love-terns, *itatae,* and the *bonnitiers* steered for them to find *mahi-mahi*. *Itatae* seldom flew alone. Lindy had wondered what happened to one when the other was lost in a storm.

(The sensitive lawyer, man of words and infinite feeling, had an answer for her, of course: "They find somebody else, honey. One good tern deserves another.")

He winced. He dropped his binoculars to the area of ocean beneath the birds, looking for whatever kept them over that particular spot.

There was nothing, anywhere.

CHAPTER
5

THE DAY THE TRIAL BEGAN, THE BACK SPASM SEEMED to have shortened Mitch's left leg by half an inch. He limped into court feeling more like a personal-injury plaintiff than a lawyer. He was tired of the classroom-smell of courtrooms, preferred even the bookish smell of their quiet library in the office. But he had scheduled himself to remain next to Bernie for their week of triumph, in case he was needed.

Bernie, trim and solid, wore his poverty-lawyer suit, a blue double-breasted that he had bought sometime after Korea and seemed to keep better shined than his shoes. He was immaculately clean but as shabby as the law allowed. His iron-gray hair was carefully mussed, as if concern for his client had occupied his mind while he combed it. When he regarded the jury, his dark eyes pleaded with it to understand a night-school lawyer who had come up the hard way. Their client was absent, but you could

43

feel the injustice of her own pain and suffering in every word he spoke.

Mitch felt a quiver of something like panic. A million and a half! They had gone too far. He discovered suddenly that he really didn't want Bernie to succeed too well.

Bernie charged ahead, turning in his best performance yet. He asked their star witness, a doctor from Johns Hopkins who also held a law degree, for a summation: "Then, Doctor, what are the actual odds?"

"On what, Mr. Bertelli?" the doctor asked. He radiated sincerity: he and Bernie were a beautiful team. Mitch wondered when he had last actually treated a patient: he was a neurosurgeon, impressively trained, but more lawyer than a medical man, and it had cost them five thousand dollars and expenses to get him on the stand for an hour.

"The odds," Bernie repeated, "that her paralysis could have stemmed from some mysterious virus she brought to the operating table?"

"None. Not one in a million."

The defense awakened. "Objection! Your Honor, that's an opinion!"

"Of an expert," Mitch broke in from the table, to get the heat off Bernie.

The young judge looked at him with some irritation. "An expert bookmaker?" he demanded. "Objection sustained," he ruled. "I will caution counsel for plaintiff. And Doctor, you're a member of the Maryland bar. You should know better."

At least, Bernie was keeping their jury awake. Four of them were pensioners. Bernie, a self-proclaimed master of instant analysis, had lumped them together. They were knee-jerks: they would prejudge any wealthy surgeon in favor of a plaintiff. As for the rest, there was an ex-kindergarten teacher (their client having taught math), an Italian barber, an ancient Jewish gentleman kept by his family, a retired merchant marine cook, a black janitor, and two housewives near the client's age of thirty. The only juror in which Bernie had detected the slightest threat of intelligence was an unemployed young carpenter who was a graduate of S. F. State. He had an ex-hippie, Haight-Ashbury air about him and a flowing moustache. He showed the seed of charisma that you searched for in assessing any jury. He had been at S. F. State during the riots which had closed it. U.C. Hospital, the co-defendant, was state-owned. The carpenter would influence the rest of the nebbishes all out of proportion to his vote, and might still harbor a grudge against the Establishment from the Reagan days.

Anyway, neither they nor the defendant had objected to him, and now Bernie was subtly addressing himself to him, skirting the line between offending him with schlock and keeping the rest of the jurors attention. Mitch felt a stab of pity for the white-faced, handsome surgeon, with his future in the hands of the cretins in the box and insurance-company counsel who was all reputation and no brains.

Court adjourned late. Mitch had left his car in the office garage, and there were no taxis in the rush hour. He fought his way onto a Sutter Street bus. A beautiful Chinese baby regarded him delightedly from its mother's shoulder. It squinted and sneezed full in his face. Someone broke wind silently and the captives glared at each other.

Three blocks in advance of his own stop, he began to inch his way to the door. A small man might have shoved through, but his height and strength prohibited violence. So he was two blocks past his office building by the time he was expelled to the sidewalk like a seed from a squeezed grapefruit.

It took him fifteen minutes to gentle his car up the ramps of the office garage, trailing the whole stenographic population of their building, only to join another crawl up Sutter Street.

If the City got any more crowded, traffic would someday freeze forever, glacierlike on the hills, and they would have to build a new city in Marin. Despite the fresh wind funneling through the Gate, they were even getting smog, like L.A.

He stopped at the St. Francis Yacht Club, to see if he could find, around the polished redwood bar, any oldtimers who recalled the red ketch. Everyone remembered her fouling the starting line, but no one recalled her name or who owned her.

When he got home he found that Tony had left, as instructed, on the morning bus, to Humboldt. It made him feel odd, their parting on a note of anger. After dinner he went to his study, intending to call Tony's dormitory. The phone rang first, cutting off his good intention. It was Lindy's brother, Bobby.

"Mitch, that stretch of beach you have up near Bragg?"

He felt a jab of irritation. It was more than a stretch of beach; it was a private cove sheltered by towering rocks. They had some vague idea of building a summer home on it, or a retreat for when he retired.

He felt a sudden thrill. If they won the case, in any reasonable amount, he could probably quit *now:* deep-six the traffic, the parking, depositions, conferences, office-coffee and phony secretary-smiles.

Ridiculous. To do what? He was only forty-three. At fifty, maybe, sixty, sure. Anyway, they'd need the beach. "You can't sell it, Bobby. It's the only place in the world with fresh air. Water's thicker than blood."

Bobby told him that an owner a half-mile north had won a zoning variance for a mobile-home park.

Mitch felt sick. "They're out of their minds. Trailers?"

"Not trailers, mobile homes. Some of them go for thirty thousand bucks. Anyway, for him, it's done. And you better beat the Coastal Commission. They'll freeze the beach. You got access from the highway. You ought to try for commercial zoning, before it's too late."

"What, for a hotdog stand? On *our* beach?"

"You might as well, if there's going to be one around the point anyway."

He had something there, but their beach was unique. "I'd sell *this* place first," he blurted. Now why the hell had he said that? His brother-in-law was an earnest study in tunnel-vision, and now that he had been stirred up, would never let it drop.

Sure enough, Bobby shifted gears. "Why not?" he asked softly. "It's too big. Tony's grown. You know what I can get you for it?"

They had bought their home for $60,000 fifteen years ago, when Tony was five. They had thought they had paid too much for the sloping land. To redo the house, which clung to the rock by its fingernails, had taken massive loans. He had infused his own sweat to save the plumbing and his cash to cling to land that wanted to slide. He had built, against architectural advice, an enormously expensive sunporch suspended over Raccoon Strait. It had turned out beautifully.

The challenge of perfecting their niche in the hillside was gone. He never worked on the place anymore. When a pipe burst now he groaned and simply called a plumber. But he didn't want to know what they could sell it for, not at all.

"How much?" he heard himself ask.

"A hundred and fifty, easy." Mitch stiffened. Bobby went on: "And I'd find you a nice condo to move into."

"Your sister," Mitch said drily, "would just love that."

Sarcasm was lost on Bobby. "They all do," he enthused, "once they've made the break. Hey, I even have a prospect!"

"No way," said Mitch. His mouth was dry and he was oddly nervous. He did not feel anymore like phoning Tony. Instead, he went upstairs to join Lindy in the living room. Offhandedly, his heart pounding, he told her. "Of course," he said, "if we sold it, we'd never find anything like it again. Probably never live in another house."

She had been reading the paper, and she folded it and put it down. "Are you serious? What good is the money?"

"It's not the money," he shrugged. "Tony *is* leaving, someday. We have to face it."

"He's leaving because we're practically dynamiting him loose. It's still home to him. It's home to *us.*"

He nodded and wandered to the window. She spoke from the chair: "Are you *tired* of it, Mitch?"

"I don't know," he murmured. "Hell, you know how I am."

"But it's not a camera or a motorcycle! It's home! And I love it! It's *us!* We don't want to live in a condominium!"

"That's for sure. OK, I *told* him to forget it. Let's us forget it too."

He didn't know, himself, what he'd had in mind. After the trial, he'd think it through.

Their client was rolled in in her iron lung. She was sworn before the bench. The effect on the jury was brutal. Bernie questioned her very quickly: her own testimony was unimportant; their object was to show her to the jury. Her smile, reflected in the mirror she must use to see other human beings, was heartbreaking. When she spoke of the surgeon, her eyes were tragic. His postoperative care was not even admissible as evidence, and she was suing the man who had saved her life. Her net impact was incalculable, but as she was wheeled out, Mitch sensed from the jury that it was no longer a question of *whether,* simply *how much.*

Mitch missed Bernie's summation. He was alone in the jury room, lying on a leather couch, to take the strain off his back. He had no further desire to attend Bernie's finest hour. He was jumpy and fearful. Something was changing within him. He needed a drink. When his back spasm passed he returned to find the courtroom cleared. The court had recessed until tomorrow. A note from Bernie lay on their table: *"Splash one. Enemy tried to bail out. We refused eight hundred grand. I love you. Do you love me?"*

He swore silently and limped to a phone booth in the marble corridor. He dialed his office and caught Bernie arriving.

"Listen, are you running this case all alone?"

"We're doing fine," Bernie said placidly.

"Did you explain she might get *less?*"

"I didn't ask her."

He almost dropped the phone. "Stay put," he said tightly. "I'll be right down."

"Yeah, well, I won't be here. I'm taking a little hop this afternoon."

"Where to?"

"Just flying around. Alone with my God. In ever-decreasing circles until I disappear up my own asshole."

Mitch felt as if he were playing second lead in a nightmare. "She's *my* client! What am I going to tell her when she finds out you turned down eight hundred grand? Without *consulting* her for Christ's sake!"

"Tell her you have the Cincinatti Kid for a partner."

"I may not have him," Mitch said darkly, "for very long." He hung up. Now he really needed the drink. He left the courthouse and crossed to a little bar-restaurant on Van Ness.

As the head waitress led him through the gloom inside, he glimpsed the surgeon eating alone at a table in the corner. He almost turned to leave, but the doctor glanced up and spotted him. He was damned if he would retreat after that, so he let the girl seat him at a table at the other side of the room. He was sipping a Gibson and studying the menu when he sensed someone standing over him. He knew it was the surgeon before he looked up.

"May I sit down?"

He took a deep breath. "Doctor, I'd rather you didn't. You have counsel, the case isn't over, it's a matter of propriety."

" 'Propriety,' " echoed the doctor, sitting down anyway. "You almost said 'ethics,' didn't you?" He signaled the waitress, ordered a drink, and asked Mitch if he wanted another.

Mitch shook his head. His cheeks were burning. If one of the doctor's attorneys wandered in, Mitch might be facing an ethics committee within a week. "We've said it all, Doctor. The jury's out. Your offer to settle was rejected."

The doctor smiled. He was a very handsome man, like a TV surgeon. He was a Californian, but a product of eastern private schools. He had gone to Milton Academy, as Mitch recalled, then Harvard Medical and a residency at McGill. His clothes breathed wealth and his features were chiseled WASP: Mitch could bet that his ancestors were straight Boston.

If he had been less eastern, less handsome, more in
the mold of the traditional San Francisco practitioner
that the older jurors must have known, his case would
be less precarious. The clothes were his attorney's
fault; he should have been better briefed.

"I'm told we'll probably lose," he said mildly. "And
I'm facing bankruptcy. Also, a ruined practice. And I
have some questions about it, that's all."

"I can't answer them." He searched for the waitress,
who was ignoring him. He had decided that he wanted
another drink after all.

The doctor went on: "You're an intelligent man.
So no matter what you believed when you started,
somewhere our testimony convinced you that I hadn't
caused her paralysis. But you continued. Why?"

"You're presuming you convinced me," Mitch said
thickly. "And you didn't." He reminded the doctor
that civil cases weren't criminal trials, that the defendant wasn't necessarily innocent until proven guilty. He
sounded phony, to himself. "A civil case isn't *built* on
reasonable doubt. It's built on a preponderance of
evidence. That, we submitted, I think."

The doctor's gray eyes were unblinking. "You don't
think that at all," he said softly.

"I won't discuss it," Mitch insisted. And then,
stupidly: "Your witnesses were guessing. Your lab was
guessing. They didn't know. They should! *You* don't
know. She's paralyzed. You couldn't prove *how* it happened."

"She's paralyzed, all right. But we proved how it
didn't happen. To you, I'm sure. And maybe your
partner. And to that so-called doctor you imported.
To the judge? I don't know. Not to the jury, I'm sure."

"Well, it's a jury trial," said Mitch. "Waitress, goddamn it, come over here, will you?"

She didn't hear him, turned and sauntered to the

kitchen. He slammed his hand on the table angrily. Christ, he was coming apart. He should have left the moment the doctor sat down. He saw himself explaining why he hadn't to the Committee on the Canons of Ethics. "Doctor," he blurted, "I've been polite, but we can't discuss this any further."

The doctor nodded, put his hands on the table. They were stubby, Mitch noted, not the traditional surgeon's hands, though reputedly among the surest in the city. For a moment they lay there, silent accusers. The doctor slid back his chair but still he did not rise. "You know, I saved her life."

She had gone in for an everyday procedure and come out a physical vegetable, but Bernie had made that point. "I'll concede that," Mitch said hoarsely.

"I'm rewarded with ruin. Have you thought of the effect on other doctors?"

"I've told you, damn it, I can't discuss it."

"Will it make them more careful? They're already careful. They know that whatever happened to my patient, it wasn't over medication, as you contend, or a severed nerve, or whatever else your Baltimore quack dragged in. No, just bad luck. An Act of God. Maybe psychosomatic! Or a bite from a housefly who'd been to a stable, or a mosquito, or a blood clot ready to go adrift, or undiagnosed paresis that came to life by chance."

"Doctor," broke in Mitch, "if *you're* not going, I will."

"What happens to some poor bastard in the future with a patient like mine? She comes out of anesthetic, and the next day she's paralyzed, dying. He wants to stay in practice. For his family's sake, or to save lives, or to make money, or whatever. Will he work night and day to save you a potential plaintiff?"

"What?" croaked Mitch. "You mean he'll let the patient die? That's ridiculous!"

"Your confidence in my profession is touching," said the doctor. "I wish I had the same in yours." He rose. "Because, suppose I *hadn't* been able to save her? The issue would now be a hospital bill, some funeral arrangements, a doctor's bill. Fifteen hundred, two thousand? Not enough to make the papers, even if her husband had sued."

"We'd have *advised* him to sue," Mitch said, weakly.

"Maybe," the doctor said softly. "But thirty percent contingency fee of two thousand dollars is six hundred bucks. Who would have taken the case?"

The restaurant murmur fell away. The background music faded with the clink of silverware. In one of the moments of silence which falls on any public place at the wrong instant, Mitch heard himself say, stuffily and much too loudly: "*I'd* have taken the case."

"Good. I wondered." He looked into Mitch's eyes and then headed back to his table.

Mitch got up, glared at the startled waitress, strode to the cashier's desk, and slapped down a five-dollar bill for the drink. He left without waiting for change.

CHAPTER
6

HE SWUNG IN GIANT ARCS TWENTY-FIVE FEET ABOVE the water, astride the spreader. The seas were rising. To hang onto the mast he had to face leeward, toward the sail, one foot dangling forward of the mast and one aft. To scan the swells to windward he had to twist his upper body completely, straining his belly-muscles and the ligaments in his back. He could not search the area hidden by the sail until it had passed by and lay off his port quarter.

His toes had rubbed raw on the sail, his bare scrotum stung with salt from the yardarm, and the constant twisting to see had slipped a familiar needle of pain into his back. He tried to shift position, so that both feet hung forward. He almost pitched off, so he hoisted the foot back.

He checked his watch. It was 6:40 A.M. He was reaching the northern limit of search. If she had fallen overboard just after he had gone to sleep, she was in these waters. She could be no further up the track. But he resisted the turn south along a trail already searched. He decided to stay on course another fifteen minutes, in case his navigation was off.

Until the sun was high enough for a morning shot, his dead-reckoning position would grow more and more inaccurate. Still, he must not correct his track. Although current was almost certainly setting him toward Huahine Island, somewhere to the west, the boat and Lindy were both in the same vast mass of water drifting over the ocean floor. If he tried to fight the set and return to the same geographical position at the end of each run, she would simply drift further and further from the path he patrolled.

The two terns had stayed with him since dawn. At first he had guessed that they assumed he was a *bonnitier*, fishing far from Tahiti, and that they were waiting for him to jettison bait. But, through the hours, they had become his friends and allies. They wheeled now in intricate chandelles to starboard, very high, as if searching for her in waters his eyes could not reach.

He climbed stiffly down the mast to turn south, finally admitting that she could no longer be anywhere ahead. Before he turned back to search the track again, he ducked below for an instant to try once more to call Radio Mahina in the peaks behind Papeete. Nothing came back but a crackling buzz. The invisible crags of Moorea, spiring sixty miles southeast between him and Tahiti, still blocked him.

He considered clearing out of the area to call for help. Planes and choppers from Faaa could be here in an hour, and a French destroyer in two. But it would take half the morning to move clear of interference with the hidden mountains to the east. And there was still no assurance that he would be heard. Her chances were better if he stayed.

He drew on shorts to protect his raw skin from the spreader. His raw toes were a problem. He went barefoot at sea and wore sandals ashore. It had been months since he had had on shoes, and his feet were swollen from dangling aloft. His deck-shoes would not go on, so he left his feet bare.

He considered brewing more coffee, knowing what fatigue would soon do to him. But, here below, he was getting jumpier by the moment. He glanced at his watch again. He was sailing through waters she could not be in, and he wanted to reverse course. He decided to skip the coffee.

Before he climbed topside he took another quick look for the logbook. The cabin was already a shambles from his search for his sunglasses: he completed the destruction in the new search for the log, and still found nothing. A mystery, but he had no time to mull over it now, so he scrambled to the cockpit.

He disengaged Irwin, spun the wheel, and tacked to the SSE course, hard on the wind again, and pounding.

He had been climbing down from the mast every fifteen minutes to drop something, anything floatable, overboard, for he had a gut-desire to mark his trail over the waste and to leave debris that might help her. Bunk pillows, spare timbers, life-jackets, were all strewn somewhere in his wake. Now he dumped his foam mattress overboard at the northwestern limit of his search. The southeastern limit was already marked with the strobe light and waving flag. He did not expect to find the mattress when and if he returned in six hours, but it seemed to add a needed punctuation to the track he was plowing.

Watching it, he wished instantly that he had not dropped it. It mocked his search. In less than thirty seconds it was out of sight, skidding downwind and dipping behind the purple swells. It reappeared, undulating lazily, and eased out of sight again, for keeps.

For an instant his guard dropped. He felt that she had no chance, not in these swells, none at all.

The terns swooped from aloft, apparently to inspect the invisible mattress. They discussed it in high piping voices and banked to the east. Something in their purposeful flight told him that they had given up, were returning to Moorea or, most likely, Marlon Brando's island, Tetiaroa.

He was betrayed. He had been counting on them for a startled dive that would mean that they were investigating something in the swells below. He almost shouted after them to stay, or at least, if they saw her homeward-bound, to return and lead him to the spot.

He messaged his eyeballs. He was groggy with fatigue: hardly 7 A.M. and he was ready to yell at birds. He should really make the coffee.

Instead he climbed back aloft.

CHAPTER
7

HE SAT MISERABLY IN HIS OFFICE HIGH ABOVE THE city. Neatly centered on the desk before him lay the opened file on *Roxon vs. Maguire,* an accident case due for trial next week. His client had had whiplash.

The top sheaf was a deposition he had taken last year from the defendant. Beneath the deposition, layer upon layer, would lie reports: Form 555, California Highway Patrol, Marin County Sheriff Department Report, Report from County Emergency, with x-rays. There would be a Blue Cross Report, a Report from Attending Physicians, even a report from a chiropractor. There was somewhere a series of pictures of his client's Coupe de Ville. A deposition from Ted, of Ted's Body and Fender Shop, lay in the pile. A neat diagram Mitch had drawn himself lay somewhere several strata down: braking distance, position of witnesses, location of a traffic light, all carefully ruled, scaled, and frozen in time. Below that lurked a deposition from his client's doctor and a Xerox of the defendant's blood alcohol report.

The file was three inches thick. They seemed to get thicker every year.

Below all the papers, of course, lurked the presence of his client, a beefy stockbroker, as he remembered, probably long out of his neck-brace by now, but still the innocent victim of pain and suffering then, all because of a machine-shop foreman's nightly inability to get past the local cocktail lounge.

They would probably settle the case in the corridors before it was called. But in case they did not, he must dig it all up now, like some sort of legal archeologist, and try to breathe life into an incident three years old, in which he had not the slightest interest.

His back ached. He shifted in his leather chair, squirmed, and tried to concentrate. *Q: And as you approached the light, did you see it change to yellow? A: No, sir. Q: Did you at any time observe the stoplights on the plaintiff's car—"*

Through the open window, from twenty-two stories down, he heard voices. He peered out. It was a clutch of kids in orange robes, with shaven heads. They had been chanting on the corner of Powell and Sutter for almost a month. They had become part of the scenery. He had wondered how they stood the tedium of it all: *hare krishna, hare krishna, hare krishna,* day after day. But the chanting was no more tedious than the pile of shit on his desk.

He closed the window. The telephone on his desk was flashing. It was Bernie, from the Hall of Justice.

"Mitch, you sitting down?"

"OK. What is it?"

The jury on the malpractice case had found in full. The young judge, incredibly, was letting the judgment stand. He almost dropped the phone.

"Say again?"

"The whole *million fucking five,* Mitchel!"

His hands went clammy. He tried to picture their happy client, getting the news in her iron coffin, but the surgeon's stubby hands intruded. *"Jesus!"*

Bernie began to issue orders like an admiral. Mitch was to have Kitty, Bernie's secretary, call the *Examiner,* before their deadline. Then Mitch and Lindy were to meet him at the airport. "What-ho for Cannery Row. It's champagne and lobster for lunch."

They had flown to Monterey for lunch before, to celebrate lesser victories. This time Mitch did not feel like going at all. But Lindy, who had loyally cooled on the surgeon when Mitch reported the bloodbath in the restaurant, would enjoy it, so he agreed.

They took off in Bernie's Bonanza, Lindy in back and Mitch in the copilot's seat. He got Bernie to sweep past the yacht harbor at Half Moon Bay, on the off-chance that they would spot the red ketch. Nothing they saw resembled her. They banked and sped south over wave-beaten cliffs. At Santa Cruz he saw a red ketch anchored out, and got Bernie to dive again. He buzzed her viciously, almost taking her masthead off, but it was not the same boat: too stumpy, Hannah-designed, built more like a stubby middleweight than the graceful light-heavy they were searching out.

He did not ask for futher aerobatics. They skimmed elegantly down on the Monterey runway, rented a car, and drove to Lou's Fish Grotto in the pier.

They sopped up two quarts of champagne over magnificent lobster. Lindy grew giggly, which almost never happened. Bernie lifted his glass.

"To Gordon, Bertelli, et al—"

"Who have et all," interposed Mitch. Lindy ho-hoed dutifully and Bernie looked pained.

"May its clients prosper," continued Bernie, "and

its enemies wither, and tomorrow may its name be on all tongues—"

"We didn't call the paper," Mitch cut in. He felt out of it. Lindy was having more fun than he, which wasn't fair, since she had pricked his conscience in the first place.

Bernie had been relaxed, for him, but now he stiffened. "You didn't call the *paper?* Why not?"

Arguing with Bernie was a no-win proposition. Mitch was tempted to tell him that he'd simply forgotten; instead, he blurted: "That poor damn doctor's got enough problems without coming home to a spread in the *Examiner.*"

Bernie looked at his watch. "Well, it's too late now." His cheeks had reddened, his voice had dropped ominously. He was furious but keeping it down. "Maybe they'll pick it up from their courthouse guy, tomorrow." He lifted his glass again. "Anyway, to bigger and better things."

Mitch did not lift his glass. "Not bigger."

Bernie regarded him thoughtfully. "What's that mean?"

"We're getting *too* big. And hard."

"You're right, Mitch," said Lindy. "But not now, OK?"

"Bullshit," said Mitch. "Now's as good as any."

"Aw, Mitch," she begged, "it's a *party!*"

She was right, he had picked the wrong terrain. It only made him madder. He faced Bernie. "You gambled with that poor gal's settlement—"

"*And* our fee, *and* made her a millionaire, OK?"

"Well, me, I don't like gambling. And I'm losing the joy of combat."

"You're never *in* combat anymore," Bernie pointed out. "You run the aid station. I'm the bad guy."

"Then maybe you better go it alone."

"Mitch!" Lindy exclaimed. "Not *now!*"

"Sure, now," Bernie said softly. "Let's talk about it now."

Bernie was seizing the high ground while he could. "The hell with it," muttered Mitch. "You'll start playing your goddamn violin, and—"

" 'Sing your troubles to Jesus, the Chaplain's gone ashore'?" asked Bernie significantly. "Korea, '51," he commented to Lindy. He seemed relaxed now that battle was joined. "How old were you, my child?"

"Don't talk Hemingway," Lindy said.

"Let's cut the crap," suggested Mitch. "She doesn't like sea stories."

"So she probably hasn't heard this one. She *should* hear it, to know what a callous bastard you really are."

"I've noticed that," Lindy said drily. "He hasn't got your sensitivity. You sweet old Godfather, Bernie."

"Thank you. Well, I took a few rounds over Wonsan. My wingman got hit and had to ditch. I had a disabled starboard aileron, a severed rudder cable, a main-fuel-tank-leak, also hydraulic fluid was pouring down my neck. There was no lateral stability to speak of. I reported these problems to the ship. *That* blackshoe bastard had the duty in the Combat Information Center. You know what he said?"

"I was trying," Mitch explained, sucked in against his will, "to get him to quit sobbing and listen. So we would vector him home."

"He said," Bernie reported, " 'Sing your troubles to Jesus, the padre's gone ashore.' "

"To *Jesus?*" marveled Lindy. "He said that, to an altarboy like you?"

"He's a blasphemous mother," Bernie assured her. " 'To Jesus,' he says, in his nice warm Center, sipping his coffee. To me, in *extremis* at twenty thousand feet, with ice-cold air shooting up my ass—"

"You're *here,* aren't you?" Mitch pointed out.

"Thank you," said Bernie without enthusiasm. "You're right. You saved my life. When a Chinaman saves somebody's life he's responsible for the rest of it."

"I'm no Chinaman," Mitch said tonelessly. "Your argument unmoves me." *Unmoves?* He *was* drunk. "I will *still* pick up my chips and quit."

"When?"

"I don't know."

"A year, goddamn it?" Bernie was sitting erect now. His black eyes glittered into Mitch's. "Two years?"

Outside the window, a fishing boat pulled away from the dock. She wore a jaunty red pilothouse and carried her nets hung high, like a pioneer woman crossing a puddle. A deckhand sang silently beyond the window, gesturing operatically, on her afterdeck.

With an effort, Mitch looked back into Bernie's eyes. "Three months?" he blurted. It came out as if he were asking permission.

Bernie sat back. "Over my dead fucking body."

She sat in the right-hand seat, next to Bernie, while he tested his engine and waited for takeoff clearance from the tower. Mitch had appropriated the rear seat, claiming a hard morning at the office. He began to snore. He never snored unless he was loaded.

Bernie's own eyes were bleary. He craned back and shook his head. "That's the guy who used to stack a half-dozen martinis on the bar at Happy Hour to chugalug on the way home."

"He doesn't get much practice. Can you still fly this thing?"

"I doubt it." He unlatched something and swung the controls over. "You drive."

"You're a kick in the butt," she said, swinging

the wheel back. He shrugged, answered his radio, and took off down the runway in a bounding, loping skid. Airborne, he seemed to get better. When he had the plane well settled down, winging high above the jagged coastal cliffs, he put the plane on autopilot and sat back. "Now, Lindy, what is all this crap?"

She hated to admit that it was news to her. "He just got high, I guess. The case was a strain."

"He didn't even *want* it," Bernie complained, lighting a cigarette. He glanced down at a freighter heading south. "Why not, for Christ's sake?"

"He was never sure, *you* know, about the doctor's culpability."

"Bull! He's been a lawyer too long to want *justice*." The plane bucked and he grabbed the yoke, set everything straight, and reset the autopilot. "He's not aggressive enough any more."

"Then you shouldn't mind his leaving," Lindy said hotly.

"No, only I *do*. Why's that?"

She wouldn't answer, so he did.

"I need him," he decided.

"You probably do."

"He's ten times brighter than me."

"He probably is."

"And he's my best friend?"

"So it seems."

Bernie glanced at her. "I'm asking you, Lindy. Is he?"

"How would I know?"

"You've been married twenty years!"

She shrugged. "Do you tell Jeanie everything?"

"I don't have to," Bernie said wryly. "She knows, from my face. I'm a Wop."

"When you want to be."

"Did *he* say that?"

"He's asleep. *I* said that. Look, Bernie, if he leaves, it isn't on account of you. Whatever it is, *that* isn't it."

"OK, OK," said Bernie distractedly. He pulled out a knob and took control of the plane. He tossed up a wing and started inland toward San Francisco Airport. "Goddamn it, if he doesn't like to win, why'd he study law?"

"You *know* why."

"OK, OK."

"And he likes to win," Lindy said. "Don't ever forget it."

"When he's interested. If a third of a million-five doesn't do it, how do you get him interested?"

She didn't know, and she didn't really care. The victory celebration had turned into a huge turkey, and she was tired enough to fall asleep herself.

"I don't know, maybe you change the rules." Her head ached. "Or the game."

Mitch woke up the next morning with a hangover. He left Lindy in bed and sneaked down to brew coffee. Cup in hand, he wandered to the living room. He stared down at the Bay, daydreaming that the red ketch, by simple luck, would round Angel Island to drop anchor in the cove. If she did, he would throw on a swimming suit and paddle out to her, fake a cramp to get aboard, if he had to. The boat would be as perfect close-up as she was from afar, and he, with his coming windfall, could make the owner an offer he couldn't refuse.

Lindy padded up behind him. She wore a shorty nightgown and carried a cup of coffee. She awakened more beautiful than any woman he had ever slept with, if memory served. Barring the Navy nurse in Honolulu, who didn't really count because he had known her before he was married, she had kept him absolutely faithful for twenty years. His Air Group shipmates would never have believed it.

She kissed him lightly and nodded toward the water.

"You're still looking for that ketch."

"If we find her," he blurted, "or any decent cruising boat—"

"*Cruising* boat," she repeated thoughtfully. "Let me say it?"

"Say what? Jesus, you are the sexiest frigging woman in the morning . . ." He wanted all at once to drag her back to bed, there and then. But she seemed to miss his vibes, or perhaps ignore them. She had been cool on the drive home from the airport last night, after his squabble with Bernie. "Where was I?" he asked.

"You were about to suggest," she said, "in an off-hand way, that if we find her we buy her. And some day sell out and move aboard."

He was astonished. She was right.

"Well," she continued, "weren't you? And cruise away, leaving all annoyance behind?"

"Now, how did you come up with that?"

"I *have* to guess," she said simply. "Nobody ever actually *tells* me anything."

So they were talking, really, about yesterday. He apologized for his bolt from the blue and blamed in on the champagne.

"The *news* was good," she shrugged. "I'm glad you want to leave him. But you have to admit, it was news, just the same."

"I said I'm sorry."

"Think nothing of it. If you split with Bernie, it'll be almost like my own idea. If you don't look at it too closely."

"Let's not," he murmured. She stretched. God, what a build.

"So that leaves buying the boat, if we find her?" she yawned.

His mind was in bed with her. "Um? Yeah, if we find her."

"Well, there again! I *did* say she looked slow. So, in effect, we talked about that too." Her voice had a brittle edge.

"Jesus, honey, we've talked about buying a boat for years!"

"Yes and no. A *racing* boat, off and on. It's kind of like the motorcycle." He had mentioned long ago the joys of owning a bike. She hadn't objected. So, twenty years later, he had bought the big Honda on sale and surprised her with it that night. She still grew tense when she knew he was driving it in traffic. After the sprained wrist, he supposed, he should have sold it. But he *liked* the damn thing, it made him feel good. Besides, their bikes were almost all he and Tony had in common, she ought to appreciate that. She was grumbling on:

"This boat won't race, I know that much. Oh, hell, maybe I *would* like us to buy her. But you don't *know* that, do you?"

"No. So tell me, one way or the other."

"It's just that you're so g.d. *unilateral*. She might be great, for weekends, and Easter, and summer vacations. Actually moving aboard would be another matter." She waved toward Sausalito, with its marinas and forests of masts. They had known couples who had lived aboard boats there. "Would we want to leave this to cram into that?"

"I was thinking," he said slowly, "more of the South Seas. Marquesas, Tahiti . . ."

"Every damn couple *down* there is thinking of Tahiti," she reminded him. "They never go. They get divorces instead, from living on top of each other. Remember Vivian and Joe? The guy ends up with the boat and the girl gets the kids."

"Divorce," he said stiffly, "seems a little farfetched for you and me."

"But selling our house, and beach, and leaving Tony isn't?" She managed to smile, but her voice was troubled. "If that comes up, could I maybe have a few minutes on it?"

He nodded. "We both can. Weeks, months, as long as we want."

"And it could still go either way?"

"Either way. One man, one vote."

"That's what I'm afraid of."

"One person, one vote," he promised.

She went to make coffee. She had not read his mind about heading back to bed, but somewhere during the discussion his desire had cooled, so it didn't matter anyway.

That afternoon they began in earnest to look for the red ketch. They sailed her father's sloop from Fort Point to Sausalito, around Angel Island to Alcatraz and Berkeley and back to St. Francis Yacht Club. They passed through regattas, races, and anchorages. They saw hundreds of boats. They returned sunburned and exhausted, but nowhere had they seen the red ketch.

They decided that they were wasting their time. The red ketch was not the only sea-going vessel in California. They began to look for any good cruising boat. He took a week off and they drove the Coast to San Diego, checking everywhere. They were humble before condescending young yacht brokers in elkskin Topsiders and immaculate dungarees, patient with experts who knew less than they, polite to owners who were palpably lying in their teeth.

Most of the brokers seemed ignorant of even the boats they were selling. Mitch and Lindy were already too salty. The brokers were programmed for a hard-breathing couple who had never sailed. The wife should be interested in sleeping-capacity and decor below, not pot-stowage or built-in galley-hazards in a heavy blow. The husband should be concerned with radar and navigational gimmicks, not water-capacity or frame-thickness or the impossible battery-drain of an autopilot at sea.

The brokers lost interest. They had plenty of chrome-and-plastic dogs already listed, without trying to find an old-fashioned wooden cruising boat. Mitch left his business cards to be disposed of as they drove away.

The night they returned he sat in his study under his sextant-lamp. The plans for *Gundred* he had cut from *Yachting* lay again on his desk before him. He was no boatwright, but he had earned extra money in high school by working on yachts when his father was Commodore of the St. Francis Yacht Club. He knew something of woods and boat maintenance. He called a yard in Seattle which still made wooden boats. They knew the Atkins design. They phoned back with an estimate, collect. There were orders stacked up. Delivery, not sooner than twelve months: bare-hull, un-rigged, someone else to do cabinet work, tanks, engine installation, and ship-fitting. "Thirty-one thousand, Mr. Gordon."

"Thirty-one *what?*"

"Thousand," said Seattle, amused. "Where you been? You can't find spruce, fir, oak. We have to cure our wood ourselves. Teak's out of sight. That's why your amateurs are trying to build in cement. Boat-wrights, fifteen bucks an hour. None left, hardly."

A bare hull was hardly a start. Rigging and fittings

would triple the price and add years to the time they must wait. He put down the phone, defeated. He could never get her built in America. He might try in Nova Scotia, Sweden, Tasmania, Finland, or Denmark. Taiwan, Japan, Hong Kong might be even cheaper, but oriental workmanship was risky. Besides, the Far East had turned to fiberglass too.

He did not want glass, or even steel: he wanted a boat that lived. His heart was set on wood.

He wanted the red ketch.

Sunday afternoon, he oiled the turnbuckles on his father-in-law's sloop *Invincible,* while the old man played dominoes in the yacht club bar. Then the two of them sailed out on the Bay in a whipping westerly. While the old man steered, Mitch tuned her rigging for the Honolulu race.

Armed with screwdriver, pliers, and crescent wrench, stung by spray, he attacked the fittings one by one, setting taut a stay, easing a shroud, twanging at another like a giant guitar string, craning his neck to check the curve of the mast. He had tuned the old boy's boat for years, before each Transpac. He knew which turnbuckles would resist and which would surrender, liked some and disliked others.

When he had finished, he found that Shawn, more heavy-handed on the helm each year, had somehow sailed them under the southern tower of the Golden Gate Bridge. The old man was no judge of the results of the tuning, so Mitch took the wheel to test her feel. They headed home with a failing breeze and a fierce outgoing tide.

In golden light, with the first wisps of evening fog racing toward the apartments on the crest of Pacific Heights, he paralleled the jetty and steered for the old granite lighthouse at the end of the yacht club quay. Sunday strollers on the breakwater stopped to look. The yacht would seem beautiful from the shore. He should be carrying a larger jenny shil in the light breeze. The hell with it.

He glanced up at the hills. On the crest he could see the pink-stucco tower where he had lived in his teens. He even spotted his bedroom window in the penthouse on top. With the view he had taken for granted, the rent now must be astronomical.

A cloud shadowed the sun. San Francisco sunlight seemed less bright than he remembered it from the days on the hill. As he watched, it erased the pink spire of his childhood. He felt sad.

They were abeam the Club, a rambling tile-and-stucco structure almost fifty years old. It's bay-window eyes stared dully at the tides sucking through the Gate. Behind it lay the cramped, rock-sided yacht basin he had haunted as a child. It seemed to have shrunk with the years.

He eased the sloop toward the bouldered seawall, where the tide was weaker. Yacht club members began to wander from the bar to the front porch, watching the boat and probably hoping that he would shave the seawall too closely and give them something to talk about over dominoes. Perversely, he brought her in further.

He was badly bored. His life was one long *déjà vu*. Every day was a rerun. The prospect of skippering one more Hawaiian race for Shawn wearied him in advance.

A hundred yards away he saw Commodore Russo leaning his belly on the railing of the porch. He wondered what the Commodore thought, now that the suit was over. He was standing with a young yacht-bum who bossed his crew. The kid pointed to their short-ened sail: derisively, Mitch imagined. They were carrying barely enough foresail to overcome the tide. Mitch could anticipate the effect of the gesture on Shawn, framed in the hatchway below and adjusting his yachting cap for the gallery.

"Mitch?" Shawn asked querulously.

"No," said Mitch.

"No, what?" demanded Shawn. "I didn't say anything."

"The big jenny," Mitch muttered. "I'm not setting it."

He sheered within inches of a danger-buoy, to give the membership something else to chew on. Shawn did not even notice it. Christ, if he left the old man to his own devices, he'd pile up his boat in a week.

"We'd *move* better under the jenny," complained Shawn. "Shit, *I'll* set it."

"Help yourself," Mitch offered, waving at the slippery foredeck. He was cold and his back hurt and he was in no mood for sail-drill twenty minutes from home. "Set it. Then we'll be in the slip thirty seconds earlier."

"What the hell's biting you?" Shawn wanted to know. He made a move forward, changed his mind as a green wave bounded over the forecastle. He groped through the hatch behind him, feeling for the liquor rack. He pulled out a bottle of Johnny Walker. Two wisps of white hair, escaping the cap, made horns at his temples. He held out the bottle. "Here. Warm up. And smile."

"No, thanks, not coming in, Pops." With no one but Shawn to help him, getting a fifty-foot sloop into the slip required his best reactions. He reached down and started the engine.

"Hey!" protested Shawn. Shawn always tried to berth his boat under sail, sometimes quite successfully. His self-image was that of a purist in canvas, theoretically.

In practice, the drill called for Mitch to sail *Invincible* through the tiny harbor and set up the approach. Then Mitch would turn over the helm at the last instant so that the owner could bring her in, to the plaudits of some imaginary crowd. Even if Shawn intended to cheat and use power, he never started his motor in full view of the spectators on the porch; he waited until he was hidden by the jetty. Already the gray heads in the bar must be wagging in disgust.

"I started the engine," Mitch explained cruelly, "because you seem to be in such a goddamn hurry. Why spend half an hour beating up the harbor?"

"I'm old enough for a powerboat," Shawn sulked. "Not yet."

Abruptly, Mitch cut the engine. He offered Shawn the wheel. "There you go, Captain Slocum."

There was a heavy silence. The old man had not brought his twenty-ton craft unaided into the harbor under sail for years. Waves gurgled at the bow, a gull jeered, and a foghorn roared from the Bridge. Shawn looked forlorn, frightened, and suddenly shrunken. Mitch sighed, pulled the visor over the old man's eyes, squeezed his arm, and took the wheel again.

Engine off, sails full, he pulled around the jetty and tacked through the jammed harbor. When the slip was dead ahead and he saw that Shawn could not miss, he gave him the helm and took a springline forward to leap ashore.

The old man, tense and wild-eyed as always, managed for once to release his mainsail almost on time. Mitch leaped for the dock, jarring his back, got a turn on an ancient cleat, and let the line take up the shock. When Shawn hit his usual piling, it left hardly a mark on the hull.

No one was watching anyway.

They showered in the paneled locker room. Toweling, Mitch wandered idly along the walls, which were hung with cartoons of the Club's Tinsley Island festivities from the early '30s. All were illustrated in-jokes. Even Mitch, whose father had been on the Board of Governors for years, had never understood some of them.

He began to dress. "I'm resigning my membership," he suddenly told his father-in-law, who was sitting on a wooden bench straining to pull on his socks. "Next week, before we get hit for next year's dues."

The old man sighed: "Are you still bitching about Bertelli?"

Mitch had sponsored his partner a year ago. Bernie had been mysteriously blackballed. Mitch suspected Shawn, who disliked Bernie, and had almost resigned then, but Bernie had talked him out of quitting on the ground that it was a good place for them to take clients for lunch.

"Put him up again," continued the old man. "Maybe he thinks it's because he's Italian. Hell, tell him we got Italians on the Board! We got an Italian Commodore! Christ, the town's got a wop mayor! Put him up again!"

"Bernie," Mitch said, "fights his own battles. He says wait until some employee breaks a leg down here, he'll handle us fuckers. And he will."

Shawn tugged up his pants, cinched in his gut and fastened his belt too tightly. He looked like a rooster getting ready to crow. "You wouldn't let him."

"I'd write his brief," promised Mitch, "but I think I might retire."

"Retire?" Shawn asked sharply. "What would you do?"

"Travel, maybe." Mitch tossed his towel into a basket

and adjusted Shawn's necktie. "Come on, Pops," he said. "Lindy's waiting."

The bar was closed to women, so she had waited at the old man's favorite table in the dining room, overlooking the Bay. She dug into her pocketbook and drew out two messages. One was from Peggy Slater, a tough aggressive Southern California yacht broker whose own boat was emblazoned with pink valentines and who made most of her male counterparts look like kids trading bubblegum wrappers. She was offering an English-built ketch, built to Lloyd's specifications, for $75,000 firm.

"Fiberglass or wood?"

"Glass."

Mitch shook his head, and Shawn exploded. "Talk about *club* snobbery! What's wrong with *glass?* You've been sailing the ass off *my* boat for ten years!"

Lindy smiled faintly. Shawn caught the smile and sat back, lips pursed. "OK," he muttered, quoting darkly: " 'It's a good thing the old man's got *somebody* to sail her, or she'd grow fast to the bottom while he played dominoes.' Right?"

Startled, they studied their plates. He was quoting her brother Bobby, drunk at Shawn's birthday party last year. They hadn't even known the old man had overheard.

"Dad," Lindy said softly, *"Mitch* never said that."

"Somebody did, somewhere," insisted the old man. "Who, damn it? Bobby?"

They were silent.

"OK," Shawn said wearily. "He was probably right. Anyway, you won a big case. You hit the jackpot. You got to spend it on a boat. It's got to be wood. It's got to be that red wooden ketch?"

"Not necessarily," Mitch said. "She's disappeared, anyway."

"If you find her, you'll never have time for *Invincible.*"

"No, Pops," said Mitch. "I probably won't."

The old man's eyes fell. "If you're shaking down your own boat, who navigates for me in the next Hawaii Race?"

Lindy was studying her father curiously. "Mitch would go. Or teach Bobby, or something. He wouldn't just dump you."

"Bobby can't find the Farallon Islands on a clear day," Shawn sulked. He moistened his finger and began to run it around the rim of his wineglass. He hit high G and, when the Commodore scowled from across the room, persisted more loudly. "Have I *seen* that ketch? She a San Francisco boat?"

"My God, Shawn," Mitch exclaimed, "you almost ran her down. Are you saying you don't know the boat?"

"Shh," Lindy cautioned. "Dad?"

"Yeah?"

"You remember her all right. So what's going on?"

"I'm senile," suggested Shawn tersely. "Can't remember who insults me. Can't remember the Rules of the Road. Can't recall *half* the boats I've seen."

"It's not Christmas," Lindy said sharply. "We're not little kids. What's under the tree?" Her eyes narrowed. "You've *found* her, haven't you?"

Shawn sat back, triumphantly. "She's not red anymore. She's at Cox's Yard, Sausalito. She's called *Lorelei*. Ther're painting her white. To make her look bigger, somebody said. So I guess she's for sale."

Mitch cut in angrily. "Did you see her? When was that? Suppose she's sold. How long have you known?"

"A week, ten days," Shawn shrugged. "I forget."

"Forget, hell!" flared Lindy. Her cheeks were flaming. "You just let him beat the bushes! All the way to *Dago!* Damn it, Dad—"

Shawn ignored her. "If you got her," he asked Mitch, "what would you do? She's too slow to race."

"We'd cruise her."

"Offshore? She's only forty feet."

"Hell, Shawn, you're only fifty feet yourself. Hawaii's offshore!"

"I *race*. With a six-man crew. And escort vessels." He shrugged. "Or I did . . ."

His voice trailed off. He looked indescribably sad. Lindy reached across the table and took his hand. "You'll still race, Dad."

The old man did not answer. Lips clamped, he stared stubbornly ahead. They finished dinner and left him playing dominoes at the bar.

Crossing the Bridge, Lindy sat distantly by the window. Mitch saw that her cheeks were wet.

"It isn't his *racing* he's worried about," he pointed out. "He's afraid I'll sail off with his little girl."

"Then why won't he say it?" she murmured. "Mitch?"

"Um?"

"Why doesn't anybody ever say it?"

" 'I love you?' " He thought for a moment. "*I* say it, all the time."

"When you mean 'thank you.' Why not when you mean 'I *love* you.' "

He squeezed her hand. "I love you, I love you, I *love* you."

"Watch it, Romeo, there's a cop." He slowed.

He had sounded tinny as a worn-out tape, and he didn't have the slightest idea why.

CHAPTER
8

HE CLUNG ALOFT. A SEARING SUN SOARED AND FELL
with every roll. Earlier, he had been teased with shade
from the mainsail. Now the sun had risen above the
sail and there was no relief.

She had shaved his head at Bora Bora to see how he
would look, bald. It was baking now like a potato. A
stupid, childish error in the tropics. He visualized his
brains at a slow simmer in a pan under the bare skull.
He ached for the cool of the cabin.

He needed water badly but he was afraid to leave
the mast too soon.

He was still plowing seas he had not yet searched
by daylight, nearing the southern limit of his patrol.
He was almost back at the spot where he had discovered her gone. In these waters, six hours before, he
had tossed in the strobe light and buoy and man-overboard flag. He had an unreasoning hope that he would
see them again, once he surmounted the wave ahead.

She, nestling in the horseshoe buoy, holding aloft the strobe, which she had swum to during the night . . .

He climbed the swell. Nothing. The vision fled.

Far below he heard three bells from the cabin. Nine-thirty. He glanced windward, toward the sun. It was high enough for a morning shot. With that, he would have an estimated position to transmit to Tahiti, if he ever raised them on the radio. He could brew coffee to awaken himself, shoot the sun, work it out, try Tahiti again, and be back on his perch in fifteen minutes.

He began to crawl from his position on the mast. A roll to starboard flung him against the leeward rigging and a wire shroud that seared his chest. He continued down. Below, in the gloomy chaos of the cabin, he gulped water and then primed Lindy's swinging, stainless stove. He touched it with a match and watched as the raw alcohol went off in an orange puff. He remembered her doing it, swiftly and expertly. Her long auburn hair was always too close to the flame. He would yell at her for it, and she would brush it back. She never seemed to get it singed. The flame turned blue, now, heating its vaporizer.

She must be hungry . . .

Doing the things she would have been doing was agonizing. He pumped water into her kettle, put it over the flame, and glanced at the clock. Three minutes gone from the quarter-hour he had allotted. He turned up the stove. He pumped another glass of water and gulped it, wanting more but not taking the time.

She must be dehydrating, too . . .

He began to prepare automatically for the morning observation. He slid his hack-chronometer from a drawer above the chart table, ducked forward and pulled their Transoceanic Radio from a rack. He nes-

tled it between pillows on the bunk, yanked up the
aerial. The 9:30 news from Radio Tahiti blasted from
the speaker: if *he* could hear Tahiti, why couldn't they
hear him? He caught a few words of French, too fast
for his understanding, and President Ford's name, and
Kissinger's. Quickly he switched to the nineteen-meter
band. He dialed in the high, nerve-wracking pulse of
the WWV time-signal that Lindy hated so much.

"At the tone, nineteen hours thirty-six minutes,
Coordinated Universal Time." His chronometer was
nine seconds off in two days, and the rate was changing. Something wrong there, but he couldn't worry
about it now. He was glad he had bothered to check it.
Nine seconds could mean a two-mile error in his line
of position.

He grabbed the handle of the varnished sextant
case on the shelf over his bunk. Kneeling awkwardly
on the berth, he waited. With its case, it weighed ten
pounds. He must ease it over the retaining fiddle without straining his back. He caught the sea in league
with him and hiked it over, using the roll to beat
gravity. As usual, he strained his back anyway. Each
job took twice the effort it would have taken ashore or
at the dock. That was why cruising sailors stayed thin.

He opened the case and caught a familiar whiff of
oiled mahogany. He drew out his polished-brass Plath.
With the sextant vulnerable in his hand, he turned
cautious as a father with a newborn infant. If he
banged it against anything or jarred the telescope going topside, he would be lost at sea until he readjusted
the whole instrument. Their spare sextant was a grand
old 1880 antique Lindy had bought for him in Copenhagen, to mount as a lamp in his den. They had
brought it along, because it still worked, but the engraved figures on its silver arc were almost too worn to
read, and he had not tested it in a year at sea.

His Plath would be Lindy's salvation: an old and trusted friend. He venerated it as Jean-Paul honored the Tikis he had shown them in the Marquesas, as a charm against disaster. The feel of it in his hand raised his spirits.

He reached for his stopwatch, hanging from the spice rack in her galley. She insisted on using it in cooking. Because tiny things mattered at sea, her attachment was an invasion of his private bubble, as navigator. He had bought another in Papeete for the galley. But his own kept returning to the spice rack, ready to time his eggs in the morning. He found himself frozen, stopwatch lanyard half around his neck, remembering the argument they had made of it.

He had forgotten the sextant, and it lay carelessly on the chart table. He grabbed it quickly, before it could slide. He climbed halfway out the hatch and braced himself, feet on the companionway ladder, for the morning sun-shot.

Facing the sun, jammed for support against the side of the hatch, he waited to be carried to the peak of a swell. When he felt his belly grow light at the summit, he lined up the horizon and checked his index-correction on the arc. Then he swung his heaviest filter over the lens and began to search for the sun in his telescope, swinging the sextant fore and aft while he moved the thumbscrew along the arc.

He glimpsed the great orange ball, lost it, found it again, and enticed it to the horizon. He let the lower part of his body, supported by his knees in the hatchway, wedge his torso, which he kept pliant to absorb the roll and pitch. He lost the sun again under the main boom and had to wait until it reappeared. When he had the bottom of the orange disk at the razor-edge of the horizon, he rocked the sextant with his waist, letting the sun swing up to the right, touch

the horizon, and then swing up to the left. At the pre-
cise moment that he felt in his gut the peak of an upward surge, he centered the sun again, made disk
and horizon kiss, and punched his stopwatch. He had
made his observation.

Cradling the sextant in both arms, he inched back
down the lurching companionway ladder. He pulled
sight-forms, *Nautical Almanac,* and *Tables of Com-
puted Altitude* from his navigation locker. He braced
all of them on the leeward edge of the chart table,
so that they could not slide off.

On the chart, he found the shaky, lopsided circle he
had labeled as their position at 0317, when he had
discovered that she was lost. He remeasured his track
from the star-fix of the previous evening, to make sure
that in his predawn panic he had not got it wrong. It
was OK.

He wrote down his sextant altitude and laid the sextant on the bunk, intending to stow it in its box when
he was finished working the sight. He flung open the
Nautical Almanac.

He worked for five minutes, in more and more
dread as he approached the answer. He sensed something wrong in his figures. When he was finally through,
the line of position was eighty miles away from any
conceivable spot he could be on now. It ran smack
through the center of Bora Bora, which they had left
two days before.

Dismayed, he stared at the column of numbers. Each
entry was a potential error. There were likely places
for a mistake to creep in, and less likely ones, but the
long search for this slip could be deadly. He had no
time. He should be topside.

He groaned. He was coming apart already. If he
couldn't work a simple sunsight after only six hours

aloft, when real fatigue got a bite of his brain he would dissolve completely.

He glanced at the bulkhead clock. 0945 already. He ought to have reversed course again by now and be back up on the mast, looking. He stood up, sat down again. Close to panic, he forced himself to concentrate on the figures before him.

He felt instinctively that his sextant altitude was good. He placed a tiny checkmark by that. There was no way to recheck the time: the instant of taking the sight had disappeared forever, like the strobe light tossed into their wake.

He tensed. Time . . . Greenwich Time . . . Greenwich date? He had a dim vision of himself, twenty-three years younger, on the bridge of the carrier at dusk. The Exec, a grizzled regular who had been a chief quartermaster, had glanced at his muddled chart.

"You using the right day of the year, Stud?"

It was even easier to forget the day of the year on a sailboat than on a carrier, especially when you couldn't find the logbook. As *Linda Lee* plowed south, he searched wildly again for the book. When he couldn't find it, he forced himself to sit down and count the days at sea, on his fingers, since Bora Bora. He had it. It was December twenty-second, not the twenty-first! With rising excitement he recalculated the sight.

When he replotted the sunline it was very close to his track and when he dropped a perpendicular to his track, the new estimated position lay within two miles of his dead-reckoning. He placed a tiny square around it and labeled it with the local time.

He picked off the latitude and longitude with dividers and wrote that on the chart, too, then moved to the radio. He let the transmitter warm up and began to call Mahina Radio, then Navy Papeete, then any ship or station, on the emergency frequency. He called in English and French, and ended with another blind Mayday to any ship or station.

No one answered.

She saw the white speck miles away, and lost it instantly as she sank into the next undulating valley. She felt that it was a sail, that it was Mitch, and that she was too far from him to be seen. She lost the speck each time she dipped into a trough, and most of the peaks were not high enough to bring it back into view, but everytime she thought that it was gone, it would appear. Its reappearances were growing more frequent.

It was far past whistling range, but she began to wave the jug, which at least was white, as violently as she could, whenever she would crest a wave and see the boat. Now the low, massive lines of *Linda Lee* were unmistakable; she could see not only the mainsail but the mizzensail. He was probably on the spreader, sweeping the seas with binoculars.

She could not actually see him there, but she was sure that he had seen her. She forced herself to relax. If the boat was approaching, her best chance was to save her strength to help him get her aboard. She lay back and rested. She had already forgotten chilled legs, fevered head, cracked lips, chafed armpits, and the awful thirst.

When there was no answer from Mahina Radio or Papeete he grew desperate and switched to the yachting channels, ship-to-ship. There were always twenty or thirty yachts along the Papeete quay and anchored off the Protestant Church. Those which were American, at least, would carry his frequencies if they had radios. The odds were almost zero that anyone would have his set turned on in the morning, but he tried anyway.

When a general call seemed to do no good, he began them by name, those he hoped might still be in the area: *Puffin II, Windrift, Kaiola,* and *Winston Churchill.* He called a trimaran named *Howler,* owned by a New Zealander they all detested. He called a German Ketch, *Kormorant,* and two island schooners, just in case, and a boat he remembered vaguely as having the amazing homeport of Las Vegas, Nevada.

There was no answer. He was simply not getting through. He jigged indecisively. He had to get topside, make his turn, backtrack the course again. Finally he hung up the mike.

He was nesting the Plath in its varnished wooden case when he heard a faint movement in the head. He froze, forgetting the sextant.

Jesus, had he looked in the *head?* He couldn't remember. If the trots had hit her and she had fainted on the john, been there all the time . . .

Confused, he lurched through the cabin, yanked open the door. The cat regarded him from the toilet lid, slipped past him, and raced up the companionway steps. He pressed his forehead against the varnished bulkhead, moaning. He remembered now. The head had been the first place he had looked. Then he had stuck the cat inside it to keep it below.

A premonition hit him, and he swung toward the chart table.

The open sextant case was sliding toward the edge. He lunged too late. "No!" It crashed to the cabin sole, spilling the Plath on the floorboards.

He sat cross-legged on the cabin floor and lifted it. One mirror was so far askew he could see the misalignment with his naked eye. That he could correct, given time. But he *had* no time, and now he saw that the arc itself was bent. That he could never repair. Dismally, he laid the carcass away. He was stuck with the ancient spare.

The pot he had set on the stove began to wheeze. An island of stability in the crazily tilting cabin, it jeered at him as the boat moved slowly around it.

He had no desire for coffee now, but he poured a cup and babied it to the cockpit. Watching the sea, he tried to drink the coffee. He could simply not get it down. It was too hot, and it would take too long to let it cool.

It was past time to turn. She could not be further ahead. He threw cup and coffee overboard, disengaged Irwin, reversed course, and reset Irwin's vane to steer north-northwest.

He was starting their second trip up the course. It would be harder to stay alert, retracing water he had prowled before. He climbed back to his position on the mast. The sun blasted the top of his head. As he took his seat on the spreader he realized that he'd forgotten his hat.

He refused to leave another five minutes of ocean unsearched while he went below to get it.

The ketch was still distant, a mile away perhaps, and she noticed that something in its shape had changed. She had been lying back, resting, but now she became more alert.

She was sure that she could see his body in tiny silhouette, midway up the sail. She lifted the jug and waved wildly. He had wonderful eyes, for distance, and he would never lose sight, now that he had spotted her.

The next glimpse shook her confidence. The boat had changed shape because it had changed course. It was pulling away.

"No!"

Suddenly she was in a screaming, thrashing tantrum. She shrieked and shouted, blew her whistle and waved, finally came to her senses only when she sank below the surface and swallowed water, which she vomited.

Even then, she took a few instinctive strokes after the boat. Then she lay back, cradling the jug and staring up at the cobalt sky. Her anger cooled. She had a great thirst. And she was very tired and very frightened.

CHAPTER
9

THEY PARKED IN BRIGHT CALIFORNIA SUNLIGHT OUT-
side a wooden fence: COX'S BOATYARD, HAUL-
OUT AND REPAIR. ALL TERMS CASH BEFORE
LAUNCHING.

The tiny yard lay next to a vast fiberglass boat-
factory in the backwaters of Richardson Bay. It was
tidal-flat, shipyard country, smelling of sewage, mud,
resin, and sawdust. The flats were lined with house-
boats, some flamboyant, garish, other stagnant and
rotting.

They passed into the yard through a door slatting in
a breeze from the flats. An enormous wooden loft
stood inside. A marine railway slid from the building's
mouth like a rusting tongue, lapping the shallow water
alongside a dock. The yard must need high tides to
haul out a deep-draft boat, thought Mitch; it probably
accounted for its anonymity. He'd had no idea the
place was even here.

The ways were almost empty. He guessed that the yard was on the edge of bankruptcy. A battered old schooner, for some reason chained to her scaffolding, towered outside the building. A bearded youth with a headband and earring was sanding her planks. An ancient Italian tapped calking into a fishing-boat hull. A pale, discouraged fat man was prying rot from a ketch-rigged motor-sailer that Mitch would not have tried to take across San Francisco Bay.

And at the end of the wharf lay his dream. In an outgoing tide which must barely have floated her, she strained against her lines. She was even prettier in white than red. Her varnished rails and hatches glittered in the sun. Carved on teak sideboards on the stern taffrail were gilded letters: LORELEI, and below them, SAN FRANCISCO. Her bowsprit was pointed toward the entrance of Richardson Bay and the Golden Gate beyond. To Mitch she seemed impatient. Lindy was watching him curiously.

"Isn't she beautiful?" he asked.

"*You're* beautiful." She squeezed his hand. "Yes, Mitch, she's lovely, you were right. How do we see her?"

There seemed no one aboard. A power saw was screaming inside the building, so they wandered in. They sniffed hemp and seasoned wood. The bone structure of a half-finished sloop loomed inside, her massive keel leading back into shadows. Her ribs rose high above them. Mitch saw from the layer of dust on her oaken stem that work on her had stopped some years before.

Far in the rear, in a slant of light through a dirty window, a gaunt figure worked at a carpenter's bench. He wore white overalls powdered with sawdust. He was sawing planks for a dinghy. Its little transom of flare-grained mahogany lay already shaped on the bench beside him. Frames, clamped to templates, were steaming over a caldron at the end of the bench.

"Mr. Cox?" asked Mitch.

The man flicked off his table saw. He had pale blue, steady eyes. He was bald, tall as Mitch, with a tanned lined face that must once have been handsome. Mitch sensed recent weight loss in the folds of his neck.

When Mitch met a man with eyes level with his own, he usually sensed rapport. They were tall men in a world built for averages. This time he felt between them a mutual impulse to test their strength. The vibes were very strong.

"Mr. Cox?" he asked again.

"Cox," the man said, "is no more. He died thirty years ago. John Dugan is Cox." He nodded toward a glassed cubicle at the corner of the loft. "Dugan's in there."

Mitch, who had promised himself to stay casual, found himself blurting suddenly: "Do you know who owns that ketch out there?"

The man stiffened. There was something familiar in the unbending way he carried his frame. And now his face was guarded.

"Dugan's in there," he said again. He turned away and the saw screamed into life. They moved toward the office, wondering where they had seen the man before.

Behind the office glass a man was jabbing an ancient adding machine. When Mitch tapped on the door he motioned them in. He was shorter, more solid, and older than the man at the carpenter's bench. His eyes lacked some of the other's clarity, but he resembled him. Probably brothers. He leaned on a drafting table stacked with boat-plans. The plans were as dusty as the unplanked hull in the loft. Mitch, trying to hide his eagerness, introduced himself and asked if the ketch was for sale.

"What makes you think so?"

"I heard a rumor. Wasn't she red?"

"Red, yeah. For sale? It seems to depend."

A fly attacked the dust-streaked window above him. He turned and swatted it with a rolled nautical chart. He wandered to his desk and reached down its side. He picked up a four-foot steel rod, two inches thick. An area a foot from one end was almost eaten through by corrosion. "Know what this is?" he asked Mitch suddenly.

"Keel-bolt," Mitch said. "Somebody pulled it just in time. Who owns the ketch?"

Dugan waved a hand toward the bench outside. "Andrew. My brother."

That explained why the tall man had looked familiar: from the Farallon Island start. He wondered if Dugan had recognized them. "Why'd he send us in here?"

Dugan began to swing the keel-bolt as an idle golfer swings a club. "Because *I'm* supposed to be the businessman, I guess. Selling her would be a matter of business."

Mitch was looking at the keel-bolt. "Was that drawn from *her?*" If her keel-bolts were going, it meant galvanic action, perhaps wet wood under her paint. Maybe he wasn't interested after all.

Dugan snorted. "This? Hell, no." He dropped the bolt by his desk with a clang. "Don't ask *him* that, he'll hit you with it." He opened the door. "Andrew!"

Outside, the howl of the saw continued. Dugan left the door open and moved to a rusty hotplate. Above it hung three Navy mugs. He selected the cleanest, poured Lindy coffee, and filled the others for Mitch and himself. The screeching died and the other

Dugan entered. He took a clothesbrush from a hook and carefully whisked the sawdust from his coveralls to the office floor. He washed his hands at a scummy basin, and dried them. His brother introduced them and said that Mitch was interested in *Lorelei*.

"I know," said Andrew Dugan. He hung up the towel but made no effort to shake hands.

"Could we take a look aboard?" asked Mitch. He felt a trickle of sweat run down his side. He had hardly slept last night, for fear that they would find the boat already sold or, perhaps, not really for sale. With his coming windfall he should feel like a Kennedy or a Rockefeller bargaining in a used car lot. Still, the taller brother, hostile and out of focus, made him uncomfortable. "May we see her?" he asked again. His voice was strained.

The tall man didn't answer. Instead, he commented: "This isn't exactly the Boat Show, over here. You must have gone to a lot of trouble to find her, Mr. Gordon."

If Andrew Dugan wanted to sell, he was the world's worst salesman. A chill had entered the office with him, and Mitch was becoming annoyed. If the boat was for sale, she was for sale, and if not, then not. His cheeks began to burn. Lindy, watching him, cut in swiftly.

"Mr. Dugan—Andrew? Is 'Andrew' OK? I can't keep calling you Mr. Dugan."

The tall man looked at her coldly. "Dugan's fine, Mrs. Gordon."

Mitch tensed. He put down his coffee cup, ready to leave. Nobody rejected Lindy, boat or not. He felt her hand on his sleeve, restraining him. She said: "We think she's beautiful. Can we see below?"

Andrew Dugan shook his head. "No decor, iron stove. Old-time, you wouldn't be impressed."

Lindy, pretty, friendly, and often more vulnerable than she seemed, looked as if she were about to cry. She was seldom rebuffed. Mitch slipped his arm around her waist. He faced the older brother, who sat embarrassed, staring at his desk-top.

"We got it wrong," Mitch said tersely. "We heard she was for sale. Thanks for your patience." He turned to the taller brother. "And for yours, such as it was." He started for the door but Lindy still held back. "Mr. Dugan," she repeated softly, *"could* I see below?"

Andrew Dugan studied her. Outside in the yard, the fisherman's calking hammer plunked. The bearded youth's sander whined, hesitated, whined again. Next door the factory whistle signaled a coffee-break. The carpenter suddenly reached to an array of keys hanging on the wall, picked one ring.

"All right," he said. He indicated the door and followed her out. As Mitch moved to leave, the older brother said: "That's funny. You're the third couple that's been here, plus two guys alone."

"What the hell gives?"

"Long story," said John Dugan briefly, "but you're the first ones to make it to the dock."

On the rotten wharf Lindy and Mitch removed their shoes, although Dugan had not. They followed him aboard, stepping over the rail to a deck of Port Orford cedar. For a moment the three of them, Mitch at 200 pounds, Dugan at perhaps 180, and Lindy at 115, were together, well outboard, on the starboard side of the ketch. The boat refused to roll to their weight. He wondered if her bottom was on the shoaling mud. Then he sensed a stirring as she rose to a passing wake. She was not aground, simply the stiffest boat of her size he had ever boarded.

He wondered how heavy a keel lay below them, whether there was internal ballast as well, to ease her roll at anchor, how close the builder had stuck to the plans on his own desk at home. He had lots of questions, but he was afraid that he would blow Lindy's minor triumph if he asked them. Dugan was unlocking oaken hatchboards and drawing them from their slot, carefully so as not to mar the varnish. Mitch glanced around topside.

She was very solid. A green tarnish on her old bronze winches, mounted on blocks of solid teak on either side of the cockpit, told him that she had not been sailed recently. Mitch plucked at a mizzen shroud. Plough-steel. He would replace it with stainless, if it were his boat, but still, it was strong if properly painted and maintained. And appropriate to the craft.

He slid his hand under the canvas sailcover and felt the mainsail. Fine Egyptian cotton. Nobody had used nonsynthetic sails for fifteen years. He happened to glance down. Dugan, starting down the companionway, was watching him. Neither spoke of the obsolete sails. Dugan dropped below as if disappearing into the conning tower of a submarine.

Mitch had noticed how low she sat in the water and how low the deckhouse seemed. She might be a wet boat at sea. But this meant safety. Portholes instead of a modern expanse of glass meant security in a hurricane. Seas had nowhere to get hold above deck. *Lorelei* was built to slog through heavy weather, to shed green water, dive and cleave the seas, not climb them. He hoped that her low lines and squat cabin-top didn't restrict the headroom below. Few boats were built for men six-feet-three.

As Lindy disappeared down the ladder behind
Dugan, Mitch took a last breath of outside air. His
first sniff below, with the boat freshly opened, might
bring him the moist-leaf odor of dry rot if she were
diseased. He moved down the varnished steps, sniffing.
There was no scent of rot. In the dim light below, he
saw that Dugan, sitting on the port bunk, was watching him again. The tall man looked away, withholding
some sort of judgment.

Lindy was watching Mitch too. He put his hand to
his scalp and lifted it, first test of any boat they looked
at. There was a three-inch clearance between the top
of his head and the varnished oak beams. Whatever
the boat drew—the plans at home said five-feet-ten—
she was as deep a blue-water craft as he had ever
seen. The waterline outside must be at knee-level here
below. Once down the ladder, she seemed twice as big
as one expected.

"Headroom," he murmured to Lindy.

"I'm six-four," said Dugan. "I built her for me."

They were the first words he had volunteered
aboard, and they resounded in the cabin with a
strangely hollow tone.

"By *yourself?*" Lindy asked.

Dugan nodded. Mitch looked around the main
cabin. An old wood-burning stove crouched by the
companionway on the starboard side. A massive ice-
compartment faced it, its top serving as a chart table.
On the galley sink were two pump-faucets, one for
fresh water, one for salt. The ambiance was Jack
London, turn-of-the-century, brass and leather. Kerosene lamps swung from the sides, transom-seats and
bunks were upholstered in quilted maroon. A clock
and matching barometer glittered in the dim light,
warm brass alive with years of polishing. The shelves
above the transom bunks were lined with Keats,

Tennyson, Toynbee, Henry James. A very unusual carpenter.

Apparently Dugan was not going to guide them. Mitch wandered alone to the bow. The two bunks forward were high, with barely room to crawl under the deck beams. There would be no headroom there, even for Lindy, except adjacent to the thick trunk of the mainmast. But aft of the forward cabin, the head-compartment was roomy as it seldom was in modern boats. By the stainless steel sink squatted a hand-pump with a varnished mahogany handle; no pressure system here to go wrong at sea. The toilet was manual, too, and there was not an electric light in sight.

Everywhere, the joiner-work was superb. Each mahogany plug, hiding a screw or a bolt-head, matched the grain of the wood in which it was set. Where roundhead screws showed, their slots were neatly aligned.

There were changes they would have to make, if they ever decided to live aboard. There were modifications they would need to cruise hot climates: she was obviously designed for the north. But her brutal scantlings would be as good insulation against heat as against cold.

She had a feel of granite stability. The varnished trim was simply icing on the cake.

He moved aft, past Dugan, opened the engine compartment under the companionway steps. Inside was a big Greymarine gasoline engine, shining in red paint. It looked new but was easily thirty years old. Under it sat a stainless steel drip-pan; the bilges were impeccably white.

"So," Dugan said tonelessly, as Mitch backed out of the engine compartment and into the main cabin, "how much do I want?"

Mitch seated himself across the table from Dugan.

The transaction seemed suddenly less like the sale of a boat than a child-custody case. If he dwelt on money, the man might stalk away.

"She's priceless," said Mitch. "But let's not discuss price yet."

"That's unusual," Dugan said. He seemed interested for the first time. His face even relaxed, minutely. "What would you like to discuss?"

"She must have taken years to build—"

"Five years, part-time. Eight, if you count aging her lumber."

"I don't understand why you want to sell her."

He had goofed. Dugan stiffened and rose.

"Actually, I don't. Not right now. Just something I was kicking around." He put a foot on the ladder, climbed a step, and looked down at Mitch. "She's sound. You might as well know that."

"Look," flared Mitch. "Sit down!" His own voice surprised him. It surprised Dugan too, and though the carpenter did not descend, he at least stayed where he was.

Mitch went on, swiftly: "All I meant was, *I* wouldn't sell her. I can practically *smell* she's sound."

"I noticed you trying."

To sniff this boat had been insolent. Desperately, Mitch plunged ahead: "She's *obviously* sound. I'll pay you whatever you think she's worth." The lawyer overcame the man of sudden wealth: "Within reason."

"What I think she's worth *isn't* within reason," Dugan said from the ladder. But he descended. Idly, he reached overhead to a row of rolled nautical charts nestling beneath the beams. He withdrew one and spread it on the chart table. He had long, graceful hands, but had lost a finger. For a long time he stood, apparently studying the coastline. With his back to Mitch he said quietly: "I used to take her north all the way to Alaska, most summers. I'd talk to the fishermen, you learn a lot. Put in to Eureka, or lay-to offshore. Astoria, Seattle, go all the way to Anchorage." He paused. "Planned to go back last year. Just to keep her young."

"Why didn't you?" Mitch asked. The man's longing was palpable.

"Maybe I will. I don't really *want* to sell." Dugan turned to face them. "If you bought her, would you leave her here, or what?"

"We would sell our house," Lindy said suddenly, "and move aboard, and cruise her far and wide."

Mitch's heart thumped. He glanced at her gratefully. Her cheeks were red, from embarrassment: she was not happy with theatrics. But she was looking dead into his own eyes: by Christ, she had *meant* it. She turned back to Dugan. "She would be *used,* Mr. Dugan. Believe me."

"Andy," shrugged Dugan. "Andy's OK. Far and wide? That has a nice ring. Where? The South Pacific? Every yachtsman's dream? People plan. Damn few ever leave."

"We'd leave," said Lindy staunchly. "The Marquesas, Tahiti, Les Iles sous le Vent . . ."

Dugan caressed an oaken knee over the chart table. "Northern timber, she's bred in the north for the north. The tropics might open her up."

Mitch promised him that the tropics would not. Dugan was wavering and Lindy had done it. Dugan wanted to know how he would change her.

Mitch's first impulse was to tell him that he'd leave everything the way it was. But instead he leveled. He admitted he'd paint over the varnished brightwork topside, for easier maintenance in the tropics; he'd replace the standing rigging with stainless, so that he wouldn't be fighting rust; he'd substitute dacron for manila, and get synthetic sails.

"In other words," Dugan pointed out, "you don't like work."

Christ, he couldn't win. The guy just didn't want to sell. "There'd be plenty of work for two people, just sailing her."

"She sails herself. I sailed her alone." The blue eyes pierced his own. "Would you put in a Diesel? I mean, if I *did* sell."

He nodded, and scored for the first time, even without help from Lindy. "Yes, Perkins, or a Westerbeke."

"She should have a Diesel," agreed Dugan. "Be a shame to lose her in a fire. I never seem to get enough money together . . ." A breeze set a halyard to knocking, and *Lorelei* complained of her lines. "Shame to leave her tied up another year, too."

The whistle at the plastic factory blasted lunch. Dugan glanced expectantly at the bulkhead clock. It chimed seven times: 11:30. Right on. "Well, Mr. Gordon, I'll think it over. Just don't sell your house."

In the car, Mitch hugged her. "You *read* him. You really read him!"

"I read you."

"If he sells, and we do decide to move aboard—"

"You've decided, Mitch. I'm probably lucky to go along."

"Quit that!" he warned. He thought for a moment. "We said we'd vote."

"I just voted."

"You know," he murmured, "I love you very much."

She smiled. "You're welcome."

CHAPTER
10

THE TROPICAL SUN CLIMBED HIGHER. HE SAT SWING-
ing from the spreader like a weight halfway up a
metronome forty feet high. His mass aloft actually
slowed the roll but increased its arc. The motion had
finally made him queasy.

It was not yet high noon and his skin was seared.
He was tanned and used to exposure, but he had not
spent so much time topside in months.

Longing again for the cool of the cabin, he glanced
at his watch. Eight minutes until time to go below
for his noon sight. He felt guilty. She was treading
water somewhere and he was looking for an excuse
to hide in the shade below.

A salty rivulet ran down his bare belly into his
crotch. It was acid to his raw scrotum. He tore his
thoughts from bodily miseries to more important
things.

Local Apparent Noon was at 11:49. At that instant,

he must be taking his second sunshot of the day. So he would hold out aloft until 11:15. His eyes stung from sweat and sunlight. He felt as if he had been diving in salt water without a mask. His back was weakening fast. But his discomfort was not all bad. In the last hour he had caught himself twice nodding in fatigue. If the needle of pain in his sacro had not jabbed him each time he slumped, he might have fallen, dooming Lindy too. When he returned aloft after the noon shot, he had better wear his safety belt and lash himself to the mast.

"The boy stood on the burning deck . . ." he began. He stopped short. The chanting of doggerel was a symptom of fatigue. Beating back to Bora Bora a few weeks ago, with the hurricane over but seas still wild and the steering cable broken, and Lindy too small to handle the emergency tiller, he had somehow stayed on the helm two days straight. He had recited poetry and sung to himself while she tried to keep him going with a quart of coffee a night.

"Darling? More coffee? Hey, are you all right? We're luffing up again."

"Little bastards quit."

"What little bastards?"

He had trusted tiny elves, dancing in the binnacle light, to swing the compass back on course. Her coffee had snapped the wire of exhaustion and driven the elves out of the binnacle. He needed it now.

His back stabbed him again, this time with authority. He clutched at the mast in agony. It was 11:15, and he had to leave the yardarm.

He steeled himself, waited for a roll to starboard to help him dismount the crosstree, and began to hoist his right foot over the spar.

The needle exploded in a flash of pain. He grunted, his foot locked halfway over the spreader. When he tried to inch his right leg either way, his lower back clamped. He teetered for a moment, gritted his teeth, yanked at his knee, and got the leg back over the yard.

He had regained the spreader, but reversed his position. There was nothing he could do until his back eased. He collapsed backward, sitting with his spine supported by the mast and his legs astride the yardarm.

Facing outboard, to windward, insecure and scared, he had no way to grip the mast until the pain left. The tendons at the base of his spine clenched tightly. He groaned, tried once to shift, and froze.

He was locked by his own muscles twenty-five feet aloft, so he clung to the spreader beneath him as best he could.

The sun would not wait, he must somehow get himself down before Local Apparent Noon, but he could not budge now.

Andrew Dugan, perhaps to delay his own decision, or to generate business for his brother's yard, had finally insisted that Mitch haul out and survey the boat before they talked further. Mitch and Lindy had watched her trundled from the oily water. Squealing up the marine railway, she had grown up before their eyes from a yacht to a full-sized sailing ship.

Now she towered on the ways above them, ready to return to the tide. Her long underwater hull, wineglass-shaped when seen headon, shone newly under brick-red paint. Mitch was filthy from the quick inspection he had given her; he had been afraid that if he hired a professional surveyor he would hurt Dugan's feelings. His bargaining position stank, and they all knew it. No one had mentioned price since the first day. He wanted the boat so badly, and showed

it so flagrantly, that he had set himself up for the
maritime screwing of the century. He didn't care.

He watched painters slap the last few quarts of anti-
fouling under her sweeping bow. Andrew Dugan strolled from the loft.

"You figure she's sound?" he asked tartly. He had
been distant and evasive all morning.

Mitch was nervous. The deal was not set, not at all.
He was afraid to say anything that might trigger
Dugan and give him an excuse to back out. "Beautiful.
Just beautiful."

Dugan whirled away suddenly and escaped to the
clapboard windlass-shack, where his brother was preparing to lower *Lorelei*.

Mitch touched his pocket. His checkbook was there.
Dugan was trapped in the shack, and his older brother
would be an anchor if he started to drift. He entered.
"Mr. Dugan, what *do* you want for her?"

The carpenter looked down the tracks at his boat.
His brother, face frozen, punched a circuit-breaker,
peered down the tracks, called the yard workmen to
their launching positions through a loudspeaker. The
winch motor groaned into life.

"I better ride her in," Andrew Dugan muttered,
bolting for the door. "Got to take the lines."

Mitch grabbed his arm. "Goddamn it, how much
do you *want?*"

"John?" Andrew Dugan pleaded to his brother.

"Go on down," John Dugan said softly, "and we'll
get her in the drink." He glanced at Mitch. "He wants
$16,481. And 91 cents."

Andrew Dugan, face stricken, strode from the
shack. Mitch almost called him back.

He had been ready to go thirty, perhaps thirty-five
thousand. And he did not understand the odd dollars
and cents.

But something told him not to test his luck. He braced his checkbook against the winch-housing and began to write.

He had grabbed a flood tide of fortune, it seemed. Within two weeks Lindy's brother had the house in escrow. In accordance with the tenets of his profession, he carefully kept them from meeting the phantom buyer. They paid off the mortgage and kept $95,000.

By the next week Bobby had scored again. He had lined up a buyer for the beach property at Fort Bragg. Mitch tried to salve his conscience by writing in a deed restriction prohibiting commercial zoning, but the buyer of course balked. Mitch gave up without another shot: he wanted no property taxes over his head when he cut loose. He found himself suddenly a quarter of a millionaire, and he had not yet even sold out his law partnership.

That was a problem that he and Bernie avoided. The dissolution of their business life simmered under a lid of civility. But sometimes Mitch caught Bernie at lunch with clients or in a conference with the juniors, regarding him speculatively, from under lowered brows.

In the meantime the list of items to do and get before they could leave for the South Pacific began to grow like cancer on their lives.

Outside the offices of Crowther & Son, *Marine Agents, Documents of Pratique, Licensed Agents of the Port, Export and Import Documents,* the little group gathered. Montgomery Street brokers hurried past, heedless of drama. Andrew Dugan wore a dated pinstriped suit and a dark tie. His black shoes were mirror-polished. He looked like a freshly robed scarecrow. His brother John, almost identically dressed, had

an air of unwavering finality, like a good funeral director. John's sturdy, anxious wife was there too, stuffed
into a shiny pillbox hat. Mitch knew that Lindy
regretted coming bareheaded; he wished, himself, that
he'd worn a suit instead of a sports jacket.

"Well . . ." began Mitch and John Dugan
simultaneously, and smiled. Dugan continued: "Got
your papers, Andrew?"

Andrew Dugan nodded without expression. Inside,
they stood at an ancient oaken counter while a clerk
with fierce white eyebrows and thick glasses studied
Dugan's certificate of ownership. The vessel would of
course continue to be federally documented, rather
than state-licensed. Documentation made you subject
to federal confiscation in time of war, but gave you
more protection in foreign ports. Mostly, it added
blue-water class: most racing boats, like automobiles,
were registered; deep-water cruisers got documented.

The clerk, straight out of Dickens, squeezed a yellow form into a typewriter and began anachronistically
to tap. Home port would remain San Francisco. Port
of Hail would be Sausalito.

"Name of vessel, *Lorelei*," murmured the clerk.

"Hold it." Mitch dropped his bomb. *"Linda Lee.*
For her first mate, cook, and co-owner."

The poised fingers froze. Above the glasses, aged
eyes fixed Mitch. It was as if he had suggested scuttling
her. "Pardon me?"

"Mitch!" breathed Lindy. "Do you really want to?"

"I do," he murmured, searching her eyes. "OK?"

She nodded uncertainly.

"Linda Lee," he told the clerk again. "Two words.
L . . . I . . . N . . ."

"I can *spell* it," the clerk said stiffly. "But there's
considerable paper work. Has to be published three
days running—"

"Publish it."

"Has to be recorded . . ."

"Charge me for it."

"We do. Forty dollars extra."

"I can change my wife's name to Lorelei for less than that!" protested Mitch.

Lindy winced. Her eyes were on Andrew Dugan. It was no place for a joke. Dugan said stonily: "I guess you know it's supposed to be bad luck."

Mitch, embarrassed, reacted irritably. If he was going to drive Dugan's mournful shadow from the boat, now was the time to start. "Forty bucks is bad luck in itself. There are also sideboards to change, life-rings to repaint, and Lloyds Registry to inform. But I still want her named *Linda Lee.*"

"Wait a second," begged Lindy. "Andy?"

Dugan looked away coldly. She struggled on, unsteadily: "We'll get a brass nameplate, for the bulkhead, under the clock? Something like: *Linda Lee,* ex-*Lorelei;* Andrew Dugan, builder, keel laid such-and-such a date, launched such-and-such a date?"

Andrew Dugan shrugged. "She's only a boat, and she's *your* boat. Do what you want." To his brother he said: "I'm taking a walk on the Embarcadero. I'll grab the ferry back." He turned to Mitch. "When you remember the eccentric son of a bitch who did the work, look at your brass plaque and remember something else."

Mitch looked at him silently.

"Remember, there are five years between those dates," said Dugan. He moved toward the glass door, turned, and tried to grin. It was ghastly. "Try to keep her off the rocks."

The event, even with Andrew Dugan gone, seemed to call for more than a farewell handshake with his brother. They sat at a table with the John Dugans in the Buena Vista Cafe on the edge of North Beach. The bar was jammed with tourists, homosexuals, airline stewardesses in mufti, long-haired brokers, and advertising men. Everyone was drinking Irish coffee.

Mitch asked Dugan if Andrew would be doing the carpentry he planned to have done on the boat.

"I don't think he will." He nodded at the bar. A slim, bare-chested youth in a leather vest, wearing a rigging-knife, was arguing with the Buena Vista's uniformed rent-a-cop. *The boy could be Tony, drifting, when they left . . .*

John Dugan suggested that the kid at the bar was more like what he would get, that even apprentices were hard to come by. "You teach them the difference between a reaming iron and a caulking mallet, next thing, they've taken off. Build their *own* boats, sometimes. Where they sail, God knows."

"They run pot," his wife said decisively. "Pot and dope. Anyway, you'll never get Andrew. He won't want to face her again. He's ashamed."

She told them that the boat had saved their lives. She and her husband had flown one summer to meet Andrew in Anchorage, Alaska, to sail down the coast on *Lorelei*. Off the cliffs of Oregon, the barometer had begun to drop.

"He waited too long," said John Dugan. "We tried to get into Tillamook, but it's breaking across the bar at Cape Meares Light. We're hove to under jib and mizzen and the wheel's lashed and the wind's maybe seventy knots and the seas are maybe forty feet. Three nights! Boat saved our lives!"

"How could he sell her?" Mitch wondered.

Dugan looked at him strangely. *"He'd* have to tell you about that. I'll say this, but you know it already: you're getting her awful cheap."

"Yes. Why?"

The other day, Dugan said, Andrew had asked him to add up the yellowing invoices he had kept from the years he was building her. There were paid bills for blocks, winches, 10,000 galvanized screws, galley pumps, bilge pumps, compass, clocks, barometers, switches and cables. "Lead for the keel. And lumber! Jesus, the lumber: mahogany, apitong, spruce, teak, cedar, oak for her frames, stuff you couldn't hardly find after the war. And can't find now at all. That's what you paid for. That's *all* you paid for."

"I wondered," muttered Mitch. "No labor?"

"He told me," said Dugan, "he'd already been paid for the labor."

CHAPTER
11

HE FELT THE SAIL THROBBING BEHIND HIM AS HE teetered on the yardarm. His treasonous back was still to the mast. He must somehow get down for the noon sunsight. Above him the sky was becoming a great lens, focusing on his brain.

The ketch pitched and he tottered on his perch. He was falling. He made a wild, backhanded grab at the mast behind him. He stopped the fall, gripping the sailtrack so hard that his fingertips hurt. It was 11:40. He had nine minutes to get below and get a fix on the sun.

He swept the ocean one last time. The sea had turned almost purple. The wind was picking up. There were a dozen whitecaps between him and his horizon and nothing else.

With great care, he raised his knee with his hand. The pain hit, but he somehow tolerated it long enough to hoist his foot over the spreader. He rolled a hip under his body. Groping with his toes for the shortest and highest of the rungs on the mast-shrouds, he missed. *Linda Lee* reared on a swell and he slipped.

He had a quick image of his body hurtling twenty-five feet to the deck. He hugged the spreader with knees and hands and swung to rest suspended like a giant sloth beneath the yardarm. He probed for a foothold, found a rung with his toes, and climbed down.

His heart knocked and he poured sweat, but his back felt no worse. He had apparently developed a new and relatively painless maneuver for coming off the mast, if he could find the guts to do it voluntarily. Safely on deck, he reached to the highest rung he could touch and hung for a moment, feet dangling, to stretch. This had always given him relief, and when he let himself down he found that he could stand erect.

At the hatchway he saw M. le Chat lying by the after hatch, waiting for the chirping. A midnight scenario flashed through his mind, as good a guess as any at how she had been lost.

The cat is sleeping with Lindy below. It hears the chirping rudder cable. It slinks topside. Lindy notices that it is gone. She worries. She moves quietly through the main cabin so as not to awaken him. She puts on her safety harness and goes topside. By starlight, she sees the cat ready to spring on the spray-slickened cover hatch. She has no time to clip her harness to a shroud.

She lunges to save the cat and slips. She plummets screaming into the wake, while he sleeps on. She strikes out for the trailing line, grabs it, slips astern until her fingers grasp the plastic buoy. It comes off in her hands.

All this the cat observes, bored and uncaring.

"You sneaky fucker!" he yelled. The cat flicked him

a glance and re-riveted his attention on the chirping hatch. Despite the press of time, he found himself stalking the predator. The lazy slant eyes turned toward him. At the last moment, the cat stretched, eluded him, padded around the hatch just out of reach. It moved with dignity to the dinghy. It leaped to the canvas cover and lay down, licking its fur.

"You bastard!" he screamed. The cat looked up and yawned.

Mitch came out of it. Aghast, he turned and swung down the companionway to the cabin. He did not know what he had intended to do. Toss it overboard? On no evidence? Maybe. He had somehow to get control of himself.

He reached automatically for his sextant and then remembered. He rummaged for the ancient spare and found it in its antique, pie-shaped mahogany case, made in Calcutta. He remembered, in vivid color—and this was a symptom of fatigue, too, the color—the tiny store in a Copenhagen alley where she had found it. He felt again her triumph when he had stepped outside to test it, using the Town Hall clock as the sun, and reported it usable.

He checked it now on the horizon and found it still accurate, although the figures engraved on its inlaid silver quadrant, by some Cockney craftsman a hundred years ago, were so tiny and worn that they were hardly readable.

He squinted at them in the dim light. He could not read them at all. He had four minutes left before Local Apparent Noon. He laid the sextant on the chart table and began hurriedly to rub the tarnish from the arc.

At dawn, three days before they were to vacate their home, he had awakened in their carton-cluttered bedroom. Gray light edged the slats of the Venetian blinds; the curtains had already been packed for storage.

A bird sang from the porch railing below. He recognized the voice. He would probably miss it, though he had never taken the trouble to go to the window to see what kind of bird it was.

It was easier to review the problems of the day than to get up and face them. First, the partnership. Today he would have to tackle Bernie before their pressurized silence gave both of them ulcers. But not *that* problem, not before coffee, not right now.

Instead, the boat. With some relief, his mind drifted to the decisions he must make in equipping her. First, self-steering. He had picked important legal strategies with less mental zig-zagging than he was spending on the choice between three vane-devices for steering by the wind. He suddenly decided on the smallest and most expensive.

Next, Lindy's galley. He had torn Dugan's old wood stove off the boat and tossed it into the yard's scrap pile. They still needed more data on alcohol stoves, propane, kerosene, Diesel oil. Alcohol was safe and clean, but hard to get in foreign ports, unless you burned rum. Propane tanks were unsightly topside and dangerous below. Kerosene smelled. Diesel stoves were hot in the tropics. Alcohol, then, he decided, and the stove stainless steel.

Third, ground-tackle. Lindy was insisting on an electric anchor winch, to save his back. But he doubted that he could maintain an electric motor, "marinized" or not, exposed on long passages to heavy green water on the foredeck. He decided to stick to Dugan's old hand windlass.

Next, the skylight hatch. It was a beautifully varnished period piece. It could be opened wide for ventilation in the tropics, at anchor in good weather. But Mitch was sure that it would leak in a tropical downpour, even closed. At any rate, they all leaked in any kind of sea. He mulled for a few minutes the idea of a substitution. No, it would be ugly, a sin against the whole soul of the boat. He would rather risk the leaks.

Four decisions already, even if two of them were only to do nothing, and the day had not started. Lindy flopped over beside him, close to waking.

Asleep, she usually looked eighteen, but this morning her face sagged. For weeks she had been up until 1 or 2 A.M., packing for the movers and for the boat. She could not believe that you couldn't stuff the contents of a three-bedroom house into a forty-foot ketch. The choice between a favorite pot and an omelette pan would stop her for half an hour.

He eased out of bed. He wove his way through prostrate suitcases, packing boxes, piles of blankets. The bathroom was stacked with medicines, lotions, and hairbrushes. A tiny box marked "BOAT" and a large carton marked "OUT" showed that initially she had intended to be brutal. The trouble was, the "BOAT" box was full and the "OUT" box practically empty. The medicine cabinet on the boat measured two feet by two and was only three inches deep.

He discovered that he could not find his electric razor. He realized suddenly that unless he could devise a method of generating 110 volts at sea he would have to grow a beard or use blades. He finally found the razor in the "OUT" box. Very funny, but today he was not in the mood.

They were not only giving up electric razors but frozen foods and ice-cubes, showers, hot water, Walter Cronkite, and the Raiders' games on Sunday. They were stepping outside the normal stream of their culture. He was all at once dubious of his own ability to do it, and of Lindy's.

He heard a whine outside the bathroom door. Christ, he had forgotten Justice Holmes. Today was goodbye to him, too. He let him in and began to rub his velvet ears. The dog's eyes were tragic. He had known they were leaving from the moment Mitch had dragged the first suitcases from the attic. He had been lumbering brokenly at Lindy's heels every second for the last week.

Mitch dressed himself quickly and slipped to the kitchen. He made coffee for himself and filled Justice Holmes' dish with Red Heart. The dog ignored it. Mitch backed the car out of the garage, and when he had it on the street, he whistled softly. For the first time in a week, Justice Holmes came alive. He bounded across the lawn and into the passenger seat, squealing joyfully. Mitch, feeling like a trundle-driver heading for the guillotine, reached across to close the door and saw Lindy's face at the bedroom window. In a moment, her nightgown whipping, she was at the door of the car.

"He thinks you're taking him riding," she quavered. "Mitch, he could sleep topside!"

Someone had to be firm. "Honey, we decided. Now, let me go."

"Just until we shove off?" she choked.

"No," he said. He leaned across and kissed her. He drove away, narrowly missing the neighbor's car parked at the curb. After twelve years of commuting, he forgot the toll gate on the Bridge and almost rear-ended the line of autos waiting to pay. By the time he turned Justice Holmes and his feeding schedule over to his sister-in-law in St. Francis Woods, he felt like crying himself.

He entered the marble lobby of their building. He had not been to work for three days. The ruddy, obsequious elevator dispatcher, who disliked him but saluted him every morning, the blind newsdealer in the stand who recognized him by his footsteps, the Nisei elevator-starter they'd won a case for, all filled him with guilt. Bernie and they were doomed to work here forever; he was a useless drone, a rat leaving the sinking ship of law.

In their suite high over the city, he moved like a thief past the empty receptionist's desk. He heard Bernie dictating inside his office but was not ready for confrontation. Only in the refuge of his own lair could he relax. On his desk was a note from Bernie, two days old, suggesting that they have a talk. Well, that was why he was here. He crumpled it and tossed it into the basket.

He wandered to the window and looked toward the Ferry Building. He heard the faint tinkle of the Powell-Jackson cablecar. It was his favorite car. He had ridden it interminably when he was fourteen, armed with an old German Rolleiflex, enticed by a photobook of Ansel Adams into another hobby, snapping candids of captive passengers.

Too many hobbies, everyone had said, except his dad, who patiently financed them. Photography, ship-models, cars, dinghy-sailing. A pattern of dilettantism: Chaucer, the guitar, Model A engines. Finally, master of nothing. Something seemed always pulling him on before he became an expert. He consumed interests like a fat man at a smorgasbord.

He wandered into their law library. He sensed that the bound rows of *U.S. Code,* which saw so much more of him than of Bernie, were glowering down at him. Even the coffee machine hidden between the stacks rumbled disapproval.

He poured a cup of coffee, disliking the stale cardboard smell of it, but willing to drink anything to delay facing Bernie. They used to have the girls make coffee, but they paid legal secretaries so much now that it was like hiring a neurosurgeon to pull a splinter, and cheaper to subscribe to the catering service. The result seemed to gag no one else in the firm. He sipped the coffee, sitting with his feet on the library table, until finally guilt drove him to his partner's office.

Bernie's desk hung high over Sutter Street, where, he claimed to clients, he could look down on his commercial beginnings in his father's flower stand. Mitch could not remember his ever having actually worked there, but it was part of Bernie's self-made myth of the self-made man, so he never argued. Now he let him finish dictating a complaint to the Airport Commission about a rise in hangar-rent for the "company" plane.

Bernie shut off the machine.

"Let's carry your boat as an asset," he suggested. "You'll be entertaining clients aboard—"

Mitch fixed him with a cold stare, shaking his head.

Bernie, unruffled, insisted: "Why not? A boat's more personal, like a toothbrush?"

Mitch leaned over his desk, looked into his eyes, and said with great clarity, "Bernie, are you listening? Do you read me?"

"Five-by-five. You're breathing Lavoris in my face."

He explained to Bernie that they would not be using the boat to entertain clients, because they were shagging ass out of San Francisco, they were leaving, they would not be back for years, if ever. *Do you understand?*

"Don't holler." Bernie nodded at the open door to his anteroom. "I think Kitty's come in."

Kitty, Bernie's ancient, close-mouthed secretary, might make a good referee. Nevertheless, Mitch shut the door.

"You get my note?" Bernie asked innocently. "There's something you have to know."

Mitch regarded him suspiciously: "What?"

Bernie sat back, grinning. "Western Casualty wants to retain us."

Western had insured the doctor. Mitch was ready for almost anything but this. Striking while he was off balance, Bernie skidded a letter across the desk. It was signed by the company's chief counsel. Western had apparently decided to insure themselves against future problems with Gordon, Bertelli, *et al.*, by canning their present firm and hiring the winners.

"That's ridiculous," Mitch blurted, shaken. "We're a plaintiffs' firm. Besides, there's conflict of interest. Western's appealing."

"They know they'll lose it anyway."

Mitch studied his partner curiously. "How do you know all this? You been bugging their office?"

"I had lunch with them yesterday. While you were playing boat."

A year ago, Mitch thought, he might have considered the offer a stroke of luck. He must not waver now, or Bernie would never quit trying to change his mind. He let the letter flutter to the desk. In the offer, at least, he saw a wedge and a sop to his conscience.

"No," he said.

"No what?"

"If I'd wanted to represent a corporation, I'd have been a corporation lawyer."

"And besides," Bernie pointed out, "you're looking for an out."

"All right, I am. Anyway," he offered swiftly, "you negotiate with them. By yourself." He sketched the outline of their dissolution. Fifty-fifty, right down the middle, even though eighteen years ago he had put up most of the cash from his father's estate. And Bernie could continue to use his name if he wanted, as an unpaid consultant. "Unpaid," he warned, *"and* unconsulted." He would agree, if it made Bernie more secure, not to practice law in San Francisco for the next ten years. By the time he had finished he had probably cost himself fifty thousand dollars, but he felt as if he had laid down a ten-ton load. "And you'll still get Western."

When he had finished, Bernie was smiling. "You're very generous." Idly, he picked up a desk model of the menacing dark-blue fighter he had flown in Korea. He strafed his dictating machine, with a faraway look in his eyes. "The trouble is, it won't go, not with Western."

"Why not?"

"They want *you,* not me! You're Boalt Hall, I'm night school. You're still down in CIC on the radar, I'm still the poor frigging pilot, and pilots are a dime a dozen. *You're* fighter-director, and they know it."

It was impossible to tell if he was serious. "Bernie," Mitch said uncertainly, "if bullshit were music, you'd be a brass band."

Bernie stared at him blandly. "The firm can't fly on one wing."

" 'One wing,' 'fighter director'? You can do better than that!" The figures of speech spelled rehearsal. Bernie had not been caught off balance this morning, not at all. "There's no problem, Bernie. Make Hal a senior partner. Maybe I'm Boalt, but he's *Harvard.* He knows case-law better than I do. And he's smarter. Hell, I said you can leave my name on the letterhead."

"That wouldn't be nice," Bernie pointed out piously. "Knowing Western wants *you.*"

"Anybody can retain a firm and lose one of its partners! It's a normal risk!"

"They already suspect it."

Mitch stiffened. "Who told them?"

"They know." Bernie swung his chair around, tapping his teeth with the wing of his plane. "They would stipulate no changes in management for two years. Barring death, disease, acts of God, you know."

"I *asked* you, Bernie, who told them?"

Bernie swung back, smiling happily. "Me."

"Yeah!" Mitch felt his cheeks go hot with anger. "Because you're so goddamn ethical? Well, you screwed yourself. Because I've *got* the boat, and we're going."

"Do you know what Western paid those idiots last year? A twenty-five grand retainer and 140,000 clams! You could buy the Queen Mary in two years."

Mitch's hands were sweaty. "No way," he said hoarsely.

Bernie ignored him. "Hell, if you can't wait to go to Tahiti, I'll *buy* you a month down there now. Out of my own pocket."

"Sorry."

"You can't just *shove,*" growled Bernie, "and let this place go down the drain. You got to think of Kitty, and Hal, and me, and the juniors." His face grew sad and his voice dropped. "I've got a kid to put through college."

"So have I. We're leaving."

"My old man's worse, Mitch. We're talking about a sanitarium."

"I'm sorry he is. He's also living with you in Pacific Towers, in a $100,000 apartment."

"With a yearly nut of twelve thousand bucks!"

"Sell out an move," suggested Mitch. "*We* are."

"I'm asking for two more years," Bernie said. "That's all. OK?"

"No."

Bernie began to land his airplane, over and over, on his blotter. He shook his head. "A long time, to blow it up like this."

"Like *what?* You're my best friend, we're not for Christ's sake *married.*"

Bernie's voice rose. "You can't *go* now. We've got cases as far as the eye can see. You've got an obligation to our clients!"

"There's Roxson-Maguire, and then my calendar's clear." Bernie's rising voice was a danger signal. He'd try to drag Mitch into a swamp of Latin passion, and when they were through they would be enemies.

"What are you leaving *for?* What you got to prove, this alone-against-the-sea shit? I wish you'd been *flying* off that carrier, with your asshole grabbing silk. You never had a chance to be *scared,* that's all."

"We can't all be heroes," grated Mitch. His pulse was beginning to pound.

"But we all got to try it for size, just once? At forty-two?" He sat back triumphantly. *"That's* your problem. It's too bad you have to drag Lindy along, too."

Mitch gripped the desk, fighting an impulse to vault it and jam Bernie's silly airplane down his throat. The last time he had hit Bernie, at seventeen, he had knocked him on his ass. He wanted to do it again. He forced himself to keep down his voice. "We're *going,* Bernie."

"I'm OK, pull up the ladder?" Bernie flared. "You always were a spoiled son-of a bitch! That ivory penthouse on the hill!"

For a moment Mitch thought he was talking about the Belvedere house; then he realized that Bernie meant his childhood home. "I didn't know you cared," he said tersely.

"You'd have been a better lawyer born on the Beach," snapped Bernie.

He was damned if he would let his partner get to him. He calmed himself by force of will. "Can we skip the up-from-North-Beach crap?" he proposed. "Your old man did all the groundwork anyway."

"*Yours* cut off your balls up there!"

"You live up there now."

"*I* earned it!" yelled Bernie.

"Then you won't need me to keep it," said Mitch. And softly, again: "We're shoving, Bernie."

Bernie hurled his model at the wall. It shattered and lay broken on the rug, cowering under its own wings. "Well, go," choked Bernie. "Goddamn it, go!"

Mitch picked up the plane and laid it on the desk. His partner's eyes were glittering with tears.

"I'm sorry, Bernie," he said quietly.

"Will you just get your ass *out?*"

Mitch left him there. Barring the adolescent brawl, it was the first argument between them he had won for twenty-five years. It did not feel good at all.

CHAPTER
12

THE SUN PEAKED. THE CABIN WAS BECOMING A STEAM-bath. Dripping sweat, he braced himself under the sky-light and tried to read his noon position on the silver arc of the 100-year-old sextant. Despite his polishing, the tiny figures on the quadrant were almost erased by time.

He rummaged through the navigation drawer and found a seven-dollar pair of glasses he had bought in Papeete from a Chinese druggist, who had selected them, solely on the basis of his age, from a crate on the pharmacy floor.

Combining the glasses with a magnifying glass, he read the altitude. The vernier was marked in seconds of arc, which no navigator had used for fifty years. He converted the reading to decimals, checking his work at every stage.

His sweat fell in huge greasy drops onto his sight-form, smearing his calculations. His dividers, parallel rules, and the chart grew moist. The cabin was suffocating. He would not take the time to air the cabin after last night's spray.

He moved his running-position forward on the chart to give himself a noon position, the first solid fix since she had been lost. It was close to his D.R. Good. He was putting pencil, plotter, gum-eraser, and nautical almanac away when the bulkhead clock chimed eight bells.

She had been in the water now at the least for nearly nine hours: at the most, for almost twelve.

The water was warm, eighty degrees now at noon, no less. And she had the jacket, and perhaps the plastic container.

Somewhere in the rear of the long double rank of books jammed on his bookshelf was a Navy publication he had liberated after Korea: *Survival at Sea.* In it lay predictions: water temperature versus survival time. He moved to find it, and paused.

If he looked up her chances and found that she was statistically dead, it would mean nothing anyway. The tables were drawn for men, not women, and everyone knew that women were more buoyant, fattier, hardier in the water.

In his first Honolulu Race, a crewman from another boat had been rescued after four days in a lifejacket by a passing freighter.

Compared to the average US Navy man, or yachtsman, Lindy was a fish. She outlasted him on every swim, was warm in the water long after he had crawled shivering up the boarding ladder. She was in perfect health. She had just survived, on a forty-foot boat, the worst hurricane to hit French Polynesia in fifty years. She had probably put on three pounds in Bora Bora after the storm. Three pounds of fat could add hours to her body heat.

And if the Navy tables decided she was dead, what was he going to do anyway? Abandon the search?

He didn't want to know and couldn't afford to take the time to find out. He tried the radio again. He thought he heard a voice come back, through crackling static. It was too faint for him to distinguish even the language. He dashed topside, wiped spray from an insulator on the antenna, tried again, but heard nothing now.

As he began to climb the mast again he glimpsed the cat, still lying on the dinghy. Its eyes mocked him slyly. In its pea-brain was locked the secret that could save her: what time she had gone.

He was again impelled to kill it. For a moment he rested his forehead on a rung. The teak was damp and cool. She had helped him shape the wood.

He struggled aloft to the yardarm and began his watch again.

They began to move aboard the boat in an unsteady drizzle under a corrugated sky. For a few days they returned to the empty house to sleep, until they stored their furniture. They slept one last night in bags on the living room floor, because she was reluctant to cut the cord.

Twice a day Mitch would return to the house to cram their station wagon with cartons of clothes, linens, and canned goods. Trans-Pacific races had taught him that equipping a vessel was not enough: you had to know precisely where each item was stored. If you did not, lockers, drawers, and stowage voids became tangled nests that you came to avoid at all costs. Jobs remained undone at sea simply because it was too much trouble to dig for the chisel or lightbulb or oilcan that would make everything work again.

So he had decreed a card-file. In it every item that

went into the boat was rigorously to be logged, along with its location. It began as a neat and colorful inventory, tagged with tinted indexes.

Each card, he proposed, would be typed. He set his portable up on the cabin table to type it. The typing became penciled scrawling as the typewriter itself disappeared under piles of bedding, linen, and nautical charts.

The deadline to vacate the house approached. The drizzle persisted. The cabin became engorged with pots, books, and tools. Lindy, working below as he hauled more and more gear from the house, could not keep up. He piled household effects on the dock, on two-by-fours raised above soggy planks. A bottleneck developed on the wharf. The elder Dugan found him tarpaulins to cover the stacks but the tarps began to leak as the rain continued.

On the third night Mitch drove down the hill with the last load. It was dark and the boatyard was locked as he slithered to a stop outside. He honked for Red-Dog, the bearded young boat owner who was acting as night watchman to pay off his yard-bill and release his handcuffed schooner. Red-Dog slid open the wooden gate and dove into the car next to him, smelling of wet wool and beer. The clouds had turned pregnant and the wind was high. He could barely see well enough through the slanting rain to back down the dock. The two of them grabbed armloads and sprinted down the wharf like broken-field runners. Gusts from the hills of Marin were yanking at the tarps tucked over the gear. If he didn't get it all crammed below, now, the food cans underneath would begin to rust and not stop rusting until they popped at sea. He tumbled below in a shower of rain.

He almost groaned when he saw Lindy. He had left her exhausted, in blue jeans, hair tangled, face smudged, a smear of dirt on the bridge of her nose. Now, despite the cold, she was wearing a sweeping hostess gown, and her hair was up, with two wispy curls at the temples. She had lost ten years of age in an hour.

She had somehow dragged everything forward, freeing the main salon. The cabin, after days of grime and mud, had got scrubbed and glowed warmly in candlelight. On the varnished table two glasses flanked a bucket of champagne; there was no ice in it, but the boat was cold enough to chill it. He smelled *coq-au-vin* simmering on her alcohol stove. They had first eaten it on their honeymoon. Their new Transoceanic radio throbbed symphonically. Her eyes shone.

"Welcome home," she said. "Mitch, I've been bitchy. About leaving the house, and all. So—" She studied his face. "What's wrong?"

"Honey?" he pleaded, hating the rain, the boat, himself.

"Oh, no," she murmured. "Not now?"

"Red-Dog's topside. We got to get it all below. The works."

She whirled, to hide tears. Later as he and Red-Dog passed the gear below, she had changed clothes to help, but though they gobbled the *coq-au-vin* with Red-Dog afterwards, they were all too tired for the champagne and they put it away.

The next morning the rain had stopped, though the cabin was freezing and the wind still moaned in the shrouds. It was Sunday and only the owner of the motor-sailer and Red-Dog were in the yard. Mitch dressed, shaking with cold. He scrounged some kerosene from the motor-sailer and started the cabin-heater.

Sloshing across the grimy yard enroute to the john,

he glanced up and glimpsed blue sky. In an hour he had everything topside to dry. Then he noticed that the bulkhead barometer was still low. He recalled, too late, an old racing adage: "When in doubt, wait half an hour." In another twenty minutes, just as Lindy announced breakfast, new clouds were scudding in from the west. They bolted their Sunday breakfast, and by the time they had finished, drops were falling again.

He and Lindy repeated last night's drill, without Red-Dog, who had during the morning got high on something and was sleeping it off in the rain on the deckhouse of his captive schooner.

By the time they had rejammed everything, his back was killing him. The kerosene heater, blasting in the closed cabin, had given him a headache. He collapsed on a sailbag. It smelled already of mildew. Lindy squirreled her way forward after an aspirin bottle, thought to be in one of the medicine cartons in the forepeak.

He closed his eyes and saw their house empty in the rain. It was very inviting, even to him, and he could imagine its pull on Lindy. Well, it had a mudslide threatening it, and he knew of termite damage in its pilings, and there were still plumbing problems: at least he was away from all that. He had it all together, within forty feet. He dozed off.

"Mitch? Mitch!"

He snapped awake. She was emerging from the forward cabin butt first, like a tick stung by a match. He got off the sailbag to make room for her to pass. She sucked a finger, nicked on a locker hatch. She blew a strand of hair from her face. She looked tired again, and it was only ten in the morning. "There's got to be aspirin aboard, but I can't find it. I'll have to go to the drugstore."

"Christ, it's pouring. I'll ache, instead. Headache's gone anyway," he lied. "Back's fine."

"Good. Look, will you move your legs?" He hoisted them painfully, so that she could sidle between the bunk and the table. She began to stuff pillowcases into a locker already stuffed. "We need more lights forward."

"OK."

She waited. "Put them on your list, all right?"

He cut off a groan. He kept the worklist on a legal pad and couldn't remember where he'd put it. He crawled aft across the cartons, groped through papers on the chart table. The main hatch was snugged against the rain, and the skylight, blocked topside by the dinghy, was dim. Dugan's dockside power had failed last night in the storm. Mitch couldn't find the circuit breakers in the empty shed, and the twelve-volt boat-power was growing weaker by the hour.

He found the worklist and peered at it. It was stupefying.

The chart table light dimmed and almost died, so that he could no longer read. "Let me by?" Lindy asked again.

"Christ!" He squashed himself against the chart table and she squeezed past.

"Put down 'stove lamp,' too," she called back, from somewhere forward. "I can never see into the pots on the stove."

Anger, despair at the whole mess he had got them into, clutched at his throat. He had begun fighting every change she suggested. This one he simply ignored.

"Oh," she said smugly. "It's leaking, like you said it might."

"What's leaking?" Dismay settled into his bones.

His shins ached. He was afraid he was coming down with flu.

"The skylight."

"It's just condensation," he begged.

"Drip . . . drip . . . drip . . ." she intoned, looking aloft. "Is that condensation?"

He crawled forward and reached up, feeling along the varnished moulding. It wasn't condensation, it was a leak. Well, he couldn't caulk it now, and when it stopped raining he probably wouldn't be able to find it. He put it on the list, making 350 items. Hiring help was not the answer; there were only so many carpenters, painters, and mechanics a forty-foot boat would hold, and none of them gave a damn how they fouled things up below.

Lindy had collapsed, sitting dully on a bunk. Until they had light there was nothing more, really, she could do.

"It's all just so goddamn *much*," she quavered. "We've done more fighting in an hour than we did all year!"

He had no answer. He went topside and tossed a wringing-wet tarpaulin over the skylight. It stopped the leak but killed what remained of the light below, so they could work no longer anyway. It was raining too hard to sprint for Dugan's filthy public shower, so they sprayed each other with Right Guard, dressed over their own sweat, and crossed the Bridge to have dinner at the Club.

They had really nowhere else to go.

CHAPTER
13

AT 3 P.M. PAPEETE TIME, HE WAS FIFTY-FOUR MILES northwest of Moorea, bearing down for the second time on the spot at which he had discovered her gone. Clinging to the spreader, he was especially alert and very apprehensive.

He was entering, again, the area in which he had pitched over the flag and the strobe light. Three hours northwest, he had sailed, until dawn: then three southeast, and no flag. Three northwest again, and now three southeast, and still no flag. He wondered if it had drifted further downwind than he.

Searching his horizon minutely, he became conscious of a distant white speck. It was no whitecap, for it remained. He raised his binoculars and trapped it in their circle of vision.

It was the cabin-top of a powerboat, hull-down beyond the horizon. It was cutting across his own course, apparently bound for Tahiti. In the crazy, bounding field of the binoculars, he could soon see long bamboo poles bundled on her cabin-top. He recognized her as a Tahitian *bonnitier,* a long way from home. Perhaps she had been trolling near Tubai Manu to the south.

He lost her in the binoculars in a sickening roll which almost pitched him from the spreader. He dropped the glasses and grabbed backward for the mast. He missed and flopped forward to his stomach. The binoculars dangled below.

He got back astride the spreader and found the fisherman again. Her bow flung the great swells back and hurled a white sheet of foam aside. She was charging northwest at twelve or fifteen knots, to make Papeete before dusk.

There was no way to cut her off at his own crawling speed. He scrambled down the rigging, slid below, and shouted out a Mayday on the radio.

He waited, got no answer, and called again. He found himself babbling, in English and French, into the deaf void: *"J'ai perdu ma femme!* My wife is overboard! *Mayday, Mayday, Mayday! Elle est tombeé à la mer!"*

He charged topside. The *bonnitier* had not changed course. He had been stupid to think that the fishing boats carried radios, or that a nonchalant, breezy Tahitian fisherman would guard the distress frequency even if he had one. He groped in the aft compartment, found the Very pistol and a box of flares. He pointed it straight up and fired. It kicked in his hand like a .45. The flare arose whitely, barely higher than his own mast, became lost in the blazing sky, and dropped into his wake. He fired all the flares he had. All were unspectacular. The fishing boat was almost out of sight.

He had one more card to play, a signal mirror they stowed in their life raft. He grappled for it by feel, unable to take his eyes off the retreating fisherman. He found it and lined up its peep hole with the target, but the sun was too low behind him.

He was jamming the mirror back into the raft when he felt a compact metallic box, hardly bigger than a pack of cigarettes, with a pencil-like projection at one end.

He froze, incredulous, recognizing the shape. "Shit!" he bellowed, drawing the object out.

It was a farewell gift from Bernie, a tiny emergency transmitter, preset to the international aircraft distress frequency. It was powered by little batteries. Private pilots were required to carry it in California.

Activated, it was supposed to transmit a warbling signal on international emergency frequencies, guarded by all planes in flight.

There were two flights a day between Papeete and Bora Bora, and he was hardly twenty miles from their track. And hourly flights, too, between Papeete and Moorea, all day long. He flicked it on. Its tiny red eye began to pulse, telling him that it was transmitting.

He took it aloft with him, suspended by a lanyard from his neck, along with the binoculars. Once on his position on the mast he began to tremble as the truth struck him. Washed with the most violent guilt he had known all day, he began to sweat.

All the interisland flights were daylight ones. The sun was dropping to port already.

He should have turned the little radio beacon on twelve hours ago.

As the water warmed at noon, she became more comfortable. She dropped into a rhythm of dipping her head every few minutes to ease her forehead from the blazing sun, then emptying the jug of whatever had trickled in, then lying back again and simply waiting.

Sometimes, when the swell swept her to a crest and widened her horizon, she remembered to swing her head for a quick look for the ketch.

Through the midday hours she seemed actually to have gained strength. Her thirst was awful, but if only he found her before the water cooled, she would be OK. She dreaded the chill that darkness would bring.

She raised her head, glanced at the descending sun, and heard a distant low rumble. Airplane? Boat? As she dipped again, the noise dropped, but she could hear it faintly still, through her body more than her ears.

She still saw nothing, but within five minutes she was hearing the grumble strongly. It seemed to be coming from all directions. She knew now that it was a boat engine, but too powerful for *Linda Lee*. A fishing boat, perhaps, or an interisland schooner.

All at once she spotted it. Diving into sheets of spray, its long bamboo poles lashed quivering to the cabin-top, it was less than a quarter-mile away, much closer than Mitch had come before he turned.

She was in its path, and for a crazy moment she was afraid that it might hit her. She jammed her whistle in her mouth and shrilled with all her strength. She lost sight of the boat, as she dipped, and then it was almost on her a hundred yards away. It slewed from its course, rolled, and gave her a view of a cockpit full of glistening gutted fish and an immense Mahi-Mahi.

If it didn't hit her, smash her down and carve her in the screws, it had found her, she was saved.

She began to yell, waving her arms: she whistled: she screamed and thrashed. The bow loomed in her vision. It was almost on her—no, it would leave her to starboard, but where was everyone? The roar became overpowering.

Then it was passing in a drumming crescendo of power, pounding into the swells a hundred yards away.

She finally glimpsed the helmsman behind glass in the cabin. He was a fat, serious Polynesian, braced at the wheel. She seemed actually to remember him from the Papeete quai. He was someone they might have bought tuna from.

Standing next to him, clinging to a cabin support, stood a handsome young Tahitian. The younger man saw something, in the other direction. He pointed to port. The older followed his glance and nodded. The younger raised a bottle of beer and sipped it.

"Hey!" she shrieked. "Help! *M'aidez!*"

They thundered past, leaving the smell of diesel exhaust, and then she was suddenly immersed in the brutal, rushing wake. When she fought free of that, they were far past hearing, but she whistled anyway until they were almost out of sight.

For a long while she lay exhausted.

It had taken all day long, but at last she was truly scared.

In Cox's Boatyard, Mitch sat in *Linda Lee*'s cockpit with Andrew Dugan and wrote a check for the yard-bill. Using the compass-binnacle as a desk, he filled it out for just over $6,000.

The yardwork was done, the gasoline engine replaced with diesel, the through-hull fittings changed. Tomorrow *Linda Lee* would leave the dock she had been chained to for years, and move to a modern marina.

It was the first time Andrew himself had been aboard since he had sold the boat. He took the check and stuffed it into the pocket of his immaculate overalls. "We charge too much," he said.

Mitch, having done half the work himself, agreed, but at least the major jobs were done. Lindy's new alcohol stove hung glittering in its rack. An auxiliary diesel generator snored below, charging their batteries and breaking itself in. A neat plexiglass-and-stainless steering vane, named Irwin after his accountant, sat behind the helmsman's station. They had tried it on a shakedown cruise and it worked perfectly.

Dugan asked him when they were leaving for the South Pacific. Mitch told him in a couple of months: there was still lots to do.

"Go now or you never will. Maybe if I'd done that, after the gale, I wouldn't have sold her." He arose. "The hell with it."

Mitch said: "Your brother told me about the storm. Awful."

The observation seemed to anger Dugan. "Awful? Jesus, that's where storms *are,* at sea! Nobody makes you *go* there, do they?" He was silent for a while, and his eyes drifted far away. "No, I'd been through gales before. Next summer, I headed for Alaska. Anchorage or bust. Beautiful day, everything perfect, perfect . . . Nice little twelve-knot breeze through the Golden Gate, little chop outside in the Potato Patch . . ."

He seemed puzzled. "All at once I jibed her around and came home. Tied her up and hardly sailed her since."

"We'll sail her," promised Mitch.

"Then *sail* her," growled Dugan. "Don't wait."

Mitch watched him shamble back down the dock. He did not look back.

CHAPTER
14

THE LATE SUN HUNG BRASSY ON HIS PORT SIDE. THE trades were still heavy, but were gusting, which meant that they were losing their strength for the night.

He shifted his position on the spreader, accidentally bending the tiny transmitter's antenna as he did so. He straightened it carefully, flicked its switch to "TEST" for the fifth time in the last hour. It glowed reassuringly.

But it would be useless after dark, when local flights would stop. Sunset was at 1855, only fifteen minutes away. The flights had probably stopped already.

Again he considered leaving the search area to clear himself from the radio interference of Moorea, and trying to call Papeete again. But he could not bring himself to leave her.

He squeezed his eyes shut to relieve them. The sunlight was a golden freeway leading to the west. His eyes, unable to stand the glare, slipped idly downward to rest.

The ketch was immense seen from above, and beautiful! The tapering bow and stern, with sweeping lines straight from the Vikings, were in flowing harmony with the sea. Lindy had always looked tiny from here, sunbathing on the deck at sea or sanding and scraping in port while he worked on the rigging. Without her, the boat was empty, a *Flying Dutchman* groping in a wasted sea.

He had to start the generator. He wanted bright lights tonight. He swung his foot over the yardarm, waited for the pain in his back, and, when it had passed, lay face-down along the yard. He let himself roll off, as he had recently learned, and hung suspended underneath it for a moment by hands and legs. Then he let his legs go and groped until he found a rung.

It did not work so well this time. He wondered how much longer he could overcome his weakening back to climb up and down the mast. He descended the rungs stiffly. Grasping the cabin-top handrails against the roll, he sidled crabwise to the cockpit.

He hesitated. Before starting the generator he had better plumb the fuel level in the tank that fed it. To unscrew the fuel cap, he raised the hinged cockpit seat. He grunted in surprise, then yelled exultantly.

The waterstained, battered logbook, memory of the boat, lay on the tank. She must have stuffed it there to protect it from wind and spray, before dealing with whatever had brought her topside, the cat or her half-hourly routine.

Shakily, he began to leaf through it. A dash of spray wet his face, but he did not notice. He found the last smudged page. Her penciled, rounded figures hopped up at him.

He had awakened her for her watch at midnight. Her first entry was a half-hour later, course and speed for 1230, then 0100, 0130, 0200, then another for 0230, and—he almost yelled again in relief, or pain—one for 3 A.M.

And he had discovered her gone at 0312. She had fallen in less than twelve minutes before he had awakened.

He had been covering three hours worth of track all day when he could have been searching twelve minutes worth.

Fifteen miles, skimmed shallowly, versus perhaps one mile, searched over and over, swell by swell . . . He was at the wrong end of his pattern *now;* she was three hours southeast.

He whirled and started the engine. He jammed the throttle forward to the highest RPM's he dared to use. He could smell hot metal.

He disconnected Irwin and took the wheel. *Linda Lee* slowly gathered speed and leaped ahead, straining under power and sail. He caught his breath as a sheet of spray hit him full in the face. The water was becoming colder.

The ketch crashed southeast, where he should have been searching all day.

They moved into Hurricane Hole Marina, Sausalito's newest, intending to stow their perishables and be gone in a couple of weeks.

Hurricane Hole was considerably more comfortable than Dugan's shabby wharf. There were cinder-block johns on the seawall, telephone-jacks and plastic dock-boxes at the slips, and a piratical marine-supply store, much too handy, adjoining the marina office and doubling the price of every bronze screw it sold.

When Lindy was too tired to cook on her new stove, the Ancient Mariner Restaurant offered itself. It was

one month old and reeked of tradition: varnished
hatch-cover tables, trawler-nets behind the bar, glass
fisherman balls hanging everywhere, yellowed photos
of square-rigger San Francisco on the walls. Waitresses
wore serving-wench bonnets, low-cut bodices, and
crotch-height miniskirts. In TV voices they announced
their names—mostly they seemed to be called Sherry
—and recited the menu, and begged them to have a
nice evening. The lobster was always tough.

They were certain rules at Hurricane Hole. You
learned to obey, to twist, or evade. You never pol-
luted in the daylight: you trudged down the dock, up
the gangway to the seawall, and along the seawall to
the nearest cinderblock toilet. After the first chilling
night-time hike, you began to use the head aboard,
letting the tide destroy the evidence.

As "live-aboards," native to the marina, they found
themselves superior in status. A live-aboard might
not actually move his boat six inches a year, might,
in fact, be a stockbroker or advertising man commuting to work like anyone else, but he was an expert on
all things nautical simply because he slept aboard at
night.

Surrounded by plastic, halliard-clinking modern
yachts, their own wooden ketch glowed with romance,
and they bore the brunt. She looked like a world
cruiser already, if only by comparison. Big auxiliary
fuel tanks were lashed in cradles to her deck, two stainless beer kegs of emergency water were set before
the mast, and her rigging bristled with baggy-wrinkles.

They couldn't get the nautical tire-kickers out of
their hair. The Bowsprit-Knocker was the worst. He
was usually a day-crawler, often retired. Placing a
familiar hand on the bowsprit, he would beam at the
boat.

"Tell me you folks are going to Tahiti."

"Eventually. Watch it, that rail's just been paint—Shit!"

"It's OK, hands were dirty anyway. Guess this sounds stupid, but how long'll it take, boat like this?"

"Haven't worked it out."

"Hope you got your appendix out?"

"Yes." Neither of them did, but it saved conversation.

"Pretty small island. Think you can find it? Got a radio?"

They all seemed to assume that if you had a radio, you could turn it on as you left the dock and somehow follow its nose to Tahiti. "Yes, got a radio." Where the hell had he put the paint thinner? The fog was due and he had less than a foot of rail to go, if the old bastard would just get off his back.

"Mind if I step aboard?"

He had suspected that he had a subspecies, the Mind-if-I, on his hands, but hadn't wanted to believe it. "I'd rather you didn—"

Too little and too late. He was aboard, just missing the paint bucket.

"Feels solid under your feet." A tentative soft-shoe, followed by a jolly stomp.

"Thanks. Don't sit there, please."

"Long way, Tahiti. Hey, you missed some railing. Couple of thousand miles, I guess?"

"Yeah, about four."

"How much fuel you carry?"

"Not much. Plenty of sails. Watch the bucket!"

Peering below, the Bowsprit-Knocker would glimpse Lindy. "Just the *two* of you?"

No, you stupid shit, we're taking a crew of seventy-four midgets and a dwarf to handle the sheets. "Just us two."

"You and your daughter."

"Wife."

Obligatory pause, faroff look in the eyes, and inevitably: "You know, one of these days—"

"You'll do the same thing? You should, you really should."

Maybe if he escaped below, he could shake him long enough to return and finish the painting undisturbed, afterward. "Excuse me, please." He started down.

"Seems awful small inside," his tormentor would suggest. "Mind if I take a look?"

Lindy had already promised him that if he let one more half-assed dreamer down to slow her progress, she'd disembowel them both with her bread knife. But she was just as helpless before longing eyes as he was, and he couldn't be the bad guy always, so he would lead him below, and shoot another half-hour showing him around.

Unless they learned to bite the bullet and swallow their guilt at escaping, they would grow roots to the bottom.

He awakened with a hangover the night after their last farewell party on the hill. The defendant in Roxson-Maguire had settled out of court. Within a week, they would be leaving, and it was high time: people were already asking him if he had given up the idea. He stumbled around the cabin, not wanting to wake Lindy, trying to make coffee silently and to find his business suits and shoes. He had to see Bernie this morning to sign the dissolution agreement. He struggled into his pants and shoes. It had been weeks since he had worn anything but slip-on deck shoes or sandals.

Swelling feet: a milestone in his liberation. He slipped into the head to tie his necktie before the mirror. He had trouble with it. He was unlearning beautifully. Not even Bernie's bleak predictions of what would happen to their firm—Bernie's firm—dimmed his satisfaction. At the office, he told Bernie about the shoes.

"Shoes?" Bernie commented sourly. "I *want* my shoes to fit."

"Come on, Bernie. Retire! The water's fine."

"That's a lot of crap," snapped Bernie. "You're not retired. You're working your ass off over there. Look at your fingernails, you look like a mechanic. You got to be living like a pig on that thing. I don't see how Lindy stands it."

Mitch declared, less than truthfully, that Lindy loved the life. Bernie asked him if their wills were up to date. Mitch thanked him wryly and told him that they were in the office safe. He asked Bernie to continue as executor.

Bernie professed that he was honored and promised to keep Tony out of the hog-belly market. "What's *he* think of your abandoning him?"

Mitch's sense of well-being fled. *"Abandoning* him? He'll be twenty-one in a month! Where were you and I at twenty-one?"

"Wards of the government," Bernie reminded him. "Lost, drunken idiots, chasing cunt whenever Uncle Sam would let us out. Safe from everything but the hazards of war. For some things, you got a mind like a sieve." He shrugged. "He's a sweet kid, but he's probably still thinking with his pecker. You ought to take him along."

"He wouldn't go."

"You ask him?"

"Bernie, he's got to finish college. Or he'll end up selling neckties!"

"Did you *ask* him?" persisted Bernie.

"No."

"I figured." Bernie snapped his fingers. "Hey, I got something for you."

He dug into his desk. He handed Mitch a package, gift-wrapped. Mitch found a tiny emergency radio inside, like one he had seen in Bernie's plane. Bernie explained it: "Automatic. Flick the switch and you're warbling on 121.5, like a nightingale in heat."

"Surrounded," Mitch said drily, "by circling aircraft."

If they ever got struck by a whale and had to abandon the ketch, the transmitter would be nice for Lindy's morale. But Mitch had directed enough unsuccessful searches in crowded Korean waters to know that in the untraveled South Pacific it would be as useful as a candle held aloft.

The gift succeeded, of course, in summoning the image of Lindy and him in a life raft under an empty sky. "Very interesting approach," he said ungratefully. "Italian. Machiavellian, you might say. But just a little too late."

Bernie shrugged. "Not *too* late." He produced the agreement, ready to tear it in half. "Your chair's still warm."

"Sorry," smiled Mitch. When they shook hands, Bernie suddenly hugged his shoulders.

Mitch was touched, but Bernie had already clouded the day.

Tony hitchhiked down from Humboldt to see them off. He arrived as Mitch was preparing to crawl into the engine compartment to change the oil filter. Mitch laid out his tools while Tony watched. The kid was nervous as a defendant being sworn. Mitch suspected that when he was safely crammed below, out of sight, his hands slippery with warm engine oil and his mind on nuts and bolts, his son would drop whatever bomb was balanced on the edge of his mind.

Tony had paused to leave his sleeping bag at Nancy's, and thus arrived too late to help Lindy, who'd already left to pick up a last case of canned food from the wholesale market.

"Nothing I can do, Dad?" he asked without enthusiasm. There was plenty, but Mitch regarded his son and shook his head. Tony seemed on the edge of a breakdown: he was yawning, his foot was jiggling, his fingers were tapping, and his eyes were shifting. If Mitch asked him to work on the boat, he would probably mangle a turnbuckle or drop the sail overboard.

"You might tell me what's on your mind."

Tony looked up, startled. "Nothing. Why?" There was no way to float the problem to the surface, so Mitch snaked into a hole that even his son could barely have fitted—and hadn't volunteered. He flicked on the dim worklight behind the engine and began to unscrew the filter. When there was no chance that he would reemerge to face him, Tony launched his rocket. "Dad?"

"Um?"

"I can't go back."

Mitch dropped the master nut from the filter casing. In the orange glow of his worklamp, he saw it roll along the engine bed. He grabbed for it, knocked it off, and heard it plop into the bilge, far below the pan and forever out of reach. *"Shit!"*

"I'm sorry, Dad," Tony said distantly. "I flunked biology, and soil chemistry I, and—"

Mitch's crotch felt moist and he discovered that oil was trickling onto his belly. "Son of a bitch," he growled. "Tony, look—"

"I'm *sorry,* Dad. I know how you feel, but—"

"Tony, just hand me in a towel, OK?"

"A *trowel?*"

"Towel, goddamn it! Rag, paper towel, anything. They're above the galley sink."

Tony's disembodied hand appeared with a single paper towel. Mitch patted at his crotch. "All right," he called. "You flunked out. What the hell are you going to do now?"

"Get a job, I guess."

"Where?"

"Filling station? Garage, maybe."

"Pass me my crescent wrench."

Silence without, and then a great clanking of tools, and then silence again. "What's a crescent wrench?" Mitch squirmed out. On his hands and knees, he regarded the fruit of his seed. Tony was calmer, apparently relieved by confession. He was there in the flesh, all right, but his mind had already fled to the hill and Nancy.

"Tony?" Mitch said softly, lifting a crescent wrench from his jumble of tools. "See?"

"Oh! Yeah." Tony smiled. He had a great smile.

"Lots of luck," Mitch said, "with the garage."

They took Tony and Nancy to the Ancient Mariner for a farewell dinner. Nancy was fresh-faced and clear-eyed. She had the oval face of a medieval angel and, as far back as Mitch could remember, the conversational style of a startled fawn.

She had always bored Mitch silly. She showed no hint of intelligence, and yet she was a junior at U.C., reputedly making straight A's. Besides, Tony was not stupid. Shy as she was, he must have discovered something in her.

He glanced enviously at the two. Tony, unemployed

and possibly unemployable, chewed mightily at a $7.50 sirloin: not a problem in the world. No rent to pay, no dues: look, Ma, no ring. Mitch was impelled to rock their boat.

"If Tony joins the workforce," he remarked, "you two ought to get married."

"Lovely," murmured Lindy. She looked at him as if he had lost his mind.

"Oh, wow!" Nancy's great dark eyes swam toward him. She studied his soul for a moment. "Why can't we just live together?"

"Why the hell not?" Mitch asked gruffly. The whole screwy set-up was, he supposed, a problem for Nancy's father more than himself, but he found himself angry and didn't know why.

Mitch sat on his bunk to take off his shoes. Lindy was spreading out her sleeping bag, kept rolled as a pillow for daytime use. "Move your butt," she said. "I'll make your bed."

He sidled around the table and sat on her bunk. He watched her as she moved, full of grace and youth.

Nancy and Tony tonight had evoked their own fumbled love affair twenty years ago.

He loved Lindy from the first, but, in terms of the Fifties, why buy a cow? Premed students should not marry. He traveled fastest who traveled alone. The odds against getting to a good medical school were rough enough. His dad had been telling him that for years.

His father was tall and lanky, and tanned from racing his sloop. He had returned from the South Pacific eight years before, drier and harder than Mitch remembered him. They had lost their rapport while his father picked up the shambles of his interrupted practice. But one night in Mitch's fraternity room they had several quarts of Psi U home-brew, and gradually reached a humming, resonant level of communication they had known long ago, sailing a dinghy on the Bay. The tumor that would kill his dad must already have been sleeping under the thick white shock of hair.

Mitch mentioned Lindy, casually. He almost never spoke of girls to his father.

"Just don't get married, that's all."

"Married? Jesus, she's only eighteen."

He knew that his dad saw him as a partner some day. He had no intention of joining him, to become another society doctor in a city full of them, but, thank God, he'd never had to argue that out; his father had died six months later, disappointed that Mitch had married but still thinking he could make medical school.

Just after his drinking session with his dad, Lindy had delivered her hammer blow, smack in the middle of midterms. He had been studying for a biology exam for a week and one evening found himself too stale to go on. He had pried his roommate out of the room and gone to get Lindy. For a quarter of an hour they lay on a straw mat he had got in Japan, watching the Sid Caesar show. As always, they had been unable to keep their hands off each other. Halfway through, he had got up and moved for the set to turn it off. She smiled and her eyes went moist and then she was on her feet and looking up at him strangely out of the gold-flecked eyes.

"Lindy? What's wrong?"

She had shaken her head silently. He flicked off the TV.

"What is it?" he demanded, pressing her close. "Come on."

She was two months pregnant. She wanted to have the child, was sure it was a girl, hoped it was a girl. But she was scared to tell her father and wanted to finish college. "What'll I do?"

Not *we. I,* as if Tony had been immaculately conceived. He knew half a dozen girls her age who would have broken the news in a fit of pseudo-hysteria.

"Kill yourself?" he grinned. His knees went wobbly.

"There'd be an autopsy. He'd find out."

"You could get married." His stupid smile felt frozen. In later years, he could only blame the crummy script on Sid Caesar.

"To who . . . Whom?"

"We might stick Clem." Clem was the senior he'd snagged her away from in the first place. "You're pretty ugly, but your daddy's rich."

"Clem's unfriendly: I'd prefer a friend."

He had moved to the reefer, uncapped a home-brew beer, and taken a large slug. From the fraternity across the street came a long-drawn wail: *"Pedro . . ."* Another house across the campus took up the traditional midterm howl: *"Pedro . . ."* Always after, the name would bring back the night.

"We could be friends," he said, offering her the bottle.

She shook her head. "We're lovers. I like it that way. And you don't want to get married."

"I *didn't,"* he admitted. He had become used to making life-and-death decisions, instantly, in the carrier CIC. But they had always dealt with somebody else's life. He hesitated. He decided that he loved her very much, more than the stupid dream. He took her back into his arms. "I mean I didn't until just now. And I'm not going to let you get away."

They married the next week in Reno, against Shawn's wishes and of course against his father's. For a semester Mitch fought it out in a trailer park, refusing to move to something bigger, using the GI bill and turning down his dad's help and Shawn's, out of perversity. He hung on in premed while Lindy got bigger and bigger. He was still slugging it out when Tony arrived.

Tony rejected all known formulae. He screamed for months. Mitch's concentration wavered. He took to studying half the night in the library and the other half in his old fraternity room, while his ex-roommate snored. He found himself at 3 A.M. over an open book, worrying about Lindy and Tony in the trailer park. He began to study in the trailer again while Tony shrieked and Lindy tiptoed.

He got a D in an organic chemistry final and a C in French, ordinarily his best subject. His father died. The next semester he quit premed for prelaw.

She could never seem to get it straight that Tony, unborn, had saved his ass. He would probably have made a lousy doctor, and he was a good lawyer. He should be eternally grateful. Now Tony had his own life-and-death decisions to make and his father would be long gone when he made them.

Lindy was smoothing his bunk. "Hey, Tony's known for years about how we got married!"

"I'll be damned. From the dates?"

She nodded. "He's decided we did it to be polite."

"Son of a *bitch!* I'll wax his ass!"

"No. He's not that far wrong."

"Come on, Lindy, that's *bullshit!*"

"OK, I'm sorry. Anyway, I know he wouldn't leave Nancy. So don't feel guilty that we didn't ask him."

"Hell, I don't feel *guilty!*"

"Good." She fluffed out a pillow and kissed his forehead. "You've done your twenty years."

CHAPTER
15

CLINGING TO THE WHEEL, POUNDING TOWARD THE spot he should have been searching for the last sixteen hours, he watched the sun turn quickly into a squashed tangerine and sink below the horizon. Now that he knew where she was, he would use the last evening twilight for a star-fix to pin his own position down. He glanced east.

His stomach tensed. Evening clouds were galloping in, like ranks of black-plumed knights, from over the eastern rim of the sea. He needed a knife-edged horizon for the ancient sextant, and bright stars for its clouded scope, but mostly he needed clear skies for himself. The open seas and long free passages of the South Pacific had tempted him to rely too much on the sun. His mental map of southern stars was vague.

He seldom shot an evening round and almost never got up before dawn for morning observations. When a tricky night passage or an early-morning landfall forced him to shoot a star-fix, he used a star-finder to identify the bodies.

Picking, roughly, altitudes and zeniths from the star-finder, he would write them down for Lindy to shout up to him. The system was OK, but it was easier if you had two people to work it. And you needed clear, uncluttered skies.

If he'd learned the southern constellations properly, he could fill in the blanks in a cloudy sky and still identify the signposts. He hadn't.

At 6:15 the first dim twinkles showed. He had not much time before the horizon grew too dim to use.

His mental map grew hazier, the sky became chaotic, the dark patches above were growing, the sextant below was obsolete, and he was so tired that his mind was drifting.

Gas grumbled in his stomach. Next would come the cramps and diarrhea he got when he faced an uncertain decision. There was no time to go to the head: he would simply have to sweat it. He was unsure and scared.

He went to get the sextant.

On February 2, a little over three months after their original deadline for departure, they stood by a beer keg on the dock and played host to their own farewell party. It seemed to be the only way to take care of the friends they had promised to show aboard, and hadn't. The crowd stretched down the dock for three boats.

Linda Lee lay deep in the water, her boot-top stripe completely immersed, though they had painted her waterline three inches higher when they hauled her. The hateful lists below were only two thirds checked off. Mitch still had doubts about his planning.

He needed *Sailing Routes of the World,* a fine old volume of routes used by the clippers, but it was a

British Admiralty Publication, hard to find, and he had not found it. With two hundred charts of the South Pacific carefully rolled, corrected, and stowed aboard the boat, he had a deep conviction that he had forgotten the most important ones. He would probably find out which ones they were when they were racing toward the mouth of some coral-fouled pass.

Their boat-papers, passports with visas for French Polynesia, and international health cards lay wrapped in plastic below. He had every conceivable handbook for the boat's systems: engine, stove, Guest-lamp, radio. Half of them were too technical for his understanding, but he could always try to translate them into French for a mechanic.

Their normal water capacity was only sixty gallons, but he had ninety gallons of emergency water below the floorboards and sixty extra in the beer kegs mounted forward of the mast. He was all at once certain that it was not enough. He had an emergency solar-still, but now he doubted that it would work. He saw themselves parched in the doldrums, drinking their own urine.

He had every day been rating his Accutron watch, two bulkhead clocks, and a surplus Navy hack-chronometer. Now that they were about to leave he had a premonition that they would all fail simultaneously, along with the two radios for his time signals, and leave them lost in infinite seas.

He had remirrored his sextant, got spare parts for the toilet, and found a twelve-volt power drill. He carried spare plywood under the bunks, sheet-lead to tack below if a floating log holed their hull.

Their tiny medicine cabinet was stuffed with pills and antibiotics. Lindy had somehow found time to go to a Red Cross first-aid class. A latent Nightingale had awakened: for weeks she injected oranges, bandaged his arms and his legs, splinted fingers, and wrapped his elbows. What they would do if *she* were the victim they hadn't discussed.

They had sailed to Raccoon Strait on a weekday, when they would not feel ridiculous before other boats. They spent the day practicing nautical emergencies: fire, abandon-ship, man-over-board, collision, dismasting.

They might founder but would surely not starve. *Linda Lee* bulged with food. There were eight dozen oiled fresh eggs, all logged and stowed away. There were fifteen gallons of Fresca and five of fruit juices, a case of beer, and a case of Johnny Walker. Below were nine pounds of margarine, four cases of canned fruit, twenty-four cans of stew, three canned whole chickens, nine canned hams, one case of hash, two cases of shrimp, one case of crabmeat, twelve cans of salmon.

There were meatballs, spaghetti, half a case of sardines, two cases of sausages, twelve cans of ravioli, boned chicken, 100 cans of vegetables, a dozen boxes of breakfast cereal, twenty-four cans of applesauce, six pounds of Bisquick, six pounds of white rice, three of brown. There were ten pounds of sugar and another ten of cheeses and forty-five rolls of toilet paper so that they could delay the purchase of razor-sharp French tissue as long as possible. He had even discovered, in the bilges, two cans of grated coconut.

"Lindy, we're *going* to Coconutsville!"

"They were on special. I might want to bake a cake."

Shawn, who had brought *Invincible* across the Bay with Bobby, was wandering through the crowd like a discontented troll. He saw Mitch studying the boat and moved over, shaking his head.

"Jesus," he muttered. "You ever hear of metacentric height?"

Mitch tried to project confidence: "Don't worry, Herreschof. You couldn't knock her down with a China Sea typhoon."

They said goodbye to Bernie. Lindy hugged her father and Bobby and kissed Tony and Nancy, who had a mutual cold. There were tears in her eyes. Justice Holmes, stupidly brought to see them off, began to bark hysterically. They stepped aboard and cast off. There were too many hands on the dock per line, and too much beer in the hands, and Red-Dog fell in.

Invincible escorted them through the Golden Gate, then turned and departed, hooting madly. The moment she met the ocean swell, *Linda Lee* began to wallow horribly, as predicted. Seasickness hovered.

There was a brief, explosive conference between captain and medical officer. Brow furrowed, lips pursed, Lindy tried to recall her shopping. Finally she confessed the awful truth. He was incredulous and flipped through the cards in the first-aid section of their magnificent filing system.

In the medicine cabinet, it promised, he would find dexedrine to wake them up, seconal to make them sleep, milk of magnesia to start their bowels and lomotil to stop them, parafon forte to unclench his back and miltown to unclench their brains, enough needles, drugs, and syringes to interest the Bureau of Narcotics, and enough hemostats and scalpels to stock a field hospital.

For an appendicitis attack she had tetracycline and penicillin. She had pyribenzamine for postnasal drip. To put them to sleep if they had to set a bone she had ether. She had bandages, compresses, eyepads, gauze, sterile cotton, splints, and slings.

She had forgotten the Dramamine.

With the realization of it, she got sick instantly. He held onto her belt while she hung over the railing and vomited. Then he became sick too.

At sunset, thirty miles south and near the limit of their radio-telephone, they remembered that Justice Holmes' rabies shots were due next week. He put through a call to Bobby via the marine operator.

"Mitch?" crackled Bobby's voice. "I've been trying to raise you! I got bad news. Over."

Lindy, pale but recovering, grabbed the mike. "It's Dad?"

"He almost passed out on the boat before we got back to the Club. He's at Stanford Hospital. They don't know what's wrong. Over."

"Oh, Bobby, stop the *over* thing! Did he eat dinner?"

"What?" Bobby's voice faded and came back. "Did he what?"

"Dinner, did he eat his dinner?"

"Yeah, such as it was. Why?"

"Tell him I love him. And write us what happens, to Nuku Hiva."

Bobby's voice rattled back half an octave higher. "Lindy! Did you hear what I told you?"

"Nuku Hiva, Bobby," she said. "Over and out."

She hung up the mike. Mitch protested and reached for it. She grabbed his wrist. "He's *my* dad, it's my decision."

He didn't want to return, he really didn't, and he didn't himself believe Shawn was sick. But he couldn't take the responsibility. "You could be kicking your butt," he warned her, "the rest of your life."

"It's *my* butt."

Mitch tried all next day for more news, without success. But one hundred miles west of Catalina Island, two days later, he tried San Pedro Marine Operator and got through to Bobby, long distance.

Shawn had been discharged the next morning and was back at his Club. He was still planning on the Hawaiian Race.

He broke out two bottles of beer and went topside. Lindy, still seasick, sat huddled in the lee of the deckhouse. She shook her head greenly at the beer. He told her about her dad.

She did not seem surprised at all. "He was just trying to tell me something again. He'd rather try to die than try to learn the words."

She seemed too sick to care. He was still nauseous himself, and too busy navigating and sailing the boat to do her work as well. They sailed on in a shambles of dirty dishes and strewn bedclothes for days.

PART II

Night

CHAPTER
1

SHE FELT THE DROP IN WATER TEMPERATURE THAT dusk was bringing. Her thirst remained.

She tried to send off the night by keeping her face to the setting sun, attracted to dying light like a moth to a lantern.

Her cheeks were still feverish from the day's heat and her lips were cracked and stinging, but her body was chilled. The floatable jacket continually slithered up her sides to chafe her armpits. It had to be tugged down to retain her heat and keep her upper body bearably warm. Her legs meanwhile grew colder. She was three people: one hot, one clammy, one freezing.

Sometime after the *bonnitier* had passed, she had unlocked and let drop the useless safety belt, which had been rubbing her belly raw. She still clung to the plastic container, emptying it when she had to. It was buoyant, as long as she kept water out of it. Her jacket was becoming soggy and losing its lift. She preferred not to think of that.

She played a game which asked little effort and wasted no heat. She would lie back, face to the sky, and promise herself in the valley that at the peak of the next swell she would raise her head and find his sails bearing down on her. Sometimes he would be forward, orange life-ring in hand and ready; sometimes he would be slicing past, unaware, and she would bring him to life with her whistle: that was even better, and seemed to make up for her stupidity at falling in.

As darkness deepened, the game lost credibility. She tried another. She would lie back and become driftwood, a log, capable of floating forever until she starved or died of thirst. That would be a long, long time. She was not hungry in the least, only very thirsty.

Log or not, she was freezing. She began to shake uncontrollably. Now it was pitch black.

She began again to raise her head on the crests. All day long she had cherished an orphan hope, that the faraway flash she had glimpsed after she fell in had been the strobe.

So darkness was not all bad. She began to look for the flash again.

Braced in the red glow of the chart table lamp, he plotted his evening starsights: Achernar, which he had been sure of, Altair to the west, which he could have confused; then Peacock, uncertain, nebulous, flirting darkly behind a dead-black veil of cloud. Last, Deneb, which might not have been Deneb at all. He had not found Nunki, but he needed only three stars, crossing on the chart in a triangle, and the size of the triangle would be a clue to his accuracy.

Achernar and Altair crossed not far from his dead-reckoning position. Peacock was impossibly off. His hands began to tremble. He plotted Deneb and let out a yell of joy.

He would have settled happily for a triangle a half-inch on a side. The triangle he got, he could have covered with the eraser of his pencil. He could hardly believe his results.

He rubbed his eyes. Something had helped him pick from the mottled skies three of the stars he had been looking for. Whatever it was, he thanked it. If his luck had truly changed, they would be sipping champagne in the Tahara'a Hotel on Christmas Eve.

For the second time that day he found himself on his knees. A childhood reflex, maybe, but he didn't care. He rose, ringed the fix on the chart with a circle triumphantly small.

He had traced and retraced his path for fifteen hours and was less than a mile from his track. Two hours to go to where the logbook pinned her down. His stomach cramped nervously. He lurched to the head, barely making the toilet.

Afterward he bounced topside, adjusted Irwin's course one degree, and climbed the mast.

It was pitch dark. Just after ten, the moon would rise, if the clouds had passed. He was still too far from where he had dropped the strobe to see *it*, but he began to search anyway.

CHAPTER
2

ON THE THIRD DAY OUT OF SAN FRANCISCO, UNDER clammy skies, she tried to cook their first breakfast. Mitch, on watch in the steamer lanes topside, smelled alcohol fumes and swung down the ladder. He said she was still too sick to cook, and that soda crackers and beer would do for another day.

Obviously, he needed a hot meal. He would be up all day in the cockpit, for she was so drowsy that she could only stand watch for an hour or so at a time. Besides, she was sure that she would be seasick all the way to Nuku Hiva, with the vicious motion and no Dramamine. In the meanwhile, she had better conquer herself and cook or she would starve them both to death.

To convince him that she was OK, she somehow managed to stow the last-minute gear away and to neaten the icebox, a helter-skelter jumble of soft drinks and Fresca cans. The clothes locker was almost impossible. The inexorable roll was maddening. Everytime she let go of a handhold to stuff something in, she lurched across the cabin and got another bruise. Her buttocks were a mottled mass of blues and greens.

Her belly ached from vomiting and her arms from clinging to handholds. Her legs ached worst of all. Her neck was still stiff from scrabbling into bulkhead lockers, during stowage at the dock. She had scraped a knee somehow. Tony had given her his cold, kissing her goodbye; it was the first real kiss he had given her for fifteen years, and it had to be laden with germs.

She was miserable, and the only pace she could break down and cry was in the head, and if she stayed too long there she would get seasick again and Mitch would know and make her lie down.

In the meanwhile he had to do the work of two adults, just to keep them sailing. Blustery gales drove down from the northwest. Slanting rain and wind forced him again and again to strike their sails. He must be so tired that he could hardly move. She awakened one night with the wind moaning in the rigging and the vane in command. The boat was charging due west, in the wrong direction. Mitch was sitting on his bunk in dripping yellow oilskins, staring at a rubber boot he had got on the wrong foot, apparently unable to tackle the job of changing it. She longed to help, but knew that if she got up she would vomit. She lay there helpless while he changed the boot and climbed topside, moving like a man of sixty.

Since he wouldn't let her try to cook, she sliced canned coldcuts. She stuffed him with food she could hardly bear to look at, let alone smell. And still, she stayed sick.

One day he announced that they were clear of the steamship lanes, far off Mexico, and could abandon the continual watches topside. He showed her on the chart.

She should have been happy that now he could get more sleep. But it was dim and dank by the chart table, and the smell of diesel fuel from the engine compartment got to her very quickly. And her glance at the chart only threw her deeper into despair. They had come so minute a distance, and the way to the Marquesas stretched so far, that she was sure she would never survive.

Their peace of mind seemed balanced on a knife edge. No matter how she goofed—as in the matter of the seasick pills—he would not let her see a reaction, and she knew that the pressure must be building. Every minor error they made held the seed of catastrophe.

Irwin began to tremble ominously. Mitch prepared to reglue the base that held the vane erect. Cans, brushes, and the members of Irwin slid around the spray-swept deck, while Mitch tried to hold course and fix the vane as well.

She volunteered to crawl way up under the bow to get a can of acetone he needed to clean the base. It was like a roller coaster, rising and falling twice as far as anyplace else on the boat. In the chaos forward, she found the can of acetone.

It was a new can, closed with a metal seal. While Mitch squatted wetly on the stern, waiting, she started to lift the seal with an icepick in the galley. But she lurched at the moment of truth and speared the top of the can. She still had the acetone but had wrecked the container. There was no more acetone aboard, so somehow they must find something for the contents.

Mitch said that acetone would eat through any of her plastic food jars. The nail-polish smell of it was already making her sick. She dug in the liquor locker and found two half-filled bottles of Johnny Walker.

She opened them. That smell made her sicker. She emptied one into the other, capped the first, filled the empty bottle with acetone, and labeled it carefully. She was lurching aft with it when it struck the corner of the stove and shattered. Acetone was everywhere, and slivers of glass.

He heard the crash and came down, tired and carefully unangry. He was barefoot. She started to warn him and he stepped on a piece of glass. She dug through bandaids, letting the acetone eat the varnished cabin sole, but got sick from the motion and smell in the head. He bandaged his own foot while she urped into the john. She staggered out to find him picking up the last of the glass. The galley deck would never be the same.

The total time, from his need for acetone to the final disaster, was a little more than an hour, and now there was no more acetone, so he glued the base without it, and both knew it would never hold.

She had been sailing virtually all her life, yet she was only five days underway and unraveling already. No wonder the novices turned back after two days at sea.

She and Mitch seemed to grow apart. Keeping their balance on their rolling, lurching little world used up so much energy they had no time for each other. She was more isolated than when he was at the office: at least, then, he was home nights. Now he was completely occupied with navigation, sails, or the engine. And sleep . . . Out of the steamship lanes, he slept all the time.

She still served cold food but did not bother to apologize for it now. They spoke little, and never discussed their condition. To admit that all the months of preparation had led to misery would have been brutal.

Everything went wrong, usually at night. They ran their engine an hour each evening to keep their batteries charged. On the fifth night it wouldn't start. Astonished, she saw him spend three hours stuffed into the smelly engine compartment, wedged between engine and bulkhead and tortured by the sickening roll. He wouldn't change the oil in their stationwagon, but he could diagnose an engine problem five hundred miles at sea.

He fixed it, just in time for the toilet to overflow. He found the spares for that, too, and replaced the flapper valve and cured it before he collapsed into sleep.

He grew leaner each day that he refused to let her cook. He was hard and sinewy, his face all sharp edges. He would not have to worry about his potbelly for a long while. But his skin was tinged with green, like the sea-worn winches topside.

He never failed to get three sun-sights a day. She knew that he was often as nauseous as she, and wondered when he would finally crack. Watching him leaning on the chart table, at an impossible angle against the heel, she could not understand how he could follow the endless figures in the *Nautical Almanac*.

She grew to hate the daily morning throb of the time-signal from Hawaii. They were both on the verge of breaking.

And then late one memorable afternoon she awakened from a nap to feel a certain warmth in the damp cabin air. They were six days out of the Golden Gate, 600 miles off the Mexican coast and far to the west of Guadalupe Island. She sensed a subtle change in the motion. She went topside. The wind had shifted. When she had dozed off, *Linda Lee* had been lurching like a drunken elephant. Now she was lifting to immense purple swells, cresting, settling gently. She had been staggering; now she waltzed.

Mitch, stripped to the waist, was sitting in the cockpit facing the late sun. He flashed her a smile.

"Mitch," she exulted, "what's *happened?*"

"Trades," he grinned. "We are now in the trade winds." His face was luminous. He had sailed the northeast trades before, on the Hawaiian Race. "And this, my sweet, is what it's all about."

They lost the trades that evening, but regained them sometime during the night. She awakened at six, starved. Mitch was already topside. She discovered that she could move without hanging on. Everything worked. The toilet flushed exuberantly. She tapped bare toes on the foot-pump. For days she had had to call Mitch to prime it. But now warm salt water poured from the spigot, just as it was supposed to. She rinsed her face and looked at herself in the mirror.

She had gone to bed haggard and drawn. Now she looked great, if pale. She scrubbed her face with a washcloth: her color returned. She brushed her teeth in salt water, worked Lubriderm into her skin so she would not get Cruising-Wife Leatheritis, and metered herself a cup of fresh water. The fresh-water pump had quit leaking.

The stove lit without a murmur, after a week of retirement. She cooked an enormous breakfast: four eggs for Mitch, three for herself, canned sausages, slabs of toast from stale bread, mountains of canned butter on each slice.

She could hear Mitch bellowing *Waltzing Matilda* in the cockpit. She had not heard him sing in years. She glanced through the hatch as she ladled out the eggs. He wore nothing but his denim skipper's hat. He was studying the swells coming down on them. He

had disengaged Irwin and was standing on the cockpit edge, clinging to a shroud. He was steering with
his bandaged foot, apparently for the joy of guiding
Linda Lee down the long sapphire slopes. His voice
rose: *"Who'll come a-waltzing Matilda with me?"* A
wave arose behind him, capped with a great white
plume. She almost shouted in alarm, but at the last
moment, as he eased the wheel over with the sole of
his foot, the crest sighed and passed under them and
they were sliding sedately down the other side of the
mountain, neatly under control.

He looked down at her. His upper lip had already
lost the greenish tinge. The early light etched his face,
beneath the battered cap, with abrupt shadows. He
had not shaved in a week. His jaw shone with a thick
golden stubble, but he looked wonderful. He was the
young student she had married.

She had brewed real coffee instead of instant. She
stirred up Tang and brought the whole mess topside
on Navy surplus trays. They ate, in the cockpit, mouth-
ing each morsel eye-to-eye like the lovers in *Tom
Jones.*

When she had washed the dishes he went below
to sleep. She took over the wheel, relieving Irwin for
a while to try to match Mitch's ease and economy of
motion.

She raced alone for hours across a sapphire, bottom-
less deep. Her hand on the varnished wheel was light:
she let the boat balance the wind and the sea and let
her body soak up the sun.

Finally she re-engaged Irwin, and then she had
nothing to do at all but to lose herself in the rolling
ride downwind.

The northeast winds were granite-steady. Day and
night they stayed, force-five, twenty knots. The swells

grew mountainous, with a length, crest-to-crest, of a quarter mile. Ahead, they looked harmless. Aft, they towered menacingly above the cockpit. Each looked as if it could broach and swamp them.

But the white rolling tops fell always just short of their stern. *Linda Lee* rose on the slope, curtsied on the peak, and dropped into the following trough as the great blue swell rolled on ahead. With the wind shifting daily further astern, Mitch reset the sails, and lashed its boom outward to a shroud. Under the foresails and main, they let her tug at the bit.

The trades never shifted. The puffy trade-wind clouds romped by, endlessly following-the-leader. Routine became unalterable and time raced faster because each trade-wind day was like the last. She would awaken every morning to the tick of the radio time-signal, as he checked his chronometer. In the trades, the sound was not nearly as nerve-wracking. After breakfast, he would wind the clocks at eight: an old Navy custom, he explained. Each half-hour, day and night, they would log the barometer reading, wind direction, and wind speed.

Every morning at ten he would get a fix on the sun, and again at noon. He would emerge with a noon position, another tiny circle to put at the end of the neat track on the pilot chart. The path inched relentlessly south and a little west, toward the Marquesas.

Now she wanted the track on the chart to stop cold. Instead, it moved faster and faster. They were logging over 120 miles a day. Once they made 137. She wanted the passage to last forever.

Time was flashing by. There were not enough hours for all the things she wanted to do. She was studying Polynesian, from a Mormon dictionary they had found in a used-book shop. She read of Tahiti and the islands west and, to please Mitch, even tackled Herman Melville, whom she'd always hated.

She continued to cook enormous meals, there was so much to use up and they had starved so long. She felt no threat to her figure; even in the gentler motion running before the trades, every muscle in her body was working for balance all day long, and even in her sleep at night.

Below, they began to move as a team. Unconsciously, she would synchronize her movements with his, tuck her feet up on the bunk if she sensed that he was passing, without even looking up from her book. Finishing his morning sunsight, he would automatically wait until she was through the dishes before crowding her with his bulk at the chart table.

They discovered one night that the plywood dinghy-cover top was a superior place to make love, under the crackling stars. But he wanted her infrequently, apparently too tired fighting motion for sex. He napped intermittently all day long.

In the afternoons she would lie on the foredeck, dozing. Sometimes porpoises would swoop in to frolic in their bow-wave. Once a school of them, babies and all, played with her for an hour, piping to her and listening to her squeak back. She tried feeding them: sardines, scraps of ham, strips of canned bacon. She never found anything they would touch: they were there to play, not to beg.

During the night, flying-fish would board them to die odorously in their scuppers, and by the time they found them in the morning, they were always too far gone to fry.

She saw few birds: they were simply too far from land. But one morning a little sparrow-sized landbird squatted on deck in the early-morning shade of the dinghy. It made no move to escape when she cuddled it. It had apparently decided that she was the least of all possible evils, but refused to drink their water. They decided that it must have been blown to sea from Clipperton Island, but there was no way to know. Anyway, when it was rested it fluttered its wings, took off chirping, and thrashed away to the east.

They tried to fish and caught nothing. The *Times Atlas* showed two thousand fathoms under the keel: over two miles, straight down, and too deep for anything but a chance encounter. A little striped pilot-fish who had adopted them somewhere skimmed along in the shade of their hull. His name was Elmer.

They were probably getting too insular, and would discuss such matters as a name for a new drink for hours, but there was no one around to sicken with their small-talk, so neither of them cared.

They were utterly alone. One glittering night Mitch called her topside, excitedly. He pointed out a satellite, streaking hurriedly from the west, arcing to the eastern horizon.

She resented it. She visualized some shadowy Russian officer, or some Pentagon bureaucrat, glancing at the image of their boat in a picture or on a TV screen and noting it ominously. Military or not, the satellite was man-made, an intrusion on their privacy, and the stars'.

The next day they saw their first and only ship, at high blazing noon. She called Mitch topside to look at it. They both waved innocently from the cockpit as it charged in from their port side. It was probably out of Panama for Auckland, New Zealand. A very conscientious gentleman, thought Lindy of the skipper, to race down to see that they were all right.

Mitch grew nervous as the ship approached. He studied it through his binoculars. Suddenly he dove for Irwin, releasing him and grabbing the wheel. "He's got no fucking lookout," he grated, coming right, "there's no fucking watch, there's nobody on the wing of the fucking *bridge!* He doesn't *see* us!"

The ship was a giant freighter, with cargo containers stacked all the way to bridge height, fore and aft. It was throwing a bow wave as high as their mizzen, overtaking them at a good twenty knots. It crossed their bow, port to starboard, 200 yards ahead.

Only then did Mitch think of the CO_2 horn. He groped in the stern compartment, found it, and pressed the lever too late. The angry blast of it was lost in the chung-chung-chung of her screws.

It was the *Southern Packer,* not some Panamanian clown under a flag of convenience, but a good American vessel out of New York under the Starbuck Line pennant. Mitch grimly logged the time, the latitude, and the longitude. He swore that when they got to civilization he would write the Coast Guard. In the meantime, they would scan the horizon, day 'and night, every thirty minutes.

She was more angry at the intrusion than the carelessness. Quite simply, she thought of the trade-wind belt as their own.

They could not, of course, stay in the trades forever. The next day the northeasterlies slackened at noon, then picked up and blew for a while, then died again. The following morning the sun rose on lazy, slapping sails.

They had run smack into the Doldrums, and it seemed for a while that they would never get out.

CHAPTER
3

SHE SOARED AND PLUMMETED IN UNSEEN SWELLS.
The sky was black velvet. She was horribly thirsty and
her teeth chattered from the cold. She had the dim
sense that some distant squall was raising the seas, but
she saw no lightning.

Furtive clouds blanked the starlight and hid the
moon, if it had risen. She was blind. When a lip of
foam would bear down on her she was helpless unless
she glimpsed a green glow as it raced down the face of
a swell. With the fading of the last faint band of
orange at sunset had gone her sense of up, down,
north, south, east, or west.

"Through caverns measureless to man," she chanted
suddenly. From *Xanadu.* With an "X." By whom?
Wordsworth? Keats? Anyway, engraved on a brass
plaque set in a massive steel frame of Jean-Paul's boat,
Xanadu.

Where Alph, the sacred river ran
Through caverns measureless to man
Down to a sunless sea . . .

Where are you, Jean-Paul, with *Xanadu,* now that
I need you? She could hear his voice, faintly accented,
quoting the poet. Not Wordsworth or Keats, Coleridge!
Sorry, Coleridge. Remember: *Cold Ridge.* As in *"a*
cold ridge of high pressure . . ."

She was past feeling cold. Her legs were numb.
She began to move them. She looked down. Her feet
trailed green bubbles of phosphorescence. She had a
sudden vision of them as seen from the ebony vastness
below, from the eyes of a cruising shark. She was a
living go-signal. She stopped moving her legs.

There was a thing about sharks, Mitch and sharks.
Like Coleridge, it lurked just behind memory, teasing
her. There was fear in it, play-fear, and warmth, too,
and safety.

It washed over her suddenly. She was a year back
in time and two thousand miles north, swimming in
flat-calm, sunlit seas.

She was floating face-down, wearing mask and snor-
kel, suspended warmly above a sapphire void. The surface was a vast blue mirror. The sun baking her bottom had chiseled out planes of light below, which
slanted as far down as she could see. She was a
thousand miles from the nearest land, in water three
miles deep, trying to cool off in the Doldrums.

She turned her head. The keel of *Linda Lee,*
battleship-solid, lay 100 feet away. The boat, seen
underwater, was always immense, and very comforting. Its brick-red paint, waving tendrils of bottom-
growth, stretched before her. The great bronze
propeller, idle and growing barnacles on its shaft, in-

creased in size underwater and looked as if it belonged
to the *Queen Mary*.

Their little black and yellow pilot fish, Elmer,
floated faithfully at the turn of the bilge. He seemed
determined to follow them all the way to the
Marquesas, swimming in their shadow. When a fish
had to look for shade, it was hot.

Usually he was busy nibbling at the tubular barnacles which grew in the green moss on the hull. But
now he was studying her thoughtfully. Something in
his gaze discomfited her. She waved at him self-
consciously. He continued to stare.

She had never seen him leave the hull, but all at
once he darted toward her. His tiger-striped body
flashed below. Surprised, she beckoned him back, but
he disappeared to the north without even a glance.

The hell with him. She returned her gaze to the
deep. She was looking for something, anything to
break the monotony and to tell Mitch, who was reading in the cockpit. She visualized a passing Russian
submarine, or another glimpse of the *voyeur* whale
which had surprised them while they were making love
on the dinghy last night, or a school of *mahi-mahi*.
But she could not concentrate.

An evil conviction grew in her that something had
chased Elmer off. *A shark?*

What in the hell was she doing, floating in water
three miles deep, a thousand miles from land?

She shivered in the lukewarm sea. Now, somehow,
she was certain a shark was there. The question was,
where? She didn't dare look down. Gently, keeping her
legs motionless, she raised her head. *Linda Lee*,
through her mask on the surface, was a blurry, smeary
mass. She pushed back the faceplate. The boat lay
frozen in time on a glassy sea. Her sails were creased
and limp.

Mitch was lying somewhere in the cockpit reading, under a canvas canopy, in jet-black shade. Sweat would be rolling down his bare chest and buttocks and pooling in his cockpit cushion, stinging his ass-rash. So in a few more minutes, as he had been doing for the last three days, he would dive into the water with her, leaving the boat unattended. The shark would feast on them both, and Elmer would pick up the scraps.

"Mitch?" she called softly. "*Mitch?*"

There was no answer. Maybe he had gone below for a drink of water, leaving her here to be torn to bits. Could sharks hear?

"*Mitch!*" she screamed suddenly, taking her life in her hands.

His head popped up. At once he was knifing into the water. In a moment he was beside her, looking into her eyes.

"What the hell *happened?*"

"Elmer—" she whispered. "Let's go back. Gently, gently . . ."

"Why?"

"A shark, maybe? Oh, never mind!"

Instead of going he ripped the mask from her head, planted it on his own, and took a long, thorough look below. He shook his head, but they swam back to the boat. He goosed her bare bottom as she climbed the swimming ladder, infuriating her. Now she could not tell him about Elmer, simply couldn't.

He asked her again what she'd seen. She shook her head. "Nothing. Damn it, I shouldn't have been so far from the boat. You don't care at all!"

She strode below, tears in her eyes. She couldn't explain her anger. It was the heat, probably, the horrible, sweaty closeness of everything in the Doldrums.

But for the next few days, when she swam alone, he watched from the cockpit, and never let her go far.

They were trapped in the Doldrums for twelve days. They had fuel for less than 500 miles under power, but each dawn they started the engine when it was coolest below, and powered for an hour: five miles, to charge the battery and for morale. The engine heated the cabin unbearably. The silence when it quit was lovely, for a while, and then boredom would grip like a vise. They would wait all day for a catspaw of wind, reading, dozing, basting in their own sweat. All work stopped. Nothing got done but the sunsights.

Each day was like the last. Only the daily log, or the radio, told them the day of the week. Time was as flat as the sea.

They were prisoners of the sun. To stay below was unbearable. Topside, under the canvas canopy, it was almost as hot, for there was no breeze at all. Overboard lay their only relief, and two minutes after they climbed the boarding ladder they felt like diving in again.

A squall raced in one afternoon, after teasing them from the horizon all morning. Mitch refused to drop the mainsail and rode it out exuberantly at the wheel.

For five minutes the boat charged blindly through rain-thrashed waters, in a froth-white chamber of wind. The squall pelted the boat with immense raindrops and created a cold breathless shower-bath, which ended just after she had lathered her hair with Halo, but before she could rinse.

Then the clouds swept off, trailing their rain behind them. They found that they had made less than a mile's progress, and that was their total, under sail, for the day.

They grew worried about water, despite all the emergency jugs. They cut themselves to a pint each a day, and wrote down every ounce.

Their new paint peeled from the hull. The rails,

though painted glossy-white against just this problem, were hot to the touch. The decks seared bare feet. Despite the canvas cockpit canopy, they broiled at noon in vertical sunlight. She was sure, despite her care, that her skin would never be the same.

They went nude and slept topside, under liquid stars, because the cabin was a hothouse even after dark. They doubled their dosage of vitamin pills, fighting salt-water boils and heat rash.

She was certain that despite her endless swims and her salt-water bucket-baths topside, she smelled. Mitch certainly did. She got used to that, but the urine smell in the head was another matter.

The boat rolled, under greasy swells, and caused him to miss the john. Then she would have to wipe up the deck—he never seemed to notice—and it was too damned hot.

"Can't you for God's sake *sit?* I'll never tell."

He would nod sheepishly and forget, and next time it would be just the same.

One day they made only twelve miles, under power and sail. Another day they actually fell backward in some vagrant current.

When she honestly thought that she could bear it no longer, they were hit by a line of squalls. The breeze freshened afterwards. Then it died. The next day it rose again and, miraculously, held.

At three degrees north, 130 west, they struck the southeast trades. All morning they scooted south under a ten-knot breeze, and by that afternoon it had increased to eighteen.

The next day they crossed the Equator, and she was cooled enough by the new trades to bake a cake to celebrate her initiation into the Ancient Order of Shellbacks. Mitch sprinkled salt water cermoniously on her forehead and they cracked their last beers.

Her moods had become puppets of the wind. Despair, boredom, peace of mind, mirth, did not come any longer from within her; she caught them from the breeze. In the blustery westerlies she had been sick and scared; in the northern trades, ecstatic; in the calms of the Doldrums, a prisoner flailing at Mitch and the heat. Now, again, she sank into the joy of trade-wind sailing.

Everything became clear-cut. Important decisions were easy, since they were a matter of life and death. If a sail began to chafe, you sewed it then and there, or you would lose it in the next blow. You replaced a whiskered halliyard instantly, even if you had to stay up all night doing it. More trivial problems were easy, too: you put them on a list and waited for the landfall.

Mitch lost his Bristol racing-yachtsman attitude: spit-and-polish was fine in a slip, but here you saved your energy for more important things, like singing and meditating, and slept as much as you could. You did not even wash down at sea: you let the squalls do it, or the odd rogue wave.

Again, she wished they would never arrive. But inevitably, as the curve on the chart arched closer to the minute dots northeast of Tahiti, he looked up from plotting his noon fix one day.

"Tomorrow morning, my sweet," he announced ponderously, picking off a distance with his dividers and measuring it on the side of the chart, "if you will climb to the spreader at precisely zero-nine-one-eight, and look dead-ahead, you will see the Island of Nuku Hiva rear its head from the limitless deep."

The next morning she clung there, waiting. For ten aching minutes she searched, while he pretended nonchalance in the cockpit. After all his hours of work, it was not fair that it hadn't appeared on the instant.

At 9:28 she raised the peak of the island, 3800 feet high. In half an hour they could smell flowers, thirty miles away.

She did not know whether she was happy or sad.

Down to a sunless sea ...

She was swallowing too much salt water: it increased her thirst, but it was hard to time her breathing to avoid whitecaps she could not even see. Fits of trembling shook her, would pass, and would grab her again. Her jacket was growing less buoyant. She thought of slipping it off and supporting herself on the jug alone. But when she fumbled with the zipper, her fingers were too cold to work, and she was afraid that if the jug somehow slipped from her hands, she would never find it again. The whistle was tied to the jacket, too; she must not let the whistle slip away.

If the jacket began actually to drag her down, she had no idea what she'd do.

She began to tread water again to warm her legs. There were no sharks, she decided suddenly, any more than in the Doldrums. The motion felt good.

She felt herself suddenly soaring into the featureless night, impelled by a force from below. It rushed her upward, and when she peaked she was hurled under as a breaker curled over her head. She surfaced, choking and gasping.

Nothing but a swell, a grandaddy swell, larger than the rest. Somewhere not far away a storm must be lashing the water. She waited for the next crest and raised her head.

She saw a stealthy, distant flash. Her first thought was lightning, since the rising swell must be coming from a squall. Not knowing north from south or east from west, confused by the aimless sea, she had no way of knowing where the storm was. Upwind and approaching, she hoped. If the full strength of a tropical squall swept down on her, she was not sure she could survive its seas, or the torrents of rain it would bring, but she would take her chances for the feel of fresh water on her lips.

She kept her eyes open. In a little while she saw the lightning again, one single flash of it.

Lightning? Or the strobe?

She thought she remembered seeing the strobe before dawn, a century ago, just after it happened.

Or had she? It didn't matter.

It *could* be a strobe, their own light in the water, or a strobe light from some other boat, called in from Papeete, and helping him search.

Tossing in rising seas, there was no way to judge the beat. But the next time she saw the flash, she began to swim toward it.

She found no way to keep her direction. She did not see it again and after a while she quit.

If it was the strobe, it would somehow just have to find her. He could not expect her to find *it*, in the rising seas.

CHAPTER
4

HE STOOD AT THE HELM AS THEY CUT CLOSE TO THE eastern tip of Nuku Hiva, sailing under the spire of Cape Martin. The boat seemed very small, dwarfed by cliffs that seemed ready to topple on them. After a month at sea, where the highest point was the crest of a following wave, the crags and pinnacles of Nuku Hiva overpowered him.

He called Lindy topside again and again, to show her formations he found beautiful. He spotted the gorge that Melville's hero, and perhaps Melville himself, had crossed escaping from the frying-pan of the whaler *Dolly* to the fire of the Vale of Typee. Lindy seemed more interested in cleaning the boat for the customs officers they expected.

With the *Sailing Directions* lying open on the deck-house, he found the large white cross it promised, formed in the strata of the mountainside, and Arch Point, and the Sentinels. They passed through the steep entrance of Taio Hae Bay, seat of Marquesan civilization, and were back in the world of people.

"Shit!" murmured Mitch. "Lindy?"

Lindy popped topside. She looked around. Seeing at first only that the dark green mountainsides cradled a bright green bay, and that the crags leading to the water shone with moss, she nodded appreciatively. After the long passage, green was twice as green and any land at all had beauty, and all the colors you never saw at sea would come alive. For Mitch it evoked childhood, the first glimpse of tints never seen. "Beautiful," Lindy breathed.

"Yeah, but look ahead," he growled.

Off a long coral beach at the head of the bay lay a tall gray ship, flying the tricolor. Above its funnels shimmered a haze of smog. Mitch sniffed the Navy-smell of baking bread and stack-gas from half a mile away. A helicopter chomped from an upper platform and thrashed toward the beach. From every mast and deck level antennae poked skyward. She must be a communications vessel of some sort, probably up from the nuclear test area to the south, for R&R for the crew. A liberty launch crammed with pompommed sailors and officers in civvies sped toward a jetty of coral-rocks.

A village peeked through the palms behind the jetty. A dusty road skirted the beach. A motorscooter popped along the road and a red jeep bounced behind it. A loudspeaker on the ship crackled in French, bringing him back to Korea: only the language was different.

"Well," Lindy said doubtfully, "its only *one* ship, anyway . . ."

"One's enough, and look at the yachts!"

Off the village, anchored helter-skelter close to the shore, a dozen cruising sailboats bobbed in the wake of the launch. He studied them through binoculars. Four flew the Stars and Stripes. He identified a Swede, a French steel ketch with an orange hull, a yawl he took to be Dutch, a Dane, two Canadian boats, and one with the black, red, and gold colors of West Germany. A tired sloop swung alone before a scrubbed and separate little beach. The Australian flag hung downheartedly near a broken windvane at her stern. A white-haired man slumped in the cockpit.

Behind this smaller beach, which appeared to be private, the Governor's mansion baked. From a flagpole before it, an immense tricolor drooped, exhausted, in the heat. Through the glasses Mitch could see two figures in white shorts batting a tennis ball on a shocking-pink court.

He swept the glasses back to the sea-gypsies clustered off the village. "Jesus," he muttered, "there were less boats anchored in front of our house!"

They raised the quarantine flag to one yardarm and the French flag for courtesy to the other. They found a spot to drop their anchor. On one side lay a fifty-foot Columbia bathtub with the salty home-port of Las Vegas, Nevada. On the other was anchored the famous schooner *Star of Peace,* out of Auckland to protest the French nuclear tests.

With Lindy at the wheel, he eased the anchor down into mushy mud, poor holding. Snubbed down, he looked around. It was hot and very sticky. They were practically landlocked, cut off from the trades by the craggy peaks. The mountains should have given him a sense of security. Instead, they seemed sullen and threatening. A drum pounded ashore, with a tom-tom rhythm. He felt oddly menaced. Melville, who had anchored here under French guns 130 years before, must have felt the same.

A nude toddler in the schooner's cockpit waved at him. Her parents were probably asleep below. On the

Columbia to starboard, a diminutive American, dressed in white shorts and holding a beaded can of beer, wandered topside. He offered his dinghy if they wanted to go ashore. He offered advice on holding: drop a second anchor. He offered the information that customs, as well as immigration, was the local gendarme. You rowed in yourself and found him. He offered a warning: the only bar in town, Henri's, was overrun with Frog Navy. He offered everything but a can of the cold beer. Then he disappeared into his plastic cabin, which was no doubt somehow air-conditioned.

Mitch began to pump up their Avon raft. He felt as deflated as it looked.

They had just sailed 2,800 miles and arrived, apparently, at Avalon Harbor on Catalina Island. No one had even bothered to ask them how the trip had been.

Lindy sat on a plain chair in the white, airy Gendarmerie. She admired Mitch's performance in French, found it titillating, as if she had sailed in with a stranger. She had to remind herself that his fluency was deceptive: he faked a lot. In Paris he had once got them to Napoleon's Tomb when they wanted their hotel on Rue Buonaparte.

The blond young gendarme, wearing starched white shorts and an open shirt, had the oval face of a saint. He stamped their passports cheerfully and stuffed them into a drawer.

His wife, petite, Parisian, and trim, emerged from the living quarters behind the office. Lindy glimpsed Sears' modern in her apartment, and an immense carved dining table, apparently local. The gendarme's wife murmured to her husband, softly: *"Le vieil Australien . . ."*

The gendarme winced. He spoke rapidly to Mitch, who looked surprised, shocked, and finally nodded. He told Lindy that the old Australian they had seen anchored alone had lost his friend, a retired New Zealand dentist. They were on their second circumnavigation of the world. The Australian was sixty-three, and the gendarme thought that his friend was even older. Three days short of Nuku Kiva, the New Zealander had fallen overboard. "Tossed him a life jacket," Mitch translated, "and then couldn't find him again."

The old man shambled in and the gendarme arose politely, something he had not done for Lindy. The Australian's face was gray and deeply lined. He nodded at Lindy and Mitch. "Saw you standing into the Bay. Very pretty, you were, sails against the cliffs, you know? Nice passage?"

His accent was more British than Australian: a retired professor or schoolmaster, she guessed. The gendarme began to fill out his report, questioning the Australian in broken English while his wife typed the answers in French. They quickly fell into a swamp of incomprehension and half-understood nuances. Mitch began to translate for them.

When they were nearly finished, the gendarme seemed to brace himself, "Captain," he mumbled, face flaming, "there is one more question, I mus' demand . . ."

"Ask," intoned Mitch. "He means 'ask.' "

"H'ask," nodded the gendarme. "My superiors, in Papeete, they say I must h'ask . . ." He stumbled, spoke to Mitch, beseeching help. Whatever question he wanted to ask, Mitch shook his head and sat mute, lips grim.

The Australian's lips began to tremble. He sighed and began to talk: "I'll go through it again. He waved, you see, and laughed, sort of. He was sure I'd get back. But flying twin headsails, with no help, it was five minutes before I could get them down . . ." He stopped for a moment, biting his lip. "Then the spray, on my eyeglasses . . . I'd try to wipe them clear, peering ahead, you know . . . And in thirty seconds they'd be bloody *useless* again, and I'd have to take them off . . . No radio. The wind-vane was broken, Ian was going to repair it, very handy with tools, he is . . ." He turned to Lindy. *"Was,* I suppose. But it's hard to imagine him gone. Kiwi, you know, from Auckland. Kiwis will fix anything. 'She'll be right, mate,' he'd say. When the silly engine would balk, you know? 'Not to worry, Cobber, she'll be right . . .' "

The gendarme broke in unhappily. To Mitch, he said: "Please, you must h'ask . . ."

The Australian seemed not to have heard. He said to Mitch: "In all events, thank this gentleman, please, for everything. They sent planes out, you know? When I got here. And a helicopter, can you imagine? Ian looking up and seeing a helicopter? Never have pulled him out, he'd pull *it* down, I imagine. Sixteen stone, he was, I think."

The gendarme gave up and thanked Mitch for his help.

Mitch invited the old man to join them for a beer, but he smiled and shook his head. They watched him row slowly out to his battered cutter, half a mile from the rest of the yachts.

"What," asked Lindy, "was the question you wouldn't ask?"

"Why he quit so soon."

"So *soon?*" He had not given up for twenty-four hours. She visualized the ponderous march of the trade-wind seas. She knew how quickly they hid a hat or a bucket knocked overboard. And she knew the fatigue that could have you babbling after four hours on the wheel. Impossible to describe, though, to the young gendarme or his superiors in Papeete.

"Well," she said, "I'm glad you didn't ask it."

The old man reached his boat, tied his dinghy off, and slowly climbed aboard.

"I might as well have asked," murmured Mitch. "He knew."

They went to see if they had any mail.

Mitch showed his driver's license for identification to a sour young Polynesian girl at *Le Bureau de Poste,* and got a little bundle of mail. Lindy's dad was fine, and Justice Holmes was thriving, and Tony had a job as an office boy at Nancy's father's TV station. They had taken an apartment in the Sunset District. A postcard edged in black gave him a scare until he read it: it was from Bernie.

"Magellan: Good news first: (1) Western Casualty bailed out, due your leaving. (2) Hal leaving us, taking the only fraternity beer stein, button-down collar, and decent law degree remaining in firm. (3) Client with Golden Snatch died of pneumonia, but after appeal denied. (4) Tony borrowed $300 from firm emergency downpayment on automobile. Will write bad news later, when Chaplain goes ashore. My love to Lindy. Have a good day. BB."

"That's our Bernie," Lindy muttered. "The bastard!"

"She died," murmured Mitch. "We *wrecked* that poor son of a bitch, and the net result is to make a millionaire out of an alcoholic husband and two crummy kids who weren't even taking care of her! Jesus!"

"Don't let Bernie wreck *this,* Mitch. It's been too hard getting here."

A breeze had come up and the afternoon sun had

turned golden. The Post Office was on a rise above the bay, and the tiny yachts clustering below seemed placed by an artist. Even the Navy ship, in the softer light, looked better.

A glowering Marquesan maiden swung by on the road, glared at them, and looked away. She wore a colorful pareu and was slim and graceful as Melville's Fayaway. Trudging along with her was her little brother, or son perhaps. The boy beamed up at them. *"Bonjour!"* he piped. *"Iorani!"*

No bullshit here: the girl hated them, the boy loved them; the vibes were so strong you could touch them. On the battered cutter below, the old Aussie slumped in his cockpit. No crap there, either: he made your throat ache, but there was truth in every line of his anguish.

He tore up the postcard and let the pieces flutter to the road. The card was black-and-white; here the world was in color.

He needed a beer very badly, so they went to find the famous *Cercle d'Or d'Henri*.

CHAPTER
5

HE WATCHED TINY ELVES APPEAR IN THE GLOW OF the compass light and march around his compass, heaving and grunting to turn the lubber's line when he let it drift from south-southeast. The engine droned a chanty for them: *heave-ho, heave-ho, heave-ho, heave* . . .

"Lindy?" he called. He needed coffee, or relief at the wheel: where the hell was she? *"Lindy!"*

She was not there. He was caught napping as he drifted right. The mizzen boom shot past an inch above his head. If he had been erect instead of sagging at the wheel, he would have been knocked unconscious.

Instantly awake, he looked around. He glanced at his watch. Still forty minutes to go to the point at which she'd gone in, four miles, at his speed under both canvas and power. But no excuse for not searching enroute.

He fought the boat around to SSE, and the canvas

190

steadied. The helm was heavy, under sail and power; too heavy to trust to Irwin, who swung idly behind him.

A dash of salt water, flung high off the port bow as she headed into the seas, stung his cheek.

He was chilled, and the water was cold. *Jesus, how must it be for her in the black emptiness ahead?* He needed his jacket. He eased the throttle a moment, so that the torque of the propeller would not take the boat too quickly off course. He dashed below and was back at the wheel wearing the jacket within seconds.

He began to sense a change in the sea. He could actually see nothing at all, but there was a heave and a drop to the swells that had not been there before. A line-squall was thrashing the water somewhere nearby.

I am coming from the northwest, he told her, I'm not far off. There were delays: for one thing, I couldn't find the goddamn logbook. But I did, and I'm on my way . . .

Now, on impulse, he closed his eyes and flipped everything on: running lights, bow-light, masthead light, spreaders. He left them on for ten or fifteen seconds. Then he turned them off and opened his eyes. In a few minutes he did it again.

If she were up ahead, and looking northwest, she might spot a glimmer and it might give her hope, and soon he would be there, OK?

She saw Jean-Paul for the first time at Henri's. Afterward, his presence vitalized the memory of the place itself, so that she found it difficult to visualize it as it actually was: a grubby little bar in a general store on a dirty road in a one-street village on an island that the world had forgotten. The building squatted behind bales of drygoods and barrels of fuel and crates of Manuia beer.

A huge white dog lay on the porch. In some ancient accident he had lost a rear leg. As she approached with Mitch, the dog arose laboriously, as if courtesy demanded it. He creaked to the pile of beer cases. He urinated. He had no leg to raise, demonstrating the uses of adversity. He hobbled back and collapsed again.

The rinky-dinky beat of French Polynesian guitar music rattled the porch. Weathered planks creaked under their feet. They passed through a deserted store, beneath shelves of French canned goods, piles of coconuts, and huge bottles of homemade wine. A musty copra smell was everywhere, with the sweet-sour odor of stale beer. They went through an inner door and found themselves behind a rough wooden bar in a room jammed with sailors, yachtsmen, and Marquesan natives.

A nut-brown half-Polynesian with sharp Gallic features looked up from a tub of beer bottles. He motioned them to the customer's side of the bar with a jerk of his head. Mitch, parched and hoarse, asked him for two beers, in French.

"I speak English," said Henri, "and better than your French." He reached into the tub and extracted two immense bottles of Hinano beer. He set them dripping on the bar. "Warm! Well, I am not Quinn's. Twelve yachts, you are thirteen, and the damn *militaire . . .*"

Mitch paid him with a twenty-dollar bill, U.S., and got the change in Polynesian francs. Later they would find the exchange rate better at Henri's than anywhere in French Polynesia, including the banks in Tahiti.

Henri asked them to sign his *Livre d'Or* of foreign yachts, promising that in it they would find news of all their friends. He requested their yacht club flag, to hang on his wall when he began to decorate, tomorrow, or the next day; anyway, *aprés demain*. They promised him, and later delivered. *Aprés demain* took a bit longer; but a year later they heard that the job had got done and the place was dripping with club burgees.

She turned to look for a place to sit. Her toes were cramped in shoes, and her arches tired from unaccustomed walking. Her cut-off Levi's, washed for weeks in salt water, felt like iron. She still had her sea legs and the room rolled and heaved beneath her feet.

There were four round tables in the room, with spindly chairs and wooden beer crates drawn up around them. At one table sat Frenchmen in civilian clothes, presumably officers from the ship, with a day's purchases of carved paddles, spears, and tikis laid out on the wet table top. The next table was full of French sailors, very drunk and very young. A third was for the local orchestra: three sweating guitarists and a spoon-clinker. The last table held a collection of weatherbeaten boat people: men, women, and children with shaggy haircuts. She was sure that she and Mitch looked just as scroungy.

None of the tables seemed to communicate with the others. She felt let down and unwelcome. The room was unbearably hot. Henri was right: the beer was warm. The music slowed. The flat, plaintive island chant and the cheerful clinking of the spoons on glass became more quiet. A handsome Polynesian, very drunk, was dancing sedately with an American girl from one of the boats. She looked bored.

One of the French officers caught Lindy's eye. If she held his gaze, she was sure he would offer them a seat; on the other hand, he might want to dance and her feet hurt. So she let her glance wander to the French sailors' table. That was worse; a slavering youngster no older than Tony, pushed his chair backward, started for her, chickened out, and headed for the door. In a moment, through the open window, she could see him urinating on a coconut tree.

She was out of it all and reluctant to dive in. Perhaps, after thirty days at sea, you built a barrier against loneliness that was hard to dismantle. She felt like asking Mitch to buy a case of the beer and going back to the boat.

And then Jean-Paul stepped through the wooden door. He swept the crowd with deep-blue eyes and looked into her own.

Her stomach soared and settled. She went warm and liquid. Her cheeks turned hot. It had happened when she first met Mitch, and never, really, since. She wanted to laugh, and cry.

"Lindy?" she heard Mitch say, as if from a distance. "Hey, kid!"

"Um?" she asked, coming back.

"I said, let's sit on the window sill."

She ripped her eyes from the shimmering blue.

"Yeah, oh, great," she said.

She wished she had worn a dress.

Mitch sat, legs swinging from the window sill, with his beer on the ledge between them, watching the blackbearded man limp across the room. He was very, very French. A huge empty wine jug dangled from his finger. Mitch had not missed the impact of the blue eyes on Lindy. Maybe, after a month at sea with a man she had slept with for twenty years, a woman was as vulnerable as any other sailor. He was a little amused, but not flattered.

Obviously, a presence had entered the bar. The blackbearded man, a head shorter than he and barely taller than Lindy, was recharging the air. When the blue eyes smiled, the place came alive. The guitarists were reborn. The spoon-clinker offered the Frenchman a half-filled beer bottle. He shook his head and placed the jug on the bar for Henri to refill. The man had even white teeth and laugh-crinkles, but his eyes were deep and thoughtful. He wore faded cut-off denims, leather sandals, and a scrimshawed pigstooth on a silver necklace. He was very solid, with broad seaman's shoulders and pink Gallic cheeks. His movements were sure, despite the limp, and young, though he was not: he might have been thirty, or forty.

A half-dozen natives had crowded into the bar, square-shouldered, lean-hipped young men of bronze, in clean Aloha shirts. They had high cheekbones and hook-noses. They were a leaner breed of cat, Mitch decided, than the Hawaiians and the occasional Tahitian he had met in Honolulu. Marquesans were cannibals, reputedly, only a few generations back: "Inveterate gormandizers of human flesh," according to Melville's not-so-tongue-in-cheek account. Anyway, from an ancient memorial to fallen French soldiers, which he had noticed by the road, he concluded that they had apparently been less digestible to French colonialism than the Tahitians further west.

The young men at the bar were trying to draw the blackbearded Frenchman into their midst, pressing their beer on him and crowding close. But his eyes were on Lindy's again, the son of a bitch, no, they flicked to his own. They were the deepest blue Mitch had ever seen. The man smiled. Mitch found himself smiling back. The Frenchman left his jug on the bar and moved across the room. His right calf was badly scarred.

"You are the white ketch, I think? An Atkins?"

He had a faint French accent, but his English was American, not British, and very good. Beneath the full black beard another vicious scar curved from his temple to his jaw; along it, the whiskers curled whitely. More closely observed, with the wrinkles better etched by the afternoon sun through the window, he looked closer to forty than thirty.

Mitch stuck out his hand. "I'm Mitch Gordon. This is my wife, Lindy. Are you anchored here?"

The Frenchman nodded and they shook hands. His clasp was firm and very un-French. He told them he had the orange ketch *Xanadu* they had passed on entering. "And that ketch, I am afraid she is *my* wife."

"That must save you a lot of confusion," remarked Lindy.

Now what the hell had she meant by that? Mitch studied her thoughtfully. The trip had toughened her; she was lithe and golden and very slender. With the Frenchman near, she glowed. He felt uncomfortable, and annoyed at himself. He was damned if he was going to be jealous of a stranger met in a bar.

Blackbeard's name was Jean-Paul, and he sailed alone or, lately, with one Tahitian crewman: "My *mahoo,* my student. A carver of wood, and he cooks, also."

"Mahoo?" asked Lindy.

"Man-woman," Jean-Paul remarked. Lindy sagged visibly, but the Frenchman's eyes were bland and steady. "Here in Polynesia, that does not matter."

It was hard to think of Jean-Paul himself as a homosexual, but Mitch found himself trying. He regarded Lindy silently. *OK, my sweet,* he thought. *That'll cool you.*

But it obviously hadn't.

She had caught Mitch's look, and it irritated her. There was nothing gay about the Frenchman: he was radiating interest in her from every pore. Her eyes

were level with his, and he was looking into them as if
the two were alone. "And your voyage," he was saying
gently, "it was bad, I think, and good, and already you
are forgetting the bad, is it not so?"

Her lips were moist but her throat was tight. She
would squeak if she talked, and could not trust herself to answer. So she nodded, and he went on, waving
his hand at the table of yachtsmen: "Some will *not*
forget how bad it was, and they will drop out at
Papeete. And some will grow too full of confidence
and lose their boats before Fiji. And some will go
round the world on the trades, like a carousel—"

"And Jean-Paul will stay in the Marquesas forever,"
Henri cut in, setting the jug, full of murderous-looking
red wine, on the window sill. "Like Gauguin, Henri
and Cape Martin. The four of us, looking always out
to sea."

"Do not count on it," Jean-Paul said softly. "Don't
bet on it, my friend."

"He must not leave," said Henri. "*Security* demands
you stay. Who will teach us to whittle spears and clubs
for the *Force Nucléaire?*"

"Your *financial* security demands me to stay," rumbled Jean-Paul. He suggested that teaching the natives
to carve what the market demanded was simply giving
them money to spend in Henri's store for chocolate to
rot their teeth or wine to rot their bellies. "If the dust
from Mururoa does not kill them all, perhaps this man
will!"

"*Merde!*" Henri snorted. He snapped his towel at
the boar's tooth dangling at Jean-Paul's bare chest and
went back to the bar.

With Jean-Paul that afternoon they met people who
would be their friends and companions for months on
the long sail west with the trades. They met a shy
young girl from the protest vessel *Star of Peace,* and

her tiny daughter, who had greeted them on anchoring.
They met a French radio officer from the nuclear test
ship *Rance,* a Dutch couple from a steel ketch and
their doll-like little girl, dressed immaculately and
seemingly of a different species than the child from
Star of Peace. They met Jack-the-Rip-Off, a piratical
young American who wore a headband and had
gentle eyes and who single-handed a tough little
double-ender he had built for himself in Costa Rica.
He was, he announced proudly, the current drug-
smuggling suspect.

"Is there a drug problem *here?*" Lindy asked.

"Yes," Jean-Paul said. "If it were not for Jack, it
would be difficult to find any pot at all."

She could never tell if Jean-Paul was serious or not,
but everything he said seemed sparkling to her. From
a souvenir stand set up for the French liberty party, he
selected her an ugly little tiki beautifully carved: the
carver refused payment from her because Jean-Paul
had been his teacher. For a moment, in a moist sweating crowd of French sailors, they stood on a village
pavilion to watch dancing: choreographed lines of
beautiful adolescents, swirling their hips and wobbling
their knees. Jean-Paul identified the *otea,* a Marquesan
war dance. But he turned away quickly. "The greatest
warriors of all Polynesia, performing like a troupe of
seals!"

It was the same old complaint she had heard and
read a hundred times, but from his lips, through the
beer they had drunk, it sounded quite profound.

He took them to the island's only restaurant, a
stucco affair with a galvanized roof, perched on the
hill above the bay. There was a line of French officers
waiting, but the native proprietor slid them in ahead,
into the best table in the place.

They said goodnight at the beach and paddled to

their respective craft. They had to sleep topside on the dinghy, it was so hot below.

"What did you think of Blue-Eyes?" Mitch asked suddenly.

"Oh, wow!" she said. He had caught her unawares, and she overreacted. "Charisma, I mean. Did you see those people, when he'd smile?"

"A charismatic Frog," he reflected, "in a very tiny pond." It was exactly the kind of red-necked generalization they both hated.

In fact, she thought, dozing off, a judgment so uncharacteristic as to be interesting. She fell asleep mulling it. In a few minutes she was awake again, writhing on the dinghy-top. From then on it was between her and the germs, whatever they were, and she had hardly a conscious thought of Jean-Paul for almost a week.

Her subconscious was another matter, and blew the whistle on her, but Jean-Paul would not tell her of that for a long time.

CHAPTER
6

SHE LAY BEDDED IN THE HEAVING WATER, CRADLING
the plastic jug. She had not seen another flash for a
long time, an hour. She was racked with deep, uncon-
trollable tremblings which passed and left her exhausted. Her thirst was agonizing. She succumbed,
sipped salt water, and gagged.

The skies had partly cleared, and she glimpsed stars
she should have learned: Mitch had tried to teach them
to her. And Jean-Paul had tried, briefly. Everyone was
always trying to teach her the stars. Why? Tonight they
were friendly but elusive; there were still enough clouds
scudding across the horizon to blot out their patterns,
just when she was about to identify one. She made out
the Southern Cross, oriented herself to face it, and then
lost it under the crest of a swell.

She began to move her legs faster, to keep her circu-
lation up and ward off the next attack of shivers. Her
jacket was more and more a hindrance. The armpit
seams were eating away at her skin and the soggy
sleeves restricted her arms.

She found the Southern Cross again and lay back to study it. She became aware of a sudden stillness. It was the sort of visceral hint that came with the sound of flapping sails in the lull before a storm. She pictured Mitch, lowering the sail as he felt the wind drop and the oily swell begin.

The Southern Cross flickered out. She had the sense of an immense anvil-cloud bearing down, towering thousands of feet into the velvet sky. She heard a gurgling rumble. When she was carried to the crest of a swell, she felt wind on her nose and cheeks. Then, in the trough, the breeze would die; she was cozy in the valleys and vulnerable on the peaks.

As her body sank into canyons, her descents became more ominous, like an elevator starting too fast. She was hurled aloft on each rise, no longer lifted gently as she had been before. In one trough, she heard a freight-train rush of water down the slope. She instinctively sucked in a breath and ducked. She was tumbled in a breaker like a surfer torn from his board. She clung to the jug through the whole wild ducking.

Great waves began to hammer her down. Hearing one coming, she would take a breath and try to dive beneath it, as if heading out from a beach. Once, the jug left her hand. She groped after it and grabbed it again as it began to sail on the wind up the slope of a swell.

The rain began with a rush, paused, and returned in torrents. For a moment, she opened her mouth like a bird and tried to drink the cold, fresh water pouring down. She grunted in relief, treaded water to cup her hands and catch more, almost lost the jug. She held it up to catch more. But it was all too much, it was in her nose, her eyes, her mouth. She began to think that, surrounded by salt water, she would drown in fresh. The rain was solid, driving her under. There was no up, down, or sideways; she was in a liquid maelstrom, with only enough air to keep her alive, strangling and coughing.

She finally sensed a slackening, and that gave her heart to fight, and then there was a calm, and when the rain began again, the guts had gone out of it, and the wind which began was from a new direction and more kindly. The dark anvil-shape had moved away from over her and she could see the Southern Cross again, crystal-clear.

The rain, cold and brutal, had almost drowned her. But her thirst was eased, and having endured the squall, she felt more confident and awake. The struggle with the breakers had warmed her. She looked around.

Below the Southern Corss she saw a flash. Perhaps lightning—but the storm had gone the other way. She rolled onto her back and began to move her legs, traveling south, imperceptibly but steadily.

She glimpsed the flash once, and again, and again. She caught a certain rhythm to it.

If it *was* lightning, it was strange lightning, because it was parked below the Southern Cross and not moving at all.

Her fish-poisoning, if that was what it was, was not the classical Polynesian variety, for her taste buds never failed and there were no tingles in her skin and no rash. The government doctor, being on rounds on another island, got back too late to diagnose its earlier stages, and never pinned it down. But her fever and diarrhea and delirium were so swift and violent that, she found later, everyone was afraid that she might die.

She had awakened on the dinghy in oppressive sultriness, hot and fevered, with a thermometer in her mouth and Mitch's hand on her forehead. She had a temperature of 104 degrees. He rowed her in and carried her in his arms up the dusty road to the island hospital.

Through clouds of fever she remembered an enormously obese Polynesian nurse in a white uniform. She turned out later to be an actual Pomare princess from Tahiti. The nurse conversed with Mitch in halting French, then lifted her in arms as thick as Lindy's legs and laid her gently on an operating table. When Lindy doubled up in cramps, she eased a rectal thermometer in and, when she read it, gasped. She took it and tried again. The last thing Lindy saw that night was her shocked liquid eyes full of fear.

She shared a stucco-walled hospital room with an injured Marquesan sailor off an island freighter. A full-blown brown-skinned nymph, wearing a *pareu* below and lacey bra above, padded in on bare feet to attend her. She wore a flower behind her ear. She stood staring. Her name was Tiare. When Lindy's temperature rose high enough, she would bring in her friends to stare too. She spoke no French that Mitch could recognize. Her deathwatch was absolutely immobile. Lindy would remember her as standing for three days by the door, never averting her gaze, never leaving except to guide her to the oriental tiled toilet, a simple hole in concrete with squat-steps and no toilet bowl, and to support her there impassively during her impressive seizures. There were no bedpans.

Mitch tried, through the gendarme, to reach the island doctor, but he was treating the chief of a tiny village on Ua Huka, beyond radio recall. From the nuclear monitor ship, Mitch got a Navy doctor, who was puzzled and prescribed immense French charcoal pills which she could hardly get down. The ship hoisted anchor and she was doctorless again.

Waves of delirium shook her and passed. She saw everything from a seat somewhere outside herself, in dissolves and fades like a bad horror movie. The enormous Pomare nurse would inflate to three times life size, and then diminish in the distance; Mitch would be cooling her forehead one moment and be a hundred yards across the room the next.

In the daytime a horse grazed outside her paneless window and at night invisible no-nos feasted on Mitch, who usually stayed ashore and slept on a sleeping bag on the floor. They left bites which did not begin to itch for hours but always became infected.

Dr. Clary, the island medico, returned from Ua Huka. He was a gentle young military surgeon, quiet and whimsical, with a tiny Van Dyke beard. He began to pump antibiotics into her. He prescribed food—although not fish—from the restaurant which had poisoned her in the first place, because he thought the hospital native fare would make her worse. Mitch would trudge across the village to get it and bring it back on a tray, under a fresh white napkin, and then she could hardly touch it.

On the fifth day she improved dramatically. They discovered on the hospital scale that she had lost six pounds. She began to get visitors: Henri, then the old Australian, still gaunt and tired. The shy, doe-eyed hippie girl from *Star of Peace* came with her daughter, the Dutch couple and their little girl, who bore boat-cooked cookies. The island's native baker brought her a bag of French pastries. Even Jack-the-Rip-Off turned up, to see, he said, if she needed pot.

Jean-Paul came, the last evening she was there. She discovered that she was hurt that he had not come before. On his entrance the impassive Tiare took life and grinned for the first time. She had perfect teeth, with one perfect gap where a front one was missing.

She thawed into motion and began to move swiftly around the room, dusting with a palm frond, her hips rolling as she swept beneath the injured Marquesan's bed. Jean-Paul might sail with a *mahoo,* but if there was anything gay about him, the news hadn't reached Tiare.

He ignored the girl. His eyes, solemn, laughing, concerned, and mischievous, stayed on Lindy. He blamed the fever on Henri's wine.

When Mitch told him that they were leaving, that they had had it with the Marquesas, he nodded. "So beautiful, and so sinister. The people entirely closed in, like the bay, by the cliffs over it. Not like Tahitians or Tuamotans. You must avoid the Tuamotos. I have dived there with the people for *nacre,* but even I, with my steel boat, am afraid of their reefs. There you would find the people flat, open, cheerful like their atolls. It is too bad, the reefs, for each little island is a paradise."

Mitch nodded but said nothing. The doctor came in, and Jean-Paul asked him something in French. The doctor looked surprised, smiled, shook his head, and left, chuckling. When Jean-Paul was ready to leave, Mitch shook his hand and thanked him. Jean-Paul's eyes widened.

"Mitch, you speak French?"

"A little. And thanks again."

Jean-Paul passed from the room. Tiare subsided, taking her place at the door and not even helping Mitch gather Lindy's clothes. Lindy asked him why he was so grateful to Jean-Paul. He moved to the window and looked out over the bay. "We dragged," he said idly. "Did you know that? Adrian came aboard and helped me set the anchor again."

Adrian was the young Dutchman. "Is that why you thanked Jean-Paul?"

"No." He picked up her bag. "Let's check out, OK?"

The doctor would accept nothing for himself or the hospital. Mitch gave him his Buck rigging knife, and Lindy gave the Pomare princess a scarf, prompting a wet-eyed scene. Lindy gave another scarf to Tiare, who stuffed it into her bra impassively and did not even nod goodbye. But as they bounced away from the hospital toward the beach in the gendarme's jeep, Lindy turned to wave, and was shocked to see Tiare crying in the nurse's arms.

It was wonderful to be home aboard, where she belonged, among her own things. It was cooler, too, in the cockpit at evening, and the *no-nos* did not like to travel over water. For the first time in a week she was free of them, although the intolerable itching would stay with them both for days and Mitch's back was scarred for life.

Mitch cooked dinner. When they finished, sitting topside, he picked his teeth, staring at the purple hills above them. The musky smell of burning copra drifted across the bay. The big American Columbia had left, but there were two more plastic boats to take its place. One had its putt-putt generator building power for its electric stove, almost drowning out a ukelele strumming from a *fare* near the beach. The Australian's battered sloop was gone: Mitch said he had left today, single-handing it for Tahiti.

"You haven't told me why you thanked Jean-Paul," she reminded him.

He seemed embarrassed. "Yeah . . . Well, he tried to get word to the doctor to come back, when the gendarme couldn't."

"How did he do that?"

Jean-Paul, he said, had hiked eight miles to a little village on Comptroller Bay. He had gone to a native psychic who had a brother on Ua Huka island. "And then," Mitch said uncomfortably, "they sent out a message."

A dog barked ashore. The generator stopped, leaving the bay silent for the throb of the uke. A flat Polynesian chant hung on the smoky air. She felt a shiver run along her arms.

"A message? How?"

"Christ, *I* don't know. Just thought long-distance, I guess."

The shiver reached her stomach, the ghost-story thrill she always felt when she heard something spooky. "And the brother *got* it? And told Dr. Clary?"

"Clary was on his way back. He says if it did get through, he missed it."

"Does *he* believe in that?"

"He's . . . well, skeptical."

"But Jean-Paul does," she murmured.

He jerked his head toward the mountains embracing the Bay. "Well, he hiked eight miles across that ridge to place the call."

She was restless, scared, and fascinated. She asked him what *he* believed. "I mean, you fell all over him, thanking him."

Mitch looked embarrassed. "So he's superstitious! He still hiked eight miles in the heat. I *do* believe," he added, looking into her eyes, "he was awful damned concerned."

He was asking her something. They were all at once communicating, and for real, and it was what she had wanted, and she found that she could not even hold his gaze, let alone answer.

"Or," she suggested awkwardly, "he's just a real nice guy."

She was very tired and soon they turned in.

CHAPTER
7

HE SAILED OUT OF TAIHOE BAY AT DAWN, INTO a long, slow swell. Lindy was clinking around in the galley, cooking an omelette. Passing under the Sentinels, he glanced back. The bay still slept under smoky copra haze. It would be hot there in two hours, but they would be well out of the lee of Nuku Hiva and into the cooling trades. He did not think they would ever return. He had come closer to losing her than she knew. The vibes here were all wrong.

Tahiti lay nearly a thousand miles away, past the Tuamotos, the Low Archipelago. The name meant "Danger Islands." They stretched like a nine hundred-mile minefield between the Marquesas and Tahiti. On the chart they were dots, quite widely spaced. To the neo-navigator who had just sailed to the high-rise Marquesas out of Los Angeles or Honolulu, it would seem perfectly safe to weave through the scattered specks. Mitch knew that the risk lay in overconfidence.

Because the dots, in the flesh, were not dots at all. They were vast coral sandspits, pounded by growling surf, impossible to see at night and even difficult to hear until too late. In daytime they hid until the last moment behind a dazzling horizon. Each crouched, more sea than land, stubbled with low coconut palms and embracing a tranquil lagoon, guarded by reefs that might run for thirty miles. The currents among them raped your navigation and you were on them without warning. All this he knew from Tahiti Race sailors and the *Sailing Directions,* Volume III.

He had heard that there was hardly one atoll among them that did not have its wreck, a ribbed carrion baking in the sun, a year old or a hundred. The whitened spines of clipper ships and the fiberglass hulls of sudden experts shared the same coral slabs. Sterling Hayden's *Wanderer* lay shattered on Rangiroa, although Hayden had not put her there, and last month a retired British merchant captain who had not scratched a freighter in forty years had deposited his own ketch on Matahiva, trying to cut the corner to Tahiti.

The atolls were so low that even radar was no help: a Decca-equipped American yawl had recently struck Tematangi, which Bligh on the *Bounty,* with more primitive instruments but better eyesight, had somehow managed to miss. A French Navy tug had pulled the yawl off, not forgetting to bill her for ecological damage to the reef itself.

Still, there was the matter of the extra 200 miles, and if he found the guts, they could stop at Takaroa or Takarava and cut the trip in half. He had never seen a coral atoll.

When Lindy handed his omelette topside, he asked her to bring up the *Sailing Directions*.

"Cut through?" she asked, when he told her. "But Jean-Paul said—" She stopped. "Mitch! *Why?*"

He gave her all the reasons, and when he was through he found that he didn't believe them himself.

At noon three days out of Nuku Hiva, she was clinging to the spreader and searching the area. It was sunny, bright, and very rough. Mitch was chasing the bounding sun with his sextant on deck below. When she looked down, she could see him dodging from one side of the mainsail to the other as she and the mast described great circles in the sky.

A squall was flailing at the jagged horizon, but there was no sign of Takarava. "No atoll at-all," she sang down. If he became discouraged, maybe he would backtrack, cut north to the course he had originally planned, avoid whatever dark danger lay ahead.

While he was working his starsights last night, she had read the general remarks in the *Sailing Directions:* "*Navigation among these islands is dangerous because of the uncertain set of the currents and the still imperfectly charted reefs and islands . . .*"

Imperfectly charted? She believed him to be an infallible navigator, but if the island itself was misplaced on the chart, they could end up like two comic-strip characters under a coconut tree, waving her panties at passing steamers. Except that here there were no steamers, not this side of Tahiti. Steamers knew better.

It was ridiculous. She swung down and faced him. He had got his observation and was heading below to work it out. She followed him and thumbed the *Sailing Directions*. She quoted: " '*It was reported in 1950 that Takarava Atoll appeared to be incorrectly charted and should be rotated clockwise through an arc of 15 degrees about the northeastern point . . .* " She looked up at him. "It *moves?*"

"You know it doesn't *move*," he growled. He told her to simmer down, that the *Sailing Directions,* for plain gloom, made the Old Testament read like *Winnie the Pooh.*

He began to work out his sight at the chart table. He seemed unconcerned. She hoped it wasn't an act. She read him another passage. " *'Six knot current in the pass, submerged reefs line both sides,'* " she chanted. " *'The pass is only eighty yards wide at the seaward end . . .'* What's eighty yards?"

"Two hundred and forty feet," he murmured, busy at the chart table. "Look, I'm trying to figure out where the fuck we are. OK?"

She drew the chart of Takarava from the chart drawer, risking his wrath as she nudged him aside to slide it out. She spread it on the salon settee and studied it. "Hey, Mitch, we don't *have* to go into the pass. The village is right at the start of it. You can tie up to a concrete wharf—"

"In a six-knot current?" He smiled, patiently enough considering the trouble she was giving him. His sight must have worked out well. "No, honey. I am hoping to anchor in a quiet little piece of a large and calm lagoon. Not the middle of the Colorado River. I am hoping for no French Navy, no frigging smog, and most of all, no other goddamn yachts. Now, you want to climb up there and see if you can find it?"

He had told her to look for a cloud-bottom which might be tinted green with reflected light from a lagoon. At 1 P.M., against all her inclinations, she was forced to study a cloud formation off their port bow.

The formation she studied was a caveman squatting with great round haunches, tending streamers of rain as if watching a fire. His bottom was tinged with green.

As she peered at the horizon beneath him, it turned, despite her hopes, to a sawtooth fringe of palm trees, much longer than she had imagined. It stretched, it seemed, across half the southern sea. The atoll enlarged with frightening speed.

"Land ho," she sang down mournfully. He popped topside and swept his eye along the comb-toothed length of the soil. She climbed down and their glances met. He seemed as impressed as she was with the sweep of the palms: the silent question was, suppose they'd come on it, or one like it, at night?

They dropped the sails and powered for an hour along the reef. Somewhere there was supposed to be a wreck, marked on the chart, which might identify the island as the right one and give them a landmark for the pass too. They stayed well offshore: there was no way to judge their distance from the palm trees without a complicated series bearings. Mitch was too busy looking for the alleged wreck to undertake them. They kept easing in to see better, and then out when they got scared, for they had no way of knowing, really, where the undersea reef began.

At three-thirty, with his glasses trained on the shore, he let out a yelp. "There she is!"

He handed her the binoculars. She ran the glasses along the monotonous palms. The wreck jumped into the field of her view: high and dry and completely naked, a brick-red hulk bleeding rust. It was steel, a trading schooner or square-rigger, piled up, probably, before her father was born.

They found the pass, with the village at its head, another hour beyond. He had worked out the tides from the phase of the moon. There should be a slack in another half hour, maybe. The *Sailing Directions* implied that here, one never knew. "Let's shoot the pass," he decided.

She begged him to stand off tonight, and try at slack tomorrow, hoping that they would drift away from the island and never see it again.

"No, honey," he said. "New moon, too dark. If the current set us *out,* we'd lose the island, and if it set us in, we'd lose the boat."

It answered her question but somehow avoided the real one, which was why the hell they were there anyway. It was on the tip of her tongue to ask it, but she did not want to add further to his problems, so she climbed to her appointed station on the yardarm.

A long herringbone rip was racing far to sea. It was the six-knot ebb, she was sure, at its ebbingest. She pointed to it, longing to ride it away from the island into open water. He merely glanced at it and shrugged.

From the spreader, she gaped down at the pass. At its mouth ran great seas. They had been unhindered, probably, since the Chilean coast five thousand miles to the east. Now, suddenly frustrated, they were trying to pound the obstacle to dust. Combers shouldered over the reefs in a deep, throbbing rhythm. Only a narrow notch in the coral seemed free of the rolling surf, and that was wrinkled with outgoing tide.

Using the exaggerated, slow-motion signals they had practiced at home, she sliced her hand toward the center of the notch, afraid that she was raising the curtain on a drama she had no desire to act in. He headed in. They began to pitch in the swell as they nosed into shallower water. The motion caught her unaware and almost flung her off the yardarm. If they grounded, she thought suddenly, she would be hurled from the mast like a boulder from a catapult.

The mouth of the pass seemed more like ten yards wide than the eighty yards the *Sailing Directions* had promised, but the pass itself was easily as long and snaky as advertised. Through binoculars, she inspected the little village and red-roofed church which nosed the channel on the left. It offered the promise of human companionship if they struck, but not much else. And it seemed deserted now. In the lull between the cannon-salvos of the surf behind her, she caught voices raised in a hymn. Church services explained the empty coral street.

Maybe the villagers had gathered to help them through the pass in the only way they could, or perhaps to warm up for a requiem.

The one street in the settlement terminated at a coral quay. On it a figure, apparently the local agnostic, studied the swirling current, ignoring them. He was joined suddenly by a little black boy, much darker than he. He was an impish child with negroid, frizzled hair. He began to jiggle, hop, and point at them. Suddenly he whirled and scampered up the village street. Good: it was time someone called the local Coast Guard. But he only dodged into a house and returned, struggling under a guitar as big as himself. He took a station on the edge of the quay and began, apparently, to strum and sing, although she could not hear a note.

She waved absently; he did not wave back. There was no further reaction from the adult or the village, so she shifted her attention to the lagoon, shimmering like Heaven beyond the gates of Hell. The one mile seemed a hundred.

The drone of the engine rose an octave. He had added full power, probably, but their speed barely increased. Something occurred to her, suddenly. Now the sun was low at her back, and she could see each brown coral-head strewn along the channel. But when, and if, they got far enough to make the left-hand turn into the lagoon, the dazzle would be in her eyes, and she knew from the *Sailing Directions* that the lagoon was pocked with barely submerged coral heads. Mitch, at the wheel, could not see the bow beyond the dinghy. He seemed carried on some inner wave of euphoria, blinded by optimism. Her eyes were the only ones he had.

She would have liked to discuss this, but there was no way, from here, over the roar of the engine, which was already sounding tired.

She wished she were back in the hospital.

CHAPTER

8

HE SEARCHED FOR HER IN SULTRY DARKNESS FROM
the wheel. He was under power and sail. The oily
smell from the southeast had persisted, and now the
shuddering mainsail and banging pulleys told him
that the storm was approaching fast. There was no
more starlight and the moon was hidden. He sensed
giant clouds to windward. He had to get the sail
down.

He threw the engine into neutral. There was not
enough wind yet for Irwin to steer, so he simply let
the boat wallow and scrambled forward along the teak
rail on the deckhouse. He got the main down. He was
so tired when he was through that he could hardly
fight his way forward for the jib. He lowered the jib
before the squall hit, but hardly got its line tied before
it was time to save the mizzen, if he could.

So he staggered aft and got the mizzen down too.
The rain began with a roar. Wind yelled through his

barren rigging. His inclination was to run before it. But now that he knew she was somewhere ahead, he refused to lose ground. He jammed the engine full forward, wheeled the boat into the wind, and began to take the waves head on. *Linda Lee* hobbyhorsed, tossing her head at the peaks and digging her bow deep in the troughs. She reared and bucked, snorting water from her forward deck at each steep short sea, and there was nothing he could do about it but hang on.

He sensed that the hastily secured jib had torn loose and was inching its way up the mast with every shake of her head. He felt the wind catch it and swing the bow to starboard. He fought the turn. He flicked on the spreader light. The jib almost up, bellied out wildly. They had turned 180 degrees now. He threw the engine into reverse. It was like trying to brake a runaway truck by dragging a foot. Under the jib alone, they were suddenly making eight, nine knots through the slashing rain. He was losing ground that it would take him hours to get back.

He whipped his rigging-knife from his jacket pocket and cut the lines that secured the jib.

The boat slowed as the sail streamed ahead like a great white flag of truce. In the glare of the spreader lights he could see it flogging itself to tatters; within seconds the head-stay was a laundry-line of shapeless snapping pennants.

But the strain was off the wheel, and he brought her bow back into the wind. He had lost half a mile, perhaps more. And if he had not found her by dawn, he would have to struggle topside with the old spare jib and bend it on. But that was tomorrow.

He began again to slog into the squall, southeast, logging nothing, but at least holding his own. In the shine from the spreader light he could see little past the hatch. He suddenly realized that it was open. His chart table, log, and instruments must be inundated, below. He clawed it closed, far too late, and turned off the light to readjust his eyes to darkness.

The rain continued, terrifying him. Earlier in the day, when the morning squalls had hit, he had not been nearly as scared, for it was easy to imagine that she was somewhere far away. But this storm, driving in from ahead, must have passed her very closely. Its rains seemed capable of slamming her under, if its waves didn't, or drowning her in the sheer cascade of water.

The wind shifted, the squall passed, and the skies began to clear. He churned onward, fighting to stay alert, searching for the flash of the strobe. Tossing it in blindly had seemed afterwards like a knee-jerk mistake. Now it was his only hope.

In the darkest corner of his mind lurked a depressing fact. He had already searched these waters twice today, at the end of each leg, in the morning and the afternoon. And he had not seen the strobe.

But that was in daylight. How could you see a strobe in the sunlight?

Well, you could, sometimes, if you watched.

Bullshit.

It had to be flashing somewhere ahead.

And he would find it. Before dawn.

And she would be waving it when he did.

He heard a heavy thump. Suddenly he was on his back, looking up from the cockpit deck at a dancing, gibbous moon.

He had passed out at the wheel and dropped behind the binnacle. The thump had been his head on the deck. He had nicked his bare scalp.

He got up and came back on course. He put a foot on the edge, one hand on his usual shroud, and pulled himself erect.

Balancing there, he could hardly fall asleep again, unless he wanted to fall in himself.

He had half an hour to go to where the logbook said she had fallen.

He wouldn't see her this soon, but he resumed the search anyway.

The sun lay low behind him as they steered through the break in the Takarava reef. His eyes were on Lindy, perched on the spreader. Her binoculars, useless now that he had committed the boat, dangled from her neck. She had seemed scared at sea, but now that the chips were down, was apparently calm. At least, she was out of easy earshot. Her passing doubts would be no problem at all.

The problem lay in a certain imbalance of nature. He was pitting a 120-cubic-inch engine against a billion cubic yards of water that, drawn by a phantom moon, had somehow to get from the 100-square-mile lagoon ahead through an eighty-yard channel to the ocean. The pass was the only neck to the bottle, and it was full of water rushing the wrong way.

Impossible, of course, but the alternatives were equally poor. Darkness threatened. He'd concealed from Lindy how crazily his navigation had suffered under the drunken currents they'd breasted so far. His sights had shown him that, last night, they had been set to the westward four miles for every hour of darkness; the night before they had been swept directly east. They were lucky to have found Takarava at all, before they ran on a reef in the dark.

He had been an idiot to try to cut through the Archipelago, but it was too late now to get them out.

They were abeam the village now, and all at once he was moving into the strength of the current. It almost stopped them dead. The channel had narrowed.

He could never get her turned around in the tidal race. He wondered if he could pick up a native from the quay to pilot him. But he was sure he could never make the dock. Besides, "local knowledge," extolled enthusiastically in the *Sailing Directions,* seemed here represented by a lethargic adult studying the water and a small black child trying to play a guitar. If they managed to make the wharf without tearing their hull in half, there was no assurance that the native would know any more about piloting a keel-draft vessel up the channel than he did. The locals were reputedly always quite surprised when a yacht they were conning hung up on a reef they had been paddling over all their lives.

He tapped the throttle forward and inched past the quay. Aloft, Lindy raised her arm, then sliced it down, a little to port. He eased the wheel to the left, waited until her hand pointed amidships, and met the swing. Her eyes still on the channel, she raised her hand and gave him an OK signal, forefinger and thumb just-so.

The village drifted aft. The little black boy bounced excitedly, beckoning them. Or warning them? Mitch hoped not, but they were well into the chute now and committed.

From his angle, with the sun low at his back, he could see nothing below the swirling surface. When they made the left turn at the far end of the pass, the sun would be glancing into Lindy's eyes and she would see nothing even from aloft. The branch of a coconut palm swished past, bound for sea. It was moving very swiftly. He added another hundred r.p.m. The smell of hot oil drifted from below.

Lindy began to point toward a danger to starboard, calmly enough at first, then in a violent, jerky motion. He swung to port and the current caught him. He

forced the bow back. There were eddies in the pass
he had not dreamed of. He came hard right, and
even from his low vantage he could see the huge
gnarled hunk of brown coral that had frightened her.
Streams of bubbles flowed from its peaks and crev-
ices.

He got the boat back to midstream and found that
at two-thirds power he was utterly halted. He jammed
the throttle forward to its stops. They might as well
burn up the engine as be swept backward into the
surf.

Imperceptibly, they drew up the channel. Around
the turn the lagoon shimmered invitingly, but the turn
was the thing, and that was up to Lindy. She signaled
him to ease to starboard, then back amidships.

He flashed her a smile and the OK signal. She
grinned back down.

She did not seem scared at all. With a girl like her,
a man could sail anywhere in the world.

She hung, terrified, to the mast. Approaching the
turn, she peered down into water which had suddenly
turned to cocoa. She tried to read the patterns of the
currents. She could not. They were dead in the water,
engine roaring. From where she clung she could not
tell if the water was six inches deep or nine feet.

She was afraid to signal the turn too soon or wait
too long. She glanced back. He was wire-taut at the
wheel, his eyes darting from her to the current to the
shore. "Now?" he yelled.

She shook her head. Now was too early, wasn't it?
Or was it? How could he *do* this to her, make her lose
his boat? It was impossible to see below the surface;
the glare of the sun was blinding; the center of the
channel could be anywhere. She leaned to port to look

more closely, lost her balance, stuck out an arm to regain it.

"Roger!" yelled Mitch. She felt the boat begin to swing.

"No!" she screamed. She turned. "Mitch, no!"

He grinned idiotically, pinched thumb and forefinger together, and continued the turn. She faced forward, wincing. The bow continued to swing, faster and faster. Thirty degrees, forty, fifty . . . God, he had better catch it now or they would go crashing into the coral to port . . . She wrapped arms and legs around the mast, closed her eyes, and waited for the impact.

Nothing happened. In a moment she heard the engine ease. Cautiously, she opened her eyes. They were slipping through emerald water, bow-wave slapping gently. They were utterly alone in a lagoon that stretched to her horizon. Even the village was hidden from sight beyond its palm grove.

She climbed down and lurched aft. Mitch was beaming at her.

"You are something," he murmured. He kissed her on her forehead. "You are really, truly something."

"Piece of cake," she shrugged.

She sat down casually, before her knees collapsed.

They moored miles from the village, in the horns of a crescent-cove hardly larger than the boat, with the stern tied to a coconut tree on one point and the bow anchor beached on the other. By the time they had furled and covered the sails against tomorrow's sun, and slipped the canvas binnacle cover on, brush strokes of crimson ringed the sky. She stowed the *Sailing Directions* and charts and mixed two gigantic scotch-and-waters. When she went topside the new moon was rising, a faint scimitar of bronze, with a golden star dotting one point. Crescent moon, crescent beach; no matter what happened, she would always have this.

The lagoon at night was an ebony mirror flashing fluorescent streaks. The surf boomed threateningly only a few yards across the rustling palms, making it all even better. A school of lagoon fish, attacked by something, jumped in a shower of blue-green sparks. Close by, there was a sudden crash in the brush.

"What was that?" she murmured.

"Coconut. Remember that, when we're walking in the grove."

For a week they stayed. They were more alone here than they had been in mid-ocean, with none of the strains and the worries. They wore no clothes, answered no schedule. They walked the beach and snorkeled the lagoon. They found an abandoned machete and Mitch sharpened it. They hacked clumsily at coconuts and drank the coconut-water and stuffed themselves on the meat. They crossed the narrow necklace of land to the sea and waded out on the reef. Even here they were protected from the thundering surf by 100 yards of shallow coral, the top of an underwater wall probably a full mile deep. They played with a baby shark stranded in a coral pocket, and finally flipped him free into a tidal rivulet.

They learned to eat *pauah,* abalone-like creatures with encrusted shells and vivid lips of green or purple or orange. They pried them off the bottom with diving knives and squatted on the boomkin slicing off the lips, which they marinated in canned lemon juice and ate raw.

They swam and dozed and ate and made love. Mitch had, somehow, got back the touch. To ask him why, she would have had to admit that she had missed it, so she did not. Why rock the boat?

At anchor they always slept in the forward bunks.

She would awaken at dawn and watch a tall, friendly palm which hung over the bow, tracing cabalistic signs above the hatch in the rising morning breeze.

The rustle of the trades never stopped, day or night. The surf drummed endlessly. Every few hours a coconut crashed in the brush. The weather was changeless: a cool morning, a searing noon, a squall after lunch, a sunset of purple and gold. They saw only three people all week: a man, a woman, and a tiny baby, far across the lagoon, droning along in an outrigger with an outboard motor. She waved and the man waved back.

She wanted to stay forever. She had only two worries: fresh water and Mitch. They had been afraid, after her fever, of Marquesas spring-water. So they had simply bought enough Vichy from Henri to reach Tahiti. Very soon, they would have to fill their tanks. And very soon, she was sure, Mitch would get bored.

At dawn on the eighth day, she awakened to the swishing of the palm, which was blessing her, Pope-like, with green fronds edged in early-morning gold. Mitch slept deeply, on his bunk a foot away. Her gaze fell from the hatch above her bunk, through the open door, to the main salon. She almost screamed.

Sitting on the companionway steps, staring at her intently, was the tiny black imp from the pier. His head was larger than the rest of his face; his jaw and snub-nose were infantile beneath a bulging forehead. His chin rested on his oversized guitar. The body was ten; the eyes were forty.

A coconut fell somewhere. The palms sighed. She sat up, stark naked, remembered, and grabbed her sheet. The little boy's glance never wavered.

"Mitch!" she whispered. She reached across and shook him. *"Mitch!"*

He awakened instantly. He followed her glance and sat up. "Get lost!"

The child regarded him soulfully. *"Bonjour, mon capitaine,"* he said, with enormous respect.

"Mon p'tit! Fiche le camp!" barked Mitch.

The little boy flinched. He hiked up his cut-offs over his ebony tummy, dropped the guitar, picked it up, and started up the companionway. He paused and turned his eyes on Lindy. She had the impression of sad and boundless wisdom.

"Bonjour, madame capitaine?" he ventured.

"Bonjour," she smiled.

"Hey!" A little-boy grin flashed on her like sudden morning sun. "Hey, you want to fuck?"

Mitch lay back. "I'll be," he muttered, "a son of a bitch."

Louie had come to lead them from the Garden of Eden. Her paradise was lost.

Mitch sat at breakfast in the salon, next to Louie. Louie had been trudging, apparently, along the reef since dawn. He was hungry. He had already eaten five of the bananas that had hung in their cockpit since the Marquesas, and he was eyeing a sixth. There were none on these atolls, and his bones must be absorbing them, for he had already exceeded his apparent volume.

He had dipped his fingers in Mitch's bowl of Ralston, tried and rejected it. Now he pointed to the cockpit. Lindy winced and tore down another stalk of bananas. He yanked one off and ate it, while his drum-tight belly swelled and Mitch began to wonder how they would clean up the mess in the cabin when he burst.

He was, he told Mitch, sent by the village chief. The chief would like it very much if the pretty yacht would tie up to the town dock, where yachts customarily stayed, and where they could be properly welcomed. But the chief was very shy and had no wish to intrude, so he had sent Louie.

Mitch doubted it: why Louie? He asked him, as delicately as he could. The enormous eyes regarded him, and the shoulders went back. The tiny chest swelled, almost matching the belly. *"Mon père,"* he announced solemnly, *"il est Américain!"*

"His father's American?" asked Lindy, from the sink.

"Hey, man, *Américain,"* repeated Louie proudly. *"C'est* bullshit, *n'est-ce-pas?"*

"Probably, Louie," sighed Mitch. The child was spooky: he claimed twelve years but seemed younger, and much older, too. In the high-domed head was a quick mind, and some secret purpose Mitch could not quite define.

"His father never taught him *that* English," Lindy said. "Somebody ought to be shot!"

Mitch delved further. Louie said his father lived beyond the pass—he pointed to sea—in Bora Bora, further even than Tahiti. His father was *bon capitaine,* too, with a yacht bigger than this, and Louie had visited him many times. Louie himself was a *bon pilote* who could take them through the reef. Were they bound for Tahiti?

He seemed to visualize Tahiti, four days sail away, as just over the horizon. His eyes shed their sadness and sparkled and danced. He had an American friend, another *bon capitaine,* Jacques.

He reached into his shirt pocket and drew out a thin package of wrapping paper, tied with a shaggy brown string. He untied it on the table, pursing his lips. In it was a Polaroid picture.

It was Jack-the-Rip-Off, sitting at the wheel of his scruffy ketch, grinning from under his headband.

Louie was standing as tall as he could beside him, his frizzled head touching the tip of Rip-Off's tangled beard, but he seemed even smaller than now. Mitch hoped Louie's English was all that Jack had screwed up.

Jacques, announced Louie, was going to take him to Tahiti when he returned. And to Raitea, and Bora Bora, too. *"Après demain."*

"Après demain?" Mitch asked gently in French. "But 'Jacques,' when was he here?"

Louie looked away. "A month?" he answered, shiftily.

Mitch knew that Jack-the-Rip-Off had anchored in Nuku Hiva over a year ago, needing, he said, repairs. He had not moved since. The gendarme had told Mitch his visa had long expired.

Not a month, he suggested in French. Perhaps a year?

"Non!" Louie's eyes grew angry. The surf growled, the palm muttered, a fish splashed somewhere in the lagoon. A stupid subject, and a stupid question, decided Mitch. Time stopped at the reef—how could the kid know?

Louie's eyes were distant. His voice dropped. Jacques did indeed seem delayed. Would *mon capitaine* and the *jolie madame* take him to Tahiti? He would guide them to it through the reef.

Mitch shook his head gently. *"Mais non, mon p'tit. Je regrette mais . . ."*

The tiny black hand darted for the last banana on the table. His forearm seemed deliberately to brush the box of Ralston. It fell and spilled on the deck: instant poltergism. Louie gnawed the banana impassively while Lindy swept the mess.

"Le quai?" he asked suddenly. His voice rang with urgency. *"Vous allez y aller, maintenant?"*

Well, he could not send the little bastard dragging home barehanded. And they needed water. "Lindy," he suggested, "let's have a go at the dock?"

She nodded resignedly. He smiled at Louie and got up to start the engine. He read relief on the black face and a crazy urgent hope, and something else.

The kid *knew* how long he had waited for Jack-the-Rip-Off. To the day.

And they had better check the bilges for a stowaway when they left.

The quay was a huge tan slab of coral-concrete with jagged edges, set on barnacled pilings. It stood in the swirling currents just a little higher than the rails of *Linda Lee*. For twenty-four wild hours they clung to it, with an anchor set in the channel forward to hold off the bow and two small anchors off the port quarter. To keep them from grinding their planks to pulp they hung out bumpers and spare tires and finally dangled a massive two-by-six beam from the side to fend them off abeam. Still, every turn of the tide was a Chinese fire drill as they shifted lines and fenders, and each was a one-man, one-woman job. The citizens were willing, and great boatmen in their outrigged *pirogues,* but no help at all with a yacht.

Mitch, when he had finally tied up, had taken one look at the copra warehouse at the foot of the dock, grabbed tin-snips, and begun to cut rat-guards for the mooring lines out of copper sheet. He should have had them ready sooner. While he snipped, the first of their two copra rats somehow scurried aboard unseen. It lodged with them for a week, until they caught it just short of Tahiti and executed it with a rolling pin in the galley.

Their first rat must have had invisible properties, for the odds were against him. There were sixty-seven pairs of human eyes in the village, and a certain percentage of them were watching *Linda Lee* from the moment she docked. They were reinforcements waiting for room to board her: the lucky ones were already aboard. There was not an instant in the twenty-four hours they were there that the boat was not being admired, serenaded, swum from, fished off, danced on, climbed on, drunk to, or used as a photo background for one of the sixty-seven Polaroid portaits that Mitch shot and gave away to a population of sixty-eight. Only the chief failed to show.

The instant they docked, Louie had taken charge, piping orders and waving his tiny arms. His moment of glory lasted only seconds, while half the village swarmed over the rail. A wiry girl with jutting breasts pushed him overboard and began to roll her hips for Mitch, to the throb of a wooden *toere* and the twang of shiny Yamaha guitars.

Louie scrambled onto the dock, his tiny face contorted. He yelled something at the world in general, turned his back on his dream of fame, and trudged down the street. Lindy almost went after him, he looked so forlorn, but the sheer weight of numbers aboard the boat was too great to ignore.

The rigging sagged with children, the water between boat and dock churned with teenagers, the salon was instantly jammed with smiling island women, immaculate in clean *pareus*. The cockpit filled with quiet, bronze men and raucous, singing adolescents.

Chaos lasted all day and into the night. No one spoke any English at all. Their French Mitch could barely follow. When he asked for the chief, they would only smile and wave toward the houses. The population was mostly Mormon, he came to understand, so no one drank but a few backsliders, which was lucky,

or they would have run out of beer in the first ten
minutes.

There was no way that Lindy could feed him, let
alone the crowd, so they did without dinner. When
he had enough, he showed in sign language that he
was sleepy. They simply crammed over to give him
room to lie down on a cockpit seat.

Long after midnight Mitch went below to use the
head. He moved through a moist, smoky press of female bodies. The door was open and a huge Polynesian
lady, skirt hiked up, sat on the toilet, in animated
conversation with those waiting in line.

Lindy was trying to play hostess. Her guests drank
her in with smiling brown eyes, chattering incompre-
hensibly and occasionally reaching out to touch her
thick bronze hair. "We're out of Coke and beer," she
choked, "I can't *communicate,* my face aches from
smiling, I can't keep my eyes open, and I'm starving
to death! Now, make a move, will you?"

"It's their island," he said weakly.

"It's our boat and it's 2 A.M. Will you in the name
of Christ do *something?*"

She glared at him, grinning all the while, and he
went topside. Louis had returned to sulk on the dock.
He was sitting with great dignity on a piling, under a
single electric bulb. He plunked his guitar, ignoring
the music from the boat, and gazed out the pass.
Mitch stepped ashore.

"Louie?" he asked, defeated.

Louie deigned to swing his eyes to him. *"Ça va
bien?"*

"Non." He asked Louie to explain to the people
avec politesse that *le bon capitaine* and *Madame
Capitaine* were *très fatigués,* and tomorrow they would
take more pictures, but tonight . . .

"You do not like these persons?" Louie wanted to know.

Of course he liked them, it was because it was so late, and they were tired.

Louie pursed his lips judiciously. *Le bon capitaine* was of course right. *"Ces gens ne sont pas gentilles,"* he announced. Always they wanted something from Americans. One had to be very careful. They were even known to steal.

That was a lot of crap, but Mitch was not going to argue with his only hope. *"Vous allez expliquer?"* he begged.

Louis shrugged. Was *le bon capitaine* going to take him to Tahiti?

"Non! C'est impossible!"

Louie reflected for a moment and relented. He got up, portraying vast patience in the face of ignorance. He patted his own tiny shoulders and pointed to Mitch's. Mitch squatted and he clambered on. He was practically weightless. With Louie on his shoulders, Mitch stepped back aboard.

From his perch, Louie delivered a short Polynesian speech to the cockpit. Then he dismounted, drew Mitch below, and addressed the women in the salon.

Everyone nodded and smiled and got up. They touched cheeks with Lindy and Mitch and in five minutes the boat was clear.

What magic phrase, Mitch asked him, had he used?

Louie pointed to Lindy and then to Mitch. He made a circle of his thumb and forefinger, inserted the middle finger of his other hand and jabbed vigorously.

"Thanks, Louie," sighed Mitch. "I'll try to remember that."

"Fine," yawned Lindy, "but not right this minute, OK?"

They let Louie sleep in the cockpit. In the morning, he was gone.

So was the Polaroid.

They would have taken on water and left without telling anyone of the camera. Louie already seemed the village outcast and there was no use making him the local juvenile delinquent. But a wizened pearl diver crippled with *tarvana* from too much pressure for too many years, shuffled to the boat for a picture in his church-suit, and a shy young island mother came asking for a photo of her baby's grave, so they had to admit the theft.

The old man was outraged. The village had been disgraced. There was nothing to do but to follow him to the chief's *fare*. He lurched painfully down the coral road, leading them down a lane of scraggly palms.

The village, after serenading them all night, was up and busy in its cookhouses. The shacks, of palm-woven walls and galvanized roofs, were windowless and wide open at waist height, gulping in the trades. They could see their guests of the night before sweeping and eating and gouging at coconuts in their neat small yards. There were waves, smiles, but no invitations inside: Mitch sensed that the island economy was dying with the pearl-diving industry, and that no one wanted to display his poverty.

The chief lived in a neat frame house at the end of the village. He was a broad-shouldered, gray-haired man in immaculate shorts, wearing a T-shirt that read: "Whup 'em, Brudah." He had an aristocratic nose and brown kindly eyes. He was a man of immense dignity and grace: he produced his slender, pretty Chinese wife and a slim son of fifteen and pulled seats from the table for Mitch and Lindy while he sat on a bed.

His English was as primitive as Mitch's French, so

they split the difference and conversed in a kind of pidgin. The chief had not visited the boat, he said, because it seemed already too crowded. Then, there was the press of administrative work for Papeete— he waved his hand at the kitchen table piled high with dusty papers. He had been standing last week on the end of the dock while the boat entered the pass, and had radioed Papeete of their arrival, and was all well? *Ça va bien?*

Mitch groped for the words to tell him but the old diver broke in in angry Tuamotuan. No one had mentioned Louie at all, but Mitch heard his name now. The chief nodded, glanced briefly at his son, and sent him on some errand. Then he faced Mitch.

The theft was unfortunate, he said. But one must realize that Louie, like himself, was not *precisely* of the island. He himself was from Takapoto, almost thirty miles away, assigned here by Papeete, perhaps unwisely, because he was neither Catholic nor Mormon, but a Witness of Jehovah. He had been here only three years, and Takarava was not Takapoto, so he did not really understand the people here. On the other hand, while they were not Jehovah's Witnesses, they were honest folk and could not have stolen the camera. Louie, though he had never left the island, was a child apart.

Louie, apparently convicted *in absentia,* obviously needed a lawyer. Lindy flushed and mentioned this, but luckily the chief did not follow her. He was watching his wife as she served them coffee. It was strong and bitter, but they drank it slowly and with a great show of relish. No one offered any to the old diver, so he stumbled over and took his own.

Louie, the chief continued, was apparently the son of a young crewman on an island schooner from Bora Bora, a half-Polynesian half-black, whose own father had been, reputedly, a wounded GI sent to recuperate in the Bora Bora rest camp during *la guerre.* Louie had never seen him, although he would tell you, *mon capitaine,* that he had visited Bora Bora many times.

The chief tapped his head, but qualified the gesture. Who knew, really, if perhaps Louie had not? If you believed *les superstitions des iles?* For Louie assuredly knew things he could not have learned here, in their little island school: French better than his own, *par exemple,* some English, too. And where had he learned *that,* from passing yachtsmen? Perhaps. But no matter, his *body* had never left the island.

The mother, with five others to care for, was *fiu,* finished: she did not have time for Louie any more. Her husband was a good fisherman, a good diver, very honest, *très stable,* but Louie did not like him and he did not understand Louie.

"Louie, he is too black, and too intelligent, and perhaps the island is too small for him." The chief sipped his coffee. "Perhaps, when the next schooner comes, at the end of the year, we shall send him to school in Papeete. There are government funds . . ."

The chief's son stalked in triumphantly, with the camera, towing Louie by one small wrist. Louie glared at his captor, yanked his hand loose, saluted Mitch, and reported to him that he had found the camera on the beach.

"C'est bullshit, Louie," Mitch said, trying not to smile.

"Abandonnée," nodded Louie. He studied the chief's son, whose mouth was working convulsively as he tried to follow Louie's French. *"Je pense,"* Louie muttered to Mitch, *"le voleur, c'est lui."*

He pointed to the son. The chief lunged for Louie and snagged a skinny arm. He said something in Tuamotuan, very low and menacing.

Louie never flinched. *"Je suis Américain!"* he shouted, turning to Mitch.

The chief said it again, louder. Mitch broke in. He agreed, he said, that it was Louie who had taken the camera. The chief's son, it was easy to see, was no *voleur*. All Mitch needed was the camera, not justice: he had to take two more pictures. Indeed, he was grateful to Louie. Louie had walked far along the reef to bring them back to the village, to meet all the islanders. They might even leave the camera with him, with the chief's permission.

That, the chief's son understood. He stamped from the room, enraged. The chief dropped Louie's arm and looked at Mitch in awe.

"Monsieur le Capitaine, vous êtes Chrétien!"

"Non!" exploded Louie. They stared at him.

A *Christian,* explained the child, would take him to Tahiti. What use had he for the camera? *"Il n' y a pas d'argent sur cette ile perdue pour acheter un sacre film!"*

"Or roughly," Mitch murmured to Lindy, "there's not enough money on this God-forsaken island to buy the goddamn film." He moved to the chief's window, looked at the growling entrance. He turned to Lindy. "Maybe," he said softly, "we *do* need a pilot to get out of that pass?"

"Oh, boy," said Lindy dubiously, studying Louie, "you *are* getting Christian. On the other hand, at least you're asking me." The child might not understand English, but he knew somehow that his fate balanced on a knife edge, and she held the knife. He gave her a dazzling smile. "You want fuck?" he asked.

"What in the world," she asked, "does he think that means?"

" 'Have a good day,' I guess. Well?"

"Whatever you say."

He asked the chief about red tape. The chief beamed incredulously. No *problem,* monsieur, he would radio ahead. Mitch wanted to know where Louie would live in Tahiti? The chief looked at him as if he were mad. Family, of course, the chief's, or the mother's perhaps; even the old pearl diver had family in Papeete. Failing that, at the government school. All would be arranged.

Mitch glanced down. The boy's eyes were shining, but his face was impassive. His little shoulders braced. *"Monsieur le capitaine?"* he piped.

"Oui?"

"Pour le pilotage, je ne vais rien vous prendre."

The chief rubbed his eyes helplessly, shaking his head. "He said," Mitch muttered, "he won't charge us a cent!"

"Louie," said Lindy, "you are just too frigging much!"

"Too frigging mawsh," agreed Louie. "Jus' too frigging mawsh."

They had signed on their first crewman, and their last.

They cast off from the wharf, weighted and wreathed in polished shell leis and loaded with coconuts. Lindy's friends of the night before were misty-eyed: she was touched, until she decided later that they were crying with joy at Louie's departure. *Linda Lee* swept into the channel in a cacophony of yells and laughter; the machine-gun rattle of *toares* and the drumming guitars followed them up the cut.

Louie blustered around the deck for the benefit of the bleachers, coiling lines backward, tiny arms pointing port and starboard as they churned straight out the channel and through the pass. At the first trade-wind swell he turned greenish-gray, looked startled, ignored the vast possibilities of the Pacific, and threw up on a cockpit cushion. If his father indeed followed the sea, Louie ignored his genes. He burrowed into the forward cabin, where the motion was worst. For hours he defied her efforts to drag him out, like their cornered copra rat.

The rat they finally conquered, but never Louie. Every hour he would emerge voluntarily, to stagger topside and look for Tahiti. As Mitch, at the chart table, sweated out *vigias* and atolls and sets and the drift, Louie chattered on, expressing his opinion. He almost wore out the chart, which he read half the time upside-down. He became worried that they had missed Tahiti the first day, became sure that they had on the second, and absolutely certain on the third.

Mitch seemed amused. He never broke under the drip of the boy's patter. He showed more patience with Louie in three days than he had with Tony in twenty years. The fourth day Louie spent at Mitch's elbow, trying to get him to turn back to search for Tahiti. When Mitch escaped for a nap forward, Lindy raised the crags of Moorea, rising majestically off their starboard bow, on schedule. In a few moments the peaks of Tahiti showed, dead ahead. She did not bother to point them out to Louie, preferring to let him make a further ass of himself.

It was all wasted on Louie. When he spotted Tahiti a half-hour later, he yelled triumphantly, waking Mitch. So it was Louie who had got them there.

For hours, he swaggered around the deck, peering over the side to study nonexistent currents, squinting professionally at the sun's elevation, nodding importantly when they felt the swell of approaching land.

She thought she knew what the peaks off their bow meant to Mitch. He had done it his way, sailed his boat to some misty dream of glens and dells and fictional waterfalls, of brown-skinned girls, probably, and garlands by Loti's Pool. She could smell the flowers already, twenty miles at sea.

Tahiti, after sixty days of sweat from San Francisco, should have meant just as much to her.

What it really meant was a fresh-water shower and getting rid of Louie.

CHAPTER
9

She moved through the water slowly, using a languorous scissor-kick until that would become too tiring, then shifting to her back and letting her legs stream, then trying a feeble breast-stroke, then simply floating.

She kept the lopsided moon to her left, heading for the Southern Cross and the rhythmic flash.

The deep, visceral attacks of shivering had become more frequent and violent; she imagined that the water was cooling more rapidly, perhaps because dawn was approaching.

She envisioned the sun over the eastern horizon, sweeping toward her. Daylight slid across the earth at 900, almost 1,000 miles an hour, Mitch had told her. It could be leaving San Francisco now, speeding to warm her. Or perhaps it was all the way to the Marquesas or Papeete, lighting the central market and kissing the spire of the Cathedral. It could be here any moment.

The seas, now that the squall had moved on, were calmer. If dawn found the seas smooth, and Mitch still in the area, he might find her very quickly.

Her right thigh muscle knotted suddenly. She grunted in pain. She ducked face-down, floating like a jellyfish, grabbed the leg, and began to knead the muscle frantically. She tried to straighten it and only made it worse. She hugged her knee to her stomach, her face underwater, and dug harder at the flesh. When she threw back her head for a breath she took a mouthful of water and gagged.

Coughing and struggling, she massaged the muscle. It finally eased. She lay back exhausted. She was afraid that if she moved the cramp would return. When she felt better, she carefully reoriented herself and faced the Southern Cross.

She craned, waiting. Finally she saw the flash once more.

Cramps or not, while the flash drew her on, she had better not stop swimming.

She began to move again.

Mitch awakened from his nap to find Louie strutting the deck and Tahiti dead ahead, all purples and hazy greens, under a broil of cumulus. Moorea rose even more grandly off the starboard bow. A plume of cloud trailed from Tahiti's Mont Oroheana, seven thousand feet high. Below it lay Venus Point, where Wallis and Cook had landed.

He caught a scent of jasmine and the heavy smell of copra. He also caught a whiff of smog. For Tahiti, you were always 100 years too late, or fifty years, or twenty. Even Cook had complained on his second voyage at the degradation of the noble savages he had corrupted on his first. Bligh, Melville, Slocum, and

Jack London had bitched, too. Tahiti was never like it used to be.

In the loom of peaks looking down on a flat blazing harbor, they drew close to the entrance to Papeete Pass. A black bell-buoy clanged at the channel. After Takarava, the clearance seemed immense. They shot under sail toward the notch in the sawtooth coral ledges, astern of a giant U.S. tanker.

As they entered the slot, a Pan Am jet labored up from a runway along the water. Louie gaped and forgot the wheel, swinging them to port toward an underwater current. Mitch grabbed the helm and straightened them out.

The jet, seen head-on, seemed to pause to gather strength. Then, climbing suddenly, it roared overhead in a gut-shaking crescendo. Louie grinned excitedly. When he saw Mitch looking at him, he composed his face.

Eh bien, he yawned. If his new school did not suit him, he might take a plane to Bora Bora to see his father, who was *un pilote,* and who flew such aircraft.

But *un pilote,* Mitch pressed him, surely only of boats, not airplanes?

Boats *and* airplanes, Louie insisted. He scanned the harbor, spotted a church by the beach, and suggested anchoring well out, off the white *église,* where they would be safe from thieves.

Mitch laughed and began to look for a slot in the long line of yachts, tied stern-to, downtown.

She stood on the bow and watched the harbor open before her. A complex of gray galvanized warehouses and work-buildings lay on a low peninsula just inside the pass. The supertanker was moving to take up moorings at the outer dock. A French warship lay at the Navy yard further into the bight of the harbor.

An enormous Russian passenger liner, flying a red
star, dominated the downtown wharf. Along her upper
deck was strung a banner: "CHAMPAGNE AND
CAVIAR CRUISE OF THE SOUTH PACIFIC."
Above it a great hammer-and-sickle gleamed on one
of her four stacks.

Lindy dropped the sails. Louie tried to help her, the
first constructive move he had made since Takarava.
In an hour or so, if all went well, he should be in the
hands of his mother's aunt, who lived in Papeete.

Dead ahead of the pass stood a half-finished natato-
rium and a simple white church with a red spire. A
modern post office sprawled on the waterfront by a
park that looked, from the blazing heart of the harbor,
very cool and dark. Anchored bow-out were so many
yachts that it seemed impossible that they could squeeze
in.

They crept under power along the boats pressed
gunwale-to-gunwale. Their sterns, to the busy street,
drooped flags of every country. At one end of the line
towered a Chinese junk, apparently converted to a restaurant. Lindy tensed. Several boats down the line from
it lay a low-slung steel ketch, painted orange.

On teak trail-boards on her bows was carved *Xanadu*.
A carved mermaid rode her stern. And waving to
Lindy from her foredeck was Jean-Paul, solid, broad-
shouldered, tanned.

Again, her stomach flipped. Her cheeks felt hot. The
feeling was ridiculous. The way to stop it was to flee.
She almost asked Mitch to anchor out.

Instead, she tossed her hair from her eyes and
smoothed it back. Jean-Paul swung his hand in an arc
along his rail, indicating room to squeeze in, and began
to tie bumpers along the side. A slender young Tahitian
emerged from the foreward hatch. He wore a flower

in his hair. He walked to the ketch's bow to wait for a
line.

Mitch dropped his bow anchor, swung his stern to
the quay, and flung the youth a looping line from aft.
The *mahoo* hauled it in, and in a few minutes Lindy
was grinning like an idiot across five feet of water into
the deep blue eyes, with no thought of fleeing at all.

The moment lasted timelessly. She became aware
that Louie was staring at her, with the wise old face,
and that there was work to do, and still, she could not
draw her glance away.

And then came Mahura. The girl popped from
Xanadu's afterhatch, dressed in the uniform of an Air
France stewardess. She was straightening her skirt
when she noticed Lindy. She read her face instantly,
flashed a look of amusement, and hurried aft. She was
Tahitian-Chinese. She made her drab suit look like a
creation of Saint-Laurent.

"Jesus," Lindy heard Mitch mutter from the cockpit.
He was standing, coil of rope in hand, gazing at the
girl. He looked as if he had been clubbed. She couldn't
blame him. The girl teetered expertly ashore on a
plank from the stern-rail to the seawall. She hopped
onto a bright motorscooter, kicked it into life, and
whipped into the traffic hurtling along the quay.

Lindy supposed she should be thankful. The problem
of her strange chemical reaction to Jean-Paul was
solved. The girl was possibly the most beautiful woman
she had ever seen.

She did not feel grateful at all. She turned away to
find Louie's eyes still on her. Screw you, she thought,
and *out* of our lives, OK?

Abruptly, she went below. With fresh water available, at least she could wash her hair.

Mitch gathered their passports and the ship's papers

and put on a clean white shirt and long pants, to go to Immigration. Louie, his tiny valise packed, trailing his guitar, was on the foredeck staring sullenly at the traffic rumbling along the Quai Bir-Hakeim.

Leading Louie down the waterfront, Mitch speculated on the child's mood. Louie had never seen a motor vehicle, outside of the chief's scooter on Takarava, and never crossed a city street. He had never seen TV or a movie, or used a toilet until he stepped aboard *Linda Lee*. And yet he was trudging stolidly along, eyes dead ahead, without a glance at what he must most want to see.

They cleared Immigration and phoned Louie's great-aunt. She arrived, piloting a belching Vespa. She was an enormous woman wearing a tent of a *pareu* and a neat straw hat. She accepted Louie gratefully, perhaps knowing no better. She smiled, showing two missing teeth. Monsieur would perhaps visit their *fare* for a *tamaaraa, après demain?*

Mitch accepted, knowing by now that in Polynesia *après demain* seldom came. He had given Louie his freedom and a camera, but you returned a gift with a gift, not thanks. The little boy reached in his hip pocket and produced the brown packet he had shown them on the boat. He unwrapped it. From the photo, now, Jack-the-Rip-Off had been removed, apparently with the tin-snips; Louie stood alone at the wheel, of the boat, lord of all he could see.

He handed the picture to Mitch. *"Pour mon capitaine."*

"Et aussi pour Madame *la capitaine?"* suggested Mitch.

Louie's face hardened. He slung his guitar over his shoulder, climbed behind the woman on the Vespa, and looked him dead in the eyes.

"No!" he said, in the first nonscatological English

phrase Mitch had ever heard him use. "She is *bad* woman."

"What?" Mitch gasped, disbelievingly.

Louie jabbed the mountain of flesh before him. *"Allez!"* he ordered. The Vespa snorted into the traffic.

"Wait a minute, you little son of a bitch—" yelled Mitch. An Australian couple off the liner, garlanded in cameras and leis, stared at him.

Angrily, he crumpled the photo and dropped it in a trash can. He hated to keep things from Lindy, but that was one message, after all she had done for the little bastard, she wasn't going to get.

CHAPTER
10

Dawn had not come. The flash, when she saw it occasionally, seemed no closer. But the cramp did not return. The dark seas were calm.

She rested again. She lay back and looked straight up. A magnificent star was overhead. It shone steadily, like a planet, but there were tiny beams radiating from it, like a star on a Christmas card. She thought that it might be Antares, at the head of Scorpio, and tried to trace the tail and the stinger.

One night at Papeete, under a gold-studded sky, Jean-Paul had shown her how easy it was to pick the star directly overhead. That was how the ancient Polynesians could find an island in an infinite sea. Their navigators would know, in summer perhaps, that a certain star peaked directly over an atoll after dusk. They would sail and paddle, using the sun and the swells as a compass by day. Each twilight they would readjust their course toward the star. When it was straight overhead just after nightfall, they would be at the island.

But how did they know there were islands out there in the first place? Very simple: *accidentellement. Par hasard,* a fisherman might be swept downwind by current or the trades. He might die of thirst. But if he survived, he might drift upon an uninhabited island. He could not sail home against the trades, but if the island was pleasant, and the fishing good, he would use the coconut radio. *Eh bien:* a brother or a son would dream of the star and the island, and know, and the whole village would launch their *pirogues* and set sail. You see?

OK, Jean-Paul. Or Mitch. Either one. Winner take all. I am here, right below the big orange star. Antares, I think, because it is big, and it is bright, and I think I see Scorpio's tail leading away. So steer for Antares, and quickly, OK? Before it begins to set?

Mitch, darling, are you coming, or not?

There was no answer. It was no use. Mitch did not really believe. Jean-Paul might receive her, but God knew where he was now.

She turned toward the Southern Cross and began to swim again. It was ages before she saw the flash, and when she did it seemed no closer.

They elbowed into the life of the quay. They were on the outskirts of "Frenchman's Row," an unofficial gathering of French yachts. It existed on the quietest end of the quayside and was relatively permanent.

Most of the other floating neighborhoods were temporary, and changed their characters as boats came and left. Some thirty American, Australian, Swedish, German, and New Zealand boats stretched along the concrete waterfront almost to the middle of town. "Cannabis Row" centered around Jack-the-Rip-Off, who had finally left the Marquesas, navigating with his alarm clock, a plastic Davis sextant, an obsolete *Nautical Almanac,* and an Ecuadorian poodle which could smell reefs.

Star of Peace and three other long-haired boats were moored in "Hippie Haven," and "Hamburg Heights" was studded with the black, red, and gold ensigns of West Germany. Kurt in *Kormorant,* an imperious Berlin carpenter, and his ex-bus-driver cook, had been tied up there for years.

The lingua franca along the quay was English. The Germans learned it of necessity, the Swedes and Danes all seemed to know it anyway. Even the French learned a little or became isolated. A handsome, quiet Czech, sailing with his government's permission, had studied it enroute through the West Indies and the Panama Canal.

Papeete authorities practiced laissez-faire with yachtsmen. If your hair was too long or you were anti-nuclear-testing, or the smell of pot from your cockpit overpowered the tourists walking along the quay, you were asked to move on when your visa expired. If not, if you wanted to stay and your finances held up, you got an extension.

The little floating communities had their own rules. No matter how tightly you were squeezed in already, you welcomed a new boat. You launched your dinghy, took her lines, and jammed her in somewhere.

A man's seamanship was measured by his modesty: the longer you sailed, the less you knew about the sea, and everyone had learned this. In Catalina, a weekend sailor might scream at a tyro for fouling his anchor line. Here, where your boat was your home, your measure was how calmly you watched a departing neighbor pull up your anchor by mistake with his own.

Within weeks Mitch and Lindy had made warmer friends than they had in twenty years in their home on the hill. Marriages and crews dissolved, loves were born, Kurt of *Kormorant* knocked his lifelong friend into the water and dove in to rescue him. A female doctor on *Mistress* saved a bungled abortion on a Chilean yawl and word never got off the quay. A young millionaire on *Foam* got religion, donated his boat to Jehovah's Witnesses, and no one laughed.

You thought of the people as their boat and the boat as the people. Mitch and Lindy evolved more fraternal feeling for the *Windrift*, the *Star of Peace*, and *Vedura* than they had for boats they had raced against for years in San Francisco Bay.

In six months Lindy was ready to stay forever. She was weary of sailing; she dreaded the day they must leave. But Mitch was getting bored.

Mitch sat at the salon table, one fan breathing down his bare neck and another, across the cabin, pointed at his face. On the opposite bunk lay Lindy, reading a paperback. Before him sat his portable typewriter, charged with paper. Stacked neatly on its left were a dozen sheets of plain bond, to be the quota for today. Face down on its right lay fifty pages of *Impossible Dream*, a chronicle of their voyage. He had been shooting pictures for it since the start of the cruise. He was tired of that, and of the writing too.

The first fifty pages had got them as far as Lindy's illness in Taio Hae Bay. Now *Linda Lee* seemed destined to lie anchored on the page forever, with the other boats frozen in limbo under the crags and Lindy in the hospital. He had not written a word in the last three days. It was simply too damn hot. He had no incentive, and he would rather be sailing. It was time to move on, but Lindy liked life along the quay and he had no heart to prod her loose.

He rattled off a sentence. His typing sounded impressively professional in the tiny cabin, but two out of three yachtsmen along the seawall seemed to be writing the same sort of thing. He stopped and read. *"The no-noes descended on the hospital room in an invisible, lethal cloud; we would not know for eight hours just how lethal . . ."*

Crap! Just crap! He ripped out the sheet. If he knew who might publish it, if he needed the money, if he even knew for sure that someone other than he and Lindy would ever read it, he was sure he could go on. He probably wouldn't.

Still, the world was stuffed with armchair adventurers, thirsting for word from Paradise. Pan-Am flew them in, the affluent ones, every day, by the score, a thousand bucks a head round-trip. The quay above him was doubtless crowded with them this very moment. There had to be a market, in the dreamers left at home, if only in *Yachting Magazine*.

He began to feed in another sheet. Its whiteness depressed him. How did you start? There were no guideposts, rules of procedure, no prior decisions. And everything he wrote read like plagiarism. Reducing the color around him to words was turning it all black and white; even freezing the locals in his camera was a species of murder or, at least, crass. Every time he pressed the shutter he felt like a potbellied tourist. He should be heading west, away from the air routes, into the real Pacific.

He heard someone pounding on the hull. Gratefully, he slid from behind the typewriter and went topside. Jean-Paul was pulling himself from the dirty water onto *Linda Lee*'s deck. Xanadu was gone from her berth, winched out from the quay, in the faint after-

noon breeze. He remembered that she was scheduled
for a haul-out today at Ellicott's yard, across the harbor. She had no engine and had been waiting all day
for wind. She was fifty yards out from the line of
yachts, with Taarii on the windlass. She was floating
strangely, bow-down, stern-up.

"Goddamn!" breathed Mitch. "We fouled?"

Jean-Paul, his hairy body glistening, puffed his
cheeks and nodded. He had a diving mask pushed up
on his forehead. "Our anchors, they seem mated for
life. *Je regrette,* Mitch."

"My fault," shrugged Mitch. He had anchored last,
six months ago. He must have dropped directly over
Jean-Paul's chain. Neither had moved since.

Worse, his scuba tanks were empty. He'd been diving with the kids from *Star of Peace* outside the reef,
and forgotten to have them refilled. So he'd have to
skin it, in thirty feet of murky Papeete mud.

At least it beat tapping at the typewriter. He put on
a mask and fins and got Lindy topside. She rowed
them over their anchors in the rubber raft. He slipped
into the water and followed the Frenchman down,
through levels of translucent green, tan, opaque brown,
until he lost sight of Jean-Paul's orange bikini trunks
in a morass of mud, chain, and anchor-flukes.

Jean-Paul, trying to work blind and alone on the
bottom while Taarii winched from above, had somehow managed to dig their anchors free. Now *Xanadu's*
anchor seemed to be hanging a few feet above the
soupy bottom. A fathom of Mitch's chain hung twisted
beneath it, under tension and disappearing into the
limbo below. Jean-Paul's hook was a seventy-pounder
and Mitch's, hidden in the murk, was a thirty-five-
pound plow. Spiraling deeper, he found the Frenchman
tunneling into the jumble, digging at *Linda Lee's*
anchor.

Mitch sank his fins into the mushy bottom and gave a few ineffectual heaves. His heart began to pound. He had a great set of lungs for poolside games. He had convinced Tony as a child that he had gills in his ears and could breathe underwater. But in Jean-Paul he had apparently met his match. Mitch quit and broke surface by the raft, a good fifteen seconds before the Frenchman.

"C'est inutile?" asked Jean-Paul. "I have it free from the mud, but perhaps we must get filled your tanks?"

"Shit, no," panted Mitch. "We can do it." He began to draw in mammoth breaths, hyperventilating.

"Mitch?" pleaded Lindy from the raft. "Let's fill the tanks?"

He pushed back his mask and glared at her. What she meant was, *"Watch it, Buster, you're forty-three."* Screw that. Jean-Paul was hardly younger, and had probably been diving the mess already for half an hour. *Xanadu* was due at the yard, and it was his own damn fault that she was snubbed where she was, missing the afternoon breeze. He was not about to let her hang here as a tribute to his own misjudgment while he charged around trying to get his tanks filled. He tugged down his mask and dove.

He seemed to plummet downward forever until he found the bottom. He felt for his chain, and followed it to his anchor. The visibility was less than a foot; the whole area was turgid with the mud they'd stirred.

Taarii, topside, had apparently eased *Xanadu*'s anchor back to the bottom. Her chain hung now in a steep angle. To untangle the mess they must somehow hoist *Linda Lee*'s hook over *Xanadu*'s chain, not once, not twice, but three times, one for each twist. Then, if they were lucky, they could drop his own anchor for him to reset when *Xanadu* had sailed away.

He grabbed the shank of his anchor, heaved mightily in the mud, and tugged it toward the surface. When he was half over Jean-Paul's chain, he felt the Frenchman helping him. They pitched it over, grabbed it again, and repeated, swimming side-by-side, stirring the murk until it was impossible to tell which way the surface lay. They heaved it over, found it again, and started to drag it upwards.

Mitch felt his lungs convulsing, but the Frenchman showed no sign of letting go. He could feel the granite body next to his own, straining. A rock-hard chest with hair like steel wool pressed him against the chain. The anchor was caught, no, free, and ready to drop, no, snagged . . .

He hung on frantically, damned if he'd give up first. He felt Jean-Paul pat his shoulder once, saying good-bye, then tug at his arm, urging him to let go too. He shrugged him off, caught a quick glimpse of the orange trunks rising through the murk, bound for the surface through a cloud of bubbles. Still he hung on, hauling the anchor over the chain with a last mighty effort.

He hated to let it fall, for then, later, he would have to haul it up from the raft, hand over hand, to reset it. Reluctantly, he began to ease his grip, then changed his mind. He had a feeling of immense and sudden power.

Flippers churning, he felt scabby links rake his thigh as he powered for the surface, weighted by anchor and chain. He fought upward through brown water to tan, glimpsed *Xanadu*'s chain leading to the distant dark hull hovering over him—he must swerve to avoid her bottom, she was encrusted with barnacles, high time for the haul-out, green sunlight somewhere, he had better let go, *the grey shape of the raft, air, he needed air . . .*

Clinging to his anchor, he broke surface a foot behind the raft. Desperately, he lunged for the handline draped on its side. He gripped it. Weighted down, both hands occupied, he managed to push back his mask against the rubber hull.

Jean-Paul was in the raft with Lindy. They were at the other end, staring down into the water. They did not see him. Jean-Paul was poised to dive. "Oh, God," he heard Lindy wail. *"Go!"*

Mitch, near fainting, took a deep breath. "Hey guys?" he managed.

Jean-Paul whirled, lumbered down the raft, and gasped: "Your *h'anchor?*" He dropped flat, plunged his arm into the water, and grappled for the shank. With Mitch's feeble help, he heaved it aboard. *"C'est formidable,"* he breathed. *"C'est impossible."*

Mitch could not find the strength to slither aboard. Hanging on to the side, he looked up at Lindy. She was ghost-white. She stared down at him, eyes wide with shock. She had never looked so angry. "You son of a bitch!"

Startled, he muttered: "Easy kid!"

"Tell me why you did that!"

"Well, we'd have had to haul it up later to reset it . . ."

"Do you really," she asked softly, "think that's what I mean?"

He felt his cheeks go hot with shame. "I guess not."

"Then why in hell pretend to?"

He winced. Jean-Paul turned scarlet and elaborately checked their anchor shackle. They dropped him at his boat, rowed out and reset the hook, and never mentioned the dive again.

They had come on a three-month visa, and extended it once. Jean-Paul was sure that they could get another extension if they wrote the governor; French bureau-

crats in Polynesia were a loose and pleasant breed, and
glad to have foreign boats decorating the quay as long
as their crews were *sobre* and their funds held up.

Funds were no problem to *Linda Lee,* although
Papeete prices were astronomical by U.S. standards.
Compared to the families in the other thirty-odd boats
tied to the Quai des Yachts or anchored close-by off
the Protestant Church, Mitch and Lindy were affluent. They held to the life-style of their neighbors so
that they would not lose their ties with the floating
community. She bought her fish fresh from the
bonnitiers at the quai, chose small Chinese shops instead of the air-conditioned French stores like Aline's
or Donald's, and felt guilty when they dined at Pitate
in sight of the boats.

The thought of the long slog west became a nightmare to her. Mitch talked of the Cooks, and Tongas,
and Fiji, then New Caledonia, where his father had
run a field hospital. She dragged her feet, projecting
less and less interest each time he mentioned it.

She was never bored with Papeete, though her
routine never varied. She awakened each morning to
the sound of the first motorscooters blasting past Parc
Bougainville, rattling the open hatch above her berth.
Showering with the hose on the quay, writhing under
its cool touch and spraying it discreetly around inside
her Bikini when she thought none of the passing traffic
was looking, she would hardly have traded the hose
for the languid warm showers of home.

None of the white-collar automotive traffic that
would later jam the quay was aboard; this was early-
morning, go-to-market time for laborers and villagers:
an hour of Lambrettas and Vespas and rocketing
Hondas. Scooters flew everywhere, carrying white-
frocked nuns and beer-bellied fishermen and bronze,

miniskirted prostitutes heading for the early-morning tourist trade.

The *bonnitiers* would be casting off from their beery section of the quay. The fish smell was carefully hosed away each evening, but the scent of Hinano beer seemed to become part of whatever it spilled on. The fishing boats churned out full-bore, bamboo poles slung on cabin tops, glittering in the morning sunlight. They left in a roar, gleefully rocking the yachts and trying to awaken anyone still asleep below. And they always came back full of fish, though the charter boats which followed them usually returned full of disgruntled tourists, empty.

One morning she finished her garden-hose shower and dressed below in a flowered print skirt. She strolled down the Bir Hakeim. She carried a palm-frond basket Louie's mother had woven and presented, along with Louie, as they pulled out from the Takarava wharf.

Early risers from the *Star of Peace* were up. The battered schooner was here on French sufferance after being slammed, ostensibly by accident, by a French destroyer off the Mururoa test grounds. Having no operating head-facilities, the protestors were crossing to the ancient Hotel Scott and brushing their teeth at the quay-side faucets. A gendarme was posted to watch them night and day.

There were other commune-boats. Skinny, bearded kids and long-haired girls from an ancient American yawl, with no visible finances, were cheerfully cooking native food topside, their galleys too full of unwashed dishes to use. On a French " 'ippie boat," the crew braved poisonous bottom-paint, harbor pollution, and unknown ingredients to scrape the growth off its hull to eat it boiled. She had seen them last night checking yacht garbage along the seawall.

The clean Dutch ketch was here, from Nuku Hiva, and the tiny girl was growing fatter every day, while her counterpart on *Star of Peace* grew thinner. Knowing no one but adults, the little Dutch girl had the poise of a lady and spoke a melange of English, French, and Dutch. The old Australian had arrived before them and was trying to sell the cutter rather than to face the trip home single-handed. He was sanding his deckhouse in the cool of the morning.

Most of their friends would be leaving soon, on the trades toward the west. Despite her feeble protests, if she read Mitch correctly, they would be with them.

She crossed the street and started toward the market. A sleepy Tahitian bartender was sweeping broken bottles off the sidewalk outside the ancient Hotel Scott, the only real relic, outside of Quinn's, of the old Papeete waterfront. A gnarled shell-lei vendor who slept under his souvenir stand outside Donald's was setting up for the day, his polished leis and engraved shell sailboats lined in neat rows on a spotless oilcloth. He greeted her with a smile and the silent lifted eyebrows of Polynesia. He walked with her wordlessly as far as the Frosty-Freeze stand where he breakfasted. He left his wares unattended: even tourists seldom stole in Papeete. Once, he had pressed a shell pocketbook on her and would not let her pay.

By the time she reached the public market she was hungry: that was the problem with her weight. Papeete, full of good French restaurants, invaded you with food too early in the day. Cooking smoke drifted from the hills, and the morning scent of squealing piglets from passing *trucs*, with a breath of yams, melons, bread-fruit, and coconut milk from the public market. She liked all she smelled and all she saw.

It was too soon to leave Tahiti: she was just getting acquainted. Tahitians never accepted you on sight:

for weeks, at first, they had endured impassive stares from waitresses and shopkeepers and the clerks in the giant gleaming post office across the street from the boat. For a month or two, they were in social quarantine.

And then, for them at least, everything had unexplainably changed. A waitress at the Viama Restaurant on the quay, who had always ignored them before, one evening rushed over and kissed her, French-general style, on either cheek. A postal clerk began to set aside their mail. The crowded sidewalks, when she would walk to market, began to blossom with smiles from Tahitians she barely knew.

Now she moved through the crowds and entered the cavernous, domed market place, carefully stepping over a shrieking piglet trussed at the entrance. She went to the bread stall, where her friend the Chinese baker had this morning saved her, out of sight, a loaf as long as her arm. Under its iron crust, she knew, beat a yielding heart of moist bread, every molecule bursting with a million calories. She did not care: it looked as if she would soon lose it all again, sailing west.

She found a table in Patisserie Pam Pam, on the *Rue Jeanne d'Arc,* where she nibbled a *croissant* and waited routinely for Jean-Paul and Mahura.

Outside, *les trucs* began to line up for a post-market exodus to the outlying districts. She studied one in bright crimson. It was bound, according to a sign painted on its wooden body, for Papeari, down the coast. A full load of passengers was already squeezed onto the wooden benches placed on either side. On its roof was a huge new washtub, an immense slab of melting ice, and a crate of breadfruit. From its rear hung a string of yams, two stalks of bananas, and a flopping chicken. On the rear step teetered a case of Hinano beer. A dented milk container and a carton of

Kellogg's cornflakes was tied on top. From every rung of the steel ladder which rose to the bus's roof hung a string of fish: little red *iihi* and *bonitas* and a black fish Jean-Paul said gave you nightmares.

The *truc* seemed burdened past all further insult, but as she watched, a giant Tahitian woman waddled grinning to the steps at the rear. She wore a flowered dress, squeaky-clean like all Tahitian clothes from a river washing along the coastal road. Sweat poured from her shining face. Her right leg was grotesque with elephantiasis. She slung a *panier* of long French loaves blindly into the crowd in the *truc*. She was clutching a monstrous tuna, which dragged on the street: someone tied that to a rung of the ladder. Two men jumped from the rear and took position behind her, one to each fabulous buttock.

The giantess and everyone else howled with laughter as they strained. They stuffed her, finally, into the bus like a mainsail into a sailbag. The *truc* sagged on its springs, started with a roar, and moved irresolutely into traffic, honking hopefully.

"C'est drôle, n'est-ce pas?" Jean-Paul murmured into her ear "And that leg like an elephant, that is part of the scene, OK? It makes it all the more colorful, and if it actually pained her, how could she laugh so?"

She was the only person in the *patisserie* who had not noticed his arrival, at least the only woman. The candy shop came to life. Even Mitch, with all his height and size, did not impact a crowd like Jean-Paul. After three months moored next to him, her damnable stomach still flipped.

Her virtue still seemed safe. At 7 A.M., Mahura was breathtakingly beautiful, if angry. Her face was flushed and her small white teeth were bared. She wore what Jean-Paul called her tiger-look, learned, he said, from the copies of *Vogue* and *McCall's* she read loafing on the airliner. They were having one of their political arguments. The girl sat down, shoved her feet ahead, and leaned back, staring blankly out the window.

"And a happy good day to you two, too," Lindy offered.

Mahura tossed her head toward Jean-Paul. "That one!" she spat.

Anger made him more Gallic, deepened the creases on his face, brought out the scar on his chin. "Today," he told Lindy, "she is Chinese. I hope tomorrow she will be Tahitienne once more."

Mahura touched her heart dramatically. "Here, I am French. Which is more than you. You *Hoopipi!*"

"What's a *Hoopipi?*" asked Lindy.

" 'Bean-fart,' approximately," said Jean-Paul. "Or gutter-Tahitian for 'Frenchman,' but she says I am not French. Which shows you how logical is her mind."

"Goddamn *Popaa*," breathed Mahura. *"Communiste! Autonimiste!"*

"And you, have you slept on a sidewalk like the Papeete lei-sellers?" Jean-Paul cut in. "I think not. *En tout cas,* not alone."

She ignored him. "I tell him, wait, if the French leave us, we will *starve* on these sidewalk!"

"Only the Tahitian part of *you* would starve," Jean-Paul said. "The Chinese part would prosper like a *champignon* in *merde de taureau.*"

"Speak English, you are not polite," Mahura said coldly. "He say, 'like a mushroom in bullshit.' "

"That is *polite?*" asked Jean-Paul. "To put in the face of an angel the tongue of *une putain,* where were you, God?"

Mahura smiled sweetly. "He was quite busy that day I was born. Saving your ass at Dien Bien Phu.

While you hide from the *communistes*. Which you love so much now!"

Jean-Paul, sipping his coffee, exploded into laughter. Tears ran down his cheeks. His was the most handsome, honest laughter Lindy had ever heard. He wiped the coffee from his beard and the tears from his eyes. "Is she not fantastic?"

Lindy nodded. "Marry her before she gets away."

"No, he is already marry-ad."

"Married?" Lindy asked, shocked.

"To his dirty little carvings, and perhaps with the *mahoo*, too." She glanced at her watch, stuffed the last of Lindy's croissant into her mouth, and stood up. She touched her cheeks to Lindy's. "I have a flight to Hono, I return too late tonight." She regarded Jean-Paul pensively. "I think," she decided, "he sleeps with Taarii when I am flying."

"You are too kind," smiled Jean-Paul. "Am I so virile?"

"You are not bad," shrugged Mahura, "for a *popaa* who has forty years."

She wheeled and marched out the door. He swirled his coffee for a moment and swept his eyes to Lindy's. Her heart jumped. How he did it, she did not know.

"And you?" he asked softly. "Do you think I sleep with Taarii?"

"I hadn't thought of it," she lied.

"To Mahura, it would only be *drôle*. To you it would be important."

"Well, *I* don't think you do. I know damn well you don't."

"*Merci, ma chérie,*" he said drily. "And Taarii, he would thank you too. He is my friend, you see. To make love, that is to him another thing. *Eh, bein. Plus de café?*"

She nodded, though it was her third cup and her bladder was bursting.

To cheat on Mitch was unthinkable, so she supposed she was leading him on.

But they had never been alone before, probably never would be again and she would wet her pants before she hollered quits.

When he awakened, Lindy was not back from the morning marketing. He stepped topside as the clock dinged eight bells: she was very late. He glanced at the boat next door.

Taarii was hacking at an adolescent coconut with a machete, as if sharpening the shell to a point. He was after the jellied, candy-like center. Jean-Paul had invited them to dinner and the *mahoo* was already starting to prepare. Mitch waved at him and his face lit for an instant; then, as if he felt he had gone too far, he nodded primly and resumed his strokes.

He was a very handsome young man, with a lithe, golden body and wide, square shoulders. Two weeks before, Mitch had bailed him out of trouble. Mitch had dropped into Quinn's for a beer. The brawling old waterfront saloon was soon to be demolished by government edict, and it was crowded with last-ditch customers. He had found Taarii backed up against the bar, tormented by a stocky, half-drunk Legionnaire, all hands, hard eyes, and *machismo*. The professional *mahoos,* beautiful in drag, were clucking in a corner like pigeons disturbed by a cat.

Word of Taarii's predicament had spread. The coconut radio apparently worked even in the city. A sympathetic circle of glowering Tahitians was gathering on the street outside, but the booths inside were jammed with French sailors, Legionnaires, and marines. Mitch, towering over the Legionnaire, had man-

aged to get the kid out before the inevitable *bagarre,*
but it had been a very scary affair, and afterward he
had shuddered to think what might have happened if
his bluff had not worked. He was out of shape, and
the Tahitians indecisive, and the Legionnaire was
hard as a rock: the Frenchman would have taken
him apart.

"Taarii is brave at sea," Jean-Paul had said, thanking him. "But he was very afraid."

"So was I."

Taarii had since grown nervous around Mitch, but
he was always quietly at hand when there was work
to be done in the rigging or a line to be snubbed on
the quay.

Jean-Paul was nowhere in sight. Neither was
Mahura, which was too bad: she could make his whole
day with one flashing grin. They had probably marketed with Lindy and were stuffing themselves at the
patisserie.

Hungry, he crossed the street, picked up the mail
from Raoul at the Post Office, and took it next door
to Cafe Vaima. He sat at a favorite sidewalk table,
shaded by a boxed fig tree, where he could watch the
line of boats beyond the traffic. Next to him two
French sailors in civvies sipped coffee and read *Paris
Match.* The harbor shimmered under a mounting sun.
A lone yoga sat cross-legged on a hatch on *Star of
Peace.* The gendarme guarding the boat strolled past,
waved, and when the young man did not respond
passed morosely on. The little Dutch girl, targeting
the gendarme, pumped furiously down the quay on
her tricycle; the gendarme skipped aside to let her
go. *Keke II* tumbled out for the morning ferry run to
Moorea, full of tourists for Club Med, drawing her
wake past the long line of yachts. *Linda Lee* and
Xanadu, which had returned from the yard wearing

an even brighter coat of orange paint, stirred restlessly side by side.

He found himself yawning. Too lethargic to open the mail, he waited in a trance for their waitress Yvonne, who had seen him sit down and had promptly hidden in the cool gloom at the bar. She finally gave up and shuffled out, a plump, warm girl in an immaculate orange *pareu* and bare feet. She took a swipe at the table with a rag and sat down with him, resting her chin on her hands and staring sadly into space.

"Je suis fiu," she sighed.

"Um." She was always *fiu:* finished with her sailor boyfriend, or the French Navy, which was sending him home, or with the burden of working five days a week almost four hours a day, to support her little girl, three cats, and five kittens.

She began to recite her woes, not in hopes of a larger tip, for like most Tahitians, she would return a tip as demeaning. She simply ran the same tape over and over, by habit, whenever Mitch or Lindy came in. He had already memorized it. He slit an envelope from Tony to forestall her. *"Le menu, s'il vous plaît?"*

She looked pained. She squinted at the sun just topping the spire of la Cathédrale. It was too early to eat, surely too early to serve. *"Un chat!"* she cried, inspired. "I have for Lindee a cat!"

"No cat," he smiled.

"A cat for eat the rat?" she begged, nodding at the boat.

"The rat is dead. *Fini,"* he explained, "before we got here."

"Another rats, when you leave. *Tahitian* rats." She rolled her eyes proudly. "Such rats! After, you could throw the cat in the sea."

"Merci, non. Le menu, la carte?"

"Le menu," she repeated, as if she had never heard

the word. She stirred only slightly. *"Tasse de café?"*
she suggested, without much hope but without getting
up. Coffee was easy; she could get that at the bar inside. If he wanted fried eggs or an omelette, as she
knew he did, it meant a trip to the kitchen. And then,
laying out all the silverware, plates, paper napkins
and other accouterments that a *popaa* thought he
needed, just to eat . . . *"De la bière?"* she proposed:
beer would be even easier.

He shook his head and glanced above her, pretend-
ing to read from the bill of fare above the entrance,
written in English and French.

"Non. Pour moi: onion soup, one cheeseburger,
pommes frites, bacon, a steak sandwich, *mahi-mahi,*
one vanilla milkshake, apple pie à la mode—"

Her eyes widened tragically. "You fool me! *Vous
plaisantez!"*

"Two scoops on the pie."

"Non! You are too . . . *gros?"*

"Fat," he agreed. She was right. The hell with the
eggs. "OK, just coffee."

She clutched his hand gratefully. She would have
crawled under the table with him out of relief. She
was up in a flash and padding toward the bar, before
he could change his mind. *"Café au lait!"* he called
after her.

She chose not to hear. The coffee would be black;
he also sensed that the next time she got at Lindy,
they would end up with a cat.

He read the mail. Tony had a second job, pumping
Texaco in Sausalito. He glanced at a letter from
Bernie, in his familiar telegraphese. Malpractice rates
had soared so high that doctors were threatening to
strike: Mitch already knew that from the *Tahiti
Times.* The press was blaming lawyers instead of medical butchers, greedy patients, or the insurance com-

panies. Even normal personal injury awards were down.

"Looks like we got last of golden eggs," Bernie concluded. *"Would head down there myself, if could strap enough gastanks on the Beech."* Which was, Mitch reflected, as close as Bernie would ever come to admitting that Mitch had the right idea.

He saw Mahura rocketing along the quay, apparently heading for the airport. She spotted him and squealed to a stop at the curb. He strolled across the sidewalk and she bussed him on both cheeks. "Lindy is at the Pam Pam," she reported. "They stuff each other with *croissants,* and you sit here alone."

"I slept late."

"Do not sleep too late in Tahiti," she warned.

"For Christ's sake, Mahura," he grinned. "What are you trying to say?"

"I do not know," she shrugged. "He makes me very angry, sometimes. Hey, she does not make you angry?"

"No. But you might. Sit down, have a cup of coffee and cut the crap. OK?"

"I have a flight," she smiled. She had perfect teeth, a short upper lip, a full lower one, a perfect nose, and skin like golden silk. There was the faintest touch of sweat on her upper lip, and she smelled of Ivory soap. He felt like climbing on the Vespa with her. *"Eh, bien,"* she decided. "You are right, *probablement.* With a man like you, how can that little Frenchman compare?"

She squeezed his hand for a long moment, laughed, and was off in a brown cloud of smoke. He returned to his table. One of the French sailors, watching her speed away, whistled softly and shook his fingers in a limp, Gallic gesture, as if they had been in water too hot.

Mitch sipped his coffee and dropped back into his reverie. In the far distance, down the quay, he could see the tiny black figure of Louie, who had once tried to tell him the same thing Mahura just had. The hell with it. He had never seen Lindy flirt before, but he had more confidence in her ultimate fidelity than his own. Especially if Mahura made another pass.

Approaching the gendarme, Louie saluted him elaborately. The gendarme shampooed his head and strolled on. When Mitch had imported Louie to Papeete, he had apparently introduced both good and evil. Louie had quit school, and now he haunted the waterfront, a tiny black entrepreneur who was everywhere at all times. He would pluck a *tiare* from a garden wall, and sell it to a tourist at a sidewalk café; he would dive for a dropped bolt off a quayside yacht; he would polish your portholes or find you a gangplank or climb your mast to untangle a line, buy your fish at a discount on the quay, or take your Polaroid picture if you caught a *mahi-mahi*. He had learned English, Mitch had heard, in about a week, and the Dutch couple claimed he had picked up gutter-Dutch and German as well, by osmosis. His aunt, stopping by, had bragged that when he quit school he had been at the head of his class.

He was scared to death of Mitch and never went near *Linda Lee,* which was exactly what Mitch wanted.

Lindy and Jean-Paul appeared finally, walking down the quay. He sat for a moment watching them. She was swinging her basket, smiling into the Frenchman's face. Jean-Paul, not much taller than she, seemed to be grinning. He wondered how he kept his gut so trim: in the sack with Mahura, perhaps. As for Lindy, she moved like an eighteen-year-old in a goddamn Pepsi commercial.

Preoccupied, the two almost passed *Linda Lee*. They stopped in confusion and parted. She stumbled coltishly, boarding on their gangway, smiled back at Jean-Paul, and went below.

She would wonder where he was, but the hell with it. She had kept him waiting long enough for breakfast, and now he was not even hungry.

He paid the bill and strolled to *Magasin Klima* on *Place Notre Dame*. It was a cool, shaded bookstore which carried a spotty collection of nautical charts: French, American, British Admiralty. He needed Huahine Island, Bora Bora, the rest of the Iles Sous le Vent, and the Cooks and Tongas, if they had them.

He was depressed. Papeete had finally got to him. He was *fiu*.

It was time to head west.

That evening he wrapped a bright green *pareu* around his waist for dinner on *Xanadu*. He wore it Tahitian-style, like a skirt, for comfort, rather than tucked up like a loincloth, as Louie had taught him. His gut hung out, but Mahura was on a flight, there was no use disguising the potbelly before Lindy, and Taarii and Jean-Paul had contributed to it with previous feasts and might as well suffer the sight. Unless he lost weight again, he would have to revert to Levi's.

He stepped topside to wait for Lindy, who had been brushing her hair for what seemed like hours. The sun was tinging the faces of dockside strollers with an odd, apricot hue. A strange silence had fallen; at this hour, there were no vehicles along the quay, and everyone seemed to move slowly. He had noticed this more and more, at sundown.

Jean-Paul claimed at first that it was the nuclear tests. "We kill the fish and perhaps the people, and the babies will be born with two heads, but for so beauti-

ful an *ambiance* in Papeete, the price is not dear,
n'est-ce pas?"

But seriously, hadn't Melville written of it and
Gauguin got it on canvas? Jean-Paul admitted that they
had: "It is caused, I think, by the coming of
mauvais temps. Soon there will be hurricanes west of
Rarotonga."

Bad news for those who had sailed for the Cooks
already. But secure here in French Polynesia, where
tropical hurricanes seldom wandered, the strange airy
quality was a gilding for Paradise. Tonight it turned
Lindy's hair to gold when she came topside. He hauled
the boats together and they stepped across.

It was like setting foot on a battleship. They had
lived fifteen feet from *Xanadu* for six months, but he
had never got used to the brute strength of the boat.
She was a storm-slogger, built to survive in any seas.
She made *Linda Lee,* rugged as a wooden boat could
be, look like a racing craft. Jean-Paul had sailed her
from Marseilles to Tahiti around the Cape of Good
Hope, and skirted the Horn to return to Cherbourg
and then done it again two years later.

Topside, she looked as if the grandaddy waves of
the Roaring Forties had washed her clean of fat. She
had no deck-house at all. An overturned aluminum
canoe was lashed to her steel flush-deck. Two immense anchors were snugged down port and starboard.
A heavy chain led to the anchor they had wrestled
with in the mud; it was set again somewhere far, he
hoped, from his own.

You tuned the shrouds with deadeyes, like a
nineteenth-century clipper ship. Jean-Paul insisted
they were better than turnbuckles, once you got the
hang.

The masts were telephone poles, not figuratively
but actually. They were unpainted, creosoted, cured,

and treated with Cuprinol. Great crack ran their length, but Jean-Paul claimed that they were stronger than the best laminated-spruce stick in the whole long line of yachts.

The masts were the only wood topside. Even the booms were steel. The decks were painted white for the tropics and the paint embedded with walnut shells for footing.

From the aft cabin protruded the only break in her deckline, a hemispheric plexiglass bubble, turret of a World War II bomber. Below it was an auxiliary steering station. Running down the Roaring Forties single-handed, Jean-Paul had steered from there, watching the graybeards coming up astern. "Watching always, one must quarter them, each as it comes. One is hurled onward like on a surfboard."

Jean-Paul seldom spoke of himself, though Mitch knew he had lived in Washington as a child and been a professional military officer in French Indo-China. He never bragged, except about his boat. "She lacks, you would say, 'lines.' She is, I think, a submarine crossed with a Sherman tank. But if I hit a berg or lost her sticks in a hurricane, I think I should grow very old before I drowned."

Having no engine, she had no electricity or radio gear. Even at the quay Jean-Paul refused the umbilical cord of shore current, and used kerosene lanterns below. She was uncluttered and ugly as a mako shark, but in any seas or collision her water-tight compartments below would keep you afloat until you starved. She was too sterile topside for Mitch's taste and much too bleak for Lindy's. Steel was dead and wood alive. But below, Mitch knew, she was a different boat.

They climbed down a hatch like a manhole cover. Austerity disappeared. Everything was sheathed from bow to stern in African mahogany, picked up in

Mozambique. Each plank was tongue-in-grooved, and there was not a steel frame showing. The glow of bulkhead lamps made the wood come alive. It throbbed with the sheen of hand-rubbed varnish.

A gimballed mahogany easy-chair rocked by a rosewood chart-table. Above ticked an ancient U.S. Navy clock. A brass-and-mahogany barograph with a cracked window was mounted beside it, tracing a wavy line of atmospheric pressure around a clockwork drum. Mitch noted that the graph was rising: no hurricane here, regardless of what was happening to the west.

Jean-Paul displayed none of his own carvings in the salon but he mounted the best he had of other carvers. A Maori three-fingered *tiki* from New Zealand, with its tongue idiotically lolling in greeting, simpered down at them from a bulkhead. An intricate tortoise. It was carved by Purvis Young of Pitcairn Island, sixth linear descendant of Fletcher Christian's lieutenant. A warclub, carved by one of Jean-Paul's Marquesan students, hung over an open bronze port. Full of fruit, on the galley counter, stood a kava bowl from Fiji, about to be flung aloft by three leaping porpoises.

On a deck-beam, engraved on a brass plate, were Coleridge's lines on Xanadu from *Kubla Khan*.

They were Mitch's favorite lines of poetry; *Xanadu* was his second favorite boat.

Dinner was *poisson cru,* taro, breadfruit, baked *fei* bananas, and *mahi mahi*. Jean-Paul poured a heavy red pinot from his home province, near Dijon. They ate Polynesian style, sucking their fingers clean. Taarii, sitting at one end of the polished teak table, had marketed for five, before Mahura learned of her flight to Honolulu. He kept pressing food on Mitch, who ate too much again.

While Lindy helped Taarii wash dishes in the galley, Jean-Paul offered Mitch a cigar.

"He has fallen in love with you," he observed, smiling. "He would, in fact, like to give you a carving."

"I can't take it."

"You must, *n'est-ce-pas?* After Quinn's?" He led Mitch into his workshop aft.

Mitch had to stoop, for the massive beams were low. A kerosene lamp flickered softly overhead. To starboard was a wide double bunk. To port, a waist-high bench of white oak, polished and scarred with use, ran the length of the compartment. A tall work-stool was set into the cabin sole. In racks behind the bench glittered chisels, knives, and gouges. A worn hand-grindstone and a series of sharpening stones were set in the workbench edge.

Tacked to a sheet of beaverboard behind the workbench were charcoal sketches of nudes, of Mahura, of lined market-crones, Chinese merchants, beer-bloated fishermen from the quays. There were anatomical sketches of hands and feet and buttocks. A magnificent Tahitian with great wide shoulders and sleek thigh muscles stood poised, casting a net.

Jean-Paul opened a drawer under the bench. From a mass of carvings he drew an intricate chess set. He opened the box. "This, someday, we will sell to a rich Parisian or a New York stockbrocker, to have brandy spilled on after dinner. I carved one side, he the other. Now, which is the master's and which the pupil's?"

The blacks were carved in *miru* wood, Polynesian kings and warrior knights with warclubs, stubby tiki-bishops. The whites were whalers, missionaries, a merchant-king. He handed the opposing queens to Mitch.

The white queen was a nordic nude of oak, with a

faint pout. She stood hands on hips, imperiously. She was a royal tramp and she breathed sex. On her coiffure sat an intricate *couronne de tiare,* studded with bits of mother-of-pearl. It was a little askew.

The black was a dusky, slender Tahitian girl, regarding him from under long tresses, as if caught showering in a waterfall. She wore no crowns: the crown was her hair, and her royalty was in all of the lines of her body.

Mitch compared them. The Polynesian queen was delightful, but on-the-nose, stereotyped, unsophisticated. The white queen was off-beat, raucous, alive. Mitch handed them back. "You did the white?"

"Thank you, but no." Taarii had carved her. His model was perhaps a Swedish tourist glimpsed in the Royal Tahitian restaurant, perhaps a French Army wife, even Taarii did not remember. She had lived within the oak, his fingers felt her there and cut her out.

Jean-Paul put the chess set back into the drawer. "So we have from a tiny *fare* in Vairao, at the end of the world on Tahiti-iti, a genius *authentique, n'est-ce pas?* A *mahoo,* like Michaelangelo. In Renaissance Rome, the Pope would steal him. Here, what shall we do with him? Show his work on a stand outside Quinn's?"

He stooped suddenly and slid back a holly plank in the cabin sole. *"Eh bien,* for you!" Between floorboards and steel skin was a compartment. "For pot, and other secret things," explained Jean-Paul. He drew out a figure wrapped in a rag. He uncovered it.

It was a two-foot-high carving of Mahura, laughing gaily, her *pareu* low on her hips and her breasts bare. It no more resembled the carved tourist-maidens on Rue Paul Gauguin than the Venus de Milo resembled a plaster statue in a Rome curio shop. It was carved in *miru,* hand-oiled. It seemed warm to the touch.

"It's too much!" protested Mitch.

"He wants for you to have it. And he cannot risk keeping it here."

At first Mitch thought that he meant the humidity would crack it. Jean-Paul, smiling faintly, turned up the kerosene lamp. Deep shadows swayed on the beams. "Study it more closely." Mitch inspected the carving under the flickering light. Suddenly he put on the glasses dangling from his neck. "Jesus," he breathed.

Scribed minutely in the grain, at the corners of the laughing eyes, around the throat, at the base of the bursting breasts, were lines of age. Mahura, like all Polynesians, would probably wear them too soon. Even in the soft light the breasts seemed suddenly to sag and the laughing face turn desperate, a skull glimpsed in the dark.

Xanadu creaked against a line. He shivered. "He's jealous?" he murmured.

Jean-Paul shrugged. "I think not. It is only that his hands cannot lie. But he is frightened to keep it."

Mitch accepted it and they stepped back through the watertight door. He moved past the galley into the main salon. He froze.

Lounging on a berth, rolling a joint as Taarii opened a porthole, was Mahura. Her uniform coat was off and her Air France shirt was unbuttoned halfway to the waist. She blew the hair out of her eyes and smiled up at them.

"I have smuggle a lid through the goddamn *douane,*" she exulted. "But the *flight,* full of tourists like *geese*—" She stared at the carving joyously. *"C'est moi?"*

Time stopped. Taarii turned slowly from the porthole and his eyes grew large. Lindy raised the cup of coffee to her lips; the motion seemed to last forever. She sensed something wrong and her eyes met Mitch's. He could only shake his head. He was watching Mahura.

"*C'est moi?*" Mahura asked again, reaching out her hand. Mitch, helpless, put the carving on the counter, out of her reach. She jumped up, flashing the heart-stopping smile at Jean-Paul. "When have you done this? *Mais je suis* jolie!"

Jean-Paul put a hand on her arm. "*Ce n'est pas fini!*"

"*Mais non, c'est joli! Je suis contente!*"

His voice lashed out. "*Arrêtez!*"

She stopped short, looking up at him curiously. "Why? When it is me, *n'est-ce pas?*"

"Not as you are!"

She freed her arm, picked up the figure and studied it. Suddenly she grew rigid. She moved closer to the light and stood, head down, tracing the lines on the face and the breasts. She turned to Jean-Paul, eyes full of tears.

"*Pourquoi?* Why have you do this to *me?*"

Jean-Paul's eyes were steady. The two stood, swept in moving light and shadow from the swaying lamp.

"*Non!*" Taarii cried suddenly. He jabbed a thumb at his chest. "*C'est* moi *qui l'ai sculptée.*"

"*C'est vrai?*" she asked Jean-Paul.

He nodded. Her eyes went hard. For an instant her face made the carving come true. She hurled the piece at Taarii. It missed, bounced from the back of the settee, and clattered to the deck.

Taarii picked it up. His face twisted, he offered the carving to Mitch. Mitch shook his head. Taarii moved to the porthole. For an instant he played his fingers along the grain of the figure. Then he flung it through the port. Mitch heard it slam against *Linda Lee* and splash into the tide.

"How much were you to pay?" Mahura spat at Mitch. She glared at Lindy, who looked like a startled doe. *"Eh bien,* Lindy. If you would mock me now, you must swim." She jerked her chin at Jean-Paul. "And that one, you can have!"

"Mahura," Lindy begged, "I don't even understand."

Mahura ignored her. She looked down at Taarii, who had slumped to a squat on the cabin sole and was staring dully ahead. Mitch thought she was going to slap him, but she bent suddenly, put her hand under his chin, and raised his face. Slowly, in ancient Polynesian style, she rubbed his nose with her own, patted his cheek, and straightened.

"Merde," she said softly, to the rest of them. Shoulders back, breasts thrust, she moved to the companionway. She looked Jean-Paul up and down. *"Popaa!"*

Then she was up through the hatch and gone. Lindy rose to follow her. Jean-Paul shook his head. "No! Believe me, please!"

For a week they did not see her. When they did, she was lunching at the Pitate with a big blond Pan Am copilot. That evening she sent him back to the boat for her things. Jean-Paul packed them, handed them over, and shook hands.

"It is well, my friend. It is no good for her, aboard here."

Mitch, lashing his dinghy topside, watched the flier leave *Xanadu.* Jean-Paul wandered forward, and sat on the bagged sails. When Mitch finished he was still sitting there, but Taarii was squatting unobtrusively by the starboard shrouds, sketching him with long, swift strokes as he stared at the strange yellow sun.

Mitch went below and checked the clocks. They were pulling out tomorrow at dawn.

CHAPTER
11

THE FLASHING LIGHT HAD GROWN STEADIER, THOUGH no stronger. She rested, floating back in the water and staring straight up. The great golden star she thought was Antares was no longer quite overhead.

Lindy is alive and well, Mitch, and living under Antares, in the sign of Scorpio. She rang you once or twice, but you never picked up the phone. Her mind rose from the swells, leaving her body floating there. First she flew east, then north, then south, then in confused circles. Finally she found the pale, starlit sails. He was moving under jib and mizzen, far too slowly.

He slumped red-eyed and half-dead at the helm. Now she forgot where to tell him to go. She had lost herself. Antares! Steer for Antares before it is too late. Forget the charts, she screamed silently: forget everything but the big golden star, hurry. If *you* can't find me, how can I?

277

She opened her eyes. The star twinkled down at her but the others were orbiting it. She was in a whirlpool of them.

She kicked upright, avoiding vertigo. Erect and treading water, she stared about. She was still disoriented and could not tell north from south. To drown would be bad enough, to drown directionless, in a void, was horrifying.

As she raised her head, the air and sea around her paled for an instant. The impression was so brief that she could not be sure that it really happened.

She sank into a trough. The strobe might be very near, or might not. She lost her fatigue. As she dropped, treading water, she pirouetted, searching the rim of her moving canyon.

There was nothing. She rose again, flailed her body full-circle around before she sank, spitting, into the next trough.

She must have imagined the flash. Her pace had been too listless all night long to have brought her anywhere near. There was no hope, she was simply losing her mind, from fatigue and fear and thirst.

The rim of her surging valley lit suddenly. A white-plumed breaker, caught slipping over its crest, posed starkly as if trapped by a flashbulb.

She yelled with joy and shipped a mouthful of water. She found herself thrashing up the side of the swell, against an avalanche of white water bearing down at her. She lost the plastic container, which swept down the gulf behind her. She did not care.

She crested the swell. She sank in the next, and rose, and sank again, and all at once was blinded by an immense white flash directly ahead.

She was suddenly in total darkness. She had lost her night vision. She could see no stars, no waves. She squinted, dreading the next explosion of light.

But when it came, she was ready. The strobe flashed, leaving imprinted on her after-vision its little orange cylinder and, much more, the man-overboard flag frozen in the full-flutter on the side of a swell, and the bright yellow horseshoe-buoy, all attached to each other by a yellow line caught snaking up the wave.

She floundered for the horseshoe-buoy. There was another searing flash to her left, before she reached it. She lunged blindly, felt the slippery plastic cover of the buoy, and lost it again in the rush of water off the crest of a swell. She took two brave strokes downhill into the white foam and snatched the buoy tumbling down the slope.

She lifted it over her head, worked her arms through, and snapped the stainless cable across its open end.

She had swallowed too much water, and now she gagged. She kept slipping through the horseshoe because her arms were too tired to stay up on the rim. And, relieved of the need to kick, she was cold again in minutes.

She had little hope that he would spot the flag at dawn. She doubted that she could hang on until then, anyway.

There was much more hope in the flash, if only he would hurry.

All night long she had waited for morning. Now she wished that it would never come.

For four hours he had been zigzagging, back and forth, over his wake. This was the area, if his navigation and the logbook were right, where she had fallen. Now that the logbook had told him this, the dark swells seemed more threatening.

He teetered on the edge of the cockpit, steering

with one foot, letting the necessity to balance keep
him awake.

The empty spreader ready to crucify him again
when he could climb the mast, raked the moon.

He had only an hour until the eastern sky would
lighten and, he hoped, bring back the trades.

He decided to heave-to in the surge, replace the
ruined jib, and take a look at the sodden chart below.

As he nudged the bow into the wind, he heard M.
le Chat mewing and saw his dark shape on the deck.
He had not had time to feed it at all. He still blamed
it for Lindy.

The cat glared up at him. Its eyes shone ruddily
in the binnacle light. It stretched, crouched, and
shifted its gaze back to the aftermost compartment.

Mitch put out a bare foot and prodded him forward,
out of danger. He didn't really want to lose it. The
cat regarded him with contempt and slunk forward.

Mitch followed him, dragged the spare jib topside
through the forward hatch, and unhanked the tatters
of the old one drooping from the forestay. He began
automatically to cut loose the hanks to save them.
They were hard to find in Tahiti, expensive anywhere. He froze, appalled.

To save the sailing gear was to give up. He was
selling the boat. Only if he didn't find her would he
sail on. He saw himself cruising endlessly, lonely in
the company of a succession of Mahura's, draining
him as they themselves grew old before his eyes.

He flung the hanks into the sea. She was there,
alive, and he would find her, and they were heading
home. He would need no hanks, or anything else.

He set the spare jib, dragged himself below to the
chart table, and found it had been drenched by the passing squall. He could barely make out his track on
the chart. But if he didn't spot the strobe by dawn,

it made no difference anyway. He was near her, if she lived. So he simply charted a rough dead-reckoning and went back topside. He jammed the engine in forward and began a square-search: fifteen minutes and a ninety-degree left turn, thirty minutes and another, forty-five minutes and another, an hour and another.

The clock chimed seven bells—0330. She had been in the water over twenty-four hours. Fifty minutes, he estimated, to first light.

He went topside. He saw nothing. He wondered if the strobe had gone out, or drifted too far, or sunk.

But until daylight, it was all he had to look for.

She left Papeete with the cat because Yvonne heard they were going. Although they said goodbye quietly to Jean-Paul and Taarii and tried to slip from their moorings before dawn to avoid farewells, the waitress was there with M. le Chat before they could warp away from the quay. Yvonne's chatter aroused the little Dutch girl, who awakened her parents, and when they actually got under way, their anchor was fouled again in *Xanadu*'s.

The whole scene got out of hand, with the *Star of Peace* kids tugging at their chain and even Kurt of *Kormorant,* whom they'd grown to detest, heaving in great Teutonic breaths and bursting his chest to dive without tanks to help. Mitch stayed on the windlass.

By the time they were free, it seemed to Lindy that half the waitresses and shopkeepers in town were waving from the quay. Farewells were part of island life. Natives were used to them, but she would never be, and as they pounded across to Moorea in the teeth of a strange *miramu* wind, she was sad for hours. She was tired of cruising, and she had wanted to stay.

They hauled and painted at Vaiare on Moorea and

spent a week in Cook's Bay and another in Robinson's Cove, loveliest of all, where they tied stern-to to a palm tree under the peaks and could step ashore from the fantail.

They cruised slowly northwest. At Huahine Island an American hotel was building a branch in a cove on a white coral beach. They anchored off it for five days. They had a few drinks at the bar, but they were not particularly welcome to the management. They returned the coolness. They had found the few American hoteliers in French Polynesia patronizing and Hollywood-phony. The hotels wanted boats anchored offshore for scenery, but they did not want the men and women who sailed them. To guests paying fifty dollars a day for a pseudo-dream, real boat-people were disturbing.

Tourists bored them both, but it was their own fault. They were becoming boat-bound and xenophobic. They could hardly carry on a conversation except with other sailors. Mitch's interests had shifted from tort and equity to varnish, diesels, and hull stability. Lindy, despite herself, was too involved in the care and feeding of eggs at sea to read about Watergate.

They touched at Raiatea. They rowed the dinghy up the river Faaroa, where the ancestors of the New Zealand Maoris had lived. She plucked hibiscus from the banks, feeling like a model in a *National Geographic* feature, as Mitch paddled lazily. They touched at Tahaa, and then, having saved the most beautiful French island for last, headed toward the craggy peak they could see only a few miles to the west, the jagged summit of Bora Bora, Michener's Bali Hai.

Mitch, trolling under power across the mirror-calm channel in the lee of Raiatea, caught a wahoo—*roroa,* the Tahitians called it. He cleaned it and hung it by its tail from the rail and it swung there as they shot the wide Bora Bora pass, steering on the range-marks.

They found only two familiar boats. The Dutch ketch, apparently racing for Samoa to beat the hurricane season, was weighing anchor off the crazy, palm-thatched Hotel Oa Oa. The *Star of Peace,* expelled from Tahiti just after *Linda Lee* had sailed, was tied to a seaplane buoy, looking for a leak in its bilges before it faced the run to Auckland.

Lindy, at the wheel, realized suddenly that she was looking for the orange steel ketch. It was not there.

They tied to the ramshackle Oa Oa dock. A swarthy young gendarme awaited them there, with a week-old radiogram in his hand.

Her father had had a stroke. He was paralyzed and speechless. Bobby begged her to fly home. Mitch pressed her in his arms. She was numb with shock, full of guilt because she could not even cry.

"Do you want me to go, too?" he murmured.

She stared at him. If he had to ask, the hell with it. And he was right to hesitate: they shouldn't leave *Linda Lee* unattended in an open lagoon this time of year anyway. Shawn wouldn't care, might not even know. She herself had things to say; maybe it was too late already. But to make Mitch fly back would be stupid.

They had her visa stamped by the gendarme and she was on a twin-engined Air Polynésie plane to Tahiti in two hours. It had taken them six months to sail from San Francisco to Bora Bora, and she was home, by Pan Am, the next morning.

Her father did not know her at all, or, if he did, could not convey it. In the hospital bed even the devil-horns of his tousled hair seemed wilted. The first evening, after Bobby and his wife had left she took his hand, drew a deep breath, and began to talk.

She told him of letters she had written him from boarding school that she had not sent. She asked forgiveness for getting pregnant before she was married, and forgetting his birthday in 1968, and being in Paris instead of home when he had a prostate operation in '69, and of course for not beating back immediately when he had his "cardiac" last year.

When she had finished her agenda, he gave no sign that he understood, but there was nothing new in that. It was a great purgative. Completed, it left nothing to do, except to help with bedpans and washings, and reading him Kipling, whom she remembered as the only poet her father had ever touched.

It was like reading to a corpse, but she persisted out of guilt for a week. Then she kissed him goodbye.

Tony and Nancy came to the airport: they were planning to marry in January. She hugged her brother, who still showed no signs of growing up, and his wife, and Justice Holmes, who after all the worry tolerated her but had obviously forgotten all about her. She said goodbye to Bernie, bought Mitch a Nikon for Christmas at the duty-free counter, and climbed on a Pan Am plane.

She found immediately that the copilot was Mahura's new boyfriend. After Honolulu, he wandered back and sat with her. He was gorgeous and she found him bland and sexless as a eunuch. He was a very naive young man, or pretended to be. And puzzled. Mahura was tender and tough, funny and sad, flighty and constant. He liked her very much.

But if the Frenchman was gay, and really preferred *mahoos,* why did she yak so much about him?

Lindy only smiled. She felt strangely disembodied and free, in other hands, and disinclined to probe her own feelings, let alone Mahura's. When he went back to the cockpit she dozed off, but the jingle of the cocktail cart awakened her. She had a martini and stared down at the infinite blue.

It was a wider, deeper ocean than the one she thought she knew. From here, it seemed a wasteland. Among the minute distant whitecaps, she searched for a sail, a freighter, a liner. There was nothing, so she simply imagined *Linda Lee,* rolling south.

One martini here was twenty-four hours below, a hundred miles of squall and sail-change, disaster and spilled soup, bruised shins, nausea, and joy. No one on the plane but she could measure a hundred miles; she knew the distance from San Francisco to Tahiti better than Mahura's lover, who probably flew it once a week. *She* knew, and she dreaded the thousands still ahead to sail.

Tahiti International, after the cool, dry cabin, was sultry. It was jammed, as usual, with Polynesians meeting relatives garlanded in leis. French military, tourists, and bored Tahitian customs officers were everywhere. Hordes of Papeete onlookers wandered through the cool, clean galleries. Whole families were there to sip Fanta and to watch the planes.

She made a reservation on the morning flight to Bora Bora. She did not cable Mitch: if he knew she was coming, he would try to meet the Bora Bora plane, and it was a long boat ride from the Oa Oa wharf to the airstrip near the pass.

She checked her suitcases for tomorrow, except for an overnight bag. She did not know why, but she ignored the taxis outside. She stood at a bus-stop on the highway and took *le truc* to Papeete. The passengers on the wooden benches scrunched together to give her room, and a Tahitian woman offered her a drink from a bottle of beer. She took it. Everyone apparently had seen her before; her face was familiar, so they loved her; she was very big on *le truc*. She wished Mitch had wanted to buy property here.

She hopped to the pavement as *le truc* squeaked to a stop at the tail of a long line of honking vehicles on Rue G. Lagarde. She moved through sidewalk crowds to the water. To the right lay Quai du Commerce, with the Royal Papeete, air conditioning, TV and a shower. To the left lay Quai des Yachts, and the battered Hotel Scott.

She hesitated, swinging the bag. She glanced left, across the street. There were new boats plugging the holes where *Star of Peace* and the Dutch ketch had been. The great schooner *Vedura,* reputedly cursed because she had taken "live" wooden tikis from the Marquesas years ago, seemed to be running out the subsequent stream of bad luck: now she had apparently had a fire: her topsides were scorched, her fine varnish peeled, her brass showcase binnacle twisted and warped.

Louie and a gang of even smaller children were diving for something off the seawall, astern of an American sloop she did not recognize. Louie was in charge, making it look as hard as possible while the owner pointed to whatever he had dropped in the water.

The quay was otherwise the same, but all was bathed in a strange ruddy light. Far down the lane of masts she could see the pitch-black poles of *Xanadu.*

She turned toward it, started to walk toward the Hotel Scott. Her head felt light and her body heavy. The air was full of tension. This was silly: she was tempting fate.

Something was happening to her, and something was happening along the quay. The whole ambience had changed. The *bonnitiers* were in, too early, sitting in their cockpits, morosely drinking beer. There were no fish on the seawall.

The yachts were heaving and falling in ponderous rhythm, as if the harbor were in deep, sound sleep. They had never risen so far or dropped so low. The line of them writhed like a giant accordian. The gangplanks were squealing and moaning in protest on the pavement. She had heard that often enough, when a chop came up from Moto Uta in the afternoon wind, but today the sound seemed sadder. She shivered.

She should go back to the Royal, where Mitch would expect her to stay, or take a taxi to the Tahara-a International Hotel, even further from the quay. Not the Scott, above the raucous bar. And above *Xanadu*.

She kept going.

She entered the rickety lobby, approached the high wooden desk, and asked the French lady behind it for a room. Her voice quavered. The old lady looked at her sharply. There was a great mulling of reservation cards, shuffling of papers, and a few more birdlike glances while the old girl tried to decide why she was here.

"You were once of the yachts?" she asked finally.

Lindy nodded. She was awarded a room with a porch. "And you will see, it is not far from the bath, *n'est-ce pas?*"

The room was immense and smelled of sweat, wicker, and old wood. A ceiling fan creaked nervously. The bed had mosquito netting draped over it. There was no breeze at all from the porch. The gangplanks wailed across the street. A Vespa stuttered by below.

She bathed and went back to the room and wrapped herself in an orange *pareu*. She stepped to the porch. Her heart was thumping, and her hands were numb.

His boat was there, but maybe he was back in the Marquesas or had flown to Moorea or France. Because she could not bear to find out, she looked past the boats, across the harbor, out at la Grande Passe. Spray was vomiting high above the reef with every swell.

Finally, she looked down at *Xanadu*. Taarii was topside, doubling her lines. Something was brewing, in the skies, or somewhere. *Xanadu,* with her massive scantlings, would be the last boat in the harbor to worry. She hoped whatever it was would miss Bora Bora.

If Taarii looked up, OK, but she refused to call out. He secured his lines and started below. Opening the hatch, he glanced idly across the street. She waved. He looked startled, called below, and in a moment Jean-Paul's head appeared. From fifty yards, she was sure she could see the blue of his eyes in the shadow.

Her legs turned weak. She turned away so that she would not have to watch him cross the street. His footsteps on the creaky stairs started her hands trembling. They were shaking so badly by the time he tapped at the door that she could hardly turn the old brass knob.

They stood facing each other for a moment. Her eyes filled, and then she was in his arms.

CHAPTER
12

THE STRANGE SLOW SWELL HAD BEEN BUILDING ALL day in the Bora Bora lagoon. It impelled Mitch to row out to *Star of Peace,* still moored to the abandoned seaplane buoy off the Oa Oa dock. He stood sipping New Zealand beer in her great cabin aft while her mate cranked up her ham radio rig.

Graham, the protest vessel's skipper, lounged on his disheveled bunk. He was a bearded young man with calm brown eyes. He was a steady, well-balanced seaman. When the French destroyer had rammed him off Mururoa, instead of abandoning *Star of Peace,* he had organized a collision drill and saved her. But now he seemed indecisive and subtly shaken.

From forward came a shriek and a groan as his ancient bilge pumps began to work. There was a squawk and a whistle from the ham rig. Graham's mate, Dennis, sitting on a crate of Leopard beer empties, jammed earphones on his head and began to make notes. A woman's voice, with a faint Canadian accent, crackled through the static. The Canadian yacht *Golden Dragon* was anchored at Nuku Hiva, 800 miles northeast. She reported mare's tails in the northern sky, a large fifteen-second swell, and a pumping barometer which was hard to average. But she thought it had dropped a tenth of an inch in the last hour. The wind was gusting to thirty knots. *Golden Dragon* was battening down and trying to decide whether to go to sea or stay in Taio Hae Bay.

Mitch spotted a greasy blue *Bowditch* in the bookcase over Graham's bunk. He found in it a table which told him that one tenth of an inch an hour meant that *Golden Dragon* was 100 miles from the eye of the hurricane.

If there *was* a hurricane. The last tropical cyclone to hit French Polynesia was in 1961. Twelve years, almost . . .

"That's the whole problem, isn't it?" complained Graham. "In the Cooks or bloody Fiji, one would know. Here, one can't tell whether to shit or go blind."

Graham slipped from his bunk, moved to a chart table, and plotted a position 100 miles north of Nuku Hiva. From it he sketched a typical southern-latitude hurricane path, southwest, then south. He did not finish the line, but if it recurved east, as hurricanes often did, Bora Bora would sit nicely astride it. Mitch's tongue felt dry.

"The French Navy started it," Dennis decided, popping a beer. "With a nuke, just to get us before we left. The rain will be radioactive and sterilize us all."

Graham flushed. He had seemed unflappable, but now he turned on his mate.

"It's not funny, you know." He drummed his fingers on the chair. "Mitch, if it *is* . . . will you run to sea, or stay?"

Mitch had been about to ask him the same question. Now, obviously, he couldn't: the kid was as confused as he. He felt sorry for him. At least *Linda Lee* was his own, and insured: *Star of Peace,* financed by donation, was a product of years of toil and begging, and the property of the Green Peace Federation. She was not Graham's to lose, and she couldn't possibly be insured: even Lloyd's wouldn't touch her. Graham had women and the little girl, too. If Graham decided to go to sea, they would probably have to stay aboard: Mitch doubted that anyone had funds to fly them to Auckland.

Mitch shook his head dubiously and climbed halfway up the ladder to study the shore. He was looking for signs that the word was out, looking for natives, perhaps, lashing their palm-thatched roofs or boarding up their gaping, paneless homes. There was no activity at all, except for a crowd of people waiting on the Air Polynésie wharf for the ferry to the Tahiti plane. The lagoon, in the afternoon shade of the crags, was like a mirror.

But the swell was still rolling onto Te Avenui Pass, the only way out; rolling much too slowly, with an authority that indicated no mere local storm. He could not see the northern sky, for the crags of Mount Pahia towered above the anchorage. The sky above was clear, but that meant nothing: it might be twelve hours before the *Golden Dragon*'s mare's tails appeared here, and then it would be too late to run.

Forward, a man and a girl, both nude, were seesawing the *Star*'s incredible pump. Since her "collision," Graham said, her bilges filled every four hours at anchor and every hour at sea. Planks had jarred loose and the French hadn't found all the leaks.

But *Star*'s leaks were not her greatest threat, now. Nothing she would hit enroute to New Zealand was likely to match the havoc right here if a typhoon hit. Here were no rivers to hide in, no bights or coves, just the mountains and valleys to anger the winds, and to seaward, low-lying *motus* and sandspits. If you dragged east you'd be hurled high and dry and if you dragged west you'd be splintered on the reefs. If you anchored and tried to ride it out aboard, no one could help you. A true sailor, if he had the guts, would probably head for open water while there was time.

If he had the guts. And valued the boat more than his life. Mitch looked at *Linda Lee,* swinging at the dock. He stepped back down.

" 'It is pleasant,' " he quoted, " 'when the sea is high and the winds are dashing the waves about, to watch from shore the struggles of another.' So said Lucretius. So say I."

"You'll stay."

"I'll leave the dock and put down every anchor I've got, and tie down the wheel. Then I'll row ashore and lash myself to a barstool and get drunk with Hans."

"You've been *in* one?" asked Graham.

Mitch shook his head.

"Well, I have," Graham murmured. "I got a yawl out of Suva for Cyclone Bebe. So she hit me dead on. Thought I'd never bloody run to sea again."

"That's what I mean," said Mitch.

"Until," added Graham sweetly, "I got back and saw Suva."

The pump creaked and the hull moaned. There seemed nothing more to say. "Thank you, Graham," muttered Mitch. He rowed ashore and helped Hans, the hotel owner, board up the Oa Oa bar. The gendarme jeeped up with a hurricane warning. Hans, a nervous, sharp-eyed Swiss-American, begged Mitch to leave the dock by noon tomorrow. Apparently he didn't want *Linda Lee* as a decoration in his lobby. They had a beer at the darkened bar and Mitch stepped aboard.

It was becoming very muggy. He was jittery and couldn't decide where to start lashing things down. He got everything moveable below. Topside, he secured everything but the dinghy, which he'd need to row back to shore, after he'd anchored. He removed his dorade scoops and screwed bronze plates in the holes they left. He doubled his lines for the night, although there wasn't a ripple on the lagoon or a cloud in the sky, and battened the skylight hatch.

He poured a drink below and tuned the Zenith to WWV out of Hawaii. The cyclone had just been christened Arlene. WWV placed its center west of the Marquesas. He wondered if *Golden Dragon* had finally put to sea.

Arlene was still an infant. Her winds were only sixty knots near her center, and she was crawling baby-like at eight knots, already too fast to outrun, but nothing to what she'd do if she matured.

WWV gave her predicted position. Six hours from now she would pass north of Takarava. He wondered how Louie's mother and the chief and the old pearl diver were preparing. A healthy hurricane wave, it seemed to him, could sweep the atoll bare.

Idly, he plotted the curve and extended it. It passed north of Tahiti but very nearly bisected Bora Bora. He erased the line. Cyclones were unpredictable, and there was no use showing this one the way.

He was glad he had not gone to Papeete to meet Lindy, as he'd planned before he began to worry about the swells. Unless Pan Am had held at Honolulu, she was at the Royal Papeete tonight. He walked to the Bureau de Poste. The postmaster was hammering boards over his windows. Mitch got him to send a cable to the Royal, telling Lindy to stay where she was.

He would rather have her in Papeete than here when the shit hit the fan.

She awakened to the midnight clang of the bell from Temple Paofai two blocks east. Jean-Paul was not in the bed. The mosquito netting stirred in a moist little gust, and then fell limp. The fan had stopped: Papeete power came and went at will. Voices sounded from the quay. She heard an anchor chain groaning as someone began to winch it up.

Then she saw him on the porch, silhouetted against the stars. She got up, drowsily, tucked a *pareu* around herself and padded out. He put an arm around her waist and drew her close. She went soft inside.

"The stars," he said. "Have you seen this before?"

She had not. They shone with a brilliance that seemed alive. She was surprised. From what he had told her last night, she would have thought that the skies would be cloudy.

"The pressure, I think, rises a little, the better to drop after. Therefore the clarity, stars like jewels . . ."

He pointed out Antares, and told her how the ancient Polynesians must have used it to navigate. But now she was fully awake, and her mind jumped to Mitch, alone with the boat.

"Is he OK at Bora Bora?" she asked.

He shrugged. "He is *homme formidable*. I think he would not fear to run to sea."

"*Run to sea?* Without me? I'd kill him!"

He looked into her eyes. "You must *not* run to sea. You *need* not run. The boat need not run." He told her of a shelter at Bora Bora, blasted into coral during the war by the Seabees, a haven against hurricane, Japanese shelling, or a passing German raider. It was big enough for a single PT boat. Or a yacht. Two meters deep, quite square, like all things *militaire*. "There are rings for lines set within the coral—"

"He's probably snugged in there now, having a beer with the local chief," she said.

He thought not. The natives would not tell him it was there. Perhaps the gendarme or Hans at the hotel, if they thought of it, but not the natives. For like all true warriors, the Seabees had ignored local protests and blasted it next to a *marae,* a *marae* most *sacre,* a kilometer south of the village in Baie Faanui. "Bad luck, the people think, to tie in there. It is too close to their burial ground. I think so also." He spread his hands. "But it is worse luck, certainly, to have to run to sea. In any case, there it is." He smiled into her eyes. *"Ma chérie?"*

"Yes?"

"I also have a boat, you know. With no engine. And there is just enough breeze for the pass."

"You're going to sea?"

He nodded. "Papeete Harbor I do not trust. Too many other boats, and too shallow, and the reefs. Listen?"

He inclined his head toward the yachts. She looked down the line of them. There were flashlights probing everywhere. She could hear voices from the new American sloop; someone was calling Louie. The swell was too high. They were all getting ready to leave the danger of the seawall. She imagined that some would run for it and some would anchor across the harbor in the lee of the Motu Uta docks. She heard a diesel engine start below, and then another.

La Grande Passe thundered at long, slow intervals. She could see plumes of greenish phosphorescence spilling over the reef past Quai au Long Cours.

"Lindy, this, tonight, with us, I knew it must happen, and you must not have bad feelings, for then it would ruin it all."

"You *knew?* I didn't."

He looked out at the harbor and smiled. "Nothing is a secret in these islands. The girl, Tiare, in l'Hôpital at Nuka Hiva, she has told me that *délirant*—when you had the delirium—you spoke of me. And it is strange, but I had already taken steps, of which you could know nothing—"

She told him that she knew about his message to the doctor, and of how far he had walked to try to get it through.

He looked embarrassed. "And of course, you do not believe in the coconut radio, so—"

"*I* believe," she said. "Where you and I are concerned, I believe."

He kissed her goodbye. She watched him cross the street. In ten minutes Taarii had winched him out to his bow-anchor. They hoisted sail easily and quickly. By the time the boats with engines had finally vacated the seawall, she could see him ghosting toward the pass. She lost his silhouette against a ship by Quai au Long Cours, but she caught it against the entrance beacon once, and then he was gone.

She crawled back under the mosquito netting and drifted into sleep.

He awakened jumpy and tired at 5 A.M. He had slept hardly at all. All night *Linda Lee* had tugged and creaked at the rotting pilings of the dock, whining for sea-room before she was caught.

The barometer, to his surprise, was high. He began to log its readings. But by six the pressure was pumping oddly, rising and falling a few hundredths of an inch almost before his eyes. He could see, above the peaks, hints of the *Golden Dragon*'s *mare's tails,*

brushstrokes converging like a great golden arrow toward the northeast. By seven the pressure was falling
steadily. At nine, it was four-hundredths of an inch
under his eight o'clock reading. WWV located Arlene a
hundred miles north of Tahiti, which it would apparently miss. Her winds were seventy knots, force
twelve. She was two hundred miles northeast of him,
and moving at fourteen knots. She had recurved. Unless she recurved again, she would hit Bora Bora in
less than twenty-four hours.

He made ready to cast off from the pier. He had the
vague intention of rounding the point and trying to find
holding ground in Faanui Bay. With storm anchors
down and all his chain out, he would stay aboard until
things got too rough. Then, if he had to, he could let
her fend for herself and try to row into Faanui Village.

The humidity rose with the sun. He had been plotting
the center every hour, using WWV. Now he shifted,
trying to follow the staccato French on Radio Mahina.
He assumed that the French had a hurricane plane following the storm, and that the location of the center
was quite accurate.

When he plotted Arlene at 10 A.M., his hand was
so slippery with the high humidity, or with fear, that he
dropped his pencil. He stepped topside to cool off. The
Star of Peace was pulling in, short on her buoy, apparently ready to move to better shelter or to sea. He
was afraid that if he rowed out to ask he might be
caught by the first gusts.

He surveyed the sky. The cirro-cumulus above
Mount Pahia had disintegrated into tangled strands,
like hair that needed combing. Far down the corridor of
clouds he could see a veil of alto-stratus.

He stepped below again and looked around. Everything seemed stowed, but there were things left undone.
He had always intended to secure the hundreds of little

blocks of pig-lead in her bilges, carried as additional ballast to ease her roll. There was a ton and a half of it, in three-inch-square pigs, packed tightly for enormous seas but not tightly enough for a knock-down. If a wave in the lagoon knocked her upside-down, the pigs would become four-pound projectiles, rocketing around the overturned cabin; when she righted herself she would be a shambles. It was too late to drill and screw down her floorboards, which came up, at a touch, for inspection. He could hammer nails through the varnished teak-and-holly, or let it go.

It was too hot to tear the boat apart looking for nails. And he was too jumpy to take time to try. Besides, the floor boards were too pretty.

He let it go.

She stood at the Air Polynésie counter at Tahiti International. The flight to Bora Bora had been canceled, put on again, canceled once more, and was now on the verge of leaving, but the little seven-passenger aircraft had not yet left the hangar.

It was hot and very sultry. Departing passengers for Huahine and Bora Bora were jittery. So was the girl at the counter. There was an un-Polynesian air of tension in the place. An easygoing young pilot Lindy had seen before, on the quay and at the Vaima, was berating a Tahitian mechanic in angry French: the mechanic glared at him, spun on his heel and stalked away.

Suddenly the flight was on and everyone piled in. She crawled into the seat behind the captain. His white shirt was soaked with sweat.

There was a sudden stir at the counter. Startled, she saw little black Louie race across the concrete. He was barefooted, and in his hand he held a ticket. They opened the door and let him in. He took the last seat, behind her.

She turned, curiously. *"Bonjour,* Louie."

His wizened little face froze. His aged eyes regarded her. They were full of contempt. Shocked, she stuttered: "Where are you going, anyway?"

"I go to help my father. And why *you* h'ask?"

Astonished, she turned back. She tried to lose herself in the beauty of the flight, down the chain of the Iles Sous le Vent: Moorea, Huahine, Raiatea, and finally the pristine beauty of Bora Bora itself, rising to threatening clouds. But she could not relax with the ebony eyes drilling the back of her head. On the little ferry across the lagoon, she sat forward on a wooden bench staring out at the glassy gray water, but she felt him glaring at her through the door at the stern, where he stood at the helmsman's elbow.

At the Air Polynésie dock, she found a van from the Hotel Bora Bora, meeting nonexistent guests. The driver would be glad to drop her at the Oa Oa.

A hundred yards down the road, they passed Louie. Her impulse was to ask the driver to pick him up, but she conquered it.

Let the little bastard walk to hell and gone.

Linda Lee tugged at the dock in a sudden gust of wind. Mitch stepped topside for perhaps the tenth time that hour, to look at the sky. Clouds to the north were sagging full-bellied over the peaks. Hans was on the wharf, obviously wondering when Mitch was going to clear his dock. The water, Hans said, was heaving like an excited virgin's breasts. "Here I think it is my hotel going to get screwed." He jerked his thumb at the slope. "When you row back in, you will find me a thousand meters up that hill."

Mitch was casting off when he heard Lindy's voice. He cleated the line and looked up. She was lugging her suitcase, two-handed, across the Oa Oa lawn, with her long bronze hair swaying and her fine legs swinging. He had not known how much he missed her. He shut off the engine, jumped ashore, and took her in his arms. He kissed her and looked into her face. She was tired. Below, she told him about her father, and why she had come back so soon.

"Honey," he scolded her, "this thing's *missing* Tahiti! And heading here. Didn't you get my cable?"

Her eyes dropped. Something about it jarred him. She looked up and said: "I *had* to come. Mitch, there's a hole here! A hurricane-hole!"

Sitting on the port settee, she almost gagged on the coffee he had made. She was sick with guilt. She'd told him the first lie in years. No, it was worse than a good old-fashioned lie: a lie took guts. He leaned on the navigation table and ran his pencil along the Bora Bora chart looking for Jean-Paul's hole.

While she was gone, he had apparently rented a Vespa and putt-putted around the island. Now, he thought he recalled glimpsing the pen behind palms, by the ancient marae. He had assumed that the notch was simply a coral-quarry, cut to repair the coastal road, too shallow for *Linda Lee*.

"I'll double-up lines to the coconut trees, bow and stern, and run breastlines—"

"We," she said weakly. "I'm back."

He studied her for a moment. "OK." He straightened, stretching exultantly. "That lovely, blue-eyed sonofabitch has saved our boat."

"He went to sea to get out of the harbor," she said. "I hope he saves his own."

The boat trembled to a gust. She heard footsteps creaking along the dock, and bare feet padding aboard. Mitch did not seem to notice and stayed at the chart table studying the line of the lagoon. A shadow fell across the open hatch above him, and Louie appeared. His hard black eyes challenged her for an instant, turned to Mitch.

" 'Allo, my captain," he said. "I have come for 'elp you for cyclone. I show you through the reef, OK?"

Mitch seemed surprised but, as always lately with Louie, curiously quite cool. "You didn't come down for *that?*"

"I sell camera, yes, for *that!*"

"We're not going through the reef, and you're not going anywhere. Not with us." He turned to Lindy and told her, after six months, that Louie's last thanks to her had been an insult.

Her heart began to hammer. She saw it all, now, the truth approaching like the hurricane. Her cheeks went hot and her hands went cold. She tried to beat Louie to the punch, but her throat was so tight that nothing came out.

"*I* will 'elp you. She is bad womans." The little black boy drew himself to his full height on the companionway steps. " 'Ees right, what I say before."

"Get lost," grated Mitch. He took a step toward Louie and jerked his thumb to the hatch. "Now!"

Louie's eyes bulged with fright, but he stood his ground. "*Non!* She is *bad!* Las' night—" His lips clenched, and his eyes filled with tears.

Mitch grabbed a skinny thigh as the child looked down at them from the steps. "Last night, *what?*" he growled.

The little boy stiffened. "With the *hoopipi* of the steel boat . . ." He made a circle of his thumb and forefinger and thrust his middle finger through it. "*Dans l'Hôtel Scott!*"

Mitch moved swiftly. He lifted the child and was up through the hatch in a flash. She lunged after them, and was barely topside as he reached the rail. He lifted

Louie overhead to hurl him to the water astern. She got
his arm.

"No!" she yelled into his ear. "Damn it! Mitch, it's
true!"

Mitch froze. Slowly he lowered Louie. Louie leaped
to the dock and turned. His face contorted. "Bad
woman!" he screamed. Mitch moved and Louie ran.

"So," muttered Mitch dully, "you didn't *get* the
cable?"

She shook her head. "No Royal Papeete," she murmured. "No cable. Mitch, I would have told you!"

"And *that* we'll never know." He stepped forward,
started the engine, and tossed off the sternline. Hans
came down from the bar and threw aboard their bow-
line. For a moment *Linda Lee* was pressed against the
dock by a cool hard gust from Mont Pahia. The bumpers squealed. He ordered Lindy ashore.

"I'm staying. To help tie her up." She grasped the
mizzen firmly.

"I'm not *going*," he said softly, "to his goddamn pen.
You know that, don't you?"

"Why not?" she begged.

"The *rent's* too fucking high."

She stayed aboard. If he wanted to anchor out, she
would take her chances too. He slammed the gearshift
viciously into reverse. The engine, still cold, screamed
in protest. He backed off, ignoring Hans waving goodby
from the dock and Louie watching from the road.

They charged full forward, full left rudder, vomiting
smoke. The stern shaved the dock by inches. *Star of
Peace* had left her mooring, heading for the pass.
Mitch, churning the lagoon at full power, overtook her
in half a mile. He cut his throttle, drew close, and yelled
to Graham at the wheel. When he was through, Jean-
Paul's hurricane-hole was lost to *Linda Lee*. *Star of*

Peace sheered off, turned back, and headed for Faanui Bay.

Lindy waited for Mitch to head for an anchorage and drop a hook. But the bow stayed granite-steady on the pass. And the seas were pounding the reef in huge, onrushing walls that spilled into the lagoon like water over a shattered dam. One out of three rollers broke in the channel itself. A mile short of the entrance she could already feel the heave.

"Mitch?" she cried, grabbing his arm.

"Sea room," he said tonelessly. His eyes were unreadable. "Shall I take you back?" She shook her head and he gently removed her hand.

At last she felt that she could cry, but she was damned if she would.

PART III

Day

CHAPTER
1

HE DREAMED THAT HE THREW THE CAT OVERBOARD. He felt himself pitching forward over the glowing binnacle light. He snapped awake. He checked his compass heading and found it had drifted ten degrees off while he dozed. He heard the clock chime once, and for a moment could not remember whether it was a half-hour past midnight or a half-hour past four. He glanced at his watch. Four-thirty. He had been on his feet or aloft and searching for over twenty-five hours. He quickly checked the eastern horizon for the first faint hint of dawn.

It was still pitch-black to the east. He did not know whether to be sorry or glad. He was still afraid that the strobe was out, or had sunk, or was simply too far away to see, and yet he kept hoping for it, as a marker if nothing else. Soon it would be too light.

The cat was glaring at him from the hatch, mewing. So at least he hadn't drowned it in his sleep. It was

307

probably starved, as he was; he could not remember
whether he had fed it yesterday, or had only intended
to.

He sent it a mental warning: you are not out of danger yet. If you think I am going to stop while I crack a
can of catfood, you're out of your silly mind. Then he
repeated the message, aloud, too loudly, in English and
French. The cat only complained more angrily. He
lunged at it, to scare it into silence. It stalked below.

To stay awake, he began to lay plans. With daylight,
Bernie's emergency radio would become potentially
useful again, as the Tahiti-Bora Bora flights began. He
had lashed the transmitter to the spreader, for elevation, and left it on all night. If the beacon was any
good, and if the pilots bothered to guard the emergency
frequency, he might well have a plane homing on him
by dawn. There might, too, be French Navy patrols
aloft on training flights out from Tahiti.

He searched for a plan to communicate, assuming
the plane slipped down to investigate. He had used up
his flares on the *bonnitier,* and the man-overboard flag
was waving from its pole somewhere in the waters sur-
rounding him, but he could hoist the national ensign,
upside-down, to buttress the signal from Bernie's transmitter.

At dawn, he would do that, while the cat saluted.

He found himself giggling. His laughter woke him
up again. He was losing his marbles, and he had somehow to hang on until dawn.

He swept the horizon. He could see a faint paling of
the eastern sky.

He tensed. He thought he had caught a distant flash
off the port bow. He dropped the wheel, rushed forward, and began to climb the mast. *Linda Lee* wobbled
off course, so that suddenly he did not know where to

look. He should have taken a compass bearing immediately.

Halfway up the mast, he paused. He had seen it again, a momentary gleam reflected on the belly of a cloud somewhere over the eastern horizon, somewhere on his port bow, infinitely distant, impossible to pinpoint, but there. He returned to the wheel, heart pounding.

Just one more flash, he begged, *just once more . . .*

He came left until he thought he was on course for it.

In five minutes the eastern sky had gone gray with morning twilight.

He stayed on course for where he thought he'd seen the flash: He did not see it again. Perhaps he'd only imagined it.

She kept drifting in the dark between trance and consciousness, and each time she returned from the void she would find herself half under the horseshoe buoy, slipping into the deep. Her jacket was pulling her down. If she managed to get it off, which seemed a tremendous effort, then she would be lighter.

She wanted to shed it, but there must be reasons why she should not. Soggy or not, it was conserving body heat, and she was very, very cold. Also, it was orange, and if she made it until daylight, it could help him spot her. Also . . . There was something else—what?

The whistle. She'd thought through that before. It was tied to the zipper, and she'd lose it.

Her whole world had compressed to the flash of the strobe on the neighboring waters. Her boundaries were herself, the yellow horseshoe, and the scruffy line that led to the man-overboard pole nodding and bobbing twenty feet away.

Her horizon was the crest of whatever watery depression she happened to be in when the strobe decided to fire. She had lost the stars and the sense of infinity she had known before she found the buoy; the instant she had touched the horseshoe she had traded vision for security.

She no longer looked for the dawn. She had no sense, even, of which way was east. From the botton of the swells, she could see the man-overboard flag silhouetted against a creamy sky, but she hardly even noticed.

The strobe seemed weaker.

But it was not. It was competing with the morning light. Soon the sun burst over the eastern horizon, upstaging the strobe so mightily that, though it was flashing two feet from her head, she forgot it was there.

She was not sure, but she thought she had been in the water for over twenty-four hours.

CHAPTER

2

GUSTS FROM MOUNT PAHIA RACED AFTER THEM across the Bora Bora lagoon. She ignored the wind. She stood in the cockpit clutching the mizzenmast, hypnotized by the surf in the pass. She still wore a dress, from the flight, but did not dare go below to change. If he entered the pass they would be hurled back, like a toy boat in a bathtub, perhaps overturned. She did not want to be trapped below.

She could not take her eyes off the entrance. Each swell began imperceptibly to rise far at sea, beyond the mouth of the channel. The interval between swells seemed interminable, but their speed of travel astonished her.

A new one stirred near Maupiti, last of the Leeward Islands, just breaking the horizon twenty miles beyond the pass. It crawled at first, gathering speed as it came. It felt coral below. Surprised, it reared. It hung suspended for an eternity. Then it pounced. The boom was visceral; it drummed into her gut before she heard it with her ears. The caldron it left on the reef spilled off. Another swell rolled in from the west.

They were half a mile short of the channel when a strong flurry from Mount Pahia heeled them and turned the lagoon into a froth of white. Mitch spun the boat around, bow to the wind. For a moment she hoped that he had given up. Instead, he hoisted the sail. Then he strode forward and raised the jib. She was grabbing the wheel to steady the boat when he dropped back into the cockpit, secured the jib, and took the helm without a word. He turned west, and once again they were headed for the pass.

She searched for something that would save them. She had refused to go back once. What if she offered now? By the time he dropped her off, the swell might rise so high that he would have to stay too. She glanced back, across the wind-torn lagoon. *Star of Peace,* under bare poles, was heeled mightily, rounding the point into Faanui Bay, heading for the hole. Behind the Oa Oa dock, a thatched roof rose from one of Hans' cottages, hovered over the lawn, and crashed headlong near the wharf.

It was too late to make the dock, and it would soon be too late to anchor safely. Besides, no matter how high the surf in the pass, he might choose to leave without her anyway. In twenty years, she had learned nothing that would help her judge his present mood.

She turned and faced him. "Is it to punish me, or what?"

He left the wheel, and handed her her safety belt. "Get it on," he said, cinching his own and snapping it to a shroud. Reluctantly, she clicked on the belt and took a turn around the mizzenmast. There was no question of going forward, as she usually did on leaving a pass: when they foundered in the surf, she wanted to be here, with him.

Two hundred yards from the entrance, passing a little *motu,* they plowed into white water from the last breaker. Feeling undertow, the boat slewed to port and picked up speed. The throb of the engine quickened. Under full power, with jib and mizzen set to angry gusts from the peaks behind, they rushed toward the pass. There was nothing to do now but hang on.

Linda Lee rose to the incoming surge. The first swell stopped them cold. They climbed, dead in the water. To either side the big blue mountains hung curled over the reef. The combers fell, first to port and then to starboard, in twin booming bellows of rage.

A central crest remained. *Linda Lee* hung tottering on it, her propeller flailing air. Her engine oversped and roared in agony. Then she was sliding down the reverse side of the swell, sails flapping as they fell into the lee of the wave, engine slowing as the propeller felt water again.

The sides of the pass inched astern, far too slowly. When the next wave broke, she was sure they would be trapped in midchannel. She could see it growing now, far at sea. It seemed bigger than the last. She found herself straining against her belt, spurring the boat onward with her toes. The oncoming swell jarred them, stopping them dead again, and *Linda Lee* threw her bow up, her stern down, and shuddered. She lost way. Mitch muttered, "Shit!" He tested the wheel for control, spinning it first to starboard, then to port. If the bow fell off either way, they would tumble broadside to the comber, and never survive the roll.

A cold gust of wind filled the jib. The boat came alive and climbed for the rim. The wave broke under them and they slid down the reverse slope. To seaward the next swell was gathering.

Linda Lee climbed that one too. It broke under them, precisely when they were cresting it. They balanced for an instant, and then the bow went down, the breaker crashed harmlessly in the entrance behind them, and they slid out of the pass.

So far as she knew, they were free of land. Maupiti, ahead of them, she could still safely see. Nothing else this side of Rarotonga in the Cooks, 500 miles to the southwest, could hurt them.

The hurricane she thought of as an overgrown gale. Andy Dugan had survived a gale on *Linda Lee* already.

She went below to change.

At the dock he had been numb with shock. The need for action in the pass had saved him from thinking. Now, temporarily out of danger, he groped for things to be done, looking for refuge from pain.

Behind them, a fine mist, untropical and northern-looking, was suddenly obscuring Mount Pahia and the crags. Bora Bora had been safety, for themselves if not the boat, and there was no way to re-enter the pass now. A thrill of fear elbowed the agony further aside.

The filmy scud astern was overtaking him. Ahead, under fat-cheeked stratus, he could see Maupiti, like a small streamlined battleship on the far horizon. It would soon be lost. He took a bearing so that he could avoid it when it disappeared. He caught a stinging slap of spray across his face. The wind had shifted dead south, opposing the swell, and the seas were rising. He set Irwin to leave Maupiti to starboard.

He let out the sails. *Linda Lee* began to gallop at six knots, under jib and mizzen. He wanted all the distance from Bora Bora, and Maupiti too, that he could earn before the wall of the cyclone hit.

A fine drizzle began. He went below to put on oil-

skins and see when the center would catch him. Lindy
was forward, changing. He surveyed the cabin. All he
had been able to lash down was secure. The hidden
lead ballast he put from his mind.

He tuned in Mahina Radio. Arlene had passed 120
miles north of Tahiti. Swells were *gigantesques* in
Papeete Harbor and there were gale winds at the airport. Satellite pictures put Arlene now fifty miles
northeast of Huahine. She was moving at eighteen
knots, three times their own speed. She seemed still to
have Bora Bora dead in her sights.

Lindy lurched from the forward compartment. She
wore torn cut-offs. She looked sick. She had apparently
lost her sea legs. She clutched a handrail against the
roll. She seemed exhausted, but calm. He suspected
that she thought of what was coming as simply another
storm. Well, he had tried to leave her behind . . .

"Mitch," she said, "you'll have to talk to me, you
know. I'm *here!*"

He studied her face in the gloom of the skylight.
There were tiny lines at her eyes that he had hardly
noticed before. But she was beautiful as ever. If only
he had gone to California, or to Tahiti to meet her, or
had shown more balls in Nuku Hiva or Papeete when
the danger-flags were flying, if only the fucking
Frenchman had run a day early for sea room . . .

The hell with that! It was not his own fault or Jean-
Paul's, or the cyclone's. It was hers.

"Get some sleep," he said. "You're tired."

"Meaning?" she flared.

"Meaning," he blurted, "you didn't get much last
night."

Predictably, her eyes grew wet. Let them. "You're
going to need your rest," he persisted. "I mean it.
Now!"

She crawled into bunk, turned her face away, and

was still. There was no reason, damn it, to comfort her, or time, even if he were flabby enough to try.

A drumroll of raindrops rattled the skylight. He would have to go topside to relieve Irwin before the vane was hurt. But he found himself delaying the move, leafing through *Bowditch,* for *Tropical Hurricanes.*

The wind and seas they would strike depended on which of Arlene's faces they would see. Her gentler, right-hand side would probably be lethal enough. But it would have gales forty knots less than her left side, the "dangerous semicircle," where her speed of advance would add to the speed of her winds.

The clue lay in the trend of the wind topside. If it shifted counterclockwise, in these latitudes, he was already on her dangerous side.

He closed the book. It was time to go up and find out.

He tugged on his sea-boots, snapped on a southwester for the first time since the California coast, and climbed the companionway ladder. A warm, heavy wind greeted him. Its direction was difficult to judge. It was backing and veering, gusting and easing. But it had been southeast when he went below, and he was very much afraid that it was more easterly now. Counterclockwise. They were in the dangerous semicircle. He looked north, toward Bora Bora.

They had floundered, so far, less than ten miles southeast, but Mount Pahia was already a blurred dark shadow flirting with him from behind a veil of fast-moving scud. The curtain lifted momentarily. "Oh, Jesus," he breathed.

Far past the island, on the northeast horizon, lay a great black mass. It seemed immovable, as if a new continent were growing there. Tiny flashes of orange lightning played against the velvet backdrop.

It was the bar of the cyclone, and behind it lay

Alrene's eye. He was twenty or thirty miles from the wall of clouds, but the sky above him seemed already to be darkening. He glanced at his watch. Just past noon.

He shortened the mizzen sail. Lines he had readied for warps were already tied in coils. An old Vespa tire for a drogue was lashed by the dinghy. The sea-anchor was ready. Airscoops were stowed below. He thanked God that he had not changed Andrew Dugan's thick little portholes, all dogged tightly, for the windows Lindy had wanted.

He stuck his head below. She was still on the bunk, apparently asleep. Again he remembered the little cubes of lead sleeping below the floorboards. He detached Irwin's vane and tossed it below; they could stow it later. He closed the hatch.

A twelve-foot wave gathered itself from somewhere astern, crested aboard, and slapped his face.

He glanced back at Arlene's black heart.

"Bitch!" he yelled at it. It made him feel better.

He took the wheel. From now on it was him and Arlene.

CHAPTER
3

HE STEERED INTO THE DAZZLE OF THE MORNING SUN, powering at three knots. This was his first daylight sweep, since he'd found the boat's logbook, of the area she must be in. The flash to the east at dawn must have been a hallucination, like the elves around the binnacle light, for he had been steering east ever since, and had seen nothing.

Then where the hell *was* the strobe? The absence of the other flotsam he understood. Pillows, life jackets, bunk mattresses, and cockpit cushions were light, high out of the water, and would quickly have sailed downwind. But not the man-overboard gear: a little nylon drogue attached to the buoy was supposed to hold it against the drift. Besides, the strobe light was heavy and low in the water and would itself resist the tug of the wind; the whole conglomeration—buoy, pole, and strobe—was supposed to stay put; that was why you carried it in the first place.

He had dropped it very near her, according to the log. She must have found it. She must be clinging to it now.

If she lived . . .

His eyes blurred with tears. He snapped alert at a squeal from below. His heart almost stopped. The cat? No, Jesus, the rat! Hunger must have hyped the cat into action. He heard a scuffle, the crash of a metal pot, a scratching of claws against varnish. He moved forward and peered down the hatch, but after the morning sun in his eyes, everything below was pitch black.

Screw it. He wished the rat well and the cat bad luck. He wouldn't stop the search to help; he didn't intend to miss searching a square inch of water.

The trades were rising. There were approaching squalls on the eastern horizon that he did not like, there were always squalls somewhere. He was intent on them when he heard an engine.

He tensed, wheeled, and looked aft. He saw nothing. The throbbing blended with the rumble of *Linda Lee*'s diesel. He throttled back, then cut his motor entirely. He searched again astern.

Dead aft, perhaps ten or fifteen miles away, he spotted a tiny silver dot, an aircraft at four thousand or five thousand feet. It seemed to stop, as if banking toward him, or away. A flash of morning sunlight, as if from an upturned wing, flicked his eyes.

He dove into the aft compartment for the Stars and Stripes. He hoisted the flag on the starboard yardarm, upside down, and clambered halfway up the shrouds. When he turned and found the plane again, it seemed to have turned back to its course, ignoring him.

He screamed, waved wildly, almost fell off, caught himself, and began to yell again. As if it heard him, the plane turned back, wavered indecisively, turned away and continued again on its original course. It was a twin-engined turboprop, and he could hear the beat of its power plants, just a little out of synch, humming to the northwest. He begged it to change its mind, to turn, to take another look into the path of the morning sun . . .

It turned toward him again, this time without hesitation. The pilot, or someone, had spotted him. It approached swiftly, descending. It passed him in a whoosh of wind, very, very closely. He glimpsed the pilot, a blond hatless young man, and, staring from the left-hand portholes, passengers craning to see. The plane climbed with a throb of quiet power, circled, and made another pass.

Mitch swept his arm around the horizon, pantomiming search. *Start looking, damn you. Start!*

Instead, the pilot drew a wing aloft and returned once again, nose high and very slow. When the aircraft was ghosting along at eye level, fifty feet from Mitch, the pilot pointed to his microphone, then southeast toward Tahiti, and banked northwest to Bora Bora.

"No!" yelled Mitch. "No, you son of a bitch! Search *yourself.*"

He watched the plane climb, wiggling its wings, and finally disappear in the haze to the west. He descended the shrouds slowly. The plane probably had fuel only for Bora Bora and return, and that was it. But at least the word was out, someone knew, and soon he would see the French Navy.

He went below to turn up the radio. He stopped, aghast. There was blood on the galley lockers, pools of it on the galley deck, broken glass from a whiskey decanter, and a pot upturned on the stove. M. le Chat glared up at him from over the body of the biggest copra rat Mitch had ever seen. The cat worried it into a corner and faced Mitch defiantly. Grimacing, Mitch picked up the body by the tail. It weighed at least a pound. He hurled it through the hatch and heard it splash impressively. The cat regarded him with pure hatred.

"Good boy," said Mitch, too late. If luck aboard *Linda Lee* was changing, he had been a fool to frustrate it. "*Bon chat!*" he said again. He promised to feed it soon. He was not forgiven. The cat stalked forward to sulk on Lindy's bunk.

He called Papeete Radio, in case the pilot's report had already filtered through and triggered action there. He got no answer. He was, apparently, still blocked by Moorea. He left the volume high and went topside.

He continued to search and waited for help.

CHAPTER
4

SHE AWAKENED CRASHING TO THE CABIN FLOOR. FOR
an instant she could not recall where she was. She was
suddenly rolled across the passageway to the foot of the
port bunk, bruising her elbow. A pillow fell on her face.
"Mitch!" she yelled.

There was no answer from topside. She sat up. A
dim light filtered through the skylight, as if it were already twilight, but time was out of kilter, it must still be
early in the afternoon. Bracing herself against the horrible roll, she struggled to her knees and flicked on the
reading light above the starboard bunk. It was 2:40 on
the bulkhead clock.

She regarded the cabin. Pillows and sleeping bags
had fallen. A chart table drawer had come open, spilling pencils, charts, rulers and old logbooks across the
galley floor. A locker to port banged open, closed, and
banged open again. She slammed it and made her way
aft. The hatch seemed jammed.

She tugged at it ineffectually. She was very weak, and afraid that she was going to be seasick. She yanked at the hatch two-handed, and it still did not budge. She felt a tug of claustrophobia. He had locked it. But suppose something happened to him, up there, and she could not get out to help? Stupid, stupid. He was losing his common sense. She pounded on the bottom of the hatch. She stopped to listen.

She was suddenly aware of creaks and groans and strains she had never heard. *Linda Lee* slewed wildly to port, as if there were no hand on the wheel. The motion hurled her across the galley. Panicked, she screamed for Mitch and began to bang on the companionway hatchboards with a pot from the stove.

Finally she heard an answering thump, and the bolt slid back. To a shriek of wind from topside, the hatch opened six inches. Mitch's face appeared, very close to the crack. She had a sense of unreality. She could hardly believe today, let alone last night. And if she did not get some air, quickly, she would be sick all over the galley.

"Let me up!" she demanded.

"We're in it," he said tersely. "But just on the edges. It's going to get worse. Stay put!"

"I'm going to be sick," she said. "Open the hatch!"

"Get your gear on first." He slammed the hatch again. She reached into the foul-weather locker. It had been so long since she had had to wear her slickers that she had trouble with the snaps. By the time she got everything on she was exhausted, and so nauseous she could hardly make it up the ladder. She banged on the hatch. He yanked it open, pulled her through, and slammed it again as a fifteen foot wave crested the stern, swarmed over the stern rail, and hit the hatch in a shower of spray. She felt salt water trickling down her neck.

He snapped her safety belt around the mizzen mast and she crawled blindly for the leeward side, where he held to the belt while she was very sick for a very long time. When she finally got off her knees and turned to sit in the cockpit she could not believe her eyes.

He had somehow, while she slept, crept forward and set their smallest storm-jib. It had never been hoisted before, except once for drill in San Francisco Bay. He had shortened the mizzen sail, too, and lashed the wheel. They were hove-to on a port tack. His feat was impressive but, she thought, futile. They were inching through the most enormous seas she had ever seen and slipping to leeward like skiers in a turn.

She looked around. There was no sun or even any sky. They were trapped like insects under a shallow, dark-gray bowl. The scud hurtling by above her seemed low enough to touch. But there seemed for a moment hardly enough wind to drive them to leeward so fast.

And then the sound of it came, a quiet, humming from aloft. At first she could not believe it was their rigging, it was so melodious. The note rose and fell and rose in pitch again. A giant swell off their port bow rose in a pyramid, and suddenly the top one-third was ripped loose, flying toward them in a stinging hail of salt. She ducked too late. Her cheeks felt as if she had been struck with splinters of glass.

The wind stopped short. She looked up again. They we're climbing, and the pyramid was passing beneath them. They balanced on the top and fell into the following trough. She heard a screech from aloft. A gust whipped her southwester from her head and sailed it fifty yards to starboard. It almost took her with it too. No calm followed this one, just a rising crescendo that heeled *Linda Lee* to starboard, heeled her further and further, until it seemed that they were going over. She

clutched at Mitch's arm, missed, and found herself
thrown into the mizzen instead. She cringed and hung
on. A wave struck, drenching her. Hundreds of gallons
of light-green water buried the deck and swirled calf-
deep in the cockpit.

The wind rose further. She could no longer face it.
She burrowed into her oilskins in the lee of the deckhouse. She looked to starboard. The seas were a tangled snowscape of foam. The wind drew her breath
from her body. She tried to turn to port now, to face
the oncoming waves. The wind seemed about to tear the
eyes from her face. Mitch was crouched behind the
lashed wheel, low in the cockpit, back to the seas.

"How long?" she mouthed. She could not hear her
own voice. "How long will it last?" she yelled.

He shook his head. He couldn't hear, or didn't know,
or didn't care to answer. He locked his eyes on hers,
pointed decisively below, and moved toward the hatch.

She tried to protest, but the wind crammed her voice
down her throat. He waited for the next wave, which
half-drowned her, suddenly unsnapped her safety belt
and slid the hatch open. With enormous strength, he
lifted her and deposited her halfway down the companionway ladder.

"Quick!" he yelled.

She did not want to leave him and waited too long.
The hatch was still open when the next wave hit. It
poured down the ladder around her, inundating the
galley and flooding forward into the main salon.

She heard the hatch slam and lock above her. She
was suddenly in another world. Two inches of solid
mahogany muted the tempest topside. Here she heard
only the groan of Linda Lee as she wrestled with the
seas, and the slosh of her bilges. She saw her pillow,
carried forward by the flood, come to rest in a pool of

swirling water over a floorboard drain. Wearily, she began to stroke the bilge-pump.

Since he didn't want her topside, she might as well work below. There was, if they should survive, a dim hope gleaming.

She would never sail again.

He huddled, tied behind the binnacle, for hours after he stuffed Lindy below. The wheel was lashed. He had no need to steer, no reason for being there, no inkling of why he was waiting it out uselessly topside. He simply preferred to keep an eye on the maelstrom.

Linda Lee took the seas like a fighter jogging in place. At each gust, the helm, hard down, forced her into the wind. Her tiny iron-hard jib would tremble as she changed course. She slopped ahead imperceptibly, still avoiding the sternway which would fold her rudder back on itself and destroy it and leave them truly helpless.

Their leeway to starboard was tremendous. He was worried about hitting Maupiti to the west. He could not pinpoint their position within ten miles. Everything beyond 100 yards was a white froth of water. If the winds blew them onto the Maupiti reef, it was simply fate. There was nothing he could do about anything except sit and wait. Only when the wind slackened could he guess its speed. Forty knots, he guessed, in lulls, perhaps sixty in the gusts.

He half-rose, staring. A mountain of heaving water rushed down on their port bow. He clung to the binnacle, trying to estimate its wave-height. It split the difference between masthead and yardarm: thirty feet high. It broke twenty-five yards off the port bow. *Linda Lee,* logging one knot, caught it slamming down from above and stopped with a mighty crash. White water cascaded over the port side and filled the cockpit; he felt it slosh over the top of his boots and pour down his legs to his toes.

But his eyes were on the wave which followed. Dead in the water, the boat was helpless, and this one would finish the job. He yelled a warning to Lindy below, but knew that she would never hear him. He kneeled and hugged the binnacle, bracing for the shock.

When it came it slammed him loose, but he had nowhere to fall but against the cockpit seat. He caught his shoulder-blade on its edge, but hardly noticed the pain.

For the boat had lost now, and her rudder was taking the brunt. Sickened with her anguish, he left *Linda Lee* shudder. The line he had lashed to the wheel sprung taut, drumming spray into his eyes. He fumbled for his knife to slash it. He was too late. The lashing held, but he heard the steering cable snap with a twang like a giant guitar. The lashing went slack and he heard her gudgeons groan below.

The huge emergency tiller was lashed near the cockpit. He cut its bindings and fumbled to jam it in the rudder-head before the next wave gathered. He got it half-in, braced his boots on the starboard side, grabbed the oaken tiller with both hands, and pulled it to him.

He could hardly budge the weight of her rudder, but slowly her bow came around. He found himself cringing. If the next wave hit now, the tiller would sweep him from his seat like a jousting knight. Somehow he hung on.

Slowly, she came downwind, picking up speed. She rose to the next wave. He put the wind off the port side and skittered down the face of the wave.

On the following wave she was surfing. By the next she was flying.

He reached with his knife as high as he could along the edge of the mizzen and slashed the dacron. With another slit in the steel-hard canvas, the foot of the sail disappeared in tatters. The sound of it was like small arms fire. He sawed at the line that secured the jib. It snapped in the key of G, and in the white chaos forward he heard the tiny jib flogging itself to death too. In seconds it was a line of ribbons climbing the forestay to point the way.

The pale seas had heightened further. But joining them had eased *Linda Lee*'s motion, and quieted the wind in her rigging. The eye of the hurricane was still to come, and the other wall after it, reputed to be the worst. They would probably not survive it. They were committed to run, now, and running would keep them in the storm. He saw no way to slow them down.

So they would simply surf each wave full-speed as it came, until he no longer had strength to fight the tiller. When the ultimate wave caught them, or Maupiti reef hove up ahead, or they speared a trough with their bowsprit and tumbled ass-over-teakettle to the bottom, at least he would not have held the boat still for the seas to rape.

When they foundered, he was damned if Lindy was going to be caught like a rat in a trap. He unlocked the hatch and pounded on the deck with his boot and she peeped out. He signaled her to get dressed and come topside.

In five minutes she was up, wearing one of his moth-eaten Navy watchcaps under the hood of her slicker. She was lost in the size of the thing. She stared for a moment at the seas astern, snapped her belt to a shroud and looked into his face.

"Mitch?"

Her voice was faint in the howling wind. He nodded, keeping his eyes on the oncoming seas.

"I love *you*. Nobody else. I want to stay your friend."

He handled the wave, tore his gaze from the next, and regarded the nut-brown face. Fleetingly, he saw it on a pillow, cupped in Jean-Paul's hands. The image faded, but he found that he could not speak.

He felt the surge of the next sea. He hauled at the helm. She put her back into it, too, and they angled left, avoiding a broach. *Linda Lee* soared, gathered herself, and hurtled, breast high and stern low, to the southwest.

He began to hum *Waltzing Matilda.*

CHAPTER

5

HE COULD MORE EASILY SEARCH THE GLARE TO THE east as the sun rose higher. The line of squalls, bearing down on the rising trades, still worried him, but he put Irwin in charge. He was under jib and mizzen. He left the mainsail down. He wanted to move slowly, so that when the French patrol planes came, or Air Polynésie returned, he would be close to where he had last been seen.

He was leaving the cockpit to climb to the spreaders when he heard the radio burst into life. It stunned him. He had not heard a word from it in thirty-six hours. "Yacht *Linda Lee! Star of Peace,* here, Zed El One Yankee Uncle—"

Star, having barely survived Arlene, even in the pen, was still at Bora Bora. Mitch dove down the hatch and grabbed the mike. "Graham! Go ahead!"

Air Polynésie, Graham said, had arrived in Bora Bora. Papeete had been informed that *Linda Lee* was in distress. Two search planes were on their way, and a French destroyer as well. Mahina Radio was trying to get him, but seemed blocked by Moorea.

Star of Peace herself was limping out the pass to help, whatever the problem was. Beating southeast, their ETA was another twelve hours, and there would be plenty of help by then.

"They aren't sure what it is, Mitch. Somebody sick? Or overboard?"

Mitch regarded the mike. He choked and could hardly speak. "Lindy," he croaked finally. "Overboard."

"When?"

He could not bring himself to tell Graham that it had been almost thirty hours. "Long time," he managed. "If you raise Papeete, tell them hurry, OK?"

A young American voice cut in, faint but perfectly readable. *"Linda Lee,* this is the yacht *Windrift,* clearing Papeete pass. The word is out on the quay. *Westerly* and *Kialoa* are following. Also *Zen,* no radio, *Xanadu,* likewise. Estimate ten hours to your area."

"Thanks, *Windrift,*" Mitch muttered.

A heavily accented German voice spoke up: "Here is *Kormorant,* coming also, Mitch. For information, two fat French aeroplanes have just took off from Faaa. So, here is Klaus, on *Kormorant,* over and out."

That call he could not even answer. Tears in his eyes, he simply climbed the companionway, mounted to the spreader, and scanned the horizon as the fat black squalls bore down.

When the eye of Arlene arrived, the wind slackened. The seas were monstrous, but they could see, for an instant, a patch of mottled blue in the tortured sky. Lindy became elated, thinking that the worst was over, and he did not tell her what was coming. He would not let her go below to try to get crackers and cheese, for he was afraid of a knockdown, and that she would be killed by flying lead from the bilge if she went.

So he kept her topside and tried to protect *Linda Lee* as best he could at the tiller. He waited for the westerly shift of wind when the trailing wall of the eye would hit.

He was unready for its brutality. It simply turned the air to foaming water. He could not see or breathe. He fought it as long as he could, trying to surf again in the chaos, but his back gave out. Lindy was half dead from fatigue, and was more hindrance than help, although she tried to lend her strength in his fight with the tiller.

Arlene had beaten them completely. There was no further way to battle the seas. He sent Lindy below, picked the longest trough he could find, and turned into it. He lashed the tiller to leeward and crawled for the hatch.

Linda Lee lay ahull, untended. A forty-foot freak wave pyramided, towered, and crashed to the deck. He dove through the hatch and slammed it closed above him. She took another monstrous wave, heeling to her beam-ends. He was flung across the chart table and jammed against the bulkhead. Very slowly she came erect.

After the noise topside, it was almost quiet below. But the boat was a sodden tangle of all they owned. Every wave that rolled down on them threatened a knockdown. They were rolling forty, fifty degrees, dead in the water, and it was impossible to hang on. The cabin sole was strewn with cans, oilskins, boots, and towels Lindy had tried to use to mop up. Oily water sloshed up from the bilges through the grills in the floorboards. There was no way he could get to his tools now, let alone nail the floorboards down.

The bunks were too precarious, so they crawled forward together and lay on the littered floor in the narrow passage between the head and the hanging locker. Water sloshed between them. He enveloped her in his arms to protect her from the wildest rolls, from the inevitable knockdown and the barrage of lead.

They both grew sick. The electrical system shorted and left them in the dark. They passed a seasick bag back and forth, alternately and regularly. He was sure they would die.

He heard a Scuba tank, lashed in the engine compartment, go adrift and begin to smash itself to pieces. He was too tired to move. A galley locker sprung open. Her crockery went in a sliding, roaring crash. They did not mention it. Somehow, *Linda Lee* avoided capsize. They did not speak at all.

He finally slept. When he awakened the motion had eased. He crawled to the porthole over the chart table. The eastern horizon was banded in a steel-gray cast. He crawled back and slept some more. When he awakened again they were in fast clearing weather. She had crept aft and was trying to light the galley stove. She felt him looking at her and gave up. She snaked back beside him. He could see her profile against the gray skylight.

"Are we OK, Mitch?" she murmured.

He knew what she meant, what she wanted him to say, and couldn't say it. Later, maybe, but Jean-Paul was too close. "Sure," he said. "It's clearing."

He slumbered again. When he finally surfaced out of a deep well of oblivion his mouth tasted of acid, his teeth were coated, his face was raw and stubbled with a two-day growth. He had slept almost eighteen hours. He moved topside. *Linda Lee* was still jogging, going nowhere. The sun was rising upwind in a mess of orange squalls. They were harmless camp-followers of Arlene, which had given up on *Linda Lee* and was probably sweeping down on Rarotonga in the Cooks.

They had taken the worst they would ever see. He would never fear weather again, not on this boat, not with Lindy. After repairs, there were the Cooks, the Tongas, Fijis, New Caledonia. Then?

Why not? Through the Indian Ocean and around the Cape of Good Hope. Around the world?

Buoyantly, he made sail. He brought the boat on course back to Bora Bora, where they could make repairs, pick up their passports, rest a while, take on stores, and go. Lindy dragged topside. She was pale and haggard, which didn't surprise him. He knew he himself looked like the tail-end of a two-week drunk. But her eyes were lifeless, and though she smiled when she saw the pretty sunrise, she saw none of her cloud-people in it. She wanted to help with the tiller, but she could not seem to keep her mind on the course, so he sent her below for more rest.

They slogged back to Bora Bora. It took them three days. *Star of Peace,* despite her shelter, had lost her mizzenmast to a flying coconut limb. Hans had lost two cottages and the pier was a pile of rotting timbers on the inland side of the road.

Mitch cleared out the chaos below, repaired the steering cable, secured the generator, and patched up Irwin, whose workings had been strained. He would have sailed then, but Lindy was not ready, so they found a lone anchorage near a *motu* at the pass. They dove and swam and fished. They made love. He exorcised Jean-Paul, in his own mind, anyway, and, she swore to him, in hers.

It became almost impossible for him to recall the details of Arlene, or the fear he must have known huddled on the cabin sole. It was all lost somewhere in the triumph of surviving. It seemed equally impossible for her to forget. A great question hung between them, and he could not bring himself to ask it.

One night in the cockpit, sipping scotch, she brought it up herself. "Let's level, Mitch. Can we?"

"I hope."

"What are we getting ready for?"

"Well, Raro, the Cooks—" Something in her face, in the light from the open hatch, stopped him. "What is it, Lindy?"

"All alone?" she gulped. "All by yourself?"

"Of course not."

She began to cry, softly. His gut felt cold. He knew, and there was no use dragging it out of her. "You're through?" he asked.

"*Fiu*, Mitch. While it balances out for me. The gales for the days in the trades, and that pass at Takarava for the lagoon inside, and the doldrums for that day rowing up the river, remember? Arlene for . . . I don't know."

"For Jean-Paul?"

"No. Arlene for the look you had when you found the boat."

A coconut crashed on the *motu*. The surf boomed into Te Avenua Pass, gently now but still with the voice to move him, belly-deep. She had been trying to tell him this, and he hadn't let her close enough to hear. "OK," he said thickly. "We'll beat back to Tahiti and sell her."

"Mitch, it's awful! I wrecked *one* dream."

He thought of her at eighteen, fat and pregnant in the trailer, trying to stay out of his way while he studied. "Bullshit! You've wrecked nothing. And I'm not going to lose you for a fucking boat."

"When," she asked softly, "did this cruise *really* begin?"

"When we spotted the boat," he lied. He reached for her glass. "Another blast?"

She did not believe him, or maybe she did. Early

next morning they winched up the anchor and powered out the pass. Lindy could recall every detail of their last mad passage through it, outward-bound. Mitch could barely remember breasting the breakers.

They began to beat back to Tahiti.

CHAPTER
6

THREE SEPARATE SQUALLS WERE SWEEPING THE search area from the east. He hung on the mast, studying their paths. He was so intent that, when an aircraft came up from astern, it caught him unaware. It roared past to starboard, filling his chest with the drumming of its engines. It wiggled its wings, banked sedately, and was back again, this time almost flicking the mast above him.

The plane was an old Lockheed P2V with French Navy markings, of the type that had patrolled the seas off Wonsan twenty years ago. It apparently had no radio channels he could receive, for it dropped a long red ribbon across his deck. When he climbed down and hauled it in, he found a waterproof bag at its end. He opened it and found a note. In schoolbook English he read that the plane's wingman was already searching five miles astern. A destroyer, steaming at flank speed, was less than an hour southeast. A frigate followed with a helicopter. The destroyer had the proper frequencies, if he wished to speak, and could relay messages to the planes. In the meanwhile, they would simply begin a standard search. If they saw anything, they would drop flares and return to lead him to the spot. He had the honor to be, at your service, Lieutenant Guy Dubois.

When he finished reading, the plane was already distant, on his port bow, sweeping the water near the squalls. As he watched, it disappeared in scud, reappeared, and dropped lower.

It could have missed her as it passed through the cloud, and it would obviously not search that area again.

For the squalls and infinite valleys and gullies they needed five planes, or ten, they needed scores of ships. The sun was peaking and even if she was still afloat she would not last another night.

He called the destroyer for more help. A voice came back immediately, in perfect English. Mitch explained that his wife was a good swimmer, that she was wearing flotation, and had probably found a lifebuoy and flag he had left, that she might have a strobe light as well.

"And how long, Captain, has it been? She has fallen in, when?"

"Thirty hours," he admitted. He became too verbal and pressed too hard. He repeated a list of those things which were saving her. Drunk with fatigue, he babbled. He finished by promising that she was still alive, and guaranteed that she was within ten miles of his own position. He begged the destroyer to send for more ships.

Perhaps, but later—*plus tard*. For now, the destroyer promised to search as long as was necessary.

He fought down his fury. He had better not push further until he calmed himself down. He thanked the

destroyer again and went topside. He trimmed the jib
and climbed to the spreader. A fast-moving squall enveloped him suddenly, drawing a white curtain between him and the world of planes and ships. For ten
minutes he simply clung to his perch, peering into driving rain. He could not see 500 yards.

The squall passed. The plane that had dropped the
message seemed even further away; his wingman, now
visible astern, was droning east.

He had felt less lonely with the two white terns.

When the sun had climbed high enough, it warmed
her forehead, but did nothing at all for the chill in her
legs. She was continually slipping through the horseshoe and having to fight her way back. It slid away
again, and now she was too tired to try to get it. Like a
lost skier freezing in the snow, she was at first too sleepy
to care.

She realized it suddenly and looked up. The buoy
was five feet away. She paddled after it and somehow
got herself in once more. If she lost it again, she would
not find the strength to reclaim it.

She had forgotten why she was in the water. She had
it somehow tied in with the hurricane, and wondered
where Mitch was, and if he were swimming beside her.
But that was stupid, the boat had survived the hurricane, the hurricane was before they had decided on
Tahiti, before Bora Bora.

No, she had fallen in, all by herself, at night. Last
night? She thought so. But why had he left her? He
should have turned back and picked her up; she had
hidden his new Nikon behind the Chunky Beef Soup,
and he'd never find it by Christmas.

It rained. Somewhere in the squall she became
aware of the drone of engines. She glimpsed a big gray
aircraft breaking from wispy clouds. It flashed through

a shaft of sunlight. She was too tired to wave. It was instantly swallowed in mist. She wished she were flying it: she'd look for the boat.

She floated for hours. She sensed the sun at its zenith, and in its descent. She dozed. She had a vivid daydream. A great red ketch bore down on her, and its figurehead was Mahura, and Jean-Paul was at its wheel, and Taarii was poised in her bows, harpoon held aloft.

She screamed at them silently. She was not a fish, or a whale, she was Lindy . . .

A coltish whitecap slurped into her face, up her nose, into her throat, strangling her. She coughed and retched. She had to have air, she was strangling. She struggled erect.

Down-sun, emerging from a squall, she was *Linda Lee*. Then it was gone. It was immense. She fumbled for her whistle, coughed out the last of the water. She blew with all her might.

The whistle was silent. She spluttered it dry and got out three feeble shrills before she ran out of air. Then she flopped back into the horseshoe. Nothing was left at all.

From the spreader, he watched the next squall approach. The drone of the aircraft put hopeless walls on the search. He was sure they would not stay past sunset, and he willed the sun to hang forever where it was.

His bare right foot, braced against the yardarm and slimy with sweat, slipped. He almost pitched from the mast. He grabbed it impulsively. But what was the difference, and why the hell not? He glanced downward. Twenty feet below, *Linda Lee* knifed heedlessly through the swells. She took a special roll and almost flung him off again. Her mainsail chuckled softly.

To port he heard the sudden shrill cry of a bird. It

was very weak. The terns? A whistle? He struggled to his feet on the yard-arm.

Bobbing in the water, 100 yards down-sun, he saw the man-overboard pole. He saw nothing else, but that was enough.

"Lindy!"

He heard nothing, saw nothing in the glare beyond the crest of the swell, only the top of the pole and the fluttering faded flag.

"*Lindy!*" he screamed. He slid down the shrouds, letting go to drop the last ten feet. He dropped the jib, loosed the mizzen as he grabbed the wheel, yanked Irwin out of command, started the engine, and spun the wheel into the plummeting sun.

He lost the flag in the glare. He spotted it again, and then the horseshoe-buoy, and her face turned skyward, and the spill of burnished hair on the rim of the buoy.

He turned well clear, brought the bow into the wind, and let the boat go dead. Lindy was twenty feet away. He cut the engine so that she could hear him, for she showed no sign of knowing that he was here. He tossed the orange life ring, attached to the boat with a long floating line, in a perfect soaring arc. It dropped within five feet of her. "Lindy!" he shouted. "Grab it!"

She raised her head. She seemed dazed. He yelled again. She seemed to see the ring. She slipped from the horseshoe and tried for it. It was not three feet away from her when she reached out, floundered, and went under.

He dove. The coolness shocked him. He surfaced. He saw her face, contorted with effort, on the face of a swell. He knifed uphill. He reached her, slid his hip under her back and his arm across her breasts, and ploughed for the orange ring. It was drifting downwind fast. He barely reached it. He jammed an arm through it, rested for a moment, holding her high. Her eyes were closed.

"Lindy," he begged. "Lindy?"

A line of mucous oozed from her nose. He wiped her face with his arm. She opened her eyes. They were very dim.

"I fell," she murmured. "Mitch—"

Her mouth went slack. She seemed to strangle. Panicked, he squeezed her nose shut, found her mouth with his lips, bent her head back, and tried to breathe into her lungs. The life ring yanked at his crooked elbow, almost pulling free. He grabbed convulsively, got his arm back through it, and found that he was forcing her head beneath the waves. He quit the mouth-to-mouth; he had to get her aboard. The ring tugged again. He glanced at the boat. His heart almost stopped.

Linda Lee was hobbyhorsing, pitching at each swell. The jib had come loose and was filling with wind at each crest. Its lines were fouled. As the sail filled, it began to climb magically up the headstay. With each gust, it would drop, then mount further on the next crest. The ketch's bow was turning downwind, and with every swell the jib climbed further and the sail grew fatter.

The life ring jerked again, almost pulling his arm from its socket as it began to tow them both. His back, supporting Lindy, went out with a shock of agony.

The boat was headed dead downwind now, and she began to pick up speed. A tiny bow wave formed at her stem, like a smile; then her bow was hidden by her buttocks and Irwin was beckoning him from astern, as if urging him to hurry.

His arm slipped again. *Linda Lee* heaved forward, towing them faster. He hung on, a link between Lindy, life ring, line, and boat. The flag, the horseshoe that had saved her, and the light were already lost astern.

The ketch began to draw a wake, half-drowning him. Across thirty feet of water, he heard a burst of static from the radio through her open hatch. The water was a giant hand, shoving against his face, tearing Lindy from his grip. He tried to shift her weight. She planed under and slithered from his grasp.

He was suddenly light in the water. If he pulled himself aboard and came back . . .

He would find her dead, if he found her at all. He twisted to look back. She was already fifteen feet away, limp on her back on the face of a cresting swell. He glimpsed her cheeks, bronze in the late sunlight. Her eyes were closed but her mouth was open and her teeth gleamed whitely.

He let go and stroked for her, head high. "Lindy!" he called.

Her eyes opened once. She saw him. A cresting wave hung over her head. She seemed to try to speak, and then she was gone.

He filled his lungs, porpoised high, and dove. He sliced downward. He saw nothing but shards of brassy sunlight lancing the depths.

Once he heard a low-pitched throb and cleared his ears: the beat remained, and he recognized the drum of distant screws.

He curved deeper. The agony of airlessness was brief; he was already through the level of no return. He recognized the edge of narcosis: for a while he was gloriously happy, soaring in a cobalt void, and then he glimpsed a pale form drifting below him.

Languidly, he spiraled down. Her body was blurred and ghostly until he reached for it. He brushed her arm and she seemed to come alive. Her skin was soft and pliant; he felt her hair sweep across his cheek. He clasped her around the waist and let her guide him down. Suddenly the depths exploded in a chaos of sapphire and gold.

And then he finally saw it all: his own body writhing in agony, hers at ease and quite content. He saw it from outside himself, with her.

Bestselling
Novels
From
POCKET BOOKS

Available at bookstores everywhere, or order direct from publisher.

FB 3-78

- -

POCKET BOOKS
Department RK
1230 Avenue of the Americas
New York, N.Y. 10020

Please send me the books I have checked above. I am enclosing
$_____ (please add 50¢ to cover postage and handling). Send check
or money order—no cash or C.O.D.'s please.

NAME_____

ADDRESS_____

CITY_____STATE/ZIP_____

FB 3-78